PRAISE FOR J.
BLACK DAGGER BI

"Frighteningly addictive."

—*Publishers Weekly*

"Ward brings on the big feels."

—*Booklist*

"J. R. Ward is the undisputed queen . . . Long live the queen."

—Steve Berry, *New York Times* bestselling author

"J. R. Ward is a master!"

—Gena Showalter, *New York Times* bestselling author

"Fearless storytelling. A league all of her own."

—Kristen Ashley, *New York Times* bestselling author

"J. R. Ward is one of the finest writers out there—in any genre."

—Sarah J. Maas, #1 *New York Times* bestselling author

"Ward is a master of her craft."

—*New York Journal of Books*

BY J. R. WARD

THE BLACK DAGGER BROTHERHOOD SERIES

THE BLACK DAGGER LEGACY SERIES

THE BLACK DAGGER BROTHERHOOD WORLD

FIREFIGHTERS SERIES

NOVELS OF THE FALLEN ANGELS

THE BOURBON KINGS SERIES

J.R. WARD

WHERE WINTER FINDS YOU

• A CALDWELL CHRISTMAS •

POCKET BOOKS

New York   London   Toronto   Sydney   New Delhi

Pocket Books
An Imprint of Simon & Schuster, Inc.
1230 Avenue of the Americas
New York, NY 10020

First Pocket Books paperback edition November 2019

POCKET and colophon are registered trademarks of Simon & Schuster, Inc.

For information about special discounts for bulk purchases, please contact Simon & Schuster Special Sales at 1-866-506-1949 or business@simonandschuster.com.

The Simon & Schuster Speakers Bureau can bring authors to your live event. For more information or to book an event contact the Simon & Schuster Speakers Bureau at 1-866-248-3049 or visit our website at www.simonspeakers.com.

Interior design by Davina Mock-Maniscalco

Manufactured in the United States of America

10 9 8 7 6 5 4 3 2 1

Library of Congress Cataloging-in-Publication Data is available.

ISBN 978-1-9821-3547-8
ISBN 978-1-5011-9518-1 (ebook)

To:

A pair of perfect souls reunited,
happily ever after.

GLOSSARY OF TERMS AND PROPER NOUNS

abstrux nohtrum (n.) Private guard with license to kill who is granted his or her position by the King.

ahvenge (v.) Act of mortal retribution, carried out typically by a male loved one.

Black Dagger Brotherhood (pr. n.) Highly trained vampire warriors who protect their species against the Lessening Society. As a result of selective breeding within the race, Brothers possess immense physical and mental strength, as well as rapid healing capabilities. They are not siblings for the most part, and are inducted into the Brotherhood upon nomination by the Brothers. Aggressive, self-reliant, and secretive by nature, they are the subjects of legend and objects of reverence within the vampire world. They may be killed only by the most serious of wounds, e.g., a gunshot or stab to the heart, etc.

blood slave (n.) Male or female vampire who has been subjugated to serve the blood needs of another. The practice of keeping blood slaves has been outlawed.

the Chosen (pr. n.) Female vampires who had been bred to serve the Scribe Virgin. In the past, they were spiritually rather than temporally focused, but that changed with the ascendance of the final Primale, who freed them from the Sanctuary. With the Scribe Virgin removing herself from her role, they are completely autonomous and learning to live on earth. They do continue to meet the blood needs of unmated members of the Brotherhood, as well as Brothers who cannot feed from their *shellans* or injured fighters.

chrih **(n.)** Symbol of honorable death in the Old Language.

cohntehst **(n.)** Conflict between two males competing for the right to be a female's mate.

Dhunhd **(pr. n.)** Hell.

doggen **(n.)** Member of the servant class within the vampire world. *Doggen* have old, conservative traditions about service to their superiors, following a formal code of dress and behavior. They are able to go out during the day, but they age relatively quickly. Life expectancy is approximately five hundred years.

ehros (n.) A Chosen trained in the matter of sexual arts.

exhile dhoble (n.) The evil or cursed twin, the one born second.

the Fade (pr. n.) Nontemporal realm where the dead reunite with their loved ones and pass eternity.

First Family (pr. n.) The King and Queen of the vampires, and any children they may have.

ghardian (n.) Custodian of an individual. There are varying degrees of *ghardians*, with the most powerful being that of a *sehcluded* female.

glymera (n.) The social core of the aristocracy, roughly equivalent to Regency England's *ton*.

hellren (n.) Male vampire who has been mated to a female. Males may take more than one female as mate.

hyslop (n. or v.) Term referring to a lapse in judgment, typically resulting in the compromise of the mechanical operations of a vehicle or otherwise motorized conveyance of some kind. For example, leaving one's keys in one's car as it is parked outside the family home overnight, whereupon said vehicle is stolen.

leahdyre (n.) A person of power and influence.

leelan (adj. or n.) A term of endearment loosely translated as "dearest one."

Lessening Society (pr. n.) Order of slayers convened by

the Omega for the purpose of eradicating the vampire species.

lesser (n.) De-souled human who targets vampires for extermination as a member of the Lessening Society. *Lessers* must be stabbed through the chest in order to be killed; otherwise they are ageless. They do not eat or drink and are impotent. Over time, their hair, skin, and irises lose pigmentation until they are blond, blushless, and pale-eyed. They smell like baby powder. Inducted into the society by the Omega, they retain a ceramic jar thereafter into which their heart was placed after it was removed.

lewlhen (n.) Gift.

lheage (n.) A term of respect used by a sexual submissive to refer to their dominant.

Lhenihan (pr. n.) A mythic beast renowned for its sexual prowess. In modern slang, refers to a male of preternatural size and sexual stamina.

lys (n.) Torture tool used to remove the eyes.

mahmen (n.) Mother. Used both as an identifier and a term of affection.

mhis (n.) The masking of a given physical environment; the creation of a field of illusion.

nalla (n., f.) or *nallum* **(n., m.)** Beloved.

needing period (n.) Female vampire's time of fertility, generally lasting for two days and accompanied by intense sexual cravings. Occurs approximately five years after a female's transition and then once a decade thereafter. All males respond to some degree if they are around a female in her need. It can be a dangerous time, with conflicts and fights breaking out between competing males, particularly if the female is not mated.

newling (n.) A virgin.

the Omega (pr. n.) Malevolent, mystical figure who has targeted the vampires for extinction out of resentment directed toward the Scribe Virgin. Exists in a nontemporal realm and has extensive powers, though not the power of creation.

phearsom (adj.) Term referring to the potency of a male's sexual organs. Literal translation something close to "worthy of entering a female."

Princeps (pr. n.) Highest level of the vampire aristocracy, second only to members of the First Family or the Scribe Virgin's Chosen. Must be born to the title; it may not be conferred.

pyrocant (n.) Refers to a critical weakness in an individual. The weakness can be internal, such as an addiction, or external, such as a lover.

rahlman (n.) Savior.

rythe (n.) Ritual manner of asserting honor, granted by one who has offended another. If accepted, the offended chooses a weapon and strikes the offender, who presents him—or herself without defenses.

the Scribe Virgin (pr. n.) Mystical force who previously was counselor to the King as well as the keeper of vampire archives and the dispenser of privileges. Existed in a nontemporal realm and had extensive powers, but has recently stepped down and given her station to another. Capable of a single act of creation, which she expended to bring the vampires into existence.

sehclusion **(n.)** Status conferred by the King upon a female of the aristocracy as a result of a petition by the female's family. Places the female under the sole direction of her *ghardian*, typically the eldest male in her household. Her *ghardian* then has the legal right to determine all manner of her life, restricting at will any and all interactions she has with the world.

shellan **(n.)** Female vampire who has been mated to a male. Females generally do not take more than one mate due to the highly territorial nature of bonded males.

symphath **(n.)** Subspecies within the vampire race characterized by the ability and desire to manipulate emotions in others (for the purposes of an energy exchange), among other traits. Historically, they have been discriminated against and, during certain eras, hunted by vampires. They are near extinction.

talhman (n.) The evil side of an individual. A dark stain on the soul that requires expression if it is not properly expunged.

the Tomb (pr. n.) Sacred vault of the Black Dagger Brotherhood. Used as a ceremonial site as well as a storage facility for the jars of *lessers*. Ceremonies performed there include inductions, funerals, and disciplinary actions against Brothers. No one may enter except for members of the Brotherhood, the Scribe Virgin, or candidates for induction.

trahyner (n.) Word used between males of mutual respect and affection. Translated loosely as "beloved friend."

transition (n.) Critical moment in a vampire's life when he or she transforms into an adult. Thereafter, he or she must drink the blood of the opposite sex to survive and is unable to withstand sunlight. Occurs generally in the mid-twenties. Some vampires do not survive their transitions, males in particular. Prior to their transitions, vampires are physically weak, sexually unaware and unresponsive, and unable to dematerialize.

vampire (n.) Member of a species separate from that of *Homo sapiens*. Vampires must drink the blood of the opposite sex to survive. Human blood will keep them alive, though the strength does not last long. Following their transitions, which occur in their mid-twenties, they are unable to go out into sunlight and must feed from the vein regularly. Vampires cannot "convert" humans through a bite or transfer of blood, though they are in rare cases able to breed with the other species. Vampires can dematerialize at will, though they must be able to calm themselves and concentrate to do so and may not carry anything heavy with them. They are able to strip the memories of humans, provided such memories are short-term. Some vampires are able to read minds. Life expectancy is upward of a thousand years, or in some cases, even longer.

wahlker (n.) An individual who has died and returned to the living from the Fade. They are accorded great respect and are revered for their travails.

whard (n.) Equivalent of a godfather or godmother to an individual.

WHERE
WINTER
FINDS
YOU

CHAPTER ONE

Raul Julia—no relation to the late, great actor—saw his first angel on a cold night in Caldwell in the middle of a December snowstorm.

And it was all because of a BMW.

He had come to a stop at the intersection of Main and Tenth, his long wool coat buttoned up to his throat, his scarf tucked in tight across his chest, the toes of his feet chilly even in his boots. Snowflakes, which had started out at lunchtime dancing in the winter air, had soon put on so much weight that they could no longer perform arabesques on the wind currents. They were also in a hurry now, wasting their freedom in a rush to get to the ground, not realizing that the fall was the very best part of their lives, and that once that descent was over, they were going to be trod upon, sped over, plowed into dirty piles like they were degenerates as opposed to floating miracles.

From one-in-a-million to a nuisance of overcrowding that had to be dealt with by Caldwell Public Works trucks.

It was a sad thing, really. Rather like children turning into adults.

As Raul stood on that corner, trapped in place by a red Do Not Cross palm that flashed in his direction, he got so tired of the cold gusts in his face that he turned and put his back to the traffic light. Due to the accommodation made to the visually impaired, a sound would alert him when it was time to go, but so would the traffic, which was slow and trudging, as if the cars didn't like the weather any more than he did. In better conditions, he would have crowded the curb and eagle-eyed any opportunity to jaywalk—he had been born in Brooklyn back before Giuliani had cleaned up the five boroughs for a short while, so he was an expert at reading traffic patterns—but in winter, the rules changed. Four-wheel drive did not mean four-wheel stop, and the skidding potential added a dangerous element to any chances you took.

And Raul was the kind of person who had a lot to live for. Especially tonight.

In his pocket, he had a small black box, leather-bound on the outside, velvet-cushioned on the inside. He had married his Ivelisse thirty-two years ago, and though their anniversary wasn't until April, and though it wasn't a special one like twenty-five or thirty or even fifty, he had passed by a jewelry store at lunch and stopped. The window had been chocked full of gold and platinum wares that were wearable, bright lights inset into the frame to make the diamonds gleam. There had been a lot of engagement rings, in preparation for the season of asking—as opposed to the season of saying I do, which, according to his youngest daughter, Alondra, was in June—but there had also been a number of crosses.

Pretty as the show was, Raul had kept on going, determined to return on time to his job as an actuary at an insurance company. Going along the packed snow with the others who had dared to venture out at noontime, he had thought of the crosses, although not one of them in particular, but rather all of them in a group. They had been relegated to a cluster down low on the right, a congregation of perhaps ten, all of them overshadowed by those rings. For some reason, he couldn't get them out of his mind, to the point where he began to become paranoid that something bad was going to happen. Even his normal workload, which was often too much, couldn't distract him away from the preoccupation.

Maybe it was a sign. Maybe it was a portent.

He had those kinds of thoughts a lot, however. Then again, he analyzed people's death rates for a living, performing the risk assessments on which life-insurance-premium calculations were based— and after you do that for twenty years, you did get a little flinchy. Every mole on his body was a melanoma, for example. Each skip of his heart was an impending myocardial infarction. Oh, and that headache he'd had when he'd been stuck in traffic coming into work this morning was definitely the precursor to a stroke.

Although put like that, maybe it was all a little crazy.

Maybe he needed to take some time off.

Still, as soon as he'd gotten his work done for the day, at a little past five, he'd put on his coat, said goodbye to his coworkers, and hurried out of the building. Instead of heading to the open-air car park six blocks over, however, he'd gone back to the jewelry store. He'd decided, as he'd slumped along in the cold, that it was going to be closed—but he should have known better. It was the Christmas season, after all, and as he'd pushed his way into the store, the narrow and relatively shallow shop was crowded with people. He'd had to wait for a good fifteen minutes before he caught a salesperson's eye, and when all she could do was shrug at him, like she couldn't promise she'd be free anytime before New Year's, he'd checked his watch and debated leaving.

The girl who'd finally waited on him had been harried and exhausted, like she'd had a long lineup of late closes just like this one, and had nothing to look forward to except more of the same. He'd decided she had to have been his Alondra's age, and she'd had a nice-sized diamond on her ring finger, no doubt something she had helped her fiancé get a store discount on. Her eyes had been tired, but she had made the effort to smile, and that, more than the time it had taken to walk to the store, or the time he had spent waiting, or even that which he was still wondering if he should purchase, was what made him stay.

When he had finished the transaction—after she had given him a nice discount—he had told her he wished her well with her nuptials. She had truly beamed then and talked about the man she was going to marry, the wedding planning, the dress. It was a deluge that he could tell she had to keep inside while she was working, and her joy, her youth, and all the things that were yet to come to her, the good and the bad, had made his eyes sting with tears.

It had been a relief to step outside and be able to blame the watering on the cold.

And now he was here, at this intersection, with a diamond cross his Ivelisse was going to kill him for buying for her, and a broken heart.

Alondra would have been twenty-three in January. And the cross wasn't about any random wedding anniversary, even though he told himself it was, even though he had to believe it was—because otherwise he'd bought the thing to commemorate his daughter's death four years ago on a snowy night just like this one, in the back of a car being driven too fast on ice, by her very best friend, who had survived.

Which would be rather morbid, wouldn't it.

As he considered the accident that had taken such a precious gift from him and his wife and the other kids, he reflected that there were a number of dangerous things that could be predicted in life. If you took too many risks with your health, with your body, with your finances, with your habits, you were, statistically speaking, liable to get caught in a situation of your own design that came out badly. He knew this. He studied this; he trended this; he understood this from an overarching, objective view-point that was god-like. Yet none of that had mat-tered when his cousin Fernando had knocked on his front door at one a.m., on that snowy December night. The instant Raul had opened that door and seen that CPD hat being removed from that head, he had known.

He and Ivelisse had had a total of three children, and there had been many, mostly from the older generation, who had felt compelled to point out after the death that at least they still had two left. As if that erased the pain or lessened it by two-thirds. He had wanted to rage at their insensitivity, scream in their faces, tear their hair out. He loved his two surviving children, as much as he had loved his Alondra, but their lives did not make up for her loss. The whims of chance had coalesced into a tragedy that night, the combination of a lead foot and some black ice, coupled with the fact that Alondra had for some reason not put her seat belt on in the rear seat, leading to exactly the phenomenon that Raul as-sessed every weekday from nine to five.

Death had taken one of his own, and for a long time, he had been terrified that he was to blame. That somehow, because of the nature of his work, he had made a lightning rod out of his family, and God was getting him back for trying to assume a role no human should ever court.

His faith had seen him through, however. His belief that there was a kind and benevolent fountainhead from whom all things flowed had helped him to absolve himself of the guilt fostered by the first, most irrational phases of his grief.

The loss did not get easier to bear with time. When he thought of his youngest daughter, he hurt just as much as he did the moment Fernando had opened his mouth and shared the sad news that Raul had already guessed at. It was just that he thought of other things, too, now.

Such as BMWs.

He had his back to the direction he wanted to go in, his body leaning against the wind, his ungloved hands crammed into the pockets of his wool coat, when the most beautiful M850i xDrive coupe he had ever seen pulled up to the stoplight on Tenth.

It was a relief to distract his mind and emotions away from his lost daughter, for he knew that when he gave his Ivelisse the cross tonight—he was not going to wait until Christmas morning because, if there was anything Alondra's death had taught him, and what he did for work underscored, it was that mortals should not wait for important things— there were going to be many tears and much bittersweet longing for their daughter. So he needed to shore his strength up. Plus it was going to be hard to drive home in the snowy dark if his eyes were all swollen from crying in the cold.

The BMW was a benediction to him, a convenient derailment just when he needed one. And the reason it worked so well was because it was not just *a* luxurious sports coupe. It was his dream car. It was *the* luxury sports coupe. Sleek and refined, with a powerful motor and comfortable seats, he had even sat in one once at a dealership last year. With a starting price of $111,900, it was out of his financial reach—and it was going to stay that way. Funny how age changed things. When you were in your late teens and looking through *Road & Track*, you could believe that the cars that were too expensive for your wallet were a temporary disappointment, something that your advancing years, and the schooling you were focused on, and the plans you were making, were going to take care of, the impossible becoming an inevitable through hard work and focus.

That avaricious optimism was nowhere to be found when you were just over the lip edge of fifty, and you had two kids in graduate school, a mortgage to finish paying off, and a wife who you liked to take care of as she deserved. The impossible stayed impossible. Maybe, if they hadn't had kids, he could have considered buying a used one. But he wouldn't trade any of his three blessings, even with the pain from the one he had lost, for the likes of a car.

Although what a car it was. The owner behind the wheel had chosen the carbon black metallic paint, and the twenty-inch M V-spoke jet-black wheels. It was hard to see inside to determine the trim choices, but Raul was willing to bet the man had customized as much of it as he could, which, according to the BMW website, would extend build time a good six to eight weeks.

Raul knew all this because he had spec'd one out for himself online just a couple of months ago. In his case, it was merely a dream he could tinker with, a fantasy that he could almost touch as he worked his mouse around and clicked on things that added thousands of dollars to that already stratospheric purchase price. That was not the case for the man behind this wheel. Whoever he was, he had had the cash to pay for the car, and Raul felt a stab of envy—

as well as some curiosity about who had cut such a check.

Leaning forward a little, he squinted. From what he could see of the driver, Raul's dream car was a reality for an incredibly handsome African American man of about thirty. The guy had a perfectly balanced face, with a strong chin, high cheekbones and deep-set eyes. His fade was perfect, the bottom completely shaved, the top allowed to grow out only so far as it blackened his skull. There wasn't much to see of his clothes, but he wasn't wearing a jacket or a coat. He had just a shirt on, one that seemed to fall as if it were silk, and a cuff link flashed in the streetlights.

He could have been an athlete, but he seemed like a businessman. Who knew his true profession, and really, did it matter? Whatever the job or wherever the money had come from, there was obviously enough of it to afford the BMW and so much more.

Too bad the man did not look happy at all.

Raul could only shake his head. Rich people. They never appreciated what they had, and that was one definition of Hell, wasn't it: to be seated at a table stacked with food, yet starving no matter how much you ate—

Without warning, the oddest thing happened,

and Raul narrowed his eyes further, taking careful note, for it was the kind of thing he was going to want to tell Ivelisse about as soon as he got home: Between one blink and the next, the interior of the car became suffused by a peridot-green glow.

At first, Raul assumed it was from a cell phone screen, something that the driver, in his frustration at having even three minutes of forward progress halted by a red light, had created by checking his email. Except no, there was no phone. No iPad. No laptop. Perhaps it was a reflection of green-means-go as the traffic light changed—no, there had been no change up there. Confused, Raul considered the possibility he was seeing things.

Which was when he noticed the figure standing directly in front of the BMW.

The lashing snow was moving around what appeared to be a man, judging by the size of the torso, the flight paths of flakes reoriented by the three dimensions of height, weight, and, at least in theory, mortality. The problem was . . . Raul could see through the figure to the buildings across the street. Everything was visible, from the corner of the intersection, to the lobby doors of the bank, to the clutch of pedestrians who were approaching the crosswalk.

Raul rubbed his eyes, although it did nothing to change what seemed to be before him, and that was when the tires of the BMW began to spin. As the light finally turned green, all four low-profile tires abruptly lost purchase, and not just in a fishtail, get-off-the-mark-in-a-sloppy-way fashion, but as in going-nowhere-at-all. Which made no sense because the M850i had the xDrive. All-wheel traction.

The powerful engine revved. And revved again.

Inside, behind the wheel, Raul could see the driver grip the steering wheel harder and tilt into the windshield as if, in his mind, he was willing the powerful car to propel forward.

And still the tires spun and the ghostly apparition blocked the way.

"'Scuse me, buddy," someone said to him.

In a reflex born of being a city dweller all of his life, Raul stepped aside without looking, assuming he had room to spare on the shoveled sidewalk. He did not. His foot landed on the edge of a snow-slicked curb, and his body lurched off balance—

Just as a semitrailer truck that was trying to stop at the red light in its lane lost control and plowed through the intersection, scattering the pedestrians who had started to cross, barreling past the BMW that was stuck, and coming right for Raul.

As his eyes swung around, he looked directly into the oncoming grille and knew, without a shadow of doubt, that he was going to die. His body was going to be impacted at a sufficient speed to do extensive internal damage, and given the forward list of his trajectory, his skull was going to be cracked wide-open.

Even though there was no hope, he whipped his hands out of the pockets of his coat, the cross in its box coming with his hand and flying free, his efforts to save himself too little, too late.

His first thought was of Alondra. He couldn't wait to see her.

His second was of his Ivelisse and his other two girls. They would be heartbroken. They had barely recovered from the family's first tragedy—how would they get through his death, too, especially as it was so random, so unlucky . . . and on another slippery, snowy night.

His third was that this was so unfair. He had led a just life. He had loved his wife and honored her. He had cherished his children. He had worked hard and been honest and done his level best to do unto others as he would have them do unto him. How could this happen—

Time stopped.

It was the best way to describe the indescribable.

Everything just halted where it was: The speeding semi, his fall, the pedestrians racing to get out of the way, the spinning tires of the BMW. Everything just . . . stopped.

Except for the snow.

The snow still fell, landing with weightless grace on what was now a tableau of chaos. And the figure in front of the BMW, the transparent, there-but-not-there figure turned its head and looked at Raul. The man's face was so beautiful that tears sprang to Raul's eyes, joining the snow, falling, falling, onto the ground he would never meet because he was going to be swept away by the truck's grille.

And that was when Raul saw the whole truth.

The man was no man, and he was no ghost, either. He was an angel, with long blond and black hair that licked up around him as if it were playing in the snow, and wings, great gossamer, shimmering, rainbow-colored wings that rose up from behind his shoulders. And he had the aura, too. The glow about him, the heavenly light emanating from his form, was just as the images had always portrayed, and that glorious illumination was evidence that the afterlife was real and whoever was in charge of the universe was a beneficent God indeed, one who sent servants unto the earth that had been created, to caretake the fragile mortals that were no mistake of the cosmos, no accident of electrons and neutrons and protons colliding in a vast, cold void, but rather a conscious choice made with love.

Thus, Raul was saved from death.

He wept openly as the angel extended a hand to him, a kind and gentle hand, to right his fall, to correct his path, to rescue his life. The contact was both made and unmade, for though there was distance between them, Raul felt the touch, and it was warm, it was both mother and father, it was that of a superior being making sure that a child was not hurt by its silly absence of attention.

As he felt his body righted and moved far back on to the sidewalk, he was flooded with relief and gratitude. This unlikely moment of deliverance now confirmed the faith that had carried him through the deaths of so many, and especially of his Alondra. Yes, he thought with joy, his beloved daughter, taken too soon, was in a safe and happy eternity, and he would see her again, and the reunion would be of such exultation that any suffering on the earth below would be as the falling snow, passing quickly and of little consequence.

The angel smiled at him.

In Raul's head, he heard a voice, deep and full of authority: *Worry not, my friend. There are good years ahead for you, and when you are called home, you will be welcomed by those you miss most.*

And then the angel disappeared and the world resumed its spin.

The truck whizzed by, horn blaring, waves of snow splashed out of its way as it careened through the intersection. The pedestrians cursed and yelled, shaking their fists, stamping their feet. The BMW's wheels gained traction, and it crossed into what would have been a path of death and destruction.

Raul slammed into something behind him. A building. A granite building. Another bank, he supposed with a dim thought.

"Hey, you okay, my man?" somebody asked. "Jesus Christ, you nearly bought the farm."

Raul said something back. Or at least he thought he did. All he could be sure of was that there was a sheet of ice on his cheeks, his tears crystallizing from the cold, the wind, the winter. He went to brush them off—

His little leather box, the one with the cross his lovely wife was going to yell at him for bringing home, was against his palm. Even though he had seen it fly from his hold in the second before he almost died.

A miracle, he thought as he looked at it.

He had received a Christmas miracle. Just in a nick of time.

CHAPTER TWO

H oly *fuck*," Trez yelled as a semitrailer truck the size of a building went blasting past the front bumper of his brand-new BMW.

Like right past. Like . . . nearly peeling off the hood of the damned car.

As his four-wheel drive, heavily treaded snow tires abruptly grabbed at that which they had been spinning on, and a pedestrian who'd slipped suddenly righted himself out of the way of the truck, Trez decided that the definition of in-the-nick-of-time was exactly what just happened. If he'd been able to go when the light had turned, if that pedestrian hadn't caught himself just when he had, they would both have been filing their termination papers tonight.

Which was kind of ironic.

Because about a split second prior to the almost-catastrophe going down, Trez had been debating whether or not to just drive on. And not merely through the intersection.

Having spent two decades in Caldwell, watching with his Shadow eyes the way a couple generations of humans built up the city, he knew exactly where this particular street in this particular section of town ended up.

At the Hudson River.

So if he hit the gas and kept on a direct, nonwavering course until the street ended, he could take a *Fast & Furious* jump off the concrete embankment under one of Caldie's two bridges. The BMW would not last long in the free fall, the sleek car having been built to fly over asphalt, not literally fly, and soon enough, both he and all this expensive steel, leather, and plastic would be sinking beneath the cold, sluggish waters of the Hudson.

As his eyes had flashed peridot, his brain had imagined what it would be like. At first, the water would infiltrate through seams and vents, a trickle, not a rush. But that would change as he used the last of the electrical system's power to lower the windows. After that, he would sit and wait for his drowning to take place, probably with his hands still on the wheel, maybe not, his seat belt remaining pulled across his chest, his clothes dampening and then clinging to his warm body with the clammy touch of the corpse he would soon become.

He would not struggle. He would keep his eyes open. He imagined himself feeling a calmness that had been missing since all the light in his world went out in that hospital room about twenty miles, and some distance underground, away from where he himself would die. He would be so relieved. Even as the water reached his throat, then proceeded over his mouth and into his nose and ears, even as his body temperature tried to rally against the icy submersion and failed to conserve any warmth, even as his air supply dwindled to that which was in his lungs and no more, he would be at peace.

The death throes, when they came—and they would, for his body was, as all were, evolutionarily adapted for survival, the conscious mind in charge only up to a dire point, whereupon autonomic function took over and things went haywire—would thrash him about in the bucket seat, throwing his head forward and back, his mouth opening and drawing in water as a reflex, as a desperate hope that his lungs were merely being denied oxygen as opposed to there being none available to them. He was under no illusions that it would be easy. There would be suffering from the suffocation, burning inside his body, perhaps even some last-moment panic kicked over his mortal transom by the lizard part of his brain.

But then it would be over. Done with. The whole miserable biological accident of his life dusted, in the bin, over and out.

A void, and nothing more.

Which was heretical.

As a Shadow, he had been raised in a slightly different belief system than regular vampires. His people, an evolutionary extension within the fanged species, relied a great deal on the stars in the sky, the traditions of the s'Hisbe a variant of what was accepted as the way the afterlife worked. The core tenets, however, were the same for both. It was like Protestants and Catholics—same essential language, but different dialects—and as such, his kind, too, had the theory that after you died, you went up unto the Fade, and lived out eternity with your loved ones under the benevolent auspices of the

Scribe Virgin. Assuming you hadn't been a total douche down on earth. If you had been an asshole, you were relegated to *Dhunhd*, also known as Hell, which was where the Omega and his minions hung out. Either way, your conduct over the course of your mortal nights determined your final zip code, and there was something after your last breath to look forward to—or dread—depending on your worthiness.

It was an okay theory, and a construct that he understood was, in its own fashion, to be found on the human side of things as well. Not the Fade or *Dhunhd*, perhaps, not the Scribe Virgin or the Omega, exactly, but rather other, similar belief systems that covered both how you treated yourself and others while you were mortal, and also considered what happened to you after your coil, so to speak, got popped. Islam, Judaism, Christianity, Buddhism, Hinduism, and countless other religions, they were all efforts to give more of a vista after death than just a coffin and a grave. Or a pyre.

He knew from pyres.

God, did he ever.

What he no longer knew from, however, what he no longer believed in, was all the rest of that stuff. He'd never been particularly spiritual, but man, you didn't know how much you had been until you were not any longer.

At all.

Anyway, prior to the whole truck/intersection/ almost-obliteration thing, he had been considering what was not exactly a sin, but rather a really, very not-so-hot idea. Assuming you were a believer. In the lexicon of both vampires and Shadows, if you took your own life, that was it. No Fade for you, motherfucker. Now, no one had been able to provide him with a good explanation of what the alternative repercussions were—sure, lore had it you were closed-door'd on the whole Fade thing. But where did you end up? *Dhunhd?* Worm food? Who knew. Yet everyone and their uncle was damn clear on the fact that you weren't going to be elbows deep in people you liked for the next jabillion years.

The message apparently being, if you took your own life, well, then, to hell with you if you didn't appreciate the gift you were given at birth.

Yeah, like this whole breathing/heart-beating thing had been such a fucking prize, these years he'd been upright and walking around such a goddamn joy. He'd been destined for a loveless mating since the night he was born, been responsible for the senseless suffering of both his parents, watched a dear friend get tortured by a psychotic cunt for a good twenty years—that was fun—been a pimp, a drug dealer, and an enforcer.

Real partridge-in-a-pear-tree shit.

And then that heaping sundae of shit-chip ice cream—which he'd self-medicated with an outstanding sex addiction, thank you very much—had been cherry-topped by the granddaddy of all gutwrenchers.

He'd met the female of his dreams, fallen in love . . . and, after what felt like twenty minutes of happiness, had had to hold her hand as she died of a wasting disease right in front of him.

Honestly, he hadn't just been born under a bad star; he'd been born under one that kicked him in the nuts so badly, he'd coughed them out in his hand.

So now he was here, in this BMW he'd just bought, on this snowy night, during the motherfucking human season of cocksucking joy, contemplating suicide—only to have the GODDAMN ACCIDENT THAT COULD HAVE MADE IT ALL COME OUT ALL RIGHT DENIED TO HIM BY A SET OF ALL-SEASON RADIALS THAT HAD WORKED JUST FINE AT EVERY OTHER FUCKING INTERSECTION HE'D EVER DRIVEN THROUGH.

Not to put too fine a point on things.

But FFS, he couldn't even have a chance to get dead in such a way that he could both end this bullshit AND not run afoul of the maybe truth that suicide got you, literally, nowhere.

Not that he believed in the afterlife anymore anyway. No matter what he'd thought he'd seen after Selena had died.

Hell, if there was anything that the last three months had taught him, it was that death was a hard stop. Especially if you were the one left behind.

Well, Trez thought, as he sped along in the snow, *at least there was still the embankment option.*

There was that to look forward to.

CHAPTER THREE

Her shadow lover came to her once again through the dense darkness of dream, his naked body pulling free of the ether, taking form before her. Tall and strong, wide of shoulder and long of leg, he was the fantasy made real in the realm of the subconscious, the representation of secret yearnings she held so dear they were in her soul.

Holding her arms up, she reached forward from her recline, and he came unto her without any entreaty, covering her with his warm, hard flesh so readily, it was as though he required her as much as she did him. His mouth, familiar and a shock at the same time, took

her lips, drugging her with kisses, his tongue, his scent.
Hands, broad and masculine, skimmed her breasts and
her waist, going lower . . . ever lower.

As she moaned, she begged for his name without
words. Her thoughts were known to him, and she told
him through the magic that enveloped them that she
needed the completion of his name, his call, his definition. There was no separate when they were like this, no
him and her, no beginning or end. A whole.

It was ever a reunion when he came to her.

Ever the closing of a loop.

Ever a return to the home she had been thrown out of.

But he always left her. He never stayed. And it was
too soon, the departure, no matter how long they had
together.

If she only knew his name, though . . . he would be
real. He would stay with her through the wakefulness that
was the thief of him. He would be next to her rather than
inside of her. His name would change everything . . .

Their bodies fell into place, the lock and the key, the
question answered, the reason given for that which had
been illogical.

The wound healed.

Tighter, she gripped him. Stronger, she pulled him to
her. Harder, she concentrated on every shift of his body,
every penetration of his sex, every surge of pleasure.

Always the parting.

No matter how long he was with her, he was always on the verge of leaving her behind, taking with him part of her heart, the cleaving a curse as much as the union was a blessing. He was beautiful moonlight eclipsed by the cloud cover; he was the still summer night interrupted by the violent storm; he was the warmth that flared before the brutal, numbing winter's arrival.

He was the last sweet breath taken before drowning.

Tears, now. Tears torn from her.

Stay with me, she begged him. Just this once. Do not go—

For the first time, in all the years she had known him, he stopped and looked down into her eyes.

His hand trembled as he brushed her long, dark curls from her face.

When he did not reply, his silence said enough. Said it all.

There was no divide between never and ever for them. Theirs was the space in between known and unknown, between the finite and the endless, proof that love was the tie that bound, but it was a faulty trip wire, changing nothing when death created the distance.

In his silence, her heart broke.

Again . . .

. . . always.

◆ ◆ ◆

Therese, blooded daughter of who the hell knew, shoved a hand into her cheap purse and pushed her wallet, a Kleenex pack, her ChapStick, and a hairbrush around. Change rattled on the very bottom and gave her brief hope, but her keys were still missing.

God, she was exhausted and she did not have time for this. That damn dream had kept her awake even as she'd slept, the dried tears on her face when she'd surfaced something she was really frickin' sick of, thank you very much. How many years had her subconscious been coughing that stuff up?

Ever since she could remember. And even before the bad thing with her family—

Across the hall from her apartment, a muffled yell and the crash of a broken lamp—or maybe it was dishes again?—brought her head up. The door to her one-room flat was standard-sized in terms of height and width, but it didn't seem thick enough. Although considering who else lived in this rooming house? She'd need one that was a foot deep and maybe made of something flame-retardant.

Back to her key search. They were definitely not in her purse, and courtesy of that dream, she'd slept through her alarm, so she was late for work. But she had to find them. And come on, there was only like, what, three hundred square feet to cover, tops. And that included the bathroom and the galley kitchen. Plus she was a nasty-neat who cleaned up after herself with a discipline that bordered on obsession. She could do this.

As she lifted up the cushions of the worn sofa, checked all the counters again, and shook out the blankets on her murphy bed, she refused to look at her watch. She did not need confirmation that she was late, late, late. She was supposed to have been at Sal's Restaurant for her shift waiting tables about an hour ago, and she could not afford to lose that job.

Maybe she needed to take some Ambien or something. Her perennial heartache dream aside, this rooming house was loud twenty-four hours a day. If one of the tenants wasn't yelling at somebody they lived with or next to or across the hall from, then they were burning food on their stove, throwing things that broke, or stomping around in concrete overshoes.

Closing her eyes, she let the blankets fall back to rest on the thin mattress—and then had to hospital-corner everything all over again. The rooming house was a dump, and worse, it was dangerous—although at least that had gotten better in the last week. That creepy dealer down the hall was avoiding her like she was contagious, and considering the diseases she could sense were already in his bloodstream? That was saying something.

"Keys . . ."

Another crash, this time above her, made her heart pound. She really should have followed up on that offer of a relocation. But she didn't want to be anyone's charity case, and even with her getting the waitress job, she hadn't saved much yet. She was going to have to find better employment, or pull in some major tips.

As her cell phone started ringing, she cursed and debated letting her manager, Enzo, go to voice mail. It couldn't be anybody else. The burner was only to field job applications. Her other phone, the one she had used when she had been with her family, wasn't even turned on.

The reminder of how little she had, and how thin her margin of survival was, hustled her back over to her purse. Grabbing the burner, she cleared her throat.

"Hi," she answered cheerfully. "I am so sorry— yes, yes, I know. Yes. All right. Of course. No, no, I'm coming in. I'm sure. Thank you."

Ending the call, she swallowed hard and felt light-headed. The sense that things were getting away from her, and not just her keys, made her feel like she was in an out-of-control car, skidding on ice, heading for an accident she was not going to walk away from. None of this was working. Not these horrible living conditions. Not this new life she had started in Caldwell. And now, almost not the job she needed.

Unlike humans, vampires had no safety net. There was no social security for the species. No Medicare/Medicaid. No organized charities. If she couldn't keep herself afloat on her own, she was going to end up on the streets because there was no going back to Michigan where she had been raised, no returning to the fold because there was no bloodline for her there. Those people were strangers who had passed themselves off as her *mahmen*, father, and brother, and only through an accident that could easily not have happened had Therese learned the truth.

Yeah, you'd think her abandonment as an infant and subsequent adoption might have come up at one of the thousands of First Meals they'd all shared. Maybe the Last Meals. Maybe the family meetings where choices were discussed and voted on. Or how about the festival nights? But . . . nope. Nada. The fact that she had not been born unto her family was a state secret to everybody but the one who it mattered the most to.

As another wave of woozy hit her, she went over to the dorm-sized refrigerator to have a sip of apple juice and—

Found her keys.

"Sonofabitch," she muttered as she reached inside the ice box.

The slips of notched metal were cold in her palm, and tears came to her eyes as she closed her hand around them.

As a vampire, she could lock the deadbolt on her apartment's flimsy door with her will alone. Not a problem. She didn't need a key for that, and God knew that the other people in the building were too distracted with their own dramas and addictions to notice that her door locked on its own. But there was more on the unadorned loop than what she had been given when she'd signed the papers for these four walls and a ceiling.

Opening her hand, she stared at the other key. The copper one. The one that opened the front and back copper locks to the house she had grown up in.

Members of the species couldn't manipulate copper locks with their minds. They were therefore the first line of security when you had a house full of people and things you wanted to protect. People and things that were yours. That you cared for and provided for and watched over.

She had tried to give the damn copper key up a number of times. She had taken it off the ring. Thrown it in the Hefty bag she used for kitchen trash. Pitched it into the Hannaford bag that hung on the back of the bathroom door. Even paused with the thing over an open municipal litter bin in the park, as well as the Dumpster behind the restaurant.

Every time she told herself to let it go, let it fall, be done with it . . . at the last minute, her hand refused to release. How in the hell could a symbol of everything that had betrayed her be her talisman? It made no damn sense.

Still, she had had no success arguing with her emotions around it up to this point.

Grabbing her bag, she bolted for the door, stepped out, and locked things. As she proceeded to the stairs, she kept her head down, her hands in her pockets, and her arm clamped down on her purse. The smells were awful. Old cigarettes, drugs she didn't know the names of but nonetheless now recognized, and old meat that might have also been rotting human skin.

Her feet were fast as she entered the stairwell,

and she moved quick on the stairs. If a human male ever aggressed on her, she could take him in a fight even though she was hardly trained for any kind of physical conflict. But that was only if he didn't have a weapon. A knife? A gun? She would find herself in trouble fast.

At the bottom, she punched out a fire door and strode into the grungy lobby. Someone called after her, but it was not her name that they used, and she was not responding to the rude term. It was a relief to get outside, and that was saying something considering it was arctic cold and snowing.

Heading around the side of her building, she batted the falling snow out of her face and tried to ignore the wail of sirens and the sound of someone screaming far off in the distance. There was also a troubling, repeating banging sound, the kind of thing that she prayed was not a head going into a hard wall.

Closing her eyes, she thought of her shadow lover and it all went away. The memory of him made her feel as safe as if he were actually with her—and yet, as always, when she was fully awake, she couldn't picture anything about him. Not his face, not his body, not his scent . . . only his existence was known to her conscious mind, not any of the details that she saw so clearly when she was asleep.

If I just knew his name, she told herself. *It would change everything.*

That was what was on her mind as she dematerialized, and it was a relief to scatter into a loose group of molecules and ghost away to a safer place. As she resumed her corporeal form behind Salvatore's Restaurant, she released the breath she had been holding and stepped forward in the foot-deep snow. The parking lot was mostly empty, only staff cars crowded up by the rear entry of the building, and a plow was trying to keep ahead of the storm, pushing more of what was coming down from the sky into piles at the edges.

It was going to be a quiet night because of the weather, and that was probably why her absence had been noted, but fairly well tolerated. The grace period wasn't going to last long, however. She had already been late once before because she'd overslept.

Stupid humans. Always pounding around above her.

Crazy dream. That wouldn't leave her in peace.

On the approach to the back door, she stood up the collar on her parka, like that somehow might make her look less late than she was. Which was ridiculous. Pushing her way into the unadorned concrete hall, she stomped most of the snow off her boots and then hurried to the staff locker room. Peeling off her coat, she tossed it and her purse in her locker—

"Are you okay?"

She spun around at the sound of the male voice. Emile Davise was six feet four inches of human male, with blond hair, blue eyes, and a kind smile. Right from the beginning, he had showed her the ropes and a lot of patience—even though he had no idea what he was dealing with, or who he was working for. Sal's was vampire-owned and -run, although humans were employed. Members of the species kept things very discreet, however.

"Oh, God, Emile." She sat down and unlaced her boots. "I slept through my alarm again. They're going to fire me."

"They will not. I will quit if they do." He held out a pressed half apron. "I got your tables ready."

She stopped what she was doing and looked up. "Emile."

"I had extra time." He jogged the apron. "Come on, service is starting. We have two tables full, believe it or not."

Therese hurried with the shoe change, swapping her heavy treads for black server shoes, and then she took what he gave her, folding and tying the apron around her waist and tucking everything in correctly so that her formal bow tie, white pressed shirt, black slacks, and the overlay were all smooth and orderly.

"How do I look?" she asked on the fly.

When there was a pause, she glanced at the human. His lids had lowered and a flush had come out on his cheeks.

Emile cleared his throat. "You're beautiful."

Therese opened her mouth to downplay everything—the moment, the attraction he was feeling, the subtle question that was in his stare but that had not yet come out of his mouth—but then she froze.

A Shadow loomed behind the man.

Therese's pulse quickened, her body responding in a rush. And as the shift in her attention was noted, Emile pivoted around.

"Oh, hello, Mr. Latimer," the human man said. "I was . . . er, I was just leaving."

Emile glanced back at her, and there was regret in his face. As if he knew things he wished he didn't. "I'll see you out on the floor, Therese."

"Thanks, Emile."

After the human left, she looked up, way up, into the eyes of a male that she had not been able to get out of her mind. Trez Latimer was more than a vampire. He was a Shadow, his dark skin and black eyes integral to the venerable heritage of the s'Hisbe, his heavy shoulders and long powerful legs the kind of thing you never saw except in warriors.

He was extraordinary. In all ways.

And he was staring at her with a kind of intensity that she had never understood, but certainly could not question. From the moment he had first seen her, he had appeared to be captivated—which made no sense at all. Therese was a middle-of-the-road female, neither beautiful nor ugly, neither fat nor thin, neither brilliant nor stupid.

Yet to this incredible male, she seemed to be of unusual interest.

There had to be a reason. But self-preservation dictated that she not go any further with him. God knew she had enough on her plate already.

"Hi," she said softly. "I wondered if you would be here tonight."

CHAPTER FOUR

And I wondered if you were dead, Trez thought to himself.

But that was hardly the kind of opener he wanted to lead with. For one, as a vampire, Therese wouldn't have been stupid like him and taken a car through the storm. She would have dematerialized here. For another, she was not his responsibility. Really. No, really, she was not.

And likewise he was not her curse.

Just because this female and his beloved Selena looked so completely similar did not give him the right to be behave as if Therese was his beloved *shellan*. So whether she was late to work on a snowy night, or if she didn't come in at all, or if she were early or on time, none of this was his problem, his fault, or his concern. And for crissakes, this paranoia he was rocking with regard to her safety was annoying.

Come on, not every female he met or came into contact with was going to die on him.

If that were true, the Black Dagger Brotherhood would all be widowers by now.

Trez cursed and looked away. Looked back. Tried not to re-memorize that which had never left his mind.

"Yes, I'm here," he heard himself say.

"Are you okay?"

Nope. Not even close. "I was just worried about you."

Yeah, wow. That pep talk he'd given himself had really stuck, hadn't it.

"That's really kind of you."

"The weather's bad out tonight." His voice sounded strange to his own ears. Tense and low. "Because of the snow."

Plus, there's that disaster zone you're living in, he tacked on in his head. And God, he really had to shut up here. He was just digging a hole he wasn't going to be able to climb out of.

"Oh, I'm fine." She made a dismissive motion with her hand. "I'm self-sufficient."

Next up: strained silence.

As the quiet persisted, Trez was aware he was staring, but his eyes refused to go anywhere else. Every time he saw this female, he found himself compulsively checking to see if he was right about what she looked like. To see if he had somehow misinterpreted something about her. And the fucked-up thing was that he couldn't decide whether he wanted his perception to be right or wrong—although it wasn't like he got a vote on that.

The likeness was stunning, and it reconnected him with everything he had lost, better than a photograph because there was movement, better than a memory because there was conversation, better than a fantasy because it was real. Therese's long, dark, curly hair, which was raked back and twisted into a tight bun per uniform requirements, was the precise color and texture of his Chosen's. And the female's pale eyes, perfectly set in her perfect face, were so like Selena's he had to force himself not to weep. And her lips . . .

Well, they were like his female's, too, and not just in terms of shape. And goddamn it, he shouldn't know what they felt like.

He shouldn't have kissed her on impulse that one

time, and he shouldn't have made this drive to see her, and he shouldn't have come here tonight on a pretense just so he could stand in front of her and get caught in this net again. She was not his dead *shellan* come back to life. She was a young female, hired by his brother, to work here in this restaurant. A stranger. Who just happened to look something like the love of his life.

"Sooooo, yes," she said slowly. "I'm fine."

Her eyebrows lifted and she leaned forward, as if she were trying to help him with the conversation. Or maybe was wondering if he'd stroked out.

"Good." Trez nodded. "I'm glad."

When she looked around him, as if she had to get to work, he knew he was going to lose his chance.

"Listen, have you given any more thought about that house I can get for you? The rental we talked about?"

Her eyes swung back up to his. When she didn't immediately answer him, he could feel his protective instinct come out, and he tried to reason with it. He didn't get far at all. His need to ensure her safety was like a charging bull, and come on, like he expected something with four clamoring hooves and anger-management issues to speak English? Listen to reason? He'd have better luck trying to convince himself she didn't look like Selena—and how far had he gotten with that one?

This whole thing was a mess. And he couldn't leave it well enough alone.

"I thought it was an apartment," she said with a frown.

"No, it was a house."

"You're really kind. But I told you last week that I've reconsidered and I'm going to stay put for now."

"I know." Okay, he was keeping his voice level. This was awesome. "But it's a good deal. An even better deal. Just like I said, you can pay what you're able now, and when you earn more, you can even it out later."

"I really appreciate it . . ." She smoothed the hair she had pulled back flat. "But I don't want to rely on you."

He put out his hand, all *Stop! In the naaaame of loooove.* Or, from her point of view, *Stop! For the love, please frickin' stop* with this rental malarkey.

"I don't expect anything in return," he said. "Just so we're clear. This is not something shady."

As her eyes dipped to his mouth, he knew exactly what she was thinking of, and dear God, he tried to hold the line with his libido. He shouldn't have engineered it so they'd been alone together, and not only because she worked for iAm. He was in no position to be taking any female out. He was chest-deep in grief, as steady as a two-legged chair, and just as likely to end up in the Hudson River as to make it home safely at the end of any given night.

Put like that? He was worse than a booby prize. He was a lit stick of dynamite, sure to cause damage and destruction in her life.

And that was before anyone got to the part about him feeling disloyal to a dead female for even thinking like this. With Selena gone, he should be a monk for the rest of his nights. No doubt the fact that they looked the same was the only reason he was able to think sexually at all. But still.

"You said you would move," he pressed. "When we were at the diner together. You said you would—"

"I know I did." Her expression turned anxious. "And I didn't mean to jerk you around. It was just, the more I thought about it, the more I felt uneasy about taking advantage of your connections."

"I can take you after work to see the place. You can do a walk-through—"

Trez sensed a presence out in the hall, and he looked in its direction. That blond human man was back again, leaning around the corner. Checking on Therese.

Trez's fangs tingled as they descended.

"She'll be right there," he clipped out.

When the guy backed off like someone was

pointing a gun at his head, Trez was disappointed for all the wrong reasons. He wanted to bare his fangs and hiss at the nosy bastard. Then maybe peel a carving knife out of the kitchen's collection and give the fucker a haircut. Starting with the feet and ankles, then working his way up.

Like any of that was going to help this situation, though? Dead bodies were inconvenient when they were created in public.

Plus, hello, body parts on the carpet were not going to help his case with Therese.

"I have to go." She offered an apologetic smile. "I was late tonight, and everyone took care of me."

Everyone? Trez thought to himself. *Or one particular guy.*

As his heart dropped and his stomach churned, he shook his head. At himself. "Look, if you're worried about . . . you know, privacy. It's fine. It's . . . whatever. I'm not going to intrude on your life."

The fuck it was whatever. But like he was in any position to criticize her choices? If she wanted to bang that human until the sonofabitch walked with a limp and needed an IV bag for fluids, then there was not a damn thing he could do about it.

Well, except go to work with that knife. Although chances were, if she actually liked that motherfucker with the flaxen fucking hair, she was going to get a little offended if a headstone was brought into the equation.

Oh, God, he needed to get out of this—

Therese put her hand on his arm, and swear to God, he felt the contact go through his entire body.

"I know this doesn't make a lot of sense, but I really want to do this on my own," she said. "I've thought about your kind offer, I really have, and I shouldn't have jumped at the chance without considering the implications. It would be so easy to rely on you, but I need to stand on my own two feet. It is why I came to Caldwell, and I am not going to compromise on that."

Trez covered her hand with his own. "I won't have a key, I promise. I won't be able to get in there—it's nothing like that. It will be your private place, for you to do . . . whatever in."

The fact that he felt like vomiting seemed a sad commentary on where he was. The desperation was, literally, nauseating.

"This is not about you," she said. "Or anybody else. I want to take care of myself. I've learned the hard way that it's best not to rely on other people, and if I don't start being independent now, when is it going to happen—"

"That shithole you're in now is not safe."

"I really appreciate your concern." Her eyes were luminous as she stared up at him. "But it's a no-thank-you. And I don't want to talk about this anymore."

Removing her hand from under his own, she patted his arm, in a classic just-a-friend kind of way, and then slipped by him. As she passed so close to his body, he closed his eyes and breathed in her scent. Then he turned and watched her go. She was going to work with that blond human all night long, and Trez was willing to bet they were going to share inside jokes, and the bastard was going to offer to take her home at the end of the shift. How far would things go at that point?

As the urge to kill resurged, Trez argued with his biochemistry. He was *not* bonding with her, goddamn it. That was crazy.

This was all crazy.

He was all crazy.

Leaning back against the cool wall, he breathed deeply and tried to ignore the smells from the kitchen, the sounds of people talking in the building, the low-level howl from the storm outside. He could not control his thoughts or his body when he was around that female, all kinds of haywire happening.

So the easy solution was to not come here. Not see her. Set up boundaries that were high and wide and accessorized with barbed wire.

And yet he kept throwing himself at this gauntlet of his own invention. To the point where that female, who had asked for none of this, and didn't even know the half of it, was the one putting up the "No Trespassing" signs.

It was too fucked up.

Forcing himself to get moving, Trez kept things slow as he went down toward the kitchen so he didn't catch up with her. The last thing he needed was to add stalking to his list of career choices. Like pimp and drug dealer weren't enough on his LinkedIn?

The back of the house was utilitarian, nothing but painted concrete walls, and serviceable spaces like iAm's office, the locker room, and the staff break room. And then there was the kitchen itself. As Trez emerged into the huge space, he blinked in the glare of the bright lights and the stainless steel. Everything was spotless, well organized, and, due to the inclement weather, nothing like the hotbed of activity that usually hustled around the stoves, the ovens, the prep counters, and the staging area.

"What the hell?" he muttered.

Something was burning on the stove, and where was his brother? Where was the sous chef?

"iAm?" he called out as he went over to the sixteen-burner and moved a pot of sauce off the heat. "iAm!—"

"—here, I'm right here." His brother came rushing out of the pantry, a twenty-pound bag of flour in one hand, a flat of eggs in the other. "Hey, how are you?"

"I'm good." *Yup, just fantastic. I've been upgraded from suicidal to self-annoying. Next stop: Lunatic.* "Where is everyone?"

"Most of them couldn't come in because of the storm." iAm dumped the bag on the counter. "I just sent Enzo home, along with my other two chefs. I'm just going to handle things myself tonight."

"Whatever's in there was burning." Trez pointed to the pot. "I moved it over."

"Thanks."

Instead of going over to check on what was up with the sauce, iAm put his egg load down like he meant to get started on whatever it was he'd intended to make. Except then he seemed to lose focus, bracing both hands on the counter and lowering his head.

Trez frowned. "What's going on? What's wrong?"

"Nothing."

"You sure about that?" Trez glanced at the pot. "When was the last time you burned something?"

There was only a heartbeat of a pause, the kind of thing that almost no one would notice. And then iAm's black eyes looked up and he appeared perfectly normal, perfectly calm, as he lied:

"I'm fine. Really."

Guess two could play at this game, Trez thought.

♦ ♦ ♦

"This is bullshit. I'm out of here."

As the words were pushed out of an angry, lipsticked mouth, Therese glanced across the water-filling station. Liza, a female human who was one of six servers supposed to be on, had evidently decided to jump ship and was determined that everyone not only know that she was leaving, but also be aware that she did not approve of the weather.

Like someone inside of Sal's was in charge of the blizzard button and had negligently greenlighted the storm.

"Fucking snow." Liza reached around to the small of her back and yanked at the ties on her half apron. "I've got rent to pay. There are two tables filled, and neither of them are in my room anyway. I swear that fucking hostess hates me."

Therese looked away. Liza Drama was something she had learned to stay out of, although God knew it was a big pool to fall into.

"Maybe more customers will come in." Emile leaned out around the ice bin and the stacks of plastic refill containers. "It's early."

"I'm not waiting around." Liza wadded up her apron and put her hands on her hips. "What are you going to do."

Therese went about her business, taking one of the pitchers, opening the ice tank, and getting some chips out. Liza was not talking to her. Liza never talked to her. The woman couldn't have made her dislike more obvious if she had tattooed her forehead with "Back Off, New Girl, He's Mine."

"I'm going to stay here," he said. "I need my shift money."

"How am I supposed to get home?"

Therese graduated from the ice bin to the water dispenser, pushing the lip of the pitcher against the toggle. The stream of cold water that came out was steady but small. She wished the damn machine peed like a racehorse so she didn't have to listen to this.

"I don't know." Emile shrugged. "Call an Uber?"

"*You* are my *ride*, Emile."

Okay. So all Therese could hear in her head was Faye Dunaway gritting out, *No more wire haaaaaaaaaangers!*

"And I am staying here."

Therese felt the sting of the woman's glare on the back of her neck so acutely, she had to roll her shoulders to release some tension.

"This is *bullshit*," Liza said. "And you better call me to make sure I get home safe."

With that, she huffed off, and it was only when the coast was clear that Therese glanced over. "You know, if you want to go, I can handle—"

"No." Emile shook his head curtly. "She needs to do her own thing. I don't know what her problem's been the last week or two."

You haven't noticed that she'd like to stab me with a fork? Therese thought. *And every shift she's denied the chance, she gets even crankier?*

Emile looked over. "We're not dating. Just so you know. She lives two streets away from my apartment and I give her rides. That's it."

Therese stepped away from the water machine. "She doesn't bother me."

Emile's smile was relieved. "That's good. That's . . . really good."

To break the eye contact, Therese took a couple of steps over and made a show of assessing the main dining room. There were twenty or so tables of various sizes and configurations, and just as Liza had reported, only two were filled, one by a human couple, and another, a four-top, by a male of the species. The bar, which had banquette seating, was totally empty, and the other front room, which was Liza's territory, was empty.

And then Therese realized something.

"Wait, are we the only servers here?"

There was the sound of ice rattling into a container. "Now that Liza's gone, yes, I think we are. The hostess left."

Therese sensed the human man staring at her, and she wanted to tell him to stop. Not because he was being offensive or invasive and not because she felt threatened. It was because she felt absolutely nothing at all—and also because he only thought he knew who she was. Humans assumed vampires were a Halloween myth, and that secret needed to be kept. But more than that, she wasn't looking for any kind of a relationship, not even a casual-dating or friends-with-benefits one.

If she was going to get involved with somebody—which she was not—it was going to be that Shadow—

Stop it, she thought. *Just frickin' stop it*—

"I'm sorry. I'm really sorry."

Therese shook herself and focused on Emile. His handsome face was stricken, his skin pale.

"What?" she said.

"Look, I don't . . ." He put his water container down on the counter. "I don't want to make things weird."

"What?"

As he stood there, looking downcast, she cursed under her breath. She must have spoken the red light out loud.

She put her hand on his shoulder. "Oh, my God. No, no. I was talking to myself. That wasn't directed to you. I'm sorry."

As his features eased and he started to smile, she almost went to find Liza and suggest she be the one to work with the guy. What the hell was going on tonight? There seemed to be trouble happening everywhere she turned, even though she hadn't dropped any trays or spilled wine on any customers.

Yet, she tacked on. She hadn't done a dropsy *yet*. The night was still young.

Before she could figure out a way to kindly pump the man's breaks—although maybe she should lead with a flash of her fangs and then dematerialize right in front of him; that would take care of things—Emile smiled like the prospects of the evening had just gotten so much better.

He nodded out to the dining room. "You see that blond guy?"

Relieved to have anything else to focus on, Therese glanced toward the hearth. "Yes?"

"You take that table. He's a great tipper."

"I don't want to cheat you out of—"

"No, you take it. And don't worry, I'll handle everyone else that comes in. I'll make it up."

"That doesn't seem fair."

"Trust me," Emile said dryly. "You're going to need the extra time with him. Even if he eats alone."

CHAPTER FIVE

And still the cold waters of the Hudson
River beckoned.

As Trez pulled his car into his reserved
space behind shAdoWs, he killed the engine and
just sat there outside of his club, watching the snowflakes clutter up the windshield that no longer was
swept clean by the wipers. When it dawned on him
that he'd turned things off with the blades halfway
up the arc of their path, he reignited the electrical
system and brought them back into their proper
place, all tucked in under the lip of the hood, a pair
of twins put to bed. It felt good to set something,

anything, into alignment, and the fact that the best he had to work with in that department was the wipers on his car?

Well, beggars, choosers, and all that shit.

He should head inside. See whether anyone had shown up either for work or for boozing and sex. Check in with Xhex.

He stayed where he was.

Meanwhile, the snow continued to fall, the heavy congregations of individual flakes making him think of people jumping out of airplanes and banding together on the descent, arms linked, bodies close. The impacts of the crystalline formations were utterly silent, and that was one of the things he had used to love about winter's version of a rainstorm. Unlike what happened in warmer months, there was no sizzle as things fell and landed on objects and people, no dripping off gutters and rooflines, no speckling tap dance on windshields.

Silence. Utter silence.

Funny, now he hated that about snow. Staring at the dapples that were closing ranks, as if his car, his club, the whole of Caldwell, was a puzzle the storm was filling in with pieces, the holes locked in, corners completed, the outside rim already done, he found that he couldn't breathe.

When he had been at his queen's deathbed, in the Brotherhood's clinic, there had been machines monitoring her body as it failed. How he had hated them. The alarms had been a countdown to her extinction, and as they went off at closer and closer intervals, he had wanted to take a baseball bat to them—or maybe a wrecking ball. But it was worse when they were switched off. The silence had been awful. Then again, medical staff only monitored patients when there was something to keep track of. Some kind of change that they could watch out for and counteract. Some course correction that could be undertaken.

When the scales tipped irrevocably to death, there was nothing to watch over anymore.

After the medical machines had been turned off, he had stepped in and become Selena's monitor. He had stayed by her side and tried to care for her. As she had been paralyzed from head to toe at the end by the Arrest, he had set up a communication system where she blinked once for *no*, twice for *yes*.

It was strange the things he remembered afterward, and that system was one of them. He had suggested one blink for the *no*s because he was most concerned that he understand what was not working for her. Can you breathe? *No.* Are you okay? *No.* Can I help you?

No.

Are you ready to go? *Yes.* Do you want help to go? *Yes.*

He'd felt as though he had to choose which answer would be more important, more critical, her *yeses* or her *nos*, because at the end, she had had so little strength that he had wanted to save her any effort if he could. One for *no.* Two for *yes.* But as if it really mattered?

Waiting for the death to occur had provided him with a new facet of torture. After what was both an eternity and a split second, the ultimate silence arrived. No more breathing from her. No more beating of her heart. No more blinking.

Gone.

Returning to the cold present, Trez exhaled as the last vacancies on his windshield were filled, a whiteout in front of him now, the view of the back of his club obscured. He had a thought that the inside of his car was probably close to freezing, but he couldn't feel anything. His mind was too far back in the past, his body left behind here in the current time, the connection between the two cut once again.

The final moments of Selena's life were something he had relived a thousand times since they had actually occurred. The constant replay was like a new part of him, a second torso, another arm, another leg. He couldn't decide whether his evidently compulsive need to go back to that exam room's bedside, that instance where her life ended and she took him along with her off the planet, was rooted in his brain or his heart. He also wondered what the purpose of the retreading was. Did he think that if he reviewed the ending enough in his mind that the finale would change? That somehow, if he just went back over those moments again and again, he might get a different result, as if maybe reality would forget? Or maybe like the past was an old-school LP record and the needle would skip at just the right place and resume the song on the far side, as if nothing had ever been wrong.

Presto! She was alive.

And so was he.

Okay . . . he really needed to go inside before he turned into a Popsicle.

Instead, the endless replay started again, and, as it always did, the sights, the smells, the sounds, eclipsed the world that was before him, sure as if they called his name in a command he had to follow.

The Brotherhood's training center had a clinical area, one that was dedicated to helping the fighters and members of the household through everything from cuts to concussions, birth to broken bones. They'd never handled a case of the Arrest before Selena. Then again, the disease was not only very rare; it was only found among the Chosen, those sacred females who served the Scribe Virgin. Selena had been well aware she suffered from it, and she had watched a couple of her sisters die from being turned into figurative stone. She had also known it was terminal and there was nothing to be done. Her body was going to fall into a rigid paralysis state that was incompatible with life.

She had been out of time long before he'd ever met her.

There were a lot of things about his life he would change. Meeting her was not one of them, however, even with all the pain that had come.

At the end of it all, when he'd been sitting beside her and holding her hand, he could remember thinking that he would have traded places with her in a heartbeat. He had always wanted to be the one to suffer instead of her, and after she was gone? He'd realized his wish had been granted. Her agony was over—either because the bullshit Fade actually existed or because she was just plain dead.

And his was permanent.

So he'd gotten what he'd prayed for.

Rubbing his eyes, he tried to pull out of the suck zone. He failed. He always failed. He didn't know why he bothered to fight it, other than the fact that each time he went back to that moment in his life, in hers, it hurt every bit as much as when it had happened.

He could picture the exam room like he was standing in it, the table in the center, the stainless steel shelves, the chair he'd been given. After the medical folks had turned the monitors off, he'd asked his queen if it was time, if she was ready to go, if she needed help. She had blinked twice at all of it. *Yes.* Still, he'd had to ask her again, just to make sure. It was the kind of thing he needed to get right. When he was sure of what she wanted, Dr. Manello had done the duty with the syringes, giving her the drugs that would ease her as death came and claimed her. Trez didn't understand then, and couldn't fathom now, what it was like to have all your mental faculties intact, but be locked into your body, unable to move, unable to communicate, unable to do anything but wait as your breathing and your heart rate slowed . . . and then stopped. The terrifying thing was that Selena's version of paralysis had not been like that of a quadriplegic, where the person felt nothing. With the Arrest, bastard disease that it was, all her nerves had functioned properly and continually. She felt everything, all the pain, all the suffocation, all the repercussions of the organ failures.

Before things had gotten acute, they had talked about what she wanted. His queen had said when it was time, she wanted help. She wanted the drugs that would bring the end a little faster and easier. He had made sure she had received them.

And then he had held her hand as his brother had held his, and he had repeated, over and over again, "I love you forever."

Over and over and over again.

He had known the instant her soul had left its broken corporeal host. He still had no clue how he'd known, but he'd felt it in his gut. And quick on her essence's departure had come unto him a crippling, shattering pain, the likes of which he had never felt before.

Selena had come to visit him once since then. Or at least his brain had coughed up a pretty damn good illusion of her, one that had basically told him everything he would have wanted to hear from her after her death. And he supposed he had got-ten a measure of temporary peace from that. But it wasn't the same as having her back. Nothing was the same.

And she hadn't come again unto him. Which was how he had lost his faith in the afterlife.

Surely, if she were somewhere in the universe, and she could come see him once, she would do it again. His *shellan* wouldn't have deserted him in his suffering. No way.

So there had to be nothing of her left.

Staring at the snow-covered windshield of his BMW and being able to see nothing on the other side made him think of Therese. He had had no real reason to go to the restaurant tonight. He had no reason to try to see that female, ever—especially now that she had drawn such a firm line about getting out of that rooming house. He needed to leave her well enough alone.

Physical similarities amplified by grief did not a relationship make.

And besides, his grief was like the snow on this car. Blinding him to what was all around, rendering him cold and sightless as to the truths he was living in. He was just starting this journey of grief, the death still so fresh, and there were no easy exit ramps off the highway he was on. From what Mary had told him, he just needed to proceed with the belief and understanding that it does get, if not better, per se, then at least more easily tolerated.

Not that he found "more easily tolerated" something to look forward to.

He didn't find anything to look forward to.

And seeking out that waitress did not count as optimism. It was a compulsion that bordered on being psychotic.

He needed to cut that shit out.

♦ ♦ ♦

Back at Sal's, Therese crossed the main dining room with a pitcher in one hand and a damask napkin in the other. As she approached the male vampire who was sitting by himself in front of the hearth, he looked up, and she nearly tripped on the carpet.

Which was what you might expect when someone saw a unicorn. Out in the wild. About to have dinner at a four-top by himself.

The male was so unusually handsome that her eyes had trouble processing the full sight of his facial features. His coloring. His incredibly big body. He had blond hair that was thick and seemed natural, not colored. His cheekbones were high and hard, balanced by the blunt cut of his chin. And she refused to even look at his lips, her peripheral vision providing her with enough of an idea of what they were like that she felt as if, were she to get a full view of them, it would be akin to staring at a naked ass that was spectacular.

"Hi, my name is Therese." As her voice squeaked, she cleared her throat. "I'll be your server tonight."

She leaned over his table, put the folded napkin on the rim of his water glass, and tipped the pitcher so that a deluge of ice and water went tumbling in. The manager, Enzo, required that all servers do the napkin trick, and at first, she'd thought it was incredibly pretentious. A couple of pours in, however, and she was grateful for the splatter shield.

"Are we waiting for others to join you?" she said as she straightened. "Perhaps a cocktail for you to pass the time—"

Therese froze and stopped talking. Her one customer of the night was staring at her with wide eyes, like someone had slapped his incredible face with a cold fish.

She glanced over her shoulder in case the good-looks police were coming to take back some of his handsome as a violation of the natural order. Or maybe it was a demogorgon from *Stranger Things*. Nope, no one was behind her. Maybe there was something wrong with her uniform? She looked down at herself to make sure everything was in proper place still, not that any kind of untucked could explain the expression of shock he was showing.

Refocusing on her customer, she held her pitcher closer to her body. "Is there something wrong?"

The male shook himself. Looked away. Looked back. Continued to stare.

Okay, so this guy might be a good tipper, she thought, but he was going to make her earn the extra money just being around the weirdness—

"I'm sorry," the male said in what was, of course, a gorgeously rich and deep voice. "You just—you remind me of someone I know."

"Oh?"

There was no reason to get braced for some kind of pickup line. For one, he was too extraordinary to need them. She was quite certain he could sneeze and women and females would come running just on the outside chance that he needed a tissue. For another, going by what he looked like, you could roll every supermodel from Dovima to Gigi Hadid into a single, incandescent vision of femininity, and a guy like him would probably only muster a casual hi-how're-ya.

The male blinked a couple of times. "Yeah, sorry. It's uncanny."

"Well, there are a lot of females around with long dark hair?"

"Yeah." Abruptly, he smiled, as if he were determined to change tracks in his head. "I'm Rhage."

As he put out his hand, Therese stared at it. Then, thinking of tips and her desire to move out of the rooming house on her own nickel, she figured, what the hell.

Shaking what he offered, she said, "Therese."

"You work here long?" he asked as they dropped palms.

"Just a little bit."

"You from Caldwell?"

"Nope. Moved here recently."

"Where's your family?"

"Back home." She cleared her throat. "So are we waiting for some more people? Or are you eating alone?"

The handsome male shook his head. "I'm waiting for my *shellan*, actually."

Okay, wow, Therese thought. Two beautiful people on his level in this dining room? They were liable to collapse gravity and suck everyone in the restaurant, maybe this whole part of town, into a black hole full of Tom Ford suits and Stella McCartney dresses.

"Well, would you like a cocktail while you wait?"

"Just this water will be—"

His unbelievably blue eyes shot to the side, and the smile that came over his face transformed that which had been gorgeous into something that defied any description with any infinite number of words. And it wasn't just his face that was affected. His big body got up as if it were operating independently and without his knowledge, his knees bumping into the lip of the table, rattling the glasses, sloshing the water that had just been poured.

Therese shored herself up as she turned to see what the *shellan* looked like. Undoubtedly, the female was going to be the kind of thing that made other carbon-based life forms of the ovarian persuasion feel like shutting themselves in a room in the dark with absolutely no mirrors and seven thousand pounds of Hershey's chocolate—

Therese recoiled. What had entered the dining room, and was taking off a rather practical wool coat, was . . . normal-looking. Like, not unattractive, but not knock-your-socks-off gorgeous. The female was small, with brown hair that was sensibly cut, and she had an open, makeup-less face that, even without knowing a thing about her, made Therese feel like she could be trusted with anything and everything.

And she wasn't a vampire. She seemed sort of human, and yet there was something else going on, although it was hard to suss out what exactly it was.

Taking a step back, Therese watched as the beautiful male walked forward and enveloped his mate in his massive arms. As he curled his body around her, you would swear they had been separated by a decade of wartime.

"I missed you," the male said.

"I just saw you an hour ago," the *shellan* murmured with a laugh.

"I know. It's been hell."

Therese dropped her eyes out of respect as the two of them said quiet things to each other and sat down at the table. The male took his *shellan*'s hand and just stared across the glasses, the china, the silverware. It was clear that he didn't know where he was and didn't care, because wherever she was was his home. And his love transformed the quiet, calmly attractive woman into something even more beautiful than he was.

Therese watched them for a moment, struck by what love can do. How it could transform. How it could connect. How it could elevate even those with the best looks and the purest hearts.

She had never thought much about matings.

Lifelong relationships. Males in particular. And not because she was a born cynic. She'd just been too busy living life to spin fantasies about her future. Now, though, she had the sense she was staring at a miracle.

And the only thing that came to her mind?

That Shadow.

Which made no sense whatsoever—

Abruptly, she became aware that the *shellan* half of the couple was staring up at her with exactly the same surprise that Mr. Perfect had.

Therese looked back and forth between them. Then she half-heartedly raised her hand in greeting. "Um, hi. I'm Therese, I'll be your server?"

The *shellan* blinked a couple of times. "Of course you are. I mean, thank you."

"Can I start you with a cocktail?" *Do you need to see my ID so you know I'm not a missing person?* "Or perhaps the menu?"

The woman's smile was sad for a reason that Therese couldn't begin to guess at. "I'd love a glass of white wine. And what did you say your name is?"

CHAPTER SIX

ShAdoWs was every club in America. You had dark corners, random lasers, booming music, and plenty of booze. The sex and drugs were BYO, and for the most part, Trez left his clientele alone on those fronts. There were two reasons for this: One, the less you hassled them, the more often they came back and dropped their cash, and two, he really didn't give a shit—and that had been true well before he had loved and lost his queen.

Staring down at the churning crowd from his second-floor office, he watched them through the kind of one-way glass that psychologists used to monitor the interviews of insane people. And this made sense. The men and women below, stimulated and stimulating each other, were not on the normal bandwidth, and that was why they came to his establishment. Most of them were young, but they were all out of college if they had gone to one, the twenty-one-year-old age requirement for drinking in New York weeding out the underclassmen. Most had low-level jobs, ones that were above menial but not by much. Most were renters in bunches of two and three. Most had STDs or were going to get them as soon as they jumped into the one-night stand pool on the dance floor.

All of them were desperate for a break from the stress in their lives.

Yeah, 'cuz there was nothing like getting away from your mistakes by making new ones.

Trez should know. After his two decades of being a pimp and an enforcer in Caldwell, nothing had changed, just the faces on those young bodies and maybe some of the politics. And for a long time, he had been down there with them, and not only in terms of security or sales of sex or drugs. He too had partaken of the women and the females. It had been a nice distraction, whether it was the sex workers who he provided a safe environment for or the women who came to dance and see what they could pull. He had always been a sure thing, and not just at the club. Everywhere. He had had sex with real estate agents, lawyers, tax accountants, personal trainers, landscapers, laundresses, mechanics, hairdressers . . .

And in spite of that track record, as he looked over the crowd, he saw nothing of interest. There were plenty of good-looking women down there, most of them half dressed and double-jointed, with willingness written all over them. But to him they were another species, and not just because they were mostly human. He'd no more have sex with them than he would a wolfen or a mailbox.

Letting go of his sex addiction had been easy. Letting go of what had taken its place, his Selena, was impossible.

Down below, the crowd's random pattern of grinding abruptly shifted and found a cohesion that rarely happened, bodies packing in tight to clear a path. Someone had come into the club and was walking through the cram of people—and whoever they were, folks were getting out of their way in a hurry, parting like the Red Sea of Fuckboys and Casual Lays.

Trez recognized the figure immediately. Then again, like anyone else on the Eastern seaboard wore a floor-length sable coat indoors, and carried a walking cane that doubled as a weapon? Rehvenge was back in his element, strolling through the club like he owned it, his Mohawk and his amethyst eyes nothing that any of the clubbers had ever seen the likes of before, the aura of don't-fuck-with-me exactly the kind of thing their survival instincts recognized as a cue to skidoo.

Trez backed off from the glass wall and went to the door to his office. As he left and proceeded down the stairs, he couldn't think of why his old boss was doing an out-and-about, especially in a club. Rehv had staged his own death a couple of years ago in a spectacular explosion, wiping out the identity he'd cultivated as a drug dealer and club owner on the scene. Why the resurrection?

Down on the floor, Trez came around the base of the staircase as Rehv broke through the last of the congregation.

"Fancy meeting you here," Trez murmured as they met face-to-face.

Rehvenge was not merely your average vampire. He was a *symphath*, and not just a Joe Schmoe one. He was king of the territory, ruler of a subspecies that made sociopaths look like family-focused nurturers. So yes, he was as dangerous as he looked.

"My man," Rehv said as they hugged it out, clapping each other on the back.

"What brings you into the riffraff?"

Rehvenge looked around. "Just checking the scene."

"Bullshit."

The smile that came over that slightly evil face was hard. "Am I not welcome here?"

"You know that's not the case." Trez nodded at the crowd, most of whom were checking out the *symphath* with barely disguised fascination—and God only knew how many phones that were discreetly sneaking pics or a video. "You're catching a lot of views, that's all. The cost-benefit analysis usually isn't there for you."

"They won't remember me."

"Not without your help, they won't."

"I'll handle it." Rehv nodded at the back stairs. "You got time to talk?"

"Depends on the subject."

"Good, I appreciate you making the time."

Rehv walked past him, like whatever conversation Trez was probably going to want to avoid had been booked on the social calendar with a Sharpie.

Great. Fucking fantastic.

As Trez followed the leader, he remembered

the way things had been, Rehv in charge, Trez and iAm's job to keep the fucker alive as he had done his dirty business with the Princess. Talk about bumping uglies. God, those had been horrible nights, Rehv going up there to that cabin in the woods with satchels of rubies bought with the money he made from drug sales and the clubs, the male turning those precious stones over before he had to give his own body to that damn bitch. Trez had always followed in the ether, staying hidden, so that after it was done, he could scrape Rehv up off the dirty floor and help him home. The male had always been so sick, the contact with that Princess making him ill, and not just because he despised the female and hated himself even more for doing what he had to. She'd been poison to him. Literally.

Instantly, Trez thought of iAm, lying through his teeth about being okay.

Maybe it was good that Rehv had come. Maybe the *symphath* knew what the hell was going on with his brother. iAm had always been the quiet one, and him finding his love with *maichen* hadn't loosened his lips. But Rehv had been known to get things out of the guy—whether iAm liked it or not. That was the problem with *symphaths*. Hiding anything from them was a losing game.

Back inside the office, Trez felt a little weird sitting behind the desk. For so long, Rehv had been the one in charge. Yet he seemed perfectly comfortable to be on the subordinate side of things.

"So," his former boss said, "how you doing?"

Trez narrowed his eyes. "Isn't this about iAm?"

"iAm? Why, what's going on with him?"

"So you haven't come because of him." When Rehv slowly shook his head and didn't go any further, Trez wanted to curse. "All right, so let's play pin the tail on the meddler. Who put you up to this? Was it my brother?"

Maybe that was why iAm had been distracted at the restaurant.

And as Trez entertained an image of himself at that traffic light, contemplating suicide in the new car that had done nothing to elevate his mood, he refused to think that his brother might have reason to worry. After all, Trez's life was his own to destroy, goddamn it. No one else was welcome at that table.

When Rehv just shook his head again, Trez considered other likely whistle-blowers. "Oh, so it was Mary, huh. I mean, she's the resident therapist, although I haven't been around her enough—wait, it was Xhex? Really?"

He would have assumed his head of security was

too much of a hard-ass to pull in reinforcements if she was worried about him. She was more the type to get up in his face and not move. But was he so bad off that even she was daunted by the idea of talking to him—

"No, it was Beth." Trez slapped his thigh. "It was because of movie night last week. She wanted me to come and asked me twice. I didn't show and she looked worried. Or maybe it was more like upset."

"Is Beth upset with you?"

"So it was her."

"The Queen has said nothing to me. I don't know whether she's worried or not."

Trez looked away, mentally reviewing the household cast of characters. Well, shit. The only people he could rule out were the *doggen*. Fritz and his staff would never be so presumptuous as to suggest so much as a wardrobe change to someone they served, much less form a consensus on a person's mental stability. Or lack thereof.

"Look," he gritted out. "Will you just get on with it? No offense, but I got business to take care of."

Not really, the club ran itself. He had to play what cards he had, however.

As the silence stretched out, Trez took an inventory of his former boss. Rehv's purple eyes were utterly level, the color reminding Trez of Rhage's GTO. And between that huge body, and all that fur, the chair that ordinarily was perfectly big enough for anyone who sat in it looked like dollhouse furniture. Worse, as the king of the *symphaths* just sat there, batting his walking stick back and forth between his knees, his white suit and white shirt like he'd worn the storm indoors, the male seemed content to ride out the bad weather. Until, like, August.

"What." Trez sat forward and fiddled with two accounts payable reports. "Can we just get this over with."

"Ehlena says hi."

"And you came all this way to tell me?"

"Well, not everything has to be on text. Have you heard about the privacy concerns going around? Smartphones are evil."

"Fuck you," Trez said in an exhausted voice. "No offense."

Rehv got to his feet and strolled over to the glass wall, that sable coat flaring out behind him, the glittering cane flashing in the dim lights from overhead. As Trez watched his old friend, he realized it had been so long since he had hung out with the male. Both of their lives had changed so much, although only Rehv's for the better.

"You know I'm still on the dopamine, right?" Rehv said as he angled his sight downward toward the dance floor.

Trez swiveled his chair around so he could face the male. "I hadn't really thought about it one way or the other."

I've been too busy playing out what drowning would be like, he added to himself. *Shit gets so hectic during this human Christmas season, dontcha know.*

But as he considered his former boss, he supposed the guy had to still be on the sauce, so to speak. *Symphaths* were known to get into things like other people's emotions, and never in a good way, never in a therapeutic, supportive fashion, more like a shove-you-off-your-ledge way. They were a subspecies that you didn't want to show your underbelly to, although the prejudice they'd been subjected to hadn't been right, either.

When Rehv had been out in the world more, he'd taken dopamine as a way to regulate himself so that his bad side stayed under wraps and his true identity remained hidden. It had been the only way for him to seem like he was just the same as everyone else. And after he was mated? Apparently, he kept on using the stuff.

Trez shrugged. "I guess I am a little surprised

you're still dosing. I mean, everyone knows what you are. Everyone who matters, that is."

And more than that, he had forged a political alliance with Wrath. He was super safe.

"It goes deeper than suppressing my identity," Rehv murmured. "My instincts are much more controllable now, it's true. My love for Ehlena is responsible for that. So are my relationships with Wrath and the Brotherhood. I am what I am, however, and if I'm going to live my fullest life with my *shellan* and allies, I want to be able to focus on things other than just curtailing my difficult side."

"Okay."

Trez ground his molars. He had no idea where this was going, and the fact that he didn't really care seemed like one more thing to add to his long list of losses. He and Rehv went way too far back for him to push the guy out, especially as Trez couldn't remember when they had sat down together last. Grief changed your priorities, however.

He thought of sitting in his BMW, out in the cold, getting buried in snow.

"So I was talking to my Ehlena," Rehv continued, "about some pharmaceutical options for you."

Trez jerked forward. "Excuse me?"

"I wanted to see if you could get some help."

Rehv's amethyst eyes swung over. "To see if you can find some relief, as I have."

An irrational anger curled in Trez's gut. "I'm not a *symphath*."

"You're suffering."

"My *shellan* fucking died. You think I should be throwing a party?"

"I know where you've been going," Rehv said calmly.

"To work, here, every night. Yeah. So—"

"In your mind." Rehv touched the center of his chest. "*Symphath*, remember? I can read your grid. You're getting worse and not better—"

Trez burst to his feet and headed for the exit, opening the door. "I gotta get back to work. Thanks for stopping by. Tell Ehlena hi—"

The door slammed shut on him, the knob ripped from his hand, the lights flickering throughout the office.

In a low, evil voice, Rehv said, "Sit the fuck down. This conversation is not a two-way."

Trez pivoted around. His former employer, one of his best friends, was looming beside the desk, his purple eyes flashing, the tremendous bulk of his body seeming to have gotten even bigger. It was a reminder that even though the big bastard was a happily mated male who had settled down, Rehv was still the kind of force you didn't want to cross.

"I know where you've been going," Rehv said in that *symphath* voice. "Down by the river. I know what you think about when you're behind the wheel of your car. I can see your emotional grid collapsing, and I am very well aware of your sudden fondness for cold fucking water."

Well, Trez thought. *Put like that, what could he say? Disneyland?*

Rehv pointed his cane at Trez. "Do you think I have any interest in living the rest of my nights in regret after I know all this and do nothing? Huh? You think that's a burden I want to strap on and carry around with me until I die?"

Trez cursed and paced around. On his second trip back and forth to the bathroom, he found himself wishing his office was big as a football field.

"In light of the way I use dopamine," Rehv continued, "I went to Ehlena and asked her if there was anything that could help you. An antidepressant. Or what I'm on. I don't fucking know. I don't know how it works. She said you should come talk to her and Jane—"

"No!" Trez put his hands up to his head and prayed he didn't get another one of his migraines.

Holding in the urge to scream was a helluva trigger. "I'm not going on some kind of drug—"

"—to see what your options are." Rehv raised his voice, talking right over the protests. "And get an assessment. They may be able to help you."

Trez sat his ass down on the sofa because he didn't trust himself not to try to push Rehv through the glass behind the desk. Then again, there was no possibility of him pulling a sneak attack. That *symphath* sonofabitch no doubt knew he had switched from suicidal to homicidal, and there was only one other bag of carbon-based molecules in the room to target that impulse on.

"Listen to me," Rehv said in a softer voice. "All those nights I had to go up to that cabin, you were with me. You were there. You protected me and you saved my life too many times to count."

"I owed you," Trez countered bitterly. "I was servicing my debt."

"That wasn't all there was to it. And don't lie just because you're pissed at me for calling you on your shit. I can read your grid."

"Please stop saying that."

"It's the truth."

"I know and that's why I don't want to hear it." Trez looked over. "I get that you think you're helping, and thanks for that. But I just want some privacy, okay?"

"So you can kill yourself in peace?"

"It's my life to take," he said roughly. "You have your own life and it's a good one. You'll get over it."

Rehv's brows came down hard. "Like you're getting over Selena so well? How's that party you're throwing, to borrow your phrase?"

"She was my *shellan*. I was just a friend to you."

"Bullshit. You're my *family*. You're iAm's blooded brother. And you're also family to a whole shitload of people who would suffer like hell if anything happened to you. And cut the shit with the past tense, asshole. You're still breathing—at least until I choke some sense into you."

Trez held that purple stare, which was every bit as angry as he himself was feeling, and as he considered where they were both at, he was really glad they hadn't taken out their weapons. Yet.

Except then he laughed . . . or Jesus, maybe it was more of a giggle.

And the levity came from God only knew where. Someplace even deeper than his grief, he supposed. But as the totally inappropriate sound came up his tight throat, he didn't have a chance in hell of keeping it in.

"You have such a way with interventions," Trez said as he tried to cough himself back to being serious. "I mean, there's tough love, and then there's the *symphath* version of it. Did you just call me an asshole while you're trying to get me not to shoot myself in the head?"

Rehv's smile was slow. "I never promised I was good at interpersonal stuff."

"Let me tell you, you're straight-up awful at it. I believe you also just threatened me with bodily harm."

"I would have sent Mary, who's a professional, but you would have given her a hug and then tossed her out."

"True."

"So you're left dealing with me. Sorry, not sorry."

Trez looked down at his hands as his mood shifted away from any levity. But at least it didn't go back into the rage. "So my grid doesn't look good, huh. Don't know why I have to even ask. I'm living it."

"I don't want you to do something stupid. That's all."

"You know what's crazy . . . even with all this? With everything that happened after my Selena died? I have no regrets about being with her. Even though she's gone and it hurts like hell . . . and there's no end in sight? I do not regret a thing."

Rehv came over and sat down on the sofa. "Listen, I don't know how else to help. That's the reason I came. I don't want you to think it's a failure if you go on some meds, either. Look at me. I'm the poster boy for better living through chemistry."

Trez shook his head back and forth. "I just don't care. About anything really."

Rehv reached out and Trez felt the male's heavy hand land on his shoulder. "But I care. And that's why I'm here."

CHAPTER SEVEN

Three prime ribs of beef. Full cuts, not the princess stuff. Two plates of the osso buco. A plate of pork pappardelle and an order of the chicken scarpariello. Seven different sides including rollatini, risotto, and the polenta—as well as a single, desultory dish of peas that the male had explained was for the fiber.

Although on that theory, Therese decided as she tallied up the check, the little side bowl was a drop in a bucket, nothing that was going to make any difference to the guy's colon.

Standing at the automated cash register, she realized she hadn't done the appetizers. Okay, so the male had had the minestrone soup. A caprese salad—more fiber there, actually. The antipasto assortment and the crostini. Wait, also the bruschetta. Was that everything? She was fairly sure. And what about dessert? He'd had the tiramisu, the cannoli, the tartufo, and profiteroles.

"I think I've got it," she said to herself. "Now, she had—"

"Don't worry about it."

Therese jumped and glanced over her shoulder. When she saw who it was, she nearly dropped her order pad.

"Oh, Chef." She inclined her head. Then bowed fully. "I'm sorry, Chef."

She had no idea what the hell she was apologizing for. But she had been late, and she needed this job, and even though the head of the house managed the waitstaff—when a storm wasn't sending him home at the start of the shift—this was the big boss, the male in charge. iAm, blooded brother of Trez.

The male smiled a little, but the expression didn't last more than a heartbeat on his handsome dark face. She had the feeling that he didn't like her, but he was never mean, and she wasn't even sure it was personal. He was a silent presence in the kitchen, unlike the stereotypical master-chef types who thundered around, red-faced and yelling—and somehow, the quiet was more powerful, more intimidating.

"They're comp'd," he said as he nodded out to the dining room, to the couple Therese had been waiting on for the two hours it took the *hellren* to be part of the clean plate(s) club.

With a quick surge of composure, she hid her disappointment, that tip she had been looking forward to going *poof*. "Of course. Certainly, Chef."

"You can leave after they're done."

"Oh. Okay. Thank you, Chef."

iAm paused, and she braced herself for a command not to come in the next night or any night thereafter. Because she had been late two times. And because . . . whatever else she'd done wrong on any shift she had ever been on in any position she had ever held, going back to the moment of her birth.

Not that she was catastrophizing. At all.

"Listen," he said. "About my brother."

Therese was aware of her heart stopping and her breath stalling in her throat. "Yes?"

"He's . . ."

"He's what?"

For some reason, she wanted to know whatever

was next with a single-minded focus that bordered on addiction.

Except iAm shook his head. "Never mind. You just finish up here and head home."

Before she could stop herself, she reached out and touched his arm. "You can tell me. Whatever it is."

"It's not my story, and that's only part of the problem."

iAm turned and went back toward the kitchen. And as she watched him go, she wanted to chase after him and make him talk to her. But that wasn't her place, and not because she was only a waitress. You didn't get between siblings. She used to live that firsthand with her own brother.

To keep from sliding down that slope of regret and recrimination, she canceled the transaction out of the register, tucked her order folder into her half apron, and headed over to the only occupied table. She wasn't sure where Emile was. The couple he had been waiting on were long gone, which was what happened when you just ate an app, an entrée, and a dessert. As opposed to four apps, seventeen entrées and the entire dessert menu.

As she came up to the table, the blond male and the human-ish female looked up at her with expectation.

"Chef is pleased to comp your meal," Therese said. "With his best regards."

The male shook his head. "iAm doesn't have to do that. Where is he?"

"I believe Chef is in the kitchen. Would you like me to get him for you?"

"Nah, it's cool. He's probably working."

"Is there anything else I can get you both?"

"We are so full. Even him." The female smiled, and tilted her head. "Tell me, where are you from?"

"Michigan."

"So you're used to the long, cold winters," the male said.

"I am."

"And what brought you to Caldwell?" the *shellan* asked.

Therese shrugged through the lancing pain that went through her chest. "I just felt like a relocation."

"Caldwell is a wonderful place to live." The female smiled. "Do you know anyone here?"

"Not really. But it's okay. I'm just getting settled."

"Well, remember to be kind to yourself. Transitions are hard even when they're exciting."

It was as she stared down into the female's eyes that she understood the male's attraction. She totally got it. There was something incredibly wise and kind about the *shellan*, a depth of knowledge and under-standing that transcended the physical and made her resplendent.

"I do what I can," Therese heard herself mumble. "Anyway, be careful out in that storm even if you aren't driving."

"Thank you. You, too."

The male indicated the table with his broad palm. "And thank you for working so hard for us."

"My pleasure. Take care."

Therese left the pair feeling defeated. Her hourly wages were low, as was to be expected. Tips were where the money was at. But her suddenly sad mood was about more than the lack of tip. The idea of going back to that rooming house made her want to cry, although that was her own fault, wasn't it. She'd had another option. Just waiting for her.

Except she'd turned that down. Out of pride. And out of the fact that anything that had to do with Trez was complicated even if it looked simple.

Her attraction was the problem.

Taking cover behind the water station, she figured she'd wait for the couple to leave, clear their coffee cups and water glasses, and then drag herself back to the hellhole. Yay. Excitement.

She passed a little time getting out some pitchers

from the cabinets under the water dispenser, mopping around the countertop, wiping down the cash register surface. The quiet of the restaurant seemed to surround her, follow her, stick close by, a stalker that kept to the shadows. And with her instincts firing for absolutely no reason, her eyes made rounds of the empty bar behind her, the empty hostess stand, the other, completely empty dining room.

Restless. So restless and anxious for no justification she could think of.

Did she want to go back to the rooming house? No. Did she wish she could be normal around that Shadow? Yes. Did she wonder what Trez's brother had been going to say? Absolutely.

But none of that explained her nagging sense of worry—

"Chef said I could go now."

Therese tried to hide her jump of surprise. "Oh, Emile. Yes, me, too. Well, as soon as they leave."

She leaned out from the water station. The couple was still there. The male had reached across the table and taken his *shellan*'s hand. He was staring into her eyes, his face rapt, a soft smile on his perfect lips.

"They're really in love," Emile said.

"They are." Therese rubbed a sore spot in the center of her chest, over her heart. "It's nice to see."

Actually, it wasn't. The two of them reminded her of her parents, and that was not anything she wanted to think about. But her brain refused to be sidetracked, memories of her *mahmen* and father holding hands, sitting close, speaking quietly, weaving into her mind and taking over. They had been so present for their children, so involved, but there had always been the sense that they had a special, private relationship—and that that connection was the true basis of the family.

Therese had felt so secure in the compass points that the four of them had formed: *hellren, shellan,* son, and daughter.

And then all of that had changed.

The bonds that she had assumed were concrete had turned out to be no more substantial than confetti. At least for her. The other three were fine, but then none of their identities had been deliberately hidden from them; none of their foundations had cracks in them.

Trust was the basis for love. Without it, you had nothing but an illusion—a pleasant illusion, it was true, an illusion that felt nice and steady. But when you thought that the lie was the real thing? Finding out the two-dimensional nature of your existence was shattering.

"—Therese?"

Shaking herself back into focus, she looked at Emile. "I'm sorry? What?"

"May I give you a ride home?"

Therese pictured Liza stamping around and demanding everything which Emile refused to provide. "Oh, that's not necessary. Thank you, though."

"So you have a ride?" Emile hesitated. "Not that I'm trying to pry."

"I'm just going to dema—" She stopped herself. Nope, not talking about ghosting out. Had she forgotten the guy was a human? "Yes, I'm going to get a ride."

"Okay, sure." He nodded and then looked at her with expectation. "Of course."

"It's just my brother." The lie hurt. Because picking her up on a snowy night was exactly the kind of thing Gareth would do. "He's like that."

She rubbed the center of her chest again. As loneliness came over her like a shroud, she took a deep breath. She had always been an independent sort, finding her own way with school, work, life, but the thing was, she had not appreciated how much her family had mattered to her, how much of a grounding it had been, what kind of a harbor those other three had offered her.

"Actually," she heard herself say, "I would like a ride."

Emile beamed. "Well. Fantastic."

As she realized she had made, yet again, a snap decision she should have thought through more, she swallowed a curse. "Except, wait, I didn't even ask where you lived. I'm downtown. Maybe that is really out of your—"

"No, it's perfect. It's just perfect."

The image of him driving her home past Liza's wherever, and the other waitress running out into the street and flagging them down so she could throw a chair through the windshield, was not a welcome thought. And then there was the hope in Emile's eyes. He was trying to be cool, but the answer he'd gotten had thrilled him. Meanwhile, he was only a Band-Aid for her sadness, for all the things she was missing . . . and so much less complicating than the Shadow who commanded all of her senses whenever he was in a hundred-foot radius of her.

Checking on her couple again, she was infinitely relieved that they had left. "I'm just going to bus my table—"

"Here, let me help—"

"No." She smiled to take the sting out of her voice. "I'm going to do it quickly, and then I'll meet you in the locker room?"

"Sure. I'll put our tickets in."

"Thank you."

She snagged one of the trays and its pop-up stand and strode across to the table. As she passed by all the empty place settings, the glasses turned rim down to the tablecloths, the napkins covering the chargers, the silverware so precisely arranged, her feeling of sadness became so overwhelming that her eyes teared up.

It had to be the storm. Something in the shift of the barometer reading, the atmospheric pressure, the wind, affecting her mood, dragging her down. Yup. That was what was happening.

Flipping the stand out, she put the tray on top and started to clear the—

With a frown, she leaned down to the plate the tiramisu had been on. It was tilted to one side, like a napkin had been put under it.

Except what she found beneath the thing was not damask.

"Oh . . . my God," she breathed.

No, it was not a napkin. It was a wad of cash, folded in half. Picking the bundle up, she fanned out the hundred-dollar bills. Ten of them.

Her head whipped up, and she looked around. Then she jogged across the empty dining room to the front entrance. Pulling things open, she went down the stairs of the ante-hall and through the outer door. The fury of the storm tore at her body with ice-cold claws, and she had to catch her balance by throwing out a hand to one of the awning's supports.

There was no hope of finding them. The couple was long gone.

Returning to the warmth and the quiet of the restaurant, she looked down at the cash in her hand. If you added up how much the couple had eaten, a thousand dollars was probably pretty close to what the bill had been, if you included tax and a tip of about 25 or 30 percent.

The couple had been comp'd and they had given her what they would have spent anyway.

A Christmas miracle from perfect strangers.

With this cash? She could make the security deposit on her own.

This was a gift the likes of which that couple couldn't possibly comprehend, and tears of gratitude entered her eyes, threatening to spill over.

It was a while before she could backtrack and re-enter the restaurant.

◆ ◆ ◆

Emile's car had four-wheel drive. It was also pretty close to the beater category, but the Subaru Outback seemed to back up its maker's assertions that an odometer with a hundred thousand miles on it was not only dog-approved, it was no big deal.

Therese passed the time looking out her window and staring at the businesses they were passing. It had been a while since she'd been in any kind of vehicle, and she had forgotten how much she enjoyed just sitting back and watching whatever was at the side of the road. Gareth had liked to go for drives, and she had been her brother's regular companion.

Although . . . the last time she had been in a car had been with Trez. His BMW. After he had briefly lost consciousness and had to be taken to get checked out.

On mutual agreement, they had abandoned that mission, and she had never asked him whether he was okay. She had just assumed so—

And he had kissed her, then.

"Are you warm enough?"

Startled by the voice next to her, she glanced at Emile. "Oh, yes, thank you."

"Here are the controls." He pointed to the . . . well, controls. "In case you want to change anything."

"Thank you."

Determined to stop thinking about that Shadow, she tried to find something to say. Funny how when you changed the environment, you changed the vibe. She had never had a hard time talking to Emile when they were at work. Now, outside of the restaurant and alone with him, things were awkward.

"The snow is stopping," she said as she leaned in to the windshield. "It's about time."

"Yes, it is."

Great, they were covering the weather. Next up—sports? Yeah, that was the last thing she wanted to talk about. During NCAA basketball season, she and Gareth had always been glued to the TV, watching the Spartans play. Never doubt the Izzo, they had always said.

She hadn't turned even one game on since she'd left.

"So," Emile said, "what kind of music do you—"

The sound of his cell phone ringing spared her from making that kind of small talk. Although as he reached into his coat and took out his phone, she figured she might as well get an answer ready.

"Liza—" He stopped as he got cut off. "Wait, I can't hear you over the noise. What?"

Therese looked over. The sound of the woman's voice was squawking out of the phone, all kinds of syllables racing into one another, to the point that even Therese's vampire hearing couldn't decipher the rush.

"Okay, okay . . ." Emile held up his hand as if the woman could see him. "Slow down. I'm not—no, I just left work. I'm giving—" He hesitated and looked at Therese.

Yeah, there was only one response to that. She shook her head.

"I'm giving Therese a ride home," he muttered.

Three, two . . . one. Boom!

Both the volume and speed of the words tripled and Therese put her head in her hands. Meanwhile, Emile was battling against a much stronger current than he could ever keep from drowning in.

"But that was in the middle of my shift, Liza. You decided to leave on your own, and I need the . . ."

When there was finally a pause on the other end, Emile jumped in with, "I don't think this is a productive conversation. You're drunk, and I'm hanging up—" He fell silent again, but now he frowned and straightened in the seat. "I'm sorry . . . what did you just say? Who was this? He did what?"

Therese frowned, and tried to hear what was being said. She was pretty sure the woman was weeping, but it seemed like the drunken kind of crying job, more alcohol than honest emotion.

"I'm coming right now," Emile said as he hit the gas harder. "Stay where you are. No, I'm going to go.

No, I want to have both hands on the wheel. The roads are slick. I want to be safe."

He ended the call and then glanced at the phone as if he were wishing a lot of things were different in his life.

"You don't have to drop me off," Therese said. "If she's in trouble, let's just go to wherever she is and I'll get myself home."

Emile glanced over again. "I swear, I've told her it's done between us. I mean, I like you. I guess that's obvious." He flushed in the dim lights of the dashboard. "I'm thinking, though . . . that that's not where this is heading on your side."

"It's not because of Liza. I just . . ."

"I know. You're interested in someone else. And given the way our boss's brother looked at me tonight? When he was talking to you? I'm pretty sure it's mutual—"

"It's not like that with us." Oh, God, it felt totally weird to "us" her and Trez Latimer, even if it was in the context of a relationship denial. "Really. I mean, I am totally not ready for any kind of anything with anybody."

Emile shrugged and refocused on the road ahead. As a sad light came into his eyes, he shrugged.

"When it happens, I'm not sure that it cares whether you want it or not."

Therese put a hand on his shoulder. "I'm sorry."

The man laughed in a short burst. "You know, I believe that. And it only makes me like you more." He put his hand out again. "But I'm not going to go overboard. I understand and respect where you're coming from."

"Thank you. I wish there was something I could do to help."

Emile put both hands on the steering wheel. Then he made a clicking sound with his teeth. "You know, actually, there is."

"Anything," Therese said. "Name it. And it's yours."

"Come with me to talk sense into Liza. Maybe if she hears from your own mouth that there's nothing going on between you and me, and no possibility of anything happening, she'll at least relax at work." He looked over pointedly. "And it'll help you, too."

Therese nodded slowly. "I see your point. I'm in."

CHAPTER EIGHT

And that was how Therese ended up walking into a club that was as dark as the inside of a hat, louder than a concert, and more blinding than a Fourth of July fireworks show. They ditched the Subaru in an open-air lot not far from whatever the place was called—shAdoWs, she thought the sign outside said?— and walked the two blocks over to the wait line. It turned out Emile knew the bouncer from his previous job, so they got right in, although that was no prize as far as she was concerned.

Bodies. Gyrating. Everywhere. Lasers shooting through the crowd like purple arrows and every single one of them landing in her eyeballs. Oh, and somewhere, there was a smoke machine.

Plus, dear God, from the music. Pounding. Thumping. Molar-rattling. How did these people stand it?

"Did she tell you where she was?" Therese yelled over the din. When Emile mouthed a *What?*, she leaned in toward his ear. "Where is she in here?"

"I don't know," Emile hollered back. Then he shrugged and pointed in some direction. "Here?"

Therese made the universal sign for *Why not?* because it was easier than trying to get heard over the music. And then she had more problems. Heading toward where he had randomly pointed turned out to be harder than communicating. There were so many humans on the floor, pushing, shoving, dancing, slipping, falling. It was as if the slick roads from the storm had come inside and there were three hundred drunk drivers careening down Caldwell's streets.

Speaking of which, how was it possible that none of these people had stayed home because of the storm? It seemed like the inclement weather had inspired them in the opposite way, no hermitting to be found anywhere.

Then again, did she really think good choices were at the top of anyone's To-Do list in here?

She was looking around, trying to locate Emile's kind-of-girlfriend's hairstyle, while at the same time not get left behind, when the fight broke out.

At first, she didn't notice the jostling because she was getting bumped into by all sorts of shoulders and elbows anyway, but then a body slammed into her and knocked her off her feet: One moment, she was upright and ambulatory; the next, she was on her ass.

After which there was a stampede's worth of boots and stilettos within inches of her face, her hands, her internal organs.

It was amazing how fast you could move when you didn't want to get hurt. As the crowd surged and retreated like a school of fish, all those humans swirling together as if they were choreographed, she jumped up—

Only to get knocked into again, this time by a human man who not only put her back on the dance floor but also used her as a cushion, his heavy weight landing on top of her. As the breath was knocked out of her lungs, she got fed up. Planting her palms on his shoulder blades, she shoved him off of her, sending him flying into the crowd, toast out of a toaster.

Therese did not mess around with vertical attempt number two. She punched herself up and stayed in a crouch, arms in front of herself, eyes sweeping around and looking for the next dodgeball.

That was when she saw the real trouble. Two human men were locked in a joint throat grab, and it looked like their posses had gotten involved—and not to peel them apart. There were spin-off fights around the center conflict, satellites of smackdown that agitated the crowd even more.

Meanwhile, Emile was not anywhere to be seen, especially as another one of those purple lasers nailed Therese right in the eye, the impact like being Three Stooges poked.

Cursing, she brought her hand up—

The gunshot was unmistakable, even with the music, a high, hot pop! that cut through the bass and the treble. And then there were screams, shrill and piercing.

In slow motion, Therese turned to the sound and held her arms up to shield herself. Although her right eye was uselessly blinded, she was able to focus her left one, and that was when she saw the muzzle of the weapon point in her direction.

The true target was a human man who had stumbled into her path, but it wasn't as if a little nuance like that was going to matter to the bullet.

There was a flash out of the tip of the gun, and Therese jumped to the side, going full Superman on the lunge, arms out ahead, body straight in the air, feet pointed. She even turned her head to track that muzzle, just to make sure she was out of range.

So she saw the man get shot.

The impact wrenched his torso to the side, as the lead slug went into the meat of his shoulder, and she yelled for him to get down—which was stupid. The shooter was closing in on the victim and about to—

The salvation tackle came from the right, and whoever it was knew what they were doing. Somehow, they managed to get control of the weapon and take the shooter down to the floor at the same time. It was one in a million, unless, of course, they had been trained to do it.

Therese hit the floor hard, her teeth clapping together, the heels of her hands skidding on the wood. One of her knees burst open with pain, and so did her left elbow, and she was worried she'd been shot.

Rolling over, she curled into a ball as the trampling feet she had tried to avoid in the first place came in what seemed to be a fleet of thousands, the size of the crowd geometrically increasing now that she was at the mercy of their panic. If she stayed like this, she was going to get seriously hurt, assuming she wasn't already, so she forced herself up, rising to all fours and scrambling as fast as she could in what she hoped was a straight line. She kept her head down to protect it as much as possible, and she prayed she could just get the hell out of the way—

Without warning, her body levitated.

She was on the floor, paddling with her hands and feet like she was in choppy water, and then she was in the air, nothing under her.

Her first thought was that someone had used her like a football and kicked her. But no. Arms were around her waist—or one arm was around her waist.

Looking forward, she saw the other of the pair thrust out in front, like one of those police battering rams that SWAT teams broke doors down with, and holy crap, it was working, clearing the path, getting her and her savior out of the crush. Determined not to be dropped, she grabbed onto the torso of whoever was carrying her, wrapping a tight hold around what turned out to be a hard, hard body.

After a few dozen feet, they were out of the chaos

and away from the panic, but whoever it was didn't stop. They seemed to want to run into the black wall—

A hidden door opened in advance of their going cartoon character through the Sheetrock, and then they were in a well-lit corridor.

The trap door slammed behind them.

Twisting around . . . she looked up into Trez Latimer's harsh face.

◆ ◆ ◆

Trez was breathing so hard, his eyesight was checker-boarding on him, although the visual optics were not the result of exertion. He had been scared fucking shitless as he'd tried to get Therese to safety.

He'd been up in his office, trying not to think about her, when he'd seen the fight break out between two asshats competing for the attention of a woman who was a sure thing either way. The men had started pushing and shoving, and then, of course, their buddies had gotten involved, the testosterone taking over and escalating everything. In a rather bored fashion, he had called down to Xhex and her team, but she was already headed in that direction, alerted by staff on the floor, and he was more than happy to stay out of it.

Except then, from his perch on high, he had seen

a familiar face in the crowd, the flash of a laser illuminating what could only be Therese.

Without wasting a second, he had dematerialized through the glass, some sixth sense of impending doom calling him into furious action.

And then the shooting had broken out.

"Are you hurt?" he asked as he laid her down on the cold concrete floor of the passageway used to bring liquor to the bar during business hours.

"It's you . . ." she said with wonder. "What are you doing here?"

Outside in the club proper, the music was abruptly cut off, the voices and yelling of the crowd taking the place of the beats.

"I own this place." He stared down at her. "Are you hurt?"

"I don't know." She pushed her upper body up and looked herself over. "I don't think so. I can't smell blood."

"Neither can I."

Therese flexed arms. Flexed legs. Turned her hands over, assessed her elbows. "I'm okay."

Annnnnnnd that was when a case of the woozies took Trez's wheel, his body weaving even though he was kneeling. To keep from passing the hell out on the female—because, one, he didn't want to crush her just after he had tried to save her from being crushed, and two, he'd pulled the fainting routine with her once already, so really, he'd prefer to keep things fresh and interesting by staying fucking conscious—he shifted to one side and sat on his ass. As they both stayed put and panted, he heard the sounds of sirens and the shuffling of feet.

"Do you need to go out there?" she asked him as she focused on the wall of the corridor.

He was momentarily distracted by looking her over himself. Her hair, previously so neat in that bun, had a halo of escaped curls, and there was a high flush on her cheeks, one that made her look especially lovely, in spite of all the drama. She also appeared to be totally not bleeding.

#bonus

Fuck. His heart rate was never going to slow down.

What had she said? Oh, right.

"Xhex is on it." Which was a good thing as he wasn't sure whether he could stand up to go out there anyway. "You did really well—getting out of the way, I mean."

"I was good until I couldn't get on my feet." She rubbed her eyes. "I was almost shot."

"I know."

As they fell silent, he was very aware that she was replaying the near miss just as he was. The idea that something like that could happen so fast—

"It happened so fast," she said.

"I was thinking exactly the same thing."

There was another slice of quiet, and then they looked at each other.

Later, when he replayed the next shock of the night, he would try to remember who reached for who first. Her? Him? He didn't recall. Couldn't recall.

Like it mattered?

All he knew for sure was that they were sitting side by side . . . and then they weren't. They were in each other's arms, and their mouths were fused, a desperate passion released, the adrenaline in their bloodstreams fueling a physical expression of the panic and the unexpected relief they both felt.

Therese's lips moved against his own, and her tongue met his with the same kind of heat he was feeling in his veins. As her hands linked around the back of his neck, she arched up to him, her breasts pressing into his chest, her body weight now in his lap. The kissing was rough, and he told himself he needed to slow down, but that warning meant nothing to him. He didn't know anything but the taste of her, the feel of her, the sense that what his brain told him was wrong was actually the rightest thing he had had since Selena's death.

Because it *was* Selena.

The kissing, the touching, the passion that thickened his blood and his cock . . . it was his mate. He had been here before, he had done this before—

He had mourned the loss of this very connection. And its return was a benediction that wiped him out.

Well, not completely out. He retained enough presence of mind to lock the door they'd come through. The last thing he needed was for one of his staff to use the hidden passageway as an escape from the CPD, who were no doubt pulling up to the club right this moment.

Spurred on by a driving need, Trez swept his palm down to her hip. Then he brought it back up, under her risen arms, over her parka. He got some sense of the curves through the down padding, but it was not enough. Not nearly enough. Finding the opening between the halves, he plowed his greedy hand underneath and—

As he cupped her breast through the thin blouse of her waitress uniform, she cried out into his mouth, her body rolling against his torso, her legs churning on the concrete.

He needed her naked. Now.

He needed his own body naked. Now—

Bang! Bang! Bang!

The two of them jerked apart and he looked toward the trap door.

At least it wasn't gunshots. And what a standard that was.

He also knew who it was. *"Do not open that."*

Xhex's voice was wry. "Just making sure you're alive."

"Affirmative." Trez knew what the next question was going to be. "I don't need help. We're—I'm fine."

"Okay." As Xhex spoke, he could picture his chief of security shaking her head. "I'm handling things out here. Police have arrived."

"Thank you."

Trez closed his eyes and cursed. Then he focused on Therese—

She was staring up at him with wide, confused eyes, her fingertips resting lightly on her mouth.

"Are you all right?" he asked. "Are you hurt?"

CHAPTER NINE

Therese couldn't concentrate on what Trez was saying to her.

She was back to when they'd been kissing, his hands on her body, his mouth on hers, his tongue penetrating her. It had not been like the quick kiss they'd shared before. That one had been a surprise. An impulse. Something that was backed away from quickly on both their parts.

But what had just happened? For one, if they hadn't been interrupted, it wouldn't have stopped until it was finished. For another . . . it was not the first time she had felt him against her. She recognized his lips, his hands, his scent.

Because he had come to her in her dreams.

This Shadow was somehow . . . her shadow lover. Except how was that possible?

"Are you sure you're okay?" Trez's eyes were worried, and he brushed a strand of her hair back from her face. "Do we need to get you medical help?"

Reaching up, she stroked his face with wonder. Maybe she was wrong, though. Maybe . . .

"Kiss me again," she breathed.

As he hesitated, she was dimly aware that they were hardly in a private place. And this was not a good time, especially as urgent voices warred outside in the club proper. And moreover, she wasn't sure where her head had gone after all that drama with the gun.

Except she didn't care about any of that.

She had a hunger to reconnect with his mouth, his body, his . . . soul. A hunger that was so deep inside of her, she couldn't understand it or determine its origin. Yes, he was a stunning male. And there was attraction on both sides. And whatever, whatever, whatever.

But this tie between them was something so much stronger than all that.

"I need you," she said in a voice she had never heard come out of herself before.

Trez's black eyes flashed peridot, and he asked no questions, made no comment. Instead, he brought his lips down on hers with a punishing passion, the heat re-flaring between them, branding her, branding them.

Groaning into his mouth, she rolled over onto the unforgiving concrete floor and pulled him on top of her. And to make sure she was very clear about where she wanted him, she parted her legs and he fit perfectly between them, his heavy weight crushing her into the hard floor, not that she cared about her spine's protest.

"Don't stop," she begged. "Faster. I need you . . ."

Her hands were sloppy as she pulled his silk shirt out of his slacks and stroked up his rib cage and then down his lower back. Without her having to ask, he started to ride her through their clothes, his pelvis thrusting, his mammoth erection rubbing her in a place that ached for him.

It was just as in her dreams, the two of them lock and key, their bodies taking over, their minds set free. In this dim light, in this unknown place, the distinction between what was real and what had come to her in her sleep was blurred, until she wasn't sure whether she was in the dream or here in this club. What she was crystal clear on?

The male she was making love with.

Oh, and the fact that she did not want this to stop. Ever.

Breaking off the kiss, Trez rolled over and brought her onto his hips. Then he stared up at her in shock and wonder—and pure, unadulterated lust. He was breathing hard, and his eyes, as they bored into hers, were both focused and strangely rattled.

He felt it, too, she thought.

"I know you," she whispered. "And I've wanted you for so long."

Dear God, what was she saying—

"Yes . . ." he breathed. "*Yes*."

Trez seemed to sag in his own skin, and she could have sworn that a sheen of tears made his stare luminous. Then his body started to shake.

"I have to . . ." He cleared his throat. "I have to . . . be in you."

"I need you."

Bending down to him, she pressed her mouth to his, and then it was on, as she lifted up off him and his hands went to his slacks. With equal haste, she took care of her side of things, wrenching her own waistband open, tearing her own zipper down. Ripping, yanking, it was as if some other force had taken over her body, but it was a force that came from within her.

It was nothing foreign. Nothing that alarmed her.

An energy was moving through her, connecting her to him, amplifying her need for him, and him alone.

As if they had been separated and this was a reunion instead of a first time.

With impatience, she kicked off one of her boots and then dragged her pants down. It was awkward maneuvering her clothes, but she didn't care. Neither did he. They were going at breakneck speed, her sex ready and open for him, his arousal hard and desperate—

The second she was free from her constraints, he stood himself up and she sat down—

They both shouted. And then she remembered no particulars, and absolutely everything about the stretching, the filling, the sex that roared to life. As she rode him, she was fully present and out of her mind, her body moving on its own, following a rhythm they jointly fell into.

"Oh, God," he groaned as he tried to recapture her mouth.

It was impossible. Faster, faster, her going up and

down, him thrusting up, the releases they were finding unstoppable forces of nature.

As an orgasm lightning'd through her, emanating out from her core, Therese gasped and then moaned. She tried to keep going, but she couldn't seem to move right. It was okay, though. Trez kept pumping.

Even as he started to fill her up.

◆ ◆ ◆

The fit was the same.

As Trez began to orgasm and then kept it up, his cock releasing jets into the body of the female on top of him, he was completely overwhelmed by the fact that not only did Therese look like his *shellan*, she felt the same, too. Her body was the same. The way their sexes locked and held . . . it was all the same. She even tasted the same.

It *was* his queen.

And she knew it, too. Somehow, she had made the connection as well.

Closing his eyes, he soaked up the sensations, refilling his empty spaces with them, his aching loneliness erased, the cold he'd been meat-lockered into falling away in the rush of warmth. With every crest of pleasure, and each pumping thrust, he was made whole . . . and when the desperation finally began to ebb, his first thought was that he just wanted to keep going. He wanted them both to get fully naked. He wanted her skin on his. He wanted to put his mouth all over her.

Except then he realized where they were. Their pants down. Still joined.

Trez stared up at the face above his. His female was almost too beautiful to look at, her dark hair loose and curling up, its binding lost, her lips red from his kisses, her face flushed and glowing. She was the most resplendent thing he had ever seen.

"You're back," he whispered.

"I haven't left." She lowered herself down and kissed him softly. "I'm here."

"Yes, you are." He took one of her hands and placed it on his heart. "You've always been here."

Therese seemed briefly confused, but the expression didn't last. "I must be crazy. How do I feel like I know you? Like we've done this before—"

"Because we have."

"In my dreams, right?" She smiled slowly. "In my dreams."

"Do I come to you?" he said, his heart starting to pound. "Did you see me when you were sleeping?"

As he waited for her to reply, he had the sense that he was on the precipice of a great revelation, something that would explain everything—the way she looked, the way she felt, the fact that he felt no guilt at all for what they had just done.

Because he did not feel as if he had been disloyal at all.

Because it had been his queen.

Her eyes searched his face. "It was absolutely you. In my dreams. You are the one who has come to me as a shadow."

"Yes, it was me. That was me." He didn't know what he was saying, but this made sense . . . even as it made no sense. "Tell me about the dream."

"It always starts the same. I am lying in a bed in a room I've never been in before. I don't recognize anything around me, and every time I have the dream, I don't remember where I am. There is a single candle on the nightstand, and a soft, warm breeze blows it out. The door opens, and a figure is there. I am not afraid, however, even though I can't see the face." With fingertips that trembled, she traced his brows, his cheeks, his jaw. "It is you, though. You come to me . . . and we make love. It is only when we are together that the room becomes familiar. It's rustic and antique, and I am safe . . . with you."

"You will always be safe with me."

"I believe you—"

Bang! Bang! Bang!

Trez wrenched his head to the side. "Xhex! I told you—"

"Oh, that you, boss?"

Shit. "Hey, Big Rob." He put his forefinger to his lips and *shhh*'d. "What's going on?"

"This door won't open."

No, shit. "What do you need?"

Blah, blah, blah. Something about liquor boxes.

"Listen, Big Rob," he said, "I'll be out in a minute. I'm helping someone. Are the police still there?"

"Yup."

"Just hang with Alex, okay?" Alex being the name Xhex used in the human world.

"Okay, boss."

Okay. Okay. Right. Right.

Meanwhile, Therese was dismounting him, his still-erect cock slapping down on his lower belly, the change in temperature along its shaft and on its head a really frickin' unpleasant shock. To make matters worse, his female was efficient in her re-dressing, which was good considering someone might be able to get in the other way, but also a disappointment because duh.

Still, they couldn't stay here forever, could they.

Sure, they could, a voice suggested in his head as she stood up and rezipped her slacks. *They absolutely could. Forever—*

Therese looked around. And cursed.

"Later, Big Rob," he said as he got to his feet and put his pants in place. Turning to Therese, he asked, "What's wrong?"

"My purse." She moved in a circle, as if the thing might be on the floor. "I think I—yup, I lost my purse when I was trying to get away from the fight."

"We'll find it." As she looked at the door they entered, he shook his head. "No, let's go the other way."

He was not about to come out of the back into a crowd of his security personnel, the human police, and whatever arrestees were cuffed—with her. She was glowing in the way of a female who had just been properly serviced by her male, and not only was he in absolutely no hurry to share that glorious sight with anybody, he didn't want people to judge her, either.

His reputation preceded him, especially with his staff and the working girls. They all knew the way he had been, and would never believe that he hadn't restarted his philandering.

Trez took her hand. "Follow me."

When she tugged at him, he stopped and looked down into her face.

His female smiled in a shy, secret way. "I . . . ah . . ."

Trez found himself smiling back at her. Then he gave her a quick kiss on that mouth. "Yes," he whispered. "I feel the same way."

CHAPTER TEN

Therese stuck close behind Trez as they made fast time down the corridor. Part of her was still back in the sex they'd had, reliving the moments that had been too quick, yet vivid enough to last a lifetime. The other part of her was in a panic over her bag.

All that tip money. Ten hundreds in cash.

What were the chances that, even if they found her purse, any of that load hadn't been lifted? Nil. But that wasn't the only thing that had been in there that she hated to lose.

She tried to recall the sequence of events. Arriving with Emile, losing him in the crowd when the fight broke out, and then . . .

"I can't remember where I dropped it." She shook her head as they hurried along. "I'm trying to think . . ."

Abruptly, Trez stopped in front of absolutely nothing—except then a panel slid back. As he dropped her hand and turned to the side to squeeze his big body through the relatively narrow exit, she had the feeling that he didn't want to be seen holding on to her. Why, though?

Except maybe she was just being paranoid, and like that wasn't understandable? She'd almost been shot, had lost her purse, and capped all that off by doing the deed in that corridor with a male she was convinced she'd seen in her dreams. As if things were going anywhere close to normal tonight?

A bar, she thought as she emerged into the club proper. They were behind the serving counter of a bar, by the liquor bottles and the stacked racks of glasses.

The lights were on in the huge warehouse space, and as her eyes adjusted, she got a clear shot of medics working on a man who was down on the floor— and it was not going well. The patient was pissed off and physically combative, batting away the nitrile-gloved hands that were attempting to diagnose and treat him. Meanwhile, in an opposite corner, human police had someone in custody, the handcuffed guy likewise arguing. There were two other people who appeared to be injured, although not critically so—and there were no dead bodies under sheets.

How that was possible, she hadn't a clue.

There were also a number of men wearing "STAFF" polos, as well as—

Oh, my God, Therese thought. *That* was the savior who had taken the shooter down.

With all the chaos, she'd assumed the figure in the muscle shirt had been a male, but that was not the case. The female had a short haircut, as well as a broad set of shoulders and well-muscled arms—and those details, along with the even harder look on her face, had led to some conclusion jumping.

"What does your purse look like?" Trez asked as he held open a break in the counter.

Therese stepped through. "It's nothing special. It's a Coach knockoff. It's brown? With some black patterning."

"Let me ask Xhex. If it's still here, it's been collected. Whenever there are big fights, there are always dropped wallets, purses, watches, other things—only some of which are legal."

"So this happens a lot? Jeez."

"Not the shooting part." He raised his hand as they started walking across the scuffed floor. "Yo, Xhex?"

The female looked over. And did a double take.

"Actually, why don't you stay here," Trez muttered.

Before Therese could ask him why, the female strode to them, her heavy boots making a loud sound in the wide-open cavern of the club, like a squadron of marching males. As she came to a halt, her dark gray eyes locked on Therese with such directness, it was like being cross-examined.

Therese glanced around. Took a step back.

"Who are you?" the female asked her.

Or demanded. Depending on how you took it.

"It doesn't matter," Trez said tightly. "None of this matters. We're looking for her purse. It's a—"

As he glanced over for some descriptive backup, Therese filled in, "A Coach knockoff. Brown and black? And I'm Therese. Nice to meet you."

She put out her hand and met that stare head-on. Undoubtedly tensions were high because of the shooting and the female must work at the club in some capacity. But dayum. And no, Therese wasn't going to be intimidated.

"Xhex," the female announced. "Good to meet you."

As the female accepted the palm that had been offered, the shake was curt and very strong. And still those eyes did not budge. Yet there was no hostility, exactly. No possessiveness over Trez, either. But still.

"Is there a problem?" Therese said. "And I don't mean that in an obnoxious way. It's just this feels . . ." She motioned between them. "A little intense."

"I apologize. Let's go see if we can find your purse."

At which point . . . absolutely nothing happened. The female just stood there, those eyes remaining fixated.

"Xhex, can I talk to you a minute," Trez said tightly. "Privately—"

He took the female's arm in a grip, but she shook her head. "You don't need to tell me a thing. I get it."

As Therese frowned, the hard-ass female smiled a little. "This way to Lost 'n' Found."

Trez said something under his breath as they all started walking, but there was no reason to get involved in whatever was going on between the pair of them. Maybe they were exes? Or . . . maybe they were lovers?

A lance of pain went through Therese's chest at that idea, but come on. In spite of the fact that she and Trez had just had sex—and she was convinced he was her shadow lover—his actual, in-person, non-lunatic love life was none of her business. And as a wave of exhaustion rolled through her, she decided she just needed to get her purse back and go home. It had been a very, very long night—

No.

The resounding negative came through so loud and clear, it was like getting tapped on the shoulder, and Therese even looked behind herself. At first, she wondered why some inner part of her was disagreeing about the fact that the combination of worrying about losing the only job she had, getting a thousand-dollar tip, setting boundaries with a co-worker, getting in the middle of a shooting, having sex with her boss's incredible brother, and losing a thousand dollars was enough to qualify for a long frickin' night.

Except then she looked at Trez's profile. His expression was tense, his brows down, his lips thin. He was staring at the back of the other female's nearly shaved head, and Therese had the sense he was having some kind of conversation with her in his own mind.

One that maybe had a lot of cursing in it—

No, the voice repeated.

And that was when the meaning became clear. Somehow, he and this powerful female with the short hair and the dark gray eyes were not lovers. Never had been lovers. Never would be lovers.

The conviction was as rock-solid as it was incomprehensible—and, arguably, irrelevant. That Therese and he had just had sex, sharing what to her was an intimate act she did not take lightly, did not change the reality that they were nothing but acquaintances. Sure, their bodies had fused for a short, intense time. Yes, she was convinced for some crazy reason that she had dreamed of him. But in the cold light of—she glanced up at the ceiling . . . well, in the cold light of these fluorescent fixtures, none of that meant that their lives were any closer than they had been at the start of the night.

With a quick shift, the female—Xhex was the name, if she got it right—glanced over her shoulder as she led the way across the dance floor, staying far from the medics, the cops, and the groups of humans giving statements.

"The recovered stuff is back here," she announced. "In one of my workrooms. The cops wanted to seal off everything. Treat this as a crime scene. Take evidence and pictures. But we are not going to allow that, of course."

"Oh," Therese said. Because she felt like she should say something, and the only thing occurring to her was, *Holy shit, you people work here every night?*

Trez shook his head as if he'd read her mind. Or maybe her expression wasn't as composed as she thought it was.

"Like I said," he muttered, "it doesn't happen all that often."

Once is enough for me, Therese thought.

"In here," Xhex said as she opened a door.

Therese went inside and was surprised to find herself in what looked like an interrogation room: There was a broad metal table with four chairs around it, and nothing else but noise-canceling, egg-carton-like padding on the walls—and wait, were those chairs bolted down? She shook herself back into focus. On the table surface, there was a clutter of all kinds of personal belongings, clothes, glasses, jewelry—

"My purse," she said as she leaned across the stuff. But she stopped before she touched anything. "Is it okay for me to pick it up?"

That female's eyes were on her again, even before she asked her question. "Yeah. Help yourself."

Therese grabbed her bag and yanked it open. There was nothing inside.

Closing her eyes, she cursed. The tip money. Her

burner phone. But more than anything . . . the keys she had tried so hard to find at the beginning of the night.

Her parents' keys.

Even as she told herself she shouldn't care, she did.

"Is your wallet gone?" Trez said as he looked inside at all the absolutely-nothing. "Oh . . . shit."

"It's all right. The keys were the only thing that really mattered. But I'm going to miss that tip money, for sure." She glanced over at him. "It was going to help me move, actually."

"I thought you said you didn't have the money?"

"Well, this blond member of the species came into the restaurant with his *shellan*? He ate like . . . I mean, almost the whole menu, and after he was comp'd by your brother, he left me this huge tip. It's okay, though. I mean . . . what am I going to do?"

Xhex nodded. "The money's probably long gone. Listen, I've got to get back to erasing memories. I'll see you both later."

With a nod, the female took her leave, and the door shut behind her. Left with Trez and the Lost 'n' Found, Therese took a deep breath. And another.

For a brief moment, she considered asking if she could go and scour the dance floor in case she could locate those keys. Then she glanced back at the table.

There were a couple of key rings scattered among the crap that had been lost, but none of them were hers.

"Well," she said. And could go no further.

"I'm really sorry."

As it was hard to know what he was apologizing for—the sex, even though it had been incredible? the strange connection, even though it had seemed so real? the shooting, even though she hadn't been injured and it was hardly his fault?—she recognized that her head was in a total tangle, and the only cure for the condition was sleep.

Assuming she would be able to get any today, and not just on account of her noisy neighbors.

"So I'm going to head back home now." She couldn't quite meet his eyes and had to force a smile. "Thanks for this—"

"I'm glad you came to see me. It was unexpected— I wish I'd known you were coming."

"I—ah . . . I didn't know this was your club, actually. Emile and I came here to calm down his girlfriend."

Trez's eyebrows lifted. "Emile. Has a girlfriend?"

◆ ◆ ◆

Well, wasn't this a happy piece of news, Trez thought. For that waiter. Because if the sonofabitch human was taken? It was going to dramatically improve his chances of seeing his next birthday.

"Yes, he's dating a woman I work with." Therese smoothed back the hair that was flowing over her shoulders. "Looks like I lost my clip, too." She shook her head. "Anyway, yes, he's with the dreaded Liza—although to be fair, I'm sure the girl's mother probably loves her."

"Is she giving you problems?"

Is she a problem I can solve for you, he thought to himself.

"No, not like you're inferring. She's just jealous."

"Does she have reason to be?" Maybe his optimism was misplaced.

"No." Those eyes, those beautiful pale eyes of hers, swung up and hung onto his stare. "There is no reason for her to be worried about me. Not on my end, at any rate. And I've made this clear to Emile."

Trez tried to keep his smile to himself. Failed miserably. "Well."

As Therese flushed, she went back to looking at the personal effects that had been thrown on the table. "Yeah, so the plan was for him and me to come talk to her. Calm her down. She was drunk and . . . whatever. It's not my problem."

He was more than happy to change the subject. "So you were going to move? Thanks to that tip?"

And P.S., there was only one blond male that

Trez could think of who would eat so much that a security deposit's worth of a tip would be warranted.

"Yup, I was going to ask you about the rental."

"It's still available," he rushed to point out.

"And I'm broke again." Therese took a defeated breath, but she didn't wallow in any kind of poor-me. "It's just a setback, though. A delay. It'll happen."

She put her purse on the table and reached inside to unzip a pocket. Taking out a cell phone that was not turned on, she shook her head. "At least they didn't get this. Maybe because it's dead. Or they just missed it."

"You out of battery? Would you like to charge it in my office?"

"Nah, this is my old one. I don't turn it on."

When she glanced at the door, he felt the way he had when they'd been talking back at the restaurant. There was something about her leaving that always made him antsy—as if, maybe, he would never see her again.

As if, maybe, he would lose her permanently. Again.

This is my queen, he thought to himself. *Back to me . . . by some kind of miracle.*

"I'm glad I am your dream," he said softly.

His female's eyes returned to his and she opened her mouth to say something. Then closed it.

As the silenced stretched out between them, he knew what she wanted. And he wanted to give it to her. For hours. For whole nights and days.

Stepping into her body, he put his arm around the small of her back and drew her against his hard muscle. He was erect again. Desperate again. But there was no chance of doing anything about it. There was too much going on on the far side of the door—and then there was Xhex and her miss-nothing *symphath* shit.

Trez lowered his mouth, but stopped with a mere half inch between them. "I want to be in you again."

Her sigh was as lovely as she was. "When?"

Now! Fucking now! his libido roared. NOWNOWNOW—

"Nightfall tomorrow. I'll come to you at the rooming house."

"I have to work."

"You can be late."

Therese shook her head. "I can't."

"Then after your shift is over. I'll come and get you."

"Okay." She reached up to his nape and put her breasts to his chest. "It's a date."

"And I'll find us some proper privacy."

"I don't know where this is going," she whispered.

"Yes, you do. And so do I."

They were talking quickly, their sentences bumping into each other's, as if she worried they would lose out on the future in the same way he did.

Trez sealed her mouth with a kiss that took him right back to when they'd been joined, so rushed, so hasty, so raw on the floor of the hidden passageway. And the next thing he knew, he put her on the corner of the table, other people's crap hitting the floor as his hands went to places that would get them into a compromising situation quick.

Places like zippers.

Trez cursed against her lips. "I need to stop before I can't."

"Me, too. This is crazy."

Getting his body to pay attention to commands was not the easiest thing he'd ever done, but he eventually managed to peel himself away. The re-tuck he had to pull was more like putting a two-by-four in a flour sack—and the way she looked at him while he was touching himself did not help him cool off in the slightest.

"I'll see you tomorrow night," he said in a guttural voice.

"Yes." She kept her eyes on his arousal. "You will."

CHAPTER ELEVEN

Xhex was scrubbing yet another human's memories when she saw the door to the interrogation room open and Trez and that female step out. It didn't take a *symphath* to know what was on both of their minds. For one thing, Trez had a tent pole in the front of his slacks. For another, that female—Therese—was looking at him under her lashes, as if she were remembering something the two of them had done, and not as in reading the paper.

More like Netflix and Chilling—without the Netflix or the chill.

It was unlikely that kind of thing had happened in that room just now, however. For one, they hadn't been alone very long, and Xhex was willing to bet her boss worked fast with the females, but not that fast. For another, they were carrying each other's scents when she had met up with them as they'd come out from the hidden passageway.

So it had already been a done deal.

Although that wasn't even the interesting part.

Narrowing her eyes, Xhex focused on the female—and not just because she was a dead ringer for Selena.

Yup. She hadn't been wrong. Therese had an extremely unusual grid.

As a *symphath*, Xhex was able to read the emotions of other people, sensing shifts in feelings and internal orientations along a three-dimensional grid pattern, the highs and lows plotted along axes. Everyone had such a superstructure. *Doggen*, regular vampires, Shadows—even *symphaths*, although most of Xhex and Rehv's kind could hide their structures from others of the subspecies. What was impossible—or should have been impossible—was for an individual to have two grids. In fact, Xhex had never seen such as thing . . .

Until she had met John Matthew, her *hellren*.

He had what was a bog-standard grid, just like everyone else, but there was something behind it, a shadow superstructure. It was like a mirror image of the primary grid, and the emotions were always plotted the same on both, the two working not in concert but identically.

To this night, Xhex had no idea what it meant.

At least not for sure.

She had her suspicions, however, ones that were too private and personal for her to share with anybody except John, but also ones that were too shattering for her to share with him. The truth was, she had started to wonder whether John was more connected with his father, Darius, than just on a sire/son basis. Except that was impossible, right? Reincarnation didn't happen.

Really. It didn't . . .

Yeah, except how else would anyone reconcile an identical copy of Trez's dead *shellan*—who had a grid like that?

"I don't want to hear it, okay."

At the sound of the terse male voice, she didn't bother shifting her eyes away from the female who was walking out of the club. "Where did you meet her?"

"I'm not talking about her."

"She looks like Selena."

"Really," he groused. "I hadn't noticed. And I am not—"

"I think she's Selena."

As he froze where he stood, she wanted to slap herself. The guy was broken by grief, and therefore primed to do things that were not in his best interest with a female who looked like that. In spite of the grid issue. Or maybe because of it.

Xhex shook her head. "I didn't mean that—"

"What do you see?" he demanded. He took her arm in a hard grip. "Xhex, what do you know?"

The sense that they were being watched made her glance around—and yes, there it was. In the far corner of the club, a dense shadow that couldn't be explained by any objects blocking any of the light. But it wasn't the Omega. It was not evil. It wasn't even a shadow.

It was an optical illusion thrown up so someone standing behind it was not seen.

And she had a feeling who it was.

And why they were here.

An abrupt sense of peacefulness came over her.

"What do you see?" Trez put her face in his. "Tell me."

The way the male's voice broke, the desperation

in his face, the painful cast of his eyes, made Xhex abruptly hug him. How could she not? His suffering had been indescribable, but the end was in sight. She knew this without a doubt.

Holding him close, Xhex said in his ear, "It's going to be okay."

"What is?"

As she eased back from her old friend, from her dear friend, she reached up to his face. "All is as it should be."

"What does that mean."

Xhex stared up at the male. Putting her hand on his heart, she opened herself to fully read his grid. It was the kind of thing she hadn't been able to do before now, and not because he locked her out. She loved him like a brother, and his loss was so painful that getting too close to his emotions, in the way of her kind, was agony.

Like putting her entire body on a red-hot grill—

Sucking a breath in through her teeth, Xhex trembled. His pain was a tidal wave that stung her very marrow, and she had to brace herself to absorb the enormity of it. But she owed him this.

Before she spoke, her eyes skipped to that corner of the club, to the shadow that was present, but couldn't technically exist.

"Do you know what you feel in here?" she whispered as she rubbed over his heart.

"What?"

"In here." She pressed in. "Here in your core." When he started to shake his head, she talked over his questions, his desperation. "Listen to me. You can trust this. Do you understand what I am saying? You can trust what is in *here*."

Trez swallowed hard. When his eyes went to the roof high above, she knew he wasn't looking at anything. He was trying to keep tears from falling, here in this public place, with so many humans and staff around.

"How do you know what I can trust?" he asked without meeting her eyes.

"I don't have a good answer for that, and not because I'm keeping anything from you. I just know . . . you can have faith in yourself. Even if it feels . . . impossible."

There was a long moment of stillness and silence, even as others in the club moved around and talked and even shouted. But she gave him all the time he needed to assess her aura and her expression. And she knew the moment he believed in what she was trying to tell him without actually telling him: Her old friend's arms shot around her and pulled her in tight, the strength that he put into the embrace nearly crushing her.

"Thank you," he gritted out.

Xhex's eyes returned to that far corner, to that inexplicable shadow that was created by magic. "Don't thank me. It's not my doing."

With a quick curse, Trez stepped back and tucked in his silk shirt. Like he was trying to tuck in his emotions.

"I, um . . . yeah, well," he said, "if you'll excuse me, I'm going to head up to my office where I am totally not going to lose it all over the fuck."

"Good plan." Xhex smiled at him. "I'll handle everything down here."

"You always do."

Trez gave her shoulder a squeeze and then he strode across the empty dance floor, a tall figure with a powerful body and a terrible heartache that had, unexpectedly, been relieved by a miracle.

Without warning, unease rippled through her, and she crossed her arms over her chest. Had she done the right thing? Had she said the right thing?

Big Rob, her second in command, approached her. "Hey, you gotta minute? That cop wants to talk to you."

"One sec. Hold him in place."

Turning from her bouncer, she walked over to the shadow, and then pivoted around so that her back was to the corner, as if she were making some kind of measurement of the dance floor.

In a quiet voice, she said, "Why can't I just tell him? I don't get it. If you've given him this gift, shouldn't he just know that she's back?"

Xhex waited. And just before she was about to give up, a disembodied answer entered her brain directly, bypassing her ear canals.

He is in the midst of his destiny the now. There are no shortcuts, even when there are gifts.

She twisted around and looked at the dense darkness. "What about John. John is the same as her, John is—"

That was before my time. I have no standing to rearrange the arrangements of my predecessor.

"So it's real?"

The shadow disappeared, but as it left, she felt a warmth come over her. Shaking her head, she had to smile.

Lassiter working magic, and taking names. As best he could.

It almost made you forget his taste in TV shows.

◆ ◆ ◆

Trez did not have a breakdown, as it turned out. Instead, he stayed up in his office until everyone, including Xhex, had left. Then, close to dawn, he went down to the club proper and stood in the huge, empty space. Slowly, he pivoted in a circle, taking in the bar, the sound booth, the interrogation rooms, the bathrooms where the fucking happened, the stairs to his private area.

He'd bought the old warehouse for a song, torn out the interior compartments, and painted all the old glass in the blocks of windows around the upper quarter of the space. He'd also built out his office space, as well as the locker room for the working girls, and those one-person, but never used that way, loos with the drains in the middle of the floor and the hose hookups behind the toilets.

He had never really thought of his business as dirty. He'd just been in it for the money.

But the idea of Selena being here? And almost getting shot?

Bringing up his hand, he placed it upon his heart, right where Xhex had put her own. *You can trust what is in here.*

Yes, he thought. *YES.*

His prayers, his desperate prayers that had been

sent up to thin ether because he had believed in nothing spiritual at all, not even the distant stars, had been answered. Xhex had proved that tonight.

She had told him, tonight, everything he had wanted to hear.

With a fresh wave of gratitude and relief, he pictured Selena in her new incarnation. Remembered them being together. Recalled the feel of her core, the taste of her lips, even the sounds she made.

His *shellan* was back to him.

His joy was so great, he could contain it no better than he had handled his grief, his emotions overspilling. Overcoming. Overtaking. Except now, he didn't mind it. He took out his phone and called up his brother's contact. He needed to tell iAm, he needed to tell the Brothers, he needed to—

A flash down on the floor caught his eye.

Frowning, he walked over and bent down. The ring of keys was nothing unusual, exactly the kind of thing that could be found any night of the week after the lights went on. There was something out of the norm, however. The unadorned ring held, in addition to a silver key of unremarkable distinction, a copper one.

The soft metal was old, utterly lacking the mellow, rose gold-like sheen of fresh copper.

So it was from a vampire house.

Bringing the thing to his nose, he breathed in deep—and caught the familiar scent of his female. These were hers. They had fallen out of her purse when her money had been taken.

Rubbing the slip of copper between his thumb and forefinger, he thought of his reincarnated Selena. Of the fact that she didn't recognize him in person, even though she knew him from her dreams, knew him from the feel of his body on hers, in hers.

This key, which warmed to his touch, was not to the door to her flat in that fucking awful rooming house. It was to another house—a home. Where she had evidently come from.

Except . . . how had that worked? How had she, as a Chosen, come from anywhere but the Sanctuary?

As much as his soul was singing, and as fervently as he wanted to proclaim to the world his queen had come back unto him, his logical side couldn't square up the past she had had without him. She was through her transition. Well through it. So how had that happened? How had his Selena died so recently, and yet been returned unto him in the body of a mature female?

There was no reconciling the two timelines. No way to make that equation add, subtract, multiply, or divide. And yet Xhex wouldn't mislead him. No way. Even though she was a *symphath*, history had proven that he could trust her, and she had very clearly confirmed what he had known all along, what had captivated him—and given that what he felt now was infinitely better than the suffering? He would take it and run with it. After all, wasn't that what faith was all about?

You believed what your soul told you even if the fallible mind struggled with the implications.

Peace. All he wanted was peace. And if he had to stop questioning and just believe to stay here in this relief? Then he was on that train, goddamn it.

Staring at his brother's contact on the screen of his cell phone, it felt all wrong not sharing this with iAm. The other male suffered as he did. Hell, maybe that was why the poor bastard had let that sauce burn on the stove tonight. He was newly mated, to a female he loved with everything in him, but he had a basket case for a nearest blood relation.

The last thing iAm needed was a crazy-ass phone call from said basket case that was full of happy tears, proclamations of reincarnation, and suggestions that they double date. This was especially true given that the guy's party line on his newest waitress was that the female was not in fact Selena. To iAm, she was Therese. From Michigan. Come to Caldwell to start a new life independent from whatever family she had left behind.

Any news flash to the contrary was not going to go well.

And iAm wasn't the only one who didn't need a conversation like that. Trez was not interested in anyone talking him out of this happiness. Trying to prove him wrong. Attempting to "reason" with him.

He was liable to go batshit, and not in an insane way. In a combative manner.

"Fuck."

As he stared at his phone, he found such irony in the fact that his good news alienated him as much as his bad news had. He had a secret he knew he couldn't share, and that made him lonely.

Maybe even when it comes to the owner of this key, he thought to himself.

His female had seen him in her dreams . . . but again, she did not recognize him in real life.

Before he became frustrated with the whole situation, he deliberately remembered the way he had felt as he had stood in front of that funeral pyre, those flames consuming the remains of his queen. How many times, during the burn, and then after it was all embers and ashes—hell, even before then, when his female had been on the lip edge of death, lingering, suffering . . . how many times had he begged for a different destiny? Promised all kinds of things, both within and without of his control, for her to come back, for his life to return to normal, for them to have years, decades, centuries ahead of them.

Instead of what they'd been granted. Which had been too short, and too tragic.

What if this was the fate he had asked for being delivered unto him? What if . . . this was the only way it could happen, the only manner in which his prayers could be answered?

The reunion with his queen granted.

But only him knowing it.

"I'll take it," he said out loud as he clicked his phone off. "I will fucking take this shit a hundred times during the week, and a thousand times on every Sunday."

CHAPTER TWELVE

The following evening, Trez all but skipped down the formal front staircase of the Brotherhood's mansion. As he descended the red-carpeted, tsar-worthy steps, he was glad no one was hanging around down in the multicolored, marble-columned foyer: Even though he was whistling, very nearly skipping, and liable to high-five anyone in range, he didn't want anybody to catch him in his good mood.

In fact, his body was bouncy and buoyant, a buoy on gentle seas, and his feet were all Fred Astaire, light and nimble. Then again, the incredible weight that had been sitting on his rib cage like an elephant had disappeared. In its absence, he could breathe for the first time since Selena's death—and hey, another bonus, his heart wasn't bleeding out in his chest anymore, either.

And it was funny. Even though he'd been so very aware of how badly off he'd been—because, hello, he'd been in so much pain, he'd had no choice but to recognize the major-organ-failure equivalent of his damage—he nonetheless had a fresh perspective on his mental and emotional states.

Not until the removal of the pain had he understood the depths of it.

Plus, check it, he was actually looking forward to something.

Someone.

Was this what Rehv had been talking about when the guy had come and pressed the drug thing? Because if a person could get this effect by popping a pill every twenty-four hours? Man, sign his shit up. He just didn't think it was that simple.

No, this optimism, this return to a normalcy he had never really had, was both complicated and simple. Soon, he was going to see his *shellan*, in the form she had been returned to him as. And what do you know, that solved so many of his problems—and the ones it created? Well, he'd spent all day lying in bed and thinking them over.

Yup, he was more than comfortable managing them.

As he hit the mosaic floor, he stopped and looked toward the cheerful sounds spilling out through the dining room's archway. There was laughter and chatter, and the soft clinking of sterling silver on porcelain, and the occasional scrape of chair legs as someone got up or sat down. He could picture the people in there. See their faces, their smiles, their bodies in those hand-carved seats. Thirty of them, including the servants.

He had been avoiding mealtimes, not because he didn't like who was in that grand room, but because he loved the people in there. And it was hard, when you were in a dark place, to be around those who were not. You didn't want to bring anybody down, but you also couldn't fake the happiness.

With his change in mood, he was tempted to go into the dining room, hug each and every one of them, and then plant himself at a vacant place setting. As he tucked into the roast beef he could smell, he would apologize for putting them all through what he had—because he knew the Brothers and their *shellans*, the other fighters, even Fritz and his staff, had worried about him. And then he would join the talking and the laughing.

Except . . . no. He couldn't do that. This resurrected mood—natch—he was sporting was like getting rhinoplasty. Everybody was going to notice, and there was no not-explaining, not to the nearest-and-dearest crew.

It was better that he made a gradual reentry.

Yes, that was how this had to go. Especially as he started bringing Selena in her new incarnation around the Brothers. Thank God at least Xhex knew what was doing and could help frame the hellos.

Taking a deep breath, he headed for the door into the vestibule, and reminded himself that him knowing the truth was enough. Reality didn't become more real just because he drew others in it—there wasn't some kind of occupancy requirement to yup-this-is-happening. Besides, if anybody challenged his good news? He was liable to get defensive in a forty-millimeter kind of way—

Trez was just about to open the vestibule's first door when something in the billiards room caught his eye.

Behind the lineup of pool tables, down on the floor, a couple dozen pages were laid out in a fan. There had to be at least twenty or so, and they were marked with splashes of bright red and green. Breathing in, he smelled paint, but not the stinky oil kind. It was sweet and—

"Bitty?" he said.

The little young, who was stretched out on her tummy and surrounded by open containers of tempera paint, looked up and smiled. "Hi, Uncle Trez."

Walking over to Rhage and Mary's daughter, he got down on his haunches. "Wow. This is some kind of work."

"I'm doing Christmas cards for everybody." She rinsed her paintbrush in a glass full of murky water. "It's a human tradition."

"So I've heard."

As he inspected her work, he thought of her hard start in life. She had lost so much, been hurt so badly. But now she was on the far side of that, having been adopted by a father and *mahmen* who loved her like nothing else. She had a good ending, and it was nice to feel like he was with her in that.

Her lovely soft face became very serious. "My mom and Auntie Beth told me all about how humans do it. You get cards for the people you love this time of year and then everyone puts them on their mantelpiece so they can look at them every night. I saved up my babysitting money, and I went to Hannaford's with my dad, but none of the cards for sale really fit any of us."

Trez smiled. "Well, vampires and all. Some things don't translate as well. But I know I would rather get a handmade card from you than a store-bought one." He put his palm up. "Not that I'm taking for granted that I'm on your list."

"But you are, Uncle Trez. Of course you are." Except then her eyes grew sad. "I mean, both of you are."

"iAm?" Trez nodded. "You know, it's more efficient to give us both one—"

"No. He gets a separate one." She hesitated. Then she sat up and leaned across her masterpieces. Picking one up, she offered it to him. "Here, this is for you. I'm sorry if it's . . . not good."

Without even looking at the artwork, Trez frowned and put his hand on her tiny shoulder. "Bitty. How can I not love what you've made me?"

She just indicated the card, so he focused on it.

As he went to take what she had made for him, his hand started to shake ever so slightly. The 8½-by-11 sheet was split in two, clearly with the intention that it was to be folded in half down the middle. Turning it around, he blinked hard. There was a pair of figures depicted, and they were holding hands, a gold star above where they were linked. On the right, the larger of the pair had dark skin, super-short hair, a green sweater, and red pants. On the left, the smaller of the pair was wearing a red blouse and a green skirt, and had long, dark hair. But instead of being flesh-colored, the arms and legs and face of the female were silver.

"I wanted Selena to be on your card." Bitty reached across her collection and pulled another page over. "So I made her like I made my *mahmen*. See? And my younger brother. They are all silver because they are not here on earth, but they are still with us."

Trez took the card she had made for her *mahmen*. There was a figure like the one that represented Selena, silver-skinned with a red-and-green dress, and in her arms, in a little red-and-green swaddling blanket, was a silver-faced young. Next to the pair, depicted with flesh-colored skin, was how Bitty saw herself, slim and in red pants and a green shirt. Bitty was not smiling, but she was holding her *mahmen*'s hand.

"I have another card, though." Bitty brought a third sheet over. "I have this one, too."

On the third one, there were three figures in the foreground, a huuuuge blond-haired one in black clothes with a red-and-green scarf, a small one that had short brown hair and green pants and a red shirt, and then the same depiction of Bitty that was on her *mahmen's* card.

In this card, Bitty was smiling. Everyone was smiling.

Rhage was standing with his big arms over Mary's and Bitty's shoulders, and the two females were holding hands across his torso. Over their heads, there was another gold star, as well as two silver figures in white robes, their arms outstretched, smiles on their faces, trails from their flying done in sparkles that fell like snow from the sky to form the ground line the little family was standing on.

"That's my *mahmen* and my brother," the girl pointed out. "Up above."

"Watching from the Fade." He looked at Bitty. "I think these are all really beautiful."

Bitty took the two cards she had done for herself back and tested the paint gently with her fingertip.

"It's dry." She carefully folded the piece of paper down the center. "See, this is how they are supposed to look."

She repeated the bend-and-flatten routine with the other, and then lined the pair up. Sitting back on her heels, she frowned.

"I don't know whether I should have done one for

Mahmen and Charlie separately." She glanced over. "I was to have a brother, you see. He came to me in a dream. So I know he'd have been a boy if he lived, and he didn't have a name, so I gave him Charlie. At least in my own head."

Bitty touched both cards, linking them as the figures were linked by hands and arms. "It felt wrong not to do a card for them. But it was a sad card. Then . . ." She pointed to the other. "Then I did this one, and I realized I could fit us all in. And this is a happy card, even if they're not with us. Because they're with us."

Grave thirteen-year-old eyes locked on his own. "When I went to do your card, I thought maybe I would put Selena up over you, but . . . I just felt like she was on the same line. Next to you."

Goose bumps ran up the back of his neck. "You have no idea how right you are. May I keep this?"

"Let me fold it so it's right."

"Of course," he murmured as he gave her artwork back.

Bitty lined up the corners precisely and then, with care to rival a brain surgeon's, drew her fingertips downward, creating a perfect crease. She made as though she were going to give it to him, but then she took the card back.

"I was supposed to write something on the inside. But I don't have the pens I was going to use. They are up in my room. I didn't expect to do the lettering yet."

Trez looked at the silver figure and the image of himself. "You know, it was made with love and I love what you've painted. So I'm not sure it needs words."

"Okay, you can have it like it is."

As he accepted the gift, the little girl threw her arms around him and squeezed. With a lump in his throat, Trez returned the hug lightly. She was such a tiny little thing, but her heart and spirit were fierce. She had more than proven that.

"Thank you, Bitty. I will treasure this always."

"I love you, Uncle Trez." Bitty pulled back. "And I don't want you to be sad anymore."

"I'm better now," he whispered. "Honest."

The sound of approaching boot falls brought Trez's head around. Rhage was striding into the billiards room, a turkey leg in one hand, a chocolate milkshake that was half finished in the other. The Brother smiled.

"Hey, Trez, what's doing?" He looked at Bitty. "And young lady, it's time for dinner. I gave you an extra ten minutes, but that's turned into twenty. You can always come back here soon as you're done."

"Okay, Dad," she said as she stood up.

"Wow, look at your cards," Hollywood murmured as he took a draw on his straw. "They are beautiful."

"She made one for me." Trez held out his as he got to his feet. "Isn't it perfect."

A shadow of sadness crossed Rhage's Bahamas-blue stare. "Yeah. It is—"

"It's perfect. Just perfect."

Rhage smiled down at this daughter. "Good job."

"Do you think George will walk on them?" Bitty asked.

"No, he sticks with his master. And as for Boo—well, that cat does its own thing. But I think you're pretty much in a paw-free zone in here."

"I don't want them to get paint on their paws and lick it off. What if it made them sick?"

"You are a very thoughtful little girl, Bits."

"I'm going to go find Mom." She waved. "Bye, Uncle Trez. I'm glad you liked the card."

"I love it!" he called out as she skipped across the mosaic floor, her long brunette hair flagging out behind her slip of a body. "Thank you again!"

When they were alone, Rhage cleared his throat. "Listen, if that's, you know, too hard for you to hold on to, you can throw it—"

"No." Trez recoiled. "I'm keeping this. I love this.

She is a talented artist, and this is my favorite card. Ever."

As Hollywood looked doubtful and tried to hide it behind taking a hunk out of that turkey leg, Trez switched subjects.

"Hey, did you happen to hit Sal's last night?" he asked.

"Yup." Hollywood took a refresh on the milk-shake, hitting his straw again. After he swallowed, he smiled. "Your brother is a helluva good cook, you know that. And actually . . ."

When the Brother didn't finish, Trez had a feeling where the male had gone in his head.

"What." Even though he knew. "You can tell me. It's okay."

◆   ◆   ◆

On time, Therese thought as she re-formed in the shadows thrown by the restaurant's far corner. *Let's hear it for being on time.*

Jumping over a low-level snowbank, she hit the shoveled part of the walkway and made her way to the staff entrance. Opening the door, she—

Stopped dead.

iAm's office was at the end of the shallow concrete hall, and she couldn't see through the open doorway for all the people crammed shoulder to shoulder in front of it. They were all facing away from her, and their voices were overlapping. It was everyone who worked at the restaurant, from the servers and the bartenders, to the sous chef and the manager. What the heck was going on?

Walking over, she tapped the pastry chef on the shoulder. "What's happening—"

"You're alive!" he called out.

The next thing she knew, he was giving her a hard hug that smelled like melted sugar and strawberries.

The staff pivoted around, and then they were all talking again, their voices loud and shouty, shock and relief warring on their faces as they looked her over as if they were searching for leaks of the arterial variety.

The next thing she knew, she was being drawn through them all, urged into iAm's utilitarian office. Emile's red-rimmed eyes were wide as he stood next to their boss. He looked awful, like he hadn't slept for a week.

"You're alive," he said. Just like the pastry chef.

Emile's embrace did not smell like shortcake with mixed berries. He was wearing a cologne of some kind, but it wasn't something he had put on fresh that night. It was in his clothes.

"I've been calling you all day," he explained. "Something happened at that club shAdoWs last night and we had to leave without you—"

Wincing, he stopped talking and brought his hand up to his temple as if he had a sudden headache. Which was characteristic when a human had had their memories stripped and replaced with some other version of events than what had actually happened. For the most part, the patches held, but when the person tried to probe past the story their minds had been supplied, they typically felt pain in their gray matter.

"Liza and I were worried," he mumbled. "And when I couldn't reach you, I panicked."

Wow, so Trez and Xhex really did take care of everything. Then again, she hadn't seen anything on the news, either. "I'm fine. But thanks for worrying about me."

iAm, who was seated behind his messy desk, cleared his throat. "Okay, guys. How about everyone but Therese head back to prep."

"I'm glad you're all right," Emile said.

"Thanks—and hey, listen, I lost my phone last night. That's why I didn't answer when you called. I wasn't avoiding you or anything, and the last thing I want is to create a problem."

"As long as you're okay." He put a hand on her shoulder. "That's all I care about."

After everybody left, Therese exhaled in frustration and turned back to her boss. "Am I in trouble or something?"

"No." He shook his head. "But what happened last night?"

She shrugged. "It was a shooting between humans. Nothing to do with us."

"At my brother's club?"

"Yes. Emile and I went there to—" She stopped herself. "That's not important. Anyway, I gather everything was . . . taken care of . . . on the human side of things. Just as they said it would be."

Now iAm was rubbing his head like it hurt. Then he muttered something under his breath and looked across that desk. When he didn't say anything, she felt as though he were trying to speak with his eyes. There was no chance to ask questions, however. The outside door opened behind Therese and—

As a blast of arctic winter air shot into the corridor, she couldn't keep the smile off her face. And forget about the flush that went through her body.

Trez was bigger, better, sexier, smarter, fitter, handsomer—every -er you could tack on to every adjective that had ever been used to describe a male of worth. Even though she had seen him a mere eighteen hours ago, the absence had gone further than making her heart grow fonder. It had turned him into a living, breathing fantasy.

And on his side? He smiled back at her. And smiled. And smiled.

Okay, she *really* needed to get another burner phone. So they could talk to each other during the day. She had wondered whether he had tried to call her—but then remembered he had been with her when she'd discovered her cell was gone—

"Allow me to break into this moment," iAm said sharply.

She and Trez snapped to attention as if a drill sergeant had threatened them with dead lifts for insubordination.

"Why didn't you tell me what had gone down at the club?" iAm demanded. Except then he put up a hand. "Wait, don't answer that. I'm just glad she's okay."

"I wasn't in any real danger," Therese said.

Hell, there had at least been three feet between the muzzle of that gun and her face. Maybe four. No problem.

iAm sat forward and pulled a folder across the

desk. Opening it, his finger went down the form she had filled out when she had first been hired.

"You never gave us your emergency contact information." He tapped one of the vacancies she had left. "I've got to know who to get in touch with if something happens to you here at work. If you're injured in an accident. If you don't come in at all."

Therese opened her mouth. Closed it.

"Me," Trez said. "Call me."

She glanced in his direction. She had been so struck by his presence, she hadn't even noticed what he was wearing. But damn . . . the male turned a white silk shirt and a set of fine black slacks into a masterpiece. Did he never wear a coat, though?

As she worried about him catching a cold that turned into pneumonia that put him on life support, Therese pulled back from the tailspin a little. It was impossible not to notice how far she had evolved in such a short time. Just twenty-four hours before, she had been all now-is-not-a-good-time-for-a-relationship and do-things-on-my-own. Now? She was totally about this male, that rare sexual connection they shared rocketing her forward on a timeline of intimacy so fast she probably should be wearing a neck brace from the whiplash.

But she couldn't argue with how she felt.

Nor did she want to.

She had been rootless, and suddenly was no longer. And the change felt too good to argue with.

"Yes," she murmured as she stared at her boss's brother. "If you could get in touch with Trez, that would be great."

CHAPTER THIRTEEN

You want to talk about fried-egg pissed? Trez thought.

Behind that desk of his, iAm was so angry, you could have cracked a yolk on his forehead, and gone scrambled with no problem at all.

Trez looked over at Selena—no, he told himself, he had to remember to refer to her as Therese, at least in public. "Would you excuse us for a second?"

"Yes, sure," she said. "Of course."

Clearly, she had picked up on the vibe. Then again, you had to have a completely different definition of a-okay, hunky-dory to miss what was doing with iAm.

"I'll just go get my tables ready," she murmured before hightailing it past Trez.

"I'll come find you before I go to work," he said.

As she glanced over her shoulder, her smile was like sunlight, and given the long winter he had been in—and he was not thinking in terms of the calendar—he soaked the warm up like he'd been frostbitten all over his body.

After she disappeared around the corner, he shut the door to his brother's office and leaned back against it. "So what's the problem."

iAm closed the folder without adding anything to the form he'd stuck his forefinger to like a dart. "What are you doing. Seriously."

"Well, at the moment, I'm holding this door up. A minute ago, I was in my car. And later, I'll be at my club." He cracked a half smile. "You want me to write this down for you? Draw a diagram—"

"What are you doing with that female," iAm snapped. "And quit it with the games."

Trez crossed his arms over his chest and told his temper to take a load off. There was no reason to fight. "Ah. So you need an anatomy lesson—"

"This is fucking serious!" iAm banged a fist on the desk, causing an adding machine to jump like the thing had been startled. "You are not in any condition to be stringing her along—"

"Excuse me?" Trez felt the tips of his fangs tingle. "Now you're a shrink?"

"She is not Selena!" iAm burst to his feet, his chef's jacket, which he had yet to button up, flapping open. "And you know she is not, and you're just using her—"

Dropping the happy-chappy act, Trez bared his fangs. "You do not know what I'm doing with her—"

"You're the one who brought up anatomy. Or are you now going to try to convince me you're only holding hands together?"

Trez stepped forward and planted his palms on the desk surface. Leaning forward, he stared directly into his brother's eyes. "It's none of your business."

"She's my employee. You're essentially an owner here. It's a violation of our HR—"

Throwing his head back, Trez laughed. "You're coming at this from a human resources angle? Really?"

"Well, I've tried the most obvious one, that she isn't your dead female, and I've gotten nowhere. The human laws protecting employees from being sexually harassed by their bosses are all I have left."

As Trez inhaled sharply, he had a thought that he was very glad this blowup hadn't happened any sooner than this very moment. Without everything Xhex had told him? Without the hope and optimism he now had in his heart? He might well have done something he really regretted.

Like pick up this desk and throw it at his brother.

"Do you just want me to be unhappy?" he said roughly.

"What?" iAm shook his head like he hadn't heard right. "Are you even kidding me?"

"Do you want me to suffer." Trez straightened. "Would you rather that than my being happy? Relieved? Living again? Does it make you feel better about your own life if mine is in the shitter?"

iAm's eyes narrowed. "I cannot believe that shit just came out of your mouth."

"Fine, then what's the other explanation for this bullshit you're talking? Because that's the only conclusion that makes any sense to me."

iAm's finger pointed through the tense air, punctuating syllables spoken with anger. "You have used and discarded hundreds upon hundreds of women and females over the course of your life. I know this because I've been on the sidelines. Watching. I've seen them pine after you, show up on our doorstep,

wander in and out of our clubs, looking for you—
and that's even after you scrub their memories, if
you remember to do so. And what I see now—"

"That's all changed—"

"—is you doing the same thing to a female who has
no one around to support her after you move on."

"—now that my *shellan* is back."

iAm recoiled. Then hung his head sadly. "So you
do think that."

"No, I don't."

Trez wanted to punch the wall as he struggled to
keep his truth inside. What he wanted to scream at
the top of his lungs was that he *knew* his *shellan* was
back.

Cursing under his breath, he muttered, "Whatever. We don't need to talk like this."

"You actually think it's her."

Trez backed up and leaned against the door
again. Recrossing his arms, he shrugged. "Hey, you
must be relieved that I'm not using her. At least you
can take that off your list of sins."

iAm shook his head. "She's not Selena."

"Talk to Xhex." Trez jabbed his thumb over his
shoulder. "Go talk to my head of security. She knows
the truth. She told me the truth. She's my best friend
and she would never lie to me."

iAm closed his eyes and rubbed them as he sat back down. When he spoke again, his voice was exhausted. "She's a *symphath*."

"Do *not* go there," Trez said in a nasty rush. "Don't you fucking shit on her for what she is. And besides, she's only ever stood by me. She's only ever been good to me. She is not evil, and you know this. You *know* her."

"I agree." iAm looked up. "She's always had your back. So it doesn't dawn on you that she gave you the information you wanted to hear just to make you feel better? I don't know what exactly she told you, but she knows how desperate you've been. How close the edge. How close to . . . certain things. You don't think maybe she manipulated you for all the right reasons?"

Trez stood up off the door and grabbed the knob. "I'm going to go. Before this gets even uglier."

"Just because a lie feels good doesn't mean it's true, and just because Xhex has good intentions doesn't mean lying to you is right. And I will tell you this right now—Therese is the one who's going to get hurt. The second it dawns on you that she's not actually Selena? You're going to lose that connection with her in a heartbeat. You're in love with someone who is not here, and self-medicating that horrible reality with a sexual stand-in is unconscionable, no matter how much it eases your pain."

Annnnnnd this is why I needed to keep the reincarnation a secret, Trez thought.

"You have no fucking clue what you're talking about." He opened the way out. "I'll talk to you later."

Like . . . maybe in a decade.

Or a thousand years, he thought as he walked off.

Back at the water station. Liza and Emile. Therese getting a pitcher to fill up so she could go out to her first table of the night. And what do you know, Liza was pissed off, Emile was apologetic, and Therese was worried about getting enough tips together to move out of that rooming house. It was just as it had been the night before.

Yet everything was completely different.

Ever since she had been with Trez in that hidden passageway, the world had reoriented itself, all the metaphorical furniture shifting three inches one way, two inches another, the new spaces between the sofas and chairs requiring a fresh assessment of a familiar room.

And what do you know, she liked the new arrangement better. Much, much better—

As long as Trez and his brother didn't get into it

too badly, she thought as she walked over to a four top of human women. He and his brother had been really tense as she'd left that office. Hopefully they cleared the air . . . instead of blew the back half of the restaurant up.

"Hi," she said to the women, "my name is Therese, I'll be your server. Can I start you off with a glass of wine or some cocktails?"

As she poured water, made small talk with her diners, and took drink orders from the quartet of old high school friends, she kept looking to the water station, and not because she was curious whether Liza and Emile had elevated their discussions and relationship to a higher level. The waiting was making her antsy, and she had a thought, in the back of her head, that she was way too emotionally invested if she couldn't make it through five or ten minutes without seeing Trez.

Try arguing with feelings, though.

She was back at the water station, having delivered the drinks and given the ladies a chance to look over the menu, when she caught a scent that went through her entire body.

"Hey," Trez whispered into her ear. "You got a minute?"

As she turned around and smiled up at him, she realized she'd been worried he'd leave without saying goodbye. Or saying anything. And again, that was a little much. If she kept up the desperate stuff, she was liable to drive him away.

Nobody wanted to be someone else's addiction.

"Absolutely I have time." Especially as she could sense the tension underneath his smiling expression. "Are you okay?"

"I am now."

There was a moment of silence, and she knew that he was kissing her in his mind—and what do you know, in hers, she was kissing him back. And here was the thing. The fact that he seemed as lost to whatever was happening as she was made her feel more secure in the crazy attraction.

Alone in it, she was lost. With him? They were on a heady journey.

"Come over here for a quick second," he said.

They stepped back into the hallway that led to the customer bathrooms, and he took something out of his pocket.

"Are these your keys?" he asked.

As he held out his palm, she couldn't believe it. "Yes! Oh, my God—how did you find them?"

Taking the ring, she singled out the copper key to her parents' house. Or rather her . . . whatever-they-were-to-her's house.

"I saw them on the floor. Before my janitorial service came in in the morning."

Putting the keys to her heart, she told herself they shouldn't matter. "Thank you so much. You have no idea how much this means to me."

"And I have something else." From the back pocket of his slacks, he took out a wad. "This is returned to you as well."

As she gasped at the sight of ten hundred-dollar bills, she was momentarily excited. But then she narrowed her eyes. "Trez. I believe you found my keys on the floor. This? You most certainly did not."

He held up his forefinger. "Before you tell me to pound sand, I'll have you know that the guy who ate here last night is a buddy of mine. When I told him what happened to the tip, he insisted on my bringing this to you. And"—when she went to interrupt, he kept talking—"as I didn't know how much he left you, you can count the bills yourself and know they're actually from him. You never told me how big the tip was. Only you and he know that."

Putting her hands on her hips, she shook her head. "I can't accept—"

"Count it." He prompted her with the cash. "Go ahead. You'll see that—"

"No." Smoothing her palms over her hair, latent anxiety caused her to fidget. "I believe you that it comes from the male. But losing the money was on me, not him. He does not need to make up for the fact that I lost it."

"You were in a shoot-out," Trez countered. "It was not your fault. And you didn't lose it, the money was stolen."

"So it's my bad luck. Not his." She reached forward and curled his hand closed. "Take this back and thank him. I really appreciate the kindness. But I'm going to keep working here, and as soon as I can, I'll fix my own problem with the housing situation."

"Does it change your mind if I tell you money is no object to the guy?"

"No." She smiled at him. "But I really appreciate you trying to take care of me. And seriously, please thank him for me."

Trez muttered some things under his breath. But he did put the cash away. And on the one hand, she was probably nuts for turning the Benjamins down. If the male was as rich as Trez was suggesting, they clearly weren't going to be missed—whereas on her side? It would change things tremendously.

She couldn't do it, though.

"I really am grateful," she said. "And to you as well."

"Can I still see you at the end of tonight?"

That flush she'd felt as he'd come through the back door to the restaurant returned. "Yes."

Trez stared at her for a long while. "I'll come pick you up after your shift. I'll just chill outside in my car until you come out."

"I can't wait," she whispered.

As they stood together in complete stillness, she knew where he was in his mind. She was there, too. Yes, it was crazy. Yes, it was intense. Yes, it had started with the adrenaline rush last night after the drama at the club. But when a craving was this strong?

You stopped asking about where it came from. And gave into it.

"I can't wait, either," he echoed before he turned away.

Thank God this isn't one-sided, Therese thought as she watched him go.

CHAPTER FOURTEEN

There were all kinds of reasons to wish the night away, but for Trez, the main one was finally getting off her shift at the restaurant in any moment. Not that he had been counting down the minutes.

Okay, fine. He'd been counting them down since he'd left her.

And he'd come early. Given that this was an average, non-holiday, non-blizzard night, dinner service at Sal's tended to grind to a halt around 10:30 at the latest. The waiters were usually off quickly thereafter. So yes, he'd shown up at 10:17 and parked in the shadows, outside the reach of the security camera by the back door.

He was not looking for a rehash with iAm. Nope. They'd both said their piece, and there was no going back from the lines that had been drawn. And besides, he was strictly on the happy train now, and anyone who had a problem with that, including his blood relative, could back off.

As Trez waited, ticking off each patron who emerged well-fed and sated into the cold, he couldn't help contrasting this shelter-in-place with the one during the storm the previous night, the one where he had cut the engine and stayed in the frosted temperatures, the snow blanketing his car, closing him in, keeping him locked and frigid.

It was still winter. But this time, he kept the engine on, and he listened to the Heat on SiriusXM, and he ran his hand around the static steering wheel, sensitizing his fingertips.

Because he wanted them ready to touch soft places. Tender places.

Wet places.

Rearranging himself in his seat, he had to pipe-down-Scotty his damn erection. He couldn't jump her the second she got in the car, for godsakes.

They had a ten-minute drive to their destination, at least.

After which the jumping could commence, assuming she would have him—

The staff door swung wide and he jerked forward, as if he could get closer her to already. Except . . . not her. It was that human man, Emile, and with him was a waitress who was talking a mile a minute.

They didn't seem particularly thrilled to be together, but as far as Trez was concerned they were the perfect frickin' couple. Total Hallmark time. Beauty and the Beast, Solo and Leia, Sheldon and Amy. Hell, go all the way back to Bogart and Bacall.

"Go forth and marry," he murmured to the windshield as they went over to an old Subaru. "I wish you maaaaaaaany years of happiness."

Abruptly, some instinct drew his attention back to the restaurant, and there his female was, coming out into the night, her parka loose—as if she trusted that he'd have a warm car waiting for her—her hair in a neat twist, a flash of lipstick on her mouth.

She had prepared herself for him, and he smiled at the thought. Because it was both sweet and totally unnecessary. He would take her any way she came.

Hell, especially if she were coming.

Opening his door, he didn't notice the cold in the slightest. "Over here."

Her head flipped around, and in the glow from the security lights, her happiness was as apparent as the noonday sun.

"Hello," she said as she walked over to his car. "How's your night—"

He meant to give her a chance to finish her sentence. His arms had a different idea. He brought her up against him and kissed her deep. And what do you know, she bent into his body and kissed him back. With a groan, he tilted her back, holding her weight, cradling her, as he lost track of everything: The winter weather. The time of night. The fact that anyone who worked there could come out at any time—the chefs, the bartender, the other servers.

Trez pulled back. "Let's go somewhere more private."

"Yes," she said.

Walking her around to the passenger side, he opened her door and gave her his arm. When she was settled in the seat, he closed her in, and hightailed it around the front bumper. He was not ashamed over being seen with her. Not in the slightest. But he worried about the consequences of her being caught with him. He didn't want any blowback gossip in her workplace—and then there was iAm's stupid HR-policy shit.

As things progressed between them, he might have to help her find another job . . . something that not only paid her more, but that used some of her talents—whatever they might be. As a Chosen, she had been sequestered all her life up in the Sanctuary until Phury had freed the Scribe Virgin's sacred class of females. She was no doubt still learning about herself and what she liked to do and what she was good at.

Maybe she'd like to go to school?

Sliding in behind the wheel, he smiled over at her. "I'm going to take us on a little field trip, if that's okay?"

"I'm game for anything."

"It's not far." He hit the gas, the four-wheel drive tires grabbed, and they shot forward through the parking lot. "And it is very private."

The farther he got away from the restaurant's back door, the more relaxed he became.

"So how was your shift?" he asked as he stopped at the main road.

"Really good. I got over two hundred in tips."

"Good." He waited for a car to pass. And then

saw another approaching. "So many humans out and about in the cold tonight."

"By the way, thank you," she said. "For understanding about your friend and the tip."

"I don't want to ever do something that makes you feel uncomfortable."

"I appreciate that."

With the coast clear, he took a right and headed down the salted road.

"So we're not going to the club?" she asked. "Not that I mind. It's an . . . intense place."

Trez laughed. "That's one word for it. And I know it's not your vibe."

"I'm sorry."

"I'm not." He reached out and took her hand, giving it a squeeze. "You like quiet spaces."

"Well, quieter places than a club, for sure." She let her head fall back on the rest and smiled at him. "And . . ."

"And what."

She just shook her head. Then she brought his hand up and kissed his knuckles. "What about your night? How's things at your work?"

"No one got shot, as far as I know."

"So you weren't at the club?" Abruptly, she sat up

and twisted toward him. "Not that I'm checking up on you. Just to make that perfectly clear—"

"You can put a tracking chip in my head if you want. It doesn't bother me. But nah, I just had some things to arrange outside of there."

As they continued along, they passed by strip malls of shops. An office park. A supermarket, gas station, DMV facility, and a real estate developer's complex. After that, the zoning turned residential, and the neighborhoods were modest but tidy, the houses cheerfully lit for the season with lots of light strings on eaves, and blow-up Santas in yards, and Christmas trees in bay windows.

"This is a beautiful car," she commented.

"I bought it on a whim." He rubbed his thumb on the inside of her wrist. "I had a different one that was much more practical. But I really like to drive, you know? It calms my mind. I realize I could dematerialize places a lot quicker, but sometimes, it's good to take the roads."

"I couldn't agree more. Do you mind if play with the radio?"

"Help yourself."

As she went through his favorites, his brows popped when she just kept going, skipping the R&B

and hip-hop stations he'd saved and going into '70s on 7.

"Do you like Led Zeppelin?" she asked him.

"Is that who this is?"

"'Ten Years Gone.' It's one of their best." She increased the volume. "I love this song."

The words rebounded around the interior, and as he listened to them, something rippled through the center of his chest. Meanwhile, she sang along, every lyric something she knew by heart, and her pitch was perfect.

The sense of being stretched in uncomfortable ways made him squirm in his seat, his muscles tightening up to the point where he had to consciously loosen things or he wasn't going to be able to drive right.

As soon as the song was over, he toggled back on the volume. "I didn't know you could sing." He also thought she was into his kind of music. From when he'd taken her to Storytown. "Did you take lessons?"

She laughed. "Oh, I don't have that kind of voice. Wait, like voice lessons, right?"

"Yes. When did you learn to sing?"

"I guess I've always known how to. It's natural. But I'm a shower singer, not anyone who belongs onstage. Can you imagine?"

Trez forced a laugh as he found himself internally arguing with her statements. She had never sung, and certainly not to Robert Plant, and of course she had never taken lessons. Before Phury had become the Primale, she hadn't been allowed outside of the Sanctuary, and afterward, all of the Chosen had been busy enough just getting used to life on this side. Voice lessons were waaaaay down on that list of things to do.

Although she had played the piano, he supposed.

Still, as for knowing all the words to that song? Maybe she had recently listened to it. Maybe she was just really quick about learning lyrics—as opposed to having heard it since the thing had first been released. In the seventies.

Trez moved around in his seat—and this time, it wasn't because of any arousal issue.

Meanwhile, his female glanced through the car windows. "You know, I've never seen this part of town before."

"It's really nice. Really safe."

"Then again, I haven't been most places in Caldwell."

Yes, he thought as he took a deep breath. That jibed with her past. See?

Abruptly, he had an image of a tennis court, versions of himself on opposite sides of the net, the proverbial ball the statements she made about her past.

Keeping his curses to himself, he made a turn. Then another. Then one more. As they went deeper into a neighborhood, he saw that not all the houses were done up for Christmas. There were Hanukkah displays, the menorahs showing two candles, and also homes that were displaying Kwanzaa symbols in preparation for the last seven days of the year.

Tracking the different expressions of the season, it made him feel a little better about the human race, that so many spiritual traditions could exist together and celebrate according to their own practices during the same season. Usually he saw only the bad sides of *Homo sapiens*, the intolerance and the injustice and the brutality—which was what happened when you were living with a secret in plain sight of all of them. It was good that vampires could be easily mistaken for their likes, but no one with a set of fangs in their upper jaw ever forgot that if humans learned the truth, things were more likely to go badly than well for the species.

So yeah, he tended to pay attention to their bad deeds, as a lot of vampires did.

But passing by these houses? He could see them

in another light—and it also made him feel better about what he'd done.

"Here we are," he said with a surge of triumph.

❖ ❖ ❖

Therese sat forward. The house Trez was pulling into was a gray-and-white Cape Cod, with glossy black shutters, a bright red front door, and cheery dormer windows in the roofline that looked like friendly eyes. Brass coach lanterns glowed on either side of the entrance, and there was a light on a stand halfway down a shoveled walkway. There was also an attached garage, a short-stack driveway that had been plowed, and bushes that had been set with strings of white lights, clearly so that the property fit in with the rest of the neighborhood.

"Is this where you live?" she asked.

"You sound so surprised." He turned the car off. "I'm not so bad, am I?"

"Oh, God, no. I mean . . . I pictured you living in an apartment in a high-rise downtown."

Trez smiled with what seemed like a curious satisfaction. "That's because I did. Come on, let's go in."

Therese got out of the car and couldn't look away from the pretty picture of the sweet house set back in its snow-covered yard, with the lights glowing and even—

"Is there a fire going?" She pointed up to the brick chimney. "There's smoke."

"I set one for us." He took her hand and led her up the walk. "Let me show you inside."

From out of his pocket, he took a copper key and put it into the front lock. As he turned the deadbolt, she frowned.

"Do you ever wear a coat?" she asked.

He glanced down at himself as if he were surprised he didn't have one on. "You know . . . I should, shouldn't I."

"It's okay. You look handsome with or without outerwear."

Instantly, he got dead serious and focused on her mouth. "How about with nothing on."

"Even better."

They were both smiling again as he opened the door, and as he let her go in first, her only thought was that they needed to finish what they had both started in their minds hours ago. Except as he willed the lights on, she gasped.

The interior of the house was done in soft dove gray and white, with pine floors that were the color of honey. Throw rugs were scattered with care in between cushioned furniture and thoughtfully arranged details, and through an archway, she saw a kitchen with stainless steel appliances and counters made of gray granite.

Her feet started walking before she was conscious of wanting to explore. Before she knew it, however, she was looking through the kitchen, going down a hall to find a study and a little bathroom, and standing at the base of the stairs and wondering what was up above.

"There are also two bedrooms and a common room underground," he said. "You can go up, if you'd like."

Therese nodded and put her hand on the varnished banister. There was no creaking underfoot as she ascended, and when she got to the top, she made a turn and learned where the fire was.

The master suite took up the entire top floor, and the bed alone would have made her never want to leave. It had a canopy of gossamer-thin white gauze that draped down onto the pale gray rug. The duvet on top of the mattress was big as a cloud and looked twice as soft, and there were so many pillows, the queen-sized expanse had little room left on it.

"What do you think?" Trez asked behind her.

She focused on the fire that was quietly crackling. "Is that a fur rug?"

"Faux fur, but yes."

"How long have you been here?"

"Not long."

Therese glanced over her shoulder. "Is it okay for me to put my bag down?"

"You can do anything you want here." He smiled. "Think of it as your own place."

She bent to the side and set her purse on the floor next to the footboard. Then she looked at her feet. "Oh, God, did I track in? I've got snow and salt—"

"Fritz loves every opportunity to clean up. Trust me."

"Fritz?"

"He's the Brotherhood's butler. He takes care of this house."

"You're connected to the Brotherhood?" She tried to keep her expression as un-fangirl as she could. But the Brotherhood? "The Black Dagger Brotherhood?"

Although come on, like there was another?

Trez crossed his arms over his huge chest and eased his shoulder onto the wall. Crossing his ankles, he gave her a remote look.

"Sorry." She smiled. "I don't mean to intrude."

"Oh, no. It's okay. I'm just . . . I'm not sure what to say."

"Well, people like me don't usually cross paths

with the likes of them." Therese indicated the heavens above. "And I am so grateful that the Scribe Virgin provided them unto the race. They have saved so many lives."

"This is very true."

Therese turned back to the fire. "That's beautiful. The flames, I mean. They're also very warm."

She shed her puffy, thigh-length parka, peeling the light weight from her torso and letting it fall to the carpet. Then she kicked off her boots. She was relieved not to find any track marks or salt stains on the treads, no matter what he said about some butler taking care of his house.

"I just want to make sure I don't hurt this nice rug," she murmured.

Turning away from him, she padded across to the hearth. The logs were burning low and slow, and as she thought about the nature of heat, she reached up to the twist she had redone in the restaurant's bathroom before she had gone out to Trez's car. The pins came out so smoothly that it was as if they wanted to work with her, and when she felt a release of tension at her temples and down on the back of her neck, she sighed. The weight of her hair tumbled, tumbled, tumbled down over her shoulders, reaching to just above her waist. She had been thinking of getting it all cut off, and going with something chin-length and easy.

Now, she was glad she had resisted the impulse.

Still with her back to him, she pulled out the tails of her work shirt and began to unbutton things from the top down. When she had released all the fastenings, she split the two halves and let the cotton fall from her torso.

The gasp from over where Trez was standing gave her the confidence to keep going. Her slacks were easy to take off, and as she kicked them to the side, she wondered how far she was willing to go. Then again, with only her underwear left? It wasn't like there was much more to remove.

And given the dark spices that emanated from behind her?

She didn't exactly suck at stripping.

Her bra had a back clasp so she torqued her hands between her shoulder blades and unclipped it. As the binding released, her breasts felt instantly fuller and heavy in a sexual way, her nipples teased as she shucked the plain, serviceable undergarment.

Therese was about to turn around when she looked down at a buzzkill and a half: She was pretty much naked . . . except for black socks she'd bought at Target. Yeah, because nothing said sexy-sexy like a female in her panties and her ankle-highs.

She had to laugh as she took them off with her toes, one . . . then the other.

After which, she looked over her bare shoulder and—

Trez's body was anything but relaxed as he leaned against that wall. His thighs were twitching underneath the fine wool of his slacks, and his pecs were spasming under his silk button-down. But it was what was doing behind his fly that she really was impressed by—

The knocking down below on the front door was loud, echoing up the open staircase.

With a squeak, she slapped her palms over her breasts even though there was no chance of anyone seeing her. "Oh, my God, tell me you do not have a roommate."

Trez had already straightened, and she was slightly alarmed when he produced a handgun from somewhere. "You stay here. No matter what you hear, do *not* come down until I get you."

She opened her mouth to tell him to pipe down with the he-man stuff. But then she decided the situation probably didn't require an untrained, mostly naked female added to the mix.

But hey, at least she had one shoot-out already under her belt.

As she wondered exactly what her life had turned into, Therese nodded. "Be careful."

Trez didn't respond to that. He was already rounding the corner and descending the stairs with that gun front and center . . . and an expression like he was used to killing on his face.

As she heard him close the door at the bottom of the staircase and lock it, she wondered exactly how he was connected to the Brotherhood. She had a feeling it wasn't just friends or drinking buddies.

He hadn't been frightened in the slightest.

So clearly, he was well familiar with conflict of the deadly variety.

CHAPTER FIFTEEN

Trez made sure the door to the upstairs was locked before he moved on the intruder. He wasn't risking his female's life for anything, and that included even his own. Getting out his phone, he dialed V's number.

One ring. Two rings . . .

As he waited for an answer, there was another series of knocking—and he was aware this was all his fault: His car was right there in the frickin' driveway. Whoever the fuck it was knew someone was in here, and if they were looking for him—if this was a disgruntled pimp, a pissed-off dealer, or some Mob-connected guy with a hard-on about something that had happened at the club—then he'd led them right to this door.

And that was sloppy.

He couldn't use that BMW anymore if his female was around—

As his call went into voice mail, someone clicked in on his other line. Taking the phone from his ear, he frowned. Accepted the call.

"Fritz?" he said.

The *doggen*'s cheerful voice came through in two places: in his ear, and on the other side of the door.

"Greetings, sire! Please excuse the interruption, I was endeavoring to get to your rental prior to your arrival. But I had to go to two places for the proper meat."

Trez blinked. "I'm sorry, what?"

"Meat, sire." There was a pause. "Forgive me, but might I enter the premises with your victuals?"

Shaking himself, Trez took two steps forward and opened the front door. There, on the other side, was the ancient butler holding four paper bags by the handles. That wrinkled face beamed.

"You're looking well, sire! And I shall not take long."

Fritz brushed by and headed for the kitchen, undisturbed in the slightest by the fact that Trez had a gun in his hand and had been considering the idea of shooting through the door.

Shaking his head, Trez reflected that there were benefits to staff who had been with the Brothers a long time. Short of an H-bomb going off in the living room, little bothered them.

Trez lamely closed the door. "You didn't have to do this."

It was as close as he could get to what he really wanted to say.

Which was something along the lines of *SHE WAS ABOUT TO TURN AROUND IN FRONT OF THE FIRE, FRITZ. TURN AROUND. IN FRONT OF THE FIRE! DO YOU THINK I CARE ABOUT FOOD RIGHT NOW?!?!?!*

Hell, on that note, someone could come and take at least one of his legs—maybe both—and he wouldn't argue with the body-part burglary as long as it got whoever it was the fuck out of this house. And he would have called upstairs and reported that all was well, but he didn't want his female to feel compromised.

"Listen, Fritz," he said as he walked through into the kitchen. "It's cool. I can put everything away."

Of course, that would be after he went back upstairs and checked on the fire—or rather the mostly naked female standing in front of said combustion.

"But the milk needs to be refrigerated." Fritz pivoted and opened the GE's door. "And the meat. And the ice cream."

Okay, so Trez didn't care if the milk curdled, the meat spoiled, and that ice cream drooled out of its container.

"As I was saying," Fritz continued on happily, "I had to go to two stores. The big Hannaford's steak offerings were not to my liking. I called my butcher."

At least the *doggen* was working fast, going back and forth to the fridge, the cupboards, those bags.

"Wait, it's almost midnight," Trez said. "You woke the guy up? I'm assuming your butcher's a human."

"Oh, you know him. Vinnie Giuffrida provides unto the restaurant Sal's, as well."

"Yeah, Vinnie you could definitely wake up. iAm swears by him."

"Indeed, he took care of us." With triumph, the butler produced a paper-wrapped bundle and then popped it into the fridge. "And now I am finished here."

Except Fritz just started to fold the paper bags. Like they were origami sheets. And he was trying to re-create the continental United States out of only one of them.

"It's okay, Fritz. I'll do that—"

Trez clapped his mouth shut as the butler recoiled like someone had cursed in front of his *grandmahmen*.

"Sorry." Trez put his palms forward. "I, ah, you're doing great. This is great. This is all so incredibly . . . great."

Once again, at least Fritz was fast, but still, the second that last bag was folded flat, Trez wanted to frog-march the butler out the front door. But if suggesting that the *doggen* needed help was a problem, actually touching the male was going to cause all this forward-motion-back-to-the-front-door to crash to a halt. Grounded in their ancient traditions, Fritz's kind couldn't handle any sort of acknowledgment, praise, or physical contact from their masters.

It was like having a hand grenade with a mop around: Very helpful, but you were extremely aware of whether the pin was where it needed to be.

"So thank you, Fritz—"

A strange sound—part thud, part thump—emanated from out behind the house, bringing their attention to the sliding glass doors on the far side of the kitchen table. Through the glass, the security lights come on and illuminated the back deck.

"I think you better go," Trez said in a low voice. "In case I have to deal with something."

Fritz bowed low. "Yes, sire."

And justlikethat the *doggen* was gone. Which, again, was the good news when it came to the male. Fritz was used to the kinds of emergencies that left bullets and knives in people. He might dawdle with paper bags, but when the shit hit the fan, he knew when to get gone.

As Trez outed his gun again, he was unaware of having reholstered it—and he killed the outside lights with his mind.

The human neighbors didn't need to see him flashing his piece all around.

Moving through the darkened kitchen, he back-flatted it against the wall by the slider and focused on the backyard—

Freezing in place, he did a double take. "What the . . ."

With a leap to the slider's handle, he unlocked the thing and shoved it back on its track. "Are you okay?"

Jumping into the snow on the deck, he tucked his gun and ran over to his female—who, for reasons he could not understand, was lying flat on her back in the snow.

And laughing.

Trez threw himself on his knees and looked up. The window in the bathroom upstairs was wide-open.

"Did you jump?" he said. Which was a ridiculous question. Like she fell out of a double-paned, closed set of Pella? "I mean, why? What—"

"I thought you needed help," she got out between laughing. "I'm sorry. I just—I don't know what I thought I would do, but I didn't hear anything like banging and crashing, so I was worried you were hurt."

His female lifted her head and indicated her fully clothed body. "I put everything back on, went into the bathroom—I was so nervous, I couldn't calm myself to dematerialize. I threw up the sash, jumped, and then panicked in midair that the snow wasn't going to be enough of a cushion. Good thing I managed to get myself turned around or I would have landed on my face—"

Lights came on in the yard next door, and a man in boxers and a flannel robe opened his own slider and piff'd out into the fluffy snow on his own deck.

"You okay over there?" he said.

Behind him, inside his kitchen, a dog the size of a throw cushion was barking in a series of high-alarm, high-register yaps that made Trez question how long that glass slider was going to survive without shattering.

"We're fine," Trez's female said with a grin. "But thanks for asking."

As the human looked suspicious and opened his mouth—no doubt to ask if 9-1-1 needed to be called—Trez lost his patience with everything and everyone. Reaching into the man's mind, he threw a patch on the memories of anything strange-noise, strange-sight related, flipped a bunch of switches relegating everything to misinterpretation, and sent Tony Soprano back into his two-story with his little dog and whatever wife was waiting for him upstairs in their bed.

"I hate the suburbs," Trez muttered as he got up and held his hand to his female. "I really do."

She accepted his help and brushed the snow off the seat of her pants. "Well, maybe you could move? Although this is a great house."

With a grunt, he checked out her mobility. "Are you sure you're okay? Do we need a doctor?"

Batting a hand, she brushed the concern aside. "Oh, God, I'm so perfectly fine. I've been jumping out of windows into snow forever."

"You have?"

"Before my transition, I used to sneak out of the

second story of my house with my brother during the days while our parents—" She stopped herself. Put her hands on her hips. Made like she was looking around. "Well, anyway. I've done this before."

She didn't want him to see her expression. Not when she talked about her family, at any rate.

"Come on," he said with exhaustion. "Let's get inside where it's warm."

As they walked back across the deck, Trez couldn't shake the feeling that the mood had been broken.

And he didn't know how to get it back.

◆ ◆ ◆

Therese entered the house feeling foolish and a little sad. As she stomped her boots on the mat just inside the slider, she hated thinking about her brother and all the good times they'd had together—so to escape all that, she replayed her brilliant, second-story-bathroom-window escape plan . . . and started laughing again. Ducking her head and trying to pull it together, she went over and stood in front of four carefully folded Hannaford paper bags—

"Wait," she said. "Groceries? That was who was at the door?"

She had jumped for a food delivery? He'd gone down those stairs all 007 . . . for a food delivery?

"Yeah," Trez said as he shut the slider.

Clapping a hand over her mouth, the absurdity of it all struck her bell so hard, she nearly snorted. And as she vowed to stop—because he was clearly not in a good mood—she really wished she was a good giggler, one of those females who managed to express oh-that's-funny in a melodic, pretty way. But nope. Not even close. She was a grunter. A chortler. A water buffalo crossed with an army tank backfiring.

Reeeeeal lovely stuff.

And given that Trez didn't seem amused as he shut the slider and double-checked its lock, she was even more determined than usual to put a cap on it. But dayum. Ever since last night, she felt like her life was in a blender, everything flying too fast and out of control, whirling around, whizzing by, sizzling along. And considering that she had just gotten 95 percent naked in front of him, he'd outed a gun, and she'd ended up jumping out of a house into a snowbank?

All over someone delivering a grub haul?

Locking her molars, she told herself to grow up—

The noise that ascended her throat was nothing she could keep down, and Trez looked over sharply. Like he was worried she'd thrown a pulmonary embolism.

"I am so sorry," she mumbled, "but this is too funny."

"Yes, it is." He smiled, but he lost the lift to his lips as he turned away. "Hey, would you like to eat something?"

Therese watched him open the refrigerator and bend down to look inside. When he stayed there, she knew he wasn't checking out all the stuff in there. His eyes had nothing but a liter of skim milk, a thing of unsalted butter, and a butcher's wrap of some kind of meat or poultry to regard.

"Trez," she said, growing serious. "What's wrong?"

"Nothing." He closed the door and went over to the cupboard. "Oh, look. Raisin Bran."

Therese took off her parka and went across to him. Putting her hand on his arm, she waited until his eyes finally swung in her direction.

"Talk to me."

He shut the cupboard and stepped back, out of reach. His expression was so intense, she was worried he was going to leave or something—or tell her to go. And sure enough, he started to pace back forth.

"Listen," she said, "if you want me to give you some privacy, just tell me. But if I stay, we're going to talk whatever this is out. I'm not going stand around in this silence all night."

Trez stopped and looked over, surprise flaring. Then he cursed. "I'm sorry. I think all the drama is just getting to me, and that has nothing to do with you. And no, I don't want you to go."

"Well, think of it this way. At least you've put your gun away for the last five minutes." When he chuckled a little, she took that as a good sign and smiled at him. "I'm hungry. How about you?"

"I ate at the club when two of my bouncers got pizza. Would you like anything?"

"I will take some of that cereal, if you don't mind."

"Let me wait on you."

Therese had the sense that he needed something to do, so she parked it at the little table. And as he got her a bowl and a spoon, the unopened box of cereal, and the milk, she liked watching him move. His body was so strong and heavy, but he was light on his feet, not cumbersome and clunky.

Now, if she could just get him to talk to her about what was really on his mind?

Because, no offense, he wasn't worried about the drama. That was just an excuse to hide behind.

When he sat down across from her, she popped open the box and poured herself a good two servings' worth. Then she glanced around, got to her feet, and went over to the sink. There was a roll of paper towels on a stand by the faucet and she pulled a section free. Back at the table, she smoothed the square flat.

"Okay, I know this is weird," she said. "But it is what it is."

As Trez cocked his head to one side, she started to pick raisins out of the bowl and put them on the paper towel. Using the spoon to help, she sifted through the flakes, making careful assessments.

"Can I ask you what you're doing?"

Therese glanced up. "One raisin per spoonful. That's the correct balance, not too sweet, not so bran-y. They overdo it with the dried fruit."

"I guess I've never thought about it like that."

"Cereal is serious business, Trez." She wagged her spoon. "It's the same thing with sundaes. You need to get the right fudge-to-ice-cream combination per spoon. It's about each delivery to the mouth."

"What about whip cream?"

"On a sundae?" As he nodded, Therese recoiled at the mere thought. "No, no, no. No nuts, no whip cream, no cherry. That's all a distraction. It's important to focus your taste buds."

"And pizza?"

"Cheese only, heavy crust, light sauce."

"Sandwiches."

Cracking the top on the milk, she poured a proper level. "Two slices of meat, no cheese, light on the mayo."

"No lettuce or tomato?"

"See also nuts, whip cream, and cherries."

"Unnecessary."

"Yup." She lifted a spoonful out of the milk. "See? Perfect proportion. And you need to get it set before you moo-juice the stuff. Otherwise things get messy."

Trez eased back in his chair. "You're very precise about your food."

She thought about her crap apartment where everything had its place. Her room back home. Her purse, her clothes, her shoes.

"Pretty much about everything, actually. It's the engineer in me." As his eyebrows went up again, she nodded. "I have a master's in civil engineering. Online school obviously. I was hoping—well, it doesn't matter now."

"You were hoping what?"

Therese moved the cereal around with her spoon. "It turns out that there are not a lot of jobs for vampires who want to build public works."

"I've never considered what civil engineers do."

"Bridges, tunnels, maintenance of natural and built environments. Large-scale stuff. When I was

little, I loved to work in the dirt. I was always building things. My father . . ." As she let that drift, she
rubbed the center of her chest and changed the subject. "Just so we're clear, I am not going to apologize
to anyone for being a waitress. Work is work. You
do everything the best you can, and it doesn't matter
what it is."

Reaching for the milk, she tipped the carton over
the bowl. "Milk percentage is off," she explained as
she felt him stare at her.

Like he'd never seen her before.

CHAPTER SIXTEEN

As iAm sat behind his desk in his office at the restaurant, he was supposed to be tallying receipts. Putting in meat and liquor orders for the upcoming week. Planning menus.

Failed it, not nailed it.

What the hell time was it anyway? he thought as he checked the digital clock on the landline phone.

Midnight-ish.

Settling back in his chair, he stretched his arms out and rotated both his shoulders. When that did absolutely nothing to relieve the tension riding up his neck and nailing him in the back of the head, he tried some office yoga by grabbing the edge of the desk and pulling against it. As his forearms roped up with muscles and veins, he reflected that as a chef, he never wore a watch. Or bracelets of any kind. Or rings. He needed to have his fingers and his wrists free of any entanglements, things that could be hard to clean, stuff that could break or be in the way, hindrances of any kind.

Then again, with Trez as his brother, he had so much existential baggage to carry around, it was a wonder he could stand the weight of his shoes and clothes.

"Damn it," he muttered as he released his hold.

That blowout between them had been bad, but it had been coming since the moment Therese had been hired. And he should have known better than to bring her on. Sure, the fact that she looked like Selena wasn't her fault, but that didn't mean he was obligated to employ her. He should have referred her to another job. With his network of contacts in the Caldwell foodie scene, he should have—

Who the hell was he kidding. Trez would still have been in bad shape.

Except the argument would have been over suicide, not some female.

And of course he wanted to see his damn brother

happy. Was the male even serious about that shit? What he did *not* want was Trez fooling himself and using someone else—and iAm stood by that message, straight up. Still, he probably could have done a helluva lot better getting the point across and now he'd driven the male off. Like he hadn't known that Trez had been outside for a good half an hour tonight? Waiting in a running car outside of the reach of the security cameras. In the cold.

For the server to get off.

No doubt so he could get her off.

And P.S., he actually didn't think Therese was going to be the one hurt most when things went tits up. Trez was. The male wasn't going to survive another crushing disappointment, but iAm hadn't wanted to put that into words. For one, it was too painful. For another, he didn't want to give the guy any ideas.

FFS, every frickin' night iAm was braced for the phone call that Trez was dead. Like that instability needed a doomed romance with a doppelganger added to it? He knew exactly where his brother was in that head of his. In that heart of his. And if Trez decided to peace out, he would make sure that somebody else found the body—he would be determined to spare iAm that trauma. So as a result, anytime iAm's cell went off, he felt like he was getting shot through the chest—and needless to say, this had given him a new hatred for telemarketers.

Groaning, he gave extending his arms over his head a try. In a way, this gut-churn over what his brother was doing, where he was, who he was with . . . was just a continuation of the way it had always been between the two of them. Trez had forever been on the run from his destiny of mating the queen of the s'Hisbe—and iAm had run after him. Someone had to protect the male. Guard his six. Make sure he didn't completely self-destruct.

Plus, there had been the reality that Trez was all he'd had in this world. With their parents and the tribe left behind, what else had there been?

Except then, the deck of destiny had ended up getting shuffled and it turned out the priests had been wrong. iAm was the one to mate the queen—a fate he had been oh, so very happy to live up to as it turned out. And you'd think with that burden lifted, all would be chill. Nope. Instead of his brother being released from the burden of pain, Trez had been saddled with the heaviest agony there was.

Selena's death had been so fucking unfair.

Maybe it was all in the stars, though. According to the tradition of the s'Hisbe, astrology determined everything, and it was clear that Trez had been born under an alignment of sorrowful portent. Back when Selena had showed up on the scene, iAm had been suspicious at first, but then, as time had passed, he'd been so sure things were finally going to change. That the sucky era was over. That the second phase, the better part, could now commence—

iAm's instincts fired, the bonded male in him overriding even the fears for his blooded kin.

Rising to his feet, he was about to go around his desk when his female materialized in between the jambs of his office doorway.

For a moment, although he had seen her merely the night before, he had to drink in everything about his mate. *maichen* was tall and regal, her dark skin set off by a spectacular set of gold-threaded robing, her hair falling down her back in hundreds of braids strung with golden beads. Her eyes were kind and worried as they sought his own, and her hands went to her belly.

iAm's heart pounded with terror. "What did they say. The priests."

"She is very healthy."

"She?" he breathed.

maichen's smile was gentle and ancient as she came unto him, moving when he was unable to.

"She. Our next queen, born unto us. As the stars had provided."

A daughter. He was going to be the father of a daughter. A princess who would be queen someday, as provided by the heavens. By the traditions. By the grace of fate.

Wrapping his arms around his mate, iAm held *maichen* close and breathed in her beautiful scent. But then he got woozy. Before he could think about sitting back down, his body made the decision for him. All at once, he fell off his feet, his chair catching his weight and holding it, when he no longer could.

"A little girl," he said with both hands on his face. And then he sat upright. "Whataboutyou?"

The words came out so fast, he was going to repeat them, but his mate just stepped in between his knees and stroked his shoulders. "I am fine. I am perfectly fine. I promise you."

Annnnnnnd cue the world going around in another circle. He was totally dizzy even though he was sitting down—it was like his body had known there was another wave on his horizon.

"You need to go see Doc Jane," he mumbled as he turned his head to put his ear to her lower belly through the royal robing. "I believe in conventional medicine, and I can't risk you or . . . our daughter."

Daughter. They were having a daughter. Provided everything went all right.

"I will go see your healer." *maichen* ran her fingertips over his skull trim, in that way he liked. "We shall go together."

"Yes. Please."

As iAm held the warm, strong body of his female, he felt like a pussy for not getting to his feet properly or sitting her in his lap. The night had been a rough one, though. He had never thought he would get mated. Never thought young were in his future. And here that amazing future was coming to him . . . with the discord around Trez the inevitable chaser of bad news.

"Did you see him tonight?" *maichen* asked.

She always seemed to know where his mind went. And there was only one "him" in his world. No name was required.

"He came by."

"How is he?"

"The same." He shook his head. "Worse, actually. And that was before we got into it."

"Did you tell Trez?" *maichen* asked while putting her hand back on her belly. "About . . ."

"I couldn't. I just . . ." He looked up at his mate. "How can I? It is too cruel. He lost everything, and now I have not only you, but a young. It's too much—and please don't take that the wrong way."

As she stared at him sadly, he reflected that when you mated someone, you took on their struggles. But man, he wished like hell he hadn't brought this shit to her door.

"I know exactly what you mean," she said.

Closing his eyes, he took a deep breath, and knew why he'd been so harsh with his brother earlier. He'd wanted to share his good news with the other most important person in his life. But with things as they were—and the way they had always been—he had no real kin of his own. He had never had kin of his own. He'd had a responsibility, one borne out of love but a weight just the same. He had a constant worry, a pit in his gut . . . a curse thanks to a fate that was his own even as it was not.

Once, just once, he'd like to be able to have the relationship flow in the other direction. In his way. He wanted to get some support and concern instead of constantly giving it.

But come on, how selfish was he? It wasn't like Trez had volunteered for any of this crap, and blaming the male for reality was a douche move. Like when their souls had been bargaining to come down onto the planet for a life span, had Trez really looked over

the Happy Days story line and decided, *Naaaaah, I'd
much rather be in the Takes a Licking section.*

Of course he hadn't. And iAm needed to be more
supportive.

"I owe my brother an apology," he said with de-
feat.

◆ ◆ ◆

Sitting across from his female, Trez was scrambled
in his head, but calm on the outside. At least he
thought he was calm. No tapping heels, drumming
fingers . . . or twitches of the eyebrows or mouth that
he could tell.

So things were looking up. And hell, not only had
there been a good ten or fifteen minutes since anybody outed a gun, there had also been a respite from
people jumping out of windows. They kept this
trend up, he might actually sleep through the day.

Yay.

"You don't really live here, do you," his female
said as she continued to consume her one-Raisin-
per-spoonful-Bran.

For a split second, he tried to configure a lie in his
head. Something about moving in soon. Just having
moved in. Trying the place out for moving in. But he
was tired, and all that fiction building seemed like

too much work. Besides, his female was smart, and it didn't take a genius to notice the lack of personal effects.

Or the total non-clothes in the closet or bureau upstairs, if she checked.

"I mean"—she motioned around the kitchen and out into the living room with her spoon—"no personal effects, no photographs. No mess."

Bingo.

And yet: "I'm pretty neat, though. Just ask my brother. He and I lived together for years."

She stirred the milk around, the spoon seeking soggy flakes that refused to be corralled. "So this is the house you want me to rent, huh."

"You do like it. You said so yourself."

"And I already know how to take my clothes off in the bedroom."

Trez felt a shot of lust go through him. That sight of her backside, her spine, her shoulders . . . with the tease that as soon as she turned around, he was going to get to see her breasts? He'd been on the verge of coming.

Except then the groceries arrived. Man, if he never heard another knock in his fucking life, it would be too soon.

"What's wrong?" she asked as she tilted her bowl and got more serious about navigating the end of the cereal. "I mean, I can—"

"I really want to have sex with you."

Her eyes flipped to his, and instantly, the chemistry was back—and he welcomed the influx of arousal. He was not lying; he did want to be inside of her. But there was another piece to it. He needed the doubts and the fears and the grief that were simmering just below his surface to shut the fuck up. He didn't want to think about his argument with iAm. He didn't want to think about her in that club of idiots last night, some asshat with a gun and a hard-on for a woman who didn't want him shooting shit up because his ego got kicked in the hey-nannies. And he didn't want to think his female was so reckless as to fly-be-free from a second-story window.

And there were other things. Things he really, really couldn't bear looking at.

The sex, however, would eclipse all that glare.

And sometimes shade was needed when the heat was on.

"Well, then," she said as she got up and took her bowl to the sink. "Maybe we need to try again?"

Trez exhaled long and slow, and focused on those

black slacks of hers, the white shirt, the hair that was so thick and curly and shiny as it ran down her shoulders.

"Yes," he said with a growl. "Let's do that."

And so help him God, if anyone—or anything—interrupted them this time, he was going to solve that problem with a fist. Or maybe a crowbar.

Trez's body got up out of the chair and went to her as if called, and the tension that had clawed into him left as if it had never been. As she reached for him, he reached for her, their mouths finding each other's, the kiss as natural and easy as everything else had been bumpy and uneven only moments before. Licking into her, he savored the feel of her breasts against his chest, her hips under his hands, her mouth moving with his own. She was all that he needed, all that he knew, and he wanted to be here again. He wanted to never leave here.

This was his female. She *was* Selena, back unto him. No matter what iAm thought or said, or how crazy it was, or all the impossibles and the doubts, Trez only needed this connection to prove the reality that his heart already knew for sure.

Just as he started to pull her shirt out from her waistband, he noticed the window over the sink. With no shutters down, they were liable to flash the entire neighborhood—if not right here, then because he was about a second and a half away from laying her out on the table in front of that slider and putting his tongue in all kinds of places other than her mouth.

"Upstairs?" he said against her lips. "Before I—"

"Yes," she moaned.

Breaking off the kiss, he took her hand and all but ran up the staircase. And as soon as they got to the top landing, he shut the stairwell's door and killed the lights with his mind—and then he drew her over to the warm, flickering glow of the fireplace. Their mouths met again, and he eased her down on the soft rug, taking his time with the descent.

Or, rather, forcing himself to.

He wanted to tear her pants off with his fangs. Rip her panties down her thighs. Mount her like a beast. Then he wanted to flip her over and take her from behind. And after that? He wanted every position physically possible, all over the bedroom floor, the bed, the bathroom—

"Oh, shit." He whipped his head around toward a cold draft that he hadn't paid any attention to. "Sorry, let me go close that."

Vampires could manipulate a lot of things with their minds, but not in a house that had been secured by Vishous. The Brother would have coppered the hell out of those puppies so that no one could use their mental powers to get in if the illusion shutters were up.

His female tugged at his shirt. "I'll will it down—"

"It's manual operation only." He kissed her lips quick. "Don't go anywhere."

"You do not have to worry about that. Trust me."

Springing to his feet, Trez tore off like there was a drowning victim in the damn tub. And as he slammed the sill back in place, all he could think of was getting back—

Out of the corner of his eye, he caught sight of his reflection in the mirror that ran across the wall above the two sinks. He stopped dead, even though he'd rather have just kept the fuck going—and not only because his female was waiting for him.

His eyes were too wide. His face was flushed and sallow at the same time. His breathing was way too heavy.

Trez hated everything about himself in that moment. And the only thing he despised more was his life. iAm was right. He was out of control, careening into something he didn't have the emotional capacity for—

It's fine, he mouthed to the image directly across from himself. *I'm fine. We're fine. It's all fine.*

With a resolve born of desperation, he looked

away. Then he strode away. Reentering the bedroom, he—

Okay. Stopping dead again. But at least this time it was for a good reason.

A fine reason. A reaaaaally fucking fine one.

"I thought I would try this one more time," his female drawled from over in front of the fire.

She was lying exactly where he had left her, on that rug, before the hearth—but she had taken off her clothes. All of them. And she was sprawled with the kind of abandon that made a male lose track of time: Her head was back, her hair spilling out around her, her neck a graceful line from her perfect chin to her collarbones . . . and her breasts were caressed by the firelight, the nipples peaked and pink, the swells creamy and full.

Trez licked his lips. And kept on looking. Her stomach was a gentle drift to her hips, and the cleft of her sex was nestled in thighs he was desperate to part. Her legs were long and graceful—and given the way they churned?

If her scent wasn't already making it clear she was ready to receive him, then the anticipation in the way they rubbed together was a big damn tip.

"You should only ever wear firelight," he groaned as his hand went to his throbbing arousal.

CHAPTER SEVENTEEN

As exposed as Therese was, as naked and vulnerable as she was, she felt nothing but free. There was no embarrassment, no anxiousness, no concern that she was less than perfect or anything less than what Trez would want. And that was when she knew how deeply she trusted him.

When he started forward, she put her hand up. "Wait."

He stopped on a dime. And to reward him, she sensuously rolled over onto her stomach. Laying her head down on her arm, she moved one of her legs up the other . . . then pivoted her hips, flashing her ass toward him.

"Fuck . . ." he breathed.

"I thought you should see the back, too."

"Just as good as the front, let me tell you."

"Perhaps you'd like to join me? And I'm not only talking about the horizontal."

Trez took the hint, yanking his silk shirt out of the waistband of his pressed slacks. Then, even though it was no doubt expensive, he tore the halves apart, buttons flying free and twinkling like falling stars. Holy . . . *crap*. Yes, what was underneath totally did not disappoint. He had a hard, ribbed stomach, and a hard, heavy set of pecs, and a hard, wide shoulder span. Oh, and talk about firelight. His dark skin was smooth across the expanse of all his muscles, and the illumination moved restlessly over the ridges and hollows of his torso. He had no tattoos that she could see, but he had scarifications across his chest and abdomen—she didn't recognize what they symbolized, but she assumed it was a Shadow tradition.

And he was a fighter. That was absolutely in his background somewhere, somehow.

Before she could get to begging, Trez's fingers went to his belt, and deftly worked the gold H buckle loose. With a slow, sexy show, he pulled the leather strap out of the loops and tossed it aside. Then he freed the button and unzipped his zipper.

When he released his hold, the pants went down in a rush—

Commando. Very commando. Totally and completely . . . commando.

As Therese focused on his erection, its incredible length and girth would have been intimidating if she hadn't known that its fit was perfect for her. In her.

Trez laughed with a guttural sound as he kicked off his loafers and stepped out of those pants. "You keep looking at me like that and I'm going to lose it right now."

"Then lose it. I want to watch."

"You do?"

Therese scooted back and patted the rug next to her. "Come. Here."

His smile was volcanic, his lids lowering to half-mast as his palm gripped his shaft. With a hiss, his fangs clamped down on his lower lip, and as he walked forward, he stroked himself in a lazy way that was anything but lazy.

Lowering himself to the floor, he put his head by hers, his long legs stretching out. "Am I doing this right?" he drawled.

His hand went up and down, pausing at the head,

squeezing. And as she watched him, she let her fingertips tickle her nipples.

"I think you need to do it faster."

"Really?" He leaned in and brushed her lips with his own. "Like this?"

As he stroked himself with more speed, she felt her body melt into the faux fur beneath her. In contrast to their first coupling, this privacy—well, now that the groceries had been delivered—and all the delicious time ahead of them took the edge off her greed. They had the rest of the night.

And maybe the day, too. Although she didn't want to think like that.

Everything was so good in this moment. She wanted to stay here forever.

"Faster," she whispered close to his mouth.

The purr that came up his throat made her vibrate inside her own skin, and she touched his chest . . . his arm, which was carved with contracted muscles . . . his stomach, which had deep cuts under his skin. As her hand moved downward, he arched up to her touch, his hips undulating, his hand pausing.

"I want to help you," she said.

Trez dropped the hold on his cock like the thing had burned his palm. "Take over. Do anything you want to me—"

"I will." She smiled as she pushed herself up, her heavy breasts swinging as she repositioned herself on all fours.

Putting her hand over the one he'd removed, she returned his grip to his shaft, and worked things up and down by guiding his wrist. "That's it. Good male."

Trez seemed momentarily disappointed that he was back to self-propulsion, so to speak. But she knew what she was doing.

Well . . . actually, she'd never done anything like what was about to happen before. But with him? With her shadow lover made flesh? She was uninhibited in ways she not only had never been, but also could never have guessed she could be.

"Keep going," she whispered, "my lover."

When he groaned and arched again, his magnificent body so aroused, so powerful in the firelight, she planted one set of hands/feet on the far side of his thighs.

Then she leaned down, bringing her face close to the tip of his erection.

"I want you to finish . . ." she said in a husky voice.

As his eyes flared wide and flashed with a mysterious peridot light, she opened her mouth.

You know, just so he was clear what she wanted.

◆ ◆ ◆

Trez lost it. Totally fucking ripped-to-the-core, out-of-his-mind, batshit lost it.

The orgasm shot out of him and went into his female, and the sight of where it ended up was so erotic, his lids slammed down. Which was exactly what he did *not* want. He wanted to watch, he wanted to see—

"Oh, fuck!" he shouted as his lids popped open again.

The wet, hot hold that slid onto the tip of his arousal meant one and only one thing—yes, oh, God, yes, she was swallowing him down, her lips stretching to accommodate his size, her eyes glowing as they looked up his body into his own. He could have watched her forever, but the pleasure was too great, the eroticism too much, the connection too close—and considering that there was a possibility both of his eyeballs were going to explode out of their sockets and scare the shit out of her, it was probably best that he caged his peepers.

Squeezing his lids shut, he growled, he bucked, he was coming again—into her mouth, her hand working him, his balls kicking out part of him into her with ever increasing cycles. Tighter, faster, draining him—

Before there was nothing left, he sprung into action, rolling her over, and pushing his way in between her legs with his hips.

"I'm sorry," he grunted.

"For what?"

As she smiled, he took her mouth with his own and he penetrated deep into her sex. "I don't know."

That was the last thing they said for a while. He meant to go slow, go easy, take his time. He couldn't. His body took over and he pounded into her, his thrusts so powerful, he pushed her along with the rug, the two of them moving across the floor.

He fucked her all the way into the corner, wedging them into the shelves.

Which had its benefits.

Throwing out a hand, he knocked books from their lineup, scattering them down his arm. They landed with a bounce, flipping open, pages asunder, as he braced himself and fucked her ever harder.

"*Yes*," his female gritted as she torqued under him.

Abruptly, he scented blood, his own, not hers— or he would have stopped and worried that he'd hurt her. But no, she had gouged his back with her short nails, and he hadn't noticed.

He was glad she did. He wanted her to mark him

up, give him wounds, make him her own in any way she wanted.

"Harder," she demanded.

Grabbing onto the vertical of a shelf, he really put the small of his back into it, shoving one of his knees up, cranking her leg into a different position, tilting her pelvis into a cradle he could dig in deep, dig in all the way to his base, dig . . . into his soul.

Their sexes slapped together. Sweat beaded his face, got into his eyes. A sound ripped out of his chest.

Trez kept going—

Until he abruptly lost his rhythm for some unknown reason. After which, without warning . . . he lost the pleasure, too.

That wasn't sweat in his eyes.

It was tears.

CHAPTER EIGHTEEN

Therese was so into the sex, so blown away, so lost to her own orgasms, that her body was reduced and elevated by turns, her flesh converted into an electrical system on an overload that seemed to make it stronger rather than weaker. And on Trez's side, he seemed to have stamina to spare, his releases ongoing, never-ending; the more she demanded of him, the more he gave her.

Except then it all changed.

At first, there was a swerve as he lost his thrusts. Then there was a curve as he started to slow. Finally, there was a stop dead.

Just as she was opening her eyes, something hit her cheeks—and with sight came hearing. There was a sound coming from him, out of him.

Not of pleasure, but of pain.

Above her, Trez's features were twisted in agony, tears rolling out of him, agony seeming to lance through him sure as if he were being stabbed.

Scared for him, she gripped his upper arms. "Trez?"

With a horrible sound, he pushed himself off her, landing in a heap, in a sprawl. He was coughing, choking, and as he crawled away on all fours, he didn't seem to have any idea where he was or where he was going. He was a mortally injured animal, dragging what was left of its life force to a place to die—and he did collapse. Not far from where they had been, he fell to the floor and curled in a ball, tucking his knees to his chest, his arms holding them in tight.

He was a grown male who rocked himself like a child.

"Trez," she said as she went to him. "What's going on?"

When she touched his shoulder, he flinched. But he opened his bloodshot, tragic eyes.

"Come here," she whispered. "Let me hold you."

She didn't know if he would let her, but he didn't resist as she gathered him up. There was so much of him that she couldn't possibly get her arms around all of him—so she held on to what she could. Cradling him, she closed her eyes and took his suffering into herself.

She had no idea what the cause was. But as he trembled against her, the only thing that went through her mind was that she wasn't leaving him. Ever. She was going to stand by him, wherever this took either of them. Because this kind of pain?

There was a terrible loss behind it.

She knew this because she had felt echoes of the same grief herself. She also knew that this was the kind of thing you kept hidden from everyone around you—kept hidden, most of the time, even from yourself. It was the sort of loss that changed the color of the night sky, and the feel of the ground beneath your feet, and the scents that entered your nose. This was new-life pain.

As in, you were living one way, and then . . .

Everything changed. You changed. The world changed.

And it was never the same again.

"It's okay," she whispered as her own eyes teared up. "I've got you . . . and I'm not letting go . . ."

Sometime later—it could have been hours—she felt him still. And as he drew in a ragged breath, she felt its exhale on her shoulder, and the sudden stillness of him scared her more than the weeping had. She wasn't sure what would come in this aftermath.

"I need . . ." His voice was nothing more than a rasp. "Bathroom."

"Okay, yeah, of course."

Releasing her hold, she moved herself out of his way as he dragged himself up off the carpet, dropped his head and stumbled out of sight. When the door closed, she wasn't surprised.

The sound of water was expected. She imagined him splashing his face with something cool, and staring at himself in the mirror as he tried to get regrounded in the present. She knew what that was like. How you got sucked back into the past, against your will, revisiting scenes you wanted to avoid. How once the past got a stranglehold on you, it was like an anchor with grasping hands, dragging you down, down, down, until you couldn't breathe and you didn't know where the surface was anymore.

As a shiver went through her, she didn't know whether it was from her own emotions or the fact that she was naked and the fire was nothing but embers now. Reaching over, she pulled the fur throw rug around her shoulders and stared at the gray ash beneath what was left of the logs that had burned so brightly. Now, there was nearly nothing left of the hardwood, the bodies eaten away, the small, twisted cores hanging together out of habit rather than structure.

Her eyes were still on the last of the fire when the bathroom door reopened.

She turned around quick.

Trez had tied a towel around his waist, and there was a gloss to his face as if he had indeed splashed himself with water. His eyes were still bloodshot. And they still would not meet her own.

As he stood in that doorway, he stared off into space as if waiting for some kind of cue.

"Tell me about her," Therese said softly.

◆ ◆ ◆

Trez heard the words spoken to him from far, far away, and he looked to the sound. The sight of his female, there, on the floor, the soft white throw rug wrapped around her bare shoulders, her lovely dark hair tangled and curled around her, took a moment to sink in

In the bathroom, braced over the sink after he had washed his face with cold water, he had hung his head and debated whether or not he was going to throw up. Then he had briefly glanced over at the window she had used so well earlier, and wondered if following her example might not be a good idea.

It certainly seemed easier than explaining himself.

Except he'd left her hanging out here, and no matter how much skipping town seemed like a plan worth serious consideration, he was not going to do that to her.

She deserved an explanation.

And sure enough, as he stood here like a zombie, she had just asked him for one.

To give himself some more time—even though he could have used a year or more, maybe eighteen months, preferably—he went over and sat on the foot of the bed. Planting his elbows on his knees, he was aware that he was pulling a classic *The Thinker* pose.

Maybe it would help.

Nope. It did not. Words continued to fail him.

Especially as, when he finally did look at her, it was Selena staring back at him.

"I'm sorry," he said in a voice that did not sound like his own.

"It's okay." She shook her head. "What I mean is . . . whatever it is, I understand."

He wasn't so sure about that.

"Trez," she said, "I want you to know that you can tell me anything."

It was as he stared into her eyes that he realized . . . of course he could explain himself. She had been separated from him as well. She had lost him . . . as well.

His female truly would understand—

For a split second his brain latched on to those details about her past—the one that didn't include the Chosen, the Scribe Virgin, the things he knew about her. The one that involved things like Michigan, and Led Zeppelin, and Raisin Bran.

He was too spent to go far with all that, however.

Shifting over to her, he knelt down on the carpet. As he reached out and stroked her face, he thought that he loved her so, and it was impossible not to speak those words. Say those syllables. Release the revelation that was no secret at all, and nothing to fear—

"I lost my parents," she said. "And what's more, I lost them even though they're still alive."

Her words made no sense so he played them back in his mind. And then did it again. In spite of the numb aftermath of him having lost it, he returned to the refrain that Chosen did not have parents. They had a sire in the Primale, and then a female who birthed them, even as their *mahmen* was the Scribe Virgin they served. How could Selena—

"I found out about it all when they decided to move." His female pulled the rug closer to herself, and her eyes drifted away. "I was helping them pack up, you see. They were leaving the home we lived in outside of Ann Arbor. The house I had grown up in. The place where they had raised me . . . and the male who I thought was my blooded brother. The papers about my adoption were in a box."

Trez tried to catch up with what she was communicating to him, but it was like translating a language that was only partially related to the ones he knew.

"A box?" he parroted.

"They were moving to a warmer place. Michigan is so cold in the winter, and my *mahmen*—the female who raised me, I mean—has a heart condition. I was packing up her things, and I found the shoebox way up on the top shelf in her closet. I didn't intend to be nosy—but I thought it was fancy shoes she never wore because she was like that." A shadow of a smile tilted his female's lips on only one side. "She rarely bought anything for herself, but when she did, something like a bag or a coat, she would never wear it because it was the 'good' one. She saved things like that for special occasions that never came."

There was a silence. "The box slipped out of my hands as I was bringing it down. What was inside went everywhere. It wasn't shoes. It was paperwork. About me."

He forced himself to get involved in what she was revealing. "They never told you . . ."

"No, they didn't. And I can remember reading the documents like . . . five times. I couldn't seem to understand what they were saying. And then . . . I couldn't understand that they were about me." She pointed to herself. "Me. I mean, surely . . . they had to be about somebody else."

As her brows tightened, it seemed as though she was still trying to come to terms with the news.

"It changed everything instantly for me." She cleared her throat. "One moment, and all the moments leading up to it, I was a daughter. And then just like that . . . I was a stranger."

"It was like a death, then," he said.

She looked at him. "Yes. Exactly. You understand."

Not really. Not . . . at all.

At least when it came to the details. Her pain, on the other hand? Yes, he recognized that for what it was, and he did not want that for her. Ever.

"I died," she said. "Who I thought I was, who I thought I belonged with, and to, died. And a ghost was left in my place." She brushed her face as if she expected tears to be there. As if there had been tears before. But there were none. "A ghost is still in my place. And that's is why I'm here in Caldwell."

"Did you ask your . . . the people who raised you about it?"

"I took the papers out into the living room and put them on the coffee table in front of my *ma*—the female who raised me."

Trez pictured the scene, conjuring out of no specific details about the house, the rooms, that box, or the other female, some approximation of the confrontation. And meanwhile, the other half of him was protesting the attempt. The story itself.

This wasn't part of their history.

Yet he could not deny that it had been part of hers.

Trying to reconcile the two versions of her life distracted him, and with force of will, he forced himself to focus on what she was saying.

In the midst of his breakdown, she had honored him, and he would do the same for her. It was the only decent thing to do. Later . . . he could try to sort it all out.

Although how much more luck was he going to have with that?

"She froze," his female murmured. "And it was the stricken expression on her face that told me it was all real. I said to her . . . something like, 'Well, this was unexpected.' Then my brother and me had a show-down in front of her and my dad. She didn't say much. She just sat on the sofa, while the male who raised me and the male who I'd been raised along-side did a lot of talking. They didn't get where I was coming from. They didn't understand that it was a violation of my history. Does that make sense? I tried to explain the betrayal to them. The hurt. The anger. Things grew even more heated and I left. I just had to leave . . . my brother and I were at each other's throats and she was upset and it was a mess."

"And then you came to Caldwell."

"As soon as I left the house, I realized I had no-where to go. Who could I stay with? My cousins? They were not my cousins." She shook her head. "My people were not my people. My own brother knew, and I didn't—so how far did the secret go? Who else knew? Who had known all along? It was like being stripped naked and everyone seeing it but yourself. Lies that are fundamental hurt fundamen-tally. Imagine if between one second and the next . . . all of the people in your life were replaced with ac-tors. Or maybe it's more . . . the parents I assumed were real were being played by actors." She shrugged. "Maybe someone else would have felt differently—"

Trez cut in. "It doesn't matter what someone else would have felt. It's you."

"That's what I tried to tell my brother. He was too busy protecting them to hear it. And you know, losing him was just as hard as losing . . . well, what I thought of as my parents." She shook her head. "I mean, families tell the truth, right? They're the only people in our lives who can really do that even when we don't want to hear it. Because blood makes us stuck with them."

He thought of iAm and felt uneasy. "Yes, but they can also be wrong."

Trez had to say that. For himself. He had to believe that . . . Fates, he didn't even know what to believe anymore. He was so damned wrung out, his thoughts totally disjointed, his body weak, his head starting to ache.

Meanwhile, she wasn't having such a great night, either. With a curse, she put her own head in her hands and shuddered. "I hurt her. That's the fucked-up thing. My *ma*—that female—looked ruined as I walked out that door. And as I dematerialized to my apartment and packed up some stuff, I blamed myself. Like it was my choice, though? I got the fallout of her decision to stay silent. Not the other way around."

When there was a long pause, he felt like he had to say something. Do something. But he couldn't seem to form anything coherent for his mouth to speak.

Grasping at straws, he mumbled, "Why did you choose Caldwell?"

She frowned. And then looked at him once more. "You know, it's funny . . . I don't have a good answer for that. I remember so many things about all of it with unbearable precision. But as for what brought me here? That . . . I don't know. I guess I was just called to Caldwell."

CHAPTER NINETEEN

Therese tried to flex her tired brain and access the piece of information about exactly why she'd ended up where she did. But there was nothing. No context for Caldwell. No contacts here. No reason to head east instead of south or west.

'Cuz God knew it was harder to get more north, unless she wanted to land in Canada. Which, granted, was a very nice place, but a change of currency and partially of language? She'd had enough to deal with.

But why this particular town? And why with such unquestionable determination? It was as if Caldwell had popped into her mind as a destination like it had been implanted there by another source—and hey, at the point she'd left home, having some direction, any direction, was better than none at all.

"So yeah," she concluded. "That's why I understand where you are. Even if I don't know the details."

During the period of silence that followed, it was Trez's opportunity to jump in the Share Pool. But he remained quiet as he sat on the floor. And it was interesting, in another era in her life, before she'd had her own awful reshuffle of things, she might have felt shut out. It was hard, though, when your emotions were strong, to plug into even yourself, much less someone else.

With a sad exhale, she reflected that the evening in this house had not started out as she'd expected. And it wasn't ending that way, either.

"Are you okay?" she asked.

When he nodded, she wanted to ask again. And again. Until she could peek into his mind and know his truth—and not just the details of the female who had come between them. She wanted to know the rest of his past, too, all of the good and the bad. She was not going to get that, however. And it was likely even he didn't know the answer to the question of whether he was all right.

One thing she was certain of was that it was a female. She knew that as surely as she could see him sitting before her, on the floor by the foot of that bed, that towel around his waist, his bare feet planted stock straight forward as if he were still considering a bolt down the stairs. Hell, he'd probably considered that bathroom window she'd used while he'd been in there. She was glad he'd decided to stay, however, even though she had been the one doing the telling, and he the listening. When she'd intended it to be the other way around.

Therese cleared her throat. "I think I'd better go—"

"Do you think we could get in bed—"

They both spoke up at the same time, and they both stopped at the same time. And then they did it again.

"Yes, I'd like that—"

"I totally understand if you want to go—"

She put her hand up. "I would like to stay."

Getting to her feet, she felt a little weird with a rug wrapped around her, the tough matting showing, the soft faux fur against her skin. But she didn't feel comfortable being naked, either. She didn't regret the sex they'd had—at all. She just didn't want him to think she was taking things in a sexual direction. He looked spent. And frankly, so was she.

"I'll be right back," she murmured.

In the bathroom, she was tempted by the shower. She didn't want him to think she was washing him off of her, though—

Stopping that train of thinking, she knew she couldn't worry about him like that. She wanted to take a shower because she had worked a shift at the restaurant, and she had just shared the most personal thing in her life with him. She needed a minute to gather herself.

And there was no better place to do it than under some hot water.

Back at the door, she ducked out. "I'm going to grab—"

He was gone.

His clothes were still where they'd been left on the floor, though. And downstairs . . . yes, she heard him moving around. A moment later, a scent drifted up the stairwell.

Toast. He was making himself some toast.

Looked like both of them were resetting in their own ways.

Reclosing the door, she cranked the shower on and yeah, wow, talk about water pressure. As she put her hand into the spray, the stuff coming out of that head was like a sandblaster. Perfect. Just . . . perfect.

As she put her rug robe aside, she stepped under the spray and exhaled more than just oxygen. The stress funneled out of her, particularly as she tilted her head back and felt the water dive into her hair. There was shampoo in a stone cut out in the wall, as well as conditioner and bodywash.

Jeez, this was like being in a hotel.

She used it all. Everything. She even shampooed twice just because she liked the smell of the Biolage whatever it was. After she was done with the cleaning thing, she backed into the spray and closed her eyes, letting the water hit her head, and flow down her hair, and fall over her shoulders, her back, her legs, and her feet.

Before she ran the hot water heater out—in case he wanted to take a shower, too—she turned things off and stepped onto the bath mat. The towels hanging on the rod across from her were fluffy and white, and as she took one off and put it to her nose, she breathed in and smelled a delicate scent of meadow flowers.

Big difference from the rough, pilled-up stuff she had at the rooming house. That one bath towel she'd bought at HomeGoods was on its last legs already. Then again, for $1.99 on clearance? What could she expect.

Once she was dried off, she took a gamble and opened a couple of drawers under the pair of sinks. Yup. Brand-new toothbrushes in every size and brush configuration Oral-B had ever thought up. As well as seven or eight different brands and kinds of toothpaste. Unbelievable. Whoever managed this house was worth every penny.

Plus they brought groceries. Even when you didn't ask them to.

As Therese brushed her teeth, she wanted to stay. She really did—and not just as in tonight. She wanted to live in a nice place like this, with clean, sweetly scented towels, and cupboards that were stocked by a thoughtful *doggen*, and rugs that were vacuumed by someone else. She wanted internet that she didn't pay for, and shelves she didn't have to dust herself, and dishes that cleaned themselves.

More than anything, though, she wanted to wake up next to Trez every night. And take coffee across from him down at that little table. And ride into work with him to her job at the restaurant. She wanted text messages from him throughout her shift, just little nothings, a meme, a stupid gif, a quick story about a crazy happening at his club. Then she wanted him to pick her up and drive her back here, the two of them chatting about what work had been like.

When they got home, she wanted to split meal prep with him. She wanted to chop vegetables on a wooden cutting board while he broiled steaks in the oven. She wanted fresh bread that smelled good, and a meal set out family-style on plates on the little table. She wanted more traded stories, from the human news or the vampire social media groups or something he'd overheard at the club from one of the bouncers.

Then cleanup. Then making love up here.

Then again, and again, until the years became decades and the decades centuries.

'Til death—in a long, long, incalculably long time off—did they part.

After which . . . the Fade. For eternity. Side by side.

"God, what am I thinking," she muttered to herself.

But yes, fine, if she were honest, she wanted the mortal version of forever on the earth with him and then the mystical one on the Other Side. And if there were young? Great. And if there were not, great.

That they were together was all that mattered.

As these wild fantasies went through her mind,

she stared at herself in the mirror over the sinks, a strange awareness rippling through her consciousness and going deeper. Much, much deeper.

It was as if she had thought these things before, and not because she was in a relationship with someone else.

It was him. For some reason . . . it had always been him.

Trez seemed, tonight at least, to be her ghost lover and her destiny, all wrapped up in one.

"And I know that's crazy," she said as she pulled a towel around herself.

Turning the lights off with her mind, she meant to turn away from her reflection. She did not. She could not.

That strange sense of connection with Trez, of bonding with him, of being fated to be with him, refused to go away—and she didn't want to go back out there until she placed it in a more reasonable context. She had learned long ago that romantic feelings were powerful—but that didn't mean they were permanent. And considering the sex they'd had? Followed by his emotional breakdown and her SuperSoul Sunday sharing stuff?

To paraphrase Oprah.

It was best to remember that anything her brain coughed up right now was the result of all the endorphins that had been released—

Out of the corner of her eye, she caught a flash of something down in the snow-covered backyard.

Frowning, she went over and looked through the double-paned glass she'd leaped free of.

Right next to her messy landing spot, there was a glow out there, and not as in a security-camera kind of thing. It was more like a residual phosphorescence, a lingering, rainbow-colored shadow, as if something—

"What. The. Fu ... dgeknuckles."

In her mind, she went all the way to "fuck." In this nice bathroom, however, with the fluffy scented towel around her and the shampoo and conditioner someone else had paid for perfuming her damp hair, she wanted to keep the cursing to a minimum even if she was alone.

And even if it was warranted.

And even though she wasn't sure that "fudge-knuckles" was a word or what it would mean if it was.

But some kind of *f*-something or another was warranted ... because right under the odd, dissipating glow was a mark in the snowpack. A large mark with two triangles on either side.

Like someone had lain down next to where she had flopped and made an angel by moving their arms and legs up and back.

To send her a message.

Abruptly, the hairs at her nape tingled and goose bumps rose on her arms. Shaking her head, she twisted the venetian blinds down so that she couldn't see out—and whoever had done that couldn't see in.

Although given that glow? She was willing to bet normal rules didn't apply. Assuming this wasn't all a figment of her unreliable mind.

Determined to put this, and so much else, behind her, she walked out of the bathroom.

Trez was in the bed on his back, his bare shoulders emerging out of the duvet that had been pulled up almost to his collarbones. His eyes were closed and his breathing was uneven, the hand he'd left out of the covers twitching, his lids fluttering as if he were dreaming.

And not of pleasant things.

Staying where she was, she watched him for a while. If he hadn't explicitly asked her to stay, she would have left him. She had a feeling he hadn't slept in a while, and surely a good day's repose could offer him more than she could when it came to help.

But she didn't want to go, and not just because she didn't want him to be alone.

Approaching the bed, she lifted the duvet and slid in between the sheets, ditching the damp towel onto the floor. Turning to face him, she was about to close her eyes when he rolled toward her. With a groan, his arms reached out and drew her into his warm, vital body, and as the contact was made, the ragged sigh he released in his sleep both broke her heart . . . and made her whole at the same time.

He needed her.

And somehow, she sensed she needed him just as much.

When Therese did close her eyes, she felt a peace come over her. And it was something she did not question.

This stranger seemed like destiny in so many ways.

Especially as she thought about her random choice to come to Caldwell when she'd left her family.

It was almost as if meeting him had been the reason.

CHAPTER TWENTY

Trez woke up at the whisper-quiet whirring of the illusion shutters as they came down over all the glass in the little house. For a split second, he knew exactly where he was. He was with his Selena, and they were in their mated bed, and the whole nightmare of her death and the pyre and the aftermath?

Nothing worth worrying about. Just ether coughed out by his subconscious, a nightmare generated by his deepest fears, a burp of terror in his brain.

Releasing his breath, he reclosed his gritty eyes

and brought his *shellan* even closer. In her sleep, her head found the place it always did on his pec, and her arm encircled him, and her hand found the dent in the side of his hip. Finally, her fingertips soothed that contour of his pelvis, just as they always did—

His lids flipped open again.

Oddly enough, the low-level irritation of his eyes was what brought it all back. They were swollen and rough because he had wept in front of her. After he had lost it while they had been having sex. And then not explained his outburst.

Shit, he mouthed into the darkness.

As the recalibration occurred, reality raising its ugly head once again, anxiety churned the two pieces of toast he'd eaten while she'd taken a shower, and he had to sit up so he didn't get sick. Carefully disentangling himself from her, he pushed his torso higher on the pillows and was glad when she rearranged herself in his lap.

The fact that she slept on reassured him.

So many things between them were complicated, but the way she sought him in her rest was simple.

Looking over at the hearth, there was nothing glowing there now, no hint of warmth or illumination left—

Light pierced through the illusion shutters, emanating from the house next door.

"What the—"

As he spoke up, his female stirred and lifted her head. "What's wrong?"

Just as he was about to throw himself on her to protect her from the sunlight, the sound of a garage door lifting and of a car not backing out to leave but driving in to stay, made him totally confused.

"Oh, shi—shoot," she said as she sat all the way up. "We slept through."

"What?" Except then he glanced at the digital clock on the bed stand. "Oh . . . it's six o'clock. At night."

Or a little before, as was the case.

With this being upstate New York, and daylight savings time having ended back in November, things got dark enough for vampire purposes by six. By even earlier. Hell, a lot of the time in December, you could be outdoors as early as five p.m.

Throwing the covers off, she jumped out of bed. "I'm going to be late again—I'm going to lose this frickin' job—"

"It's Monday. The restaurant's closed."

As she swung around to him, he did his best not to notice the way her perfect breasts settled from the movement. Or how her hair covered her shoulders and a lot of her back. Or the length of her lovely legs.

He stuck to her eyes. Meeting them, he refused to get aroused.

Okay, fine. His mind refused to go there. His erection on the other hand? Oops.

Glancing down, he made sure he was covered.

"Monday?" she said.

"Yes, Monday. I swear." Hey, she'd gotten it right on the time of night, and he was nailing the whole day-of-the-week thing. Even steven. "The snowstorm was Saturday and that's our busiest night at the club. Last night, Sunday, I didn't have to worry about a big crowd, which was why I had time to fight with my brother."

"Fight with him?"

Trez shook his head. "It doesn't matter."

Her face registered the hint of a frown. But then she looked down at herself in surprise. "Oh. Hello. Sorry, I'm in my birthday suit."

In spite of all the things unsaid between them, he had to crack a smile. "Are you seriously apologizing to me for being naked?"

"Well, it's a little much." She covered her breasts with her arm and her sex with her hand. "I mean—"

"It's just perfect, actually." Trez fiddled with the edge of the duvet. "Listen, I need to apologize about what happened last night. I didn't mean to get all dramatic."

She approached the bed. Got back in. Tucked the duvet under her arms as she propped herself up next to him. When she looked over, her face was calm and open, and he was glad. He didn't want some boatload of sympathy or oh-you-poor-baby stuff. But he also didn't want to be judged for the kind of thing he'd had absolutely no control over.

"I'm not going to ask you what happened," she said. "Just know, when, and if, you are ever ready to talk about it, I'm here for you."

"Thank you."

They sat in silence for a while. Then, when he couldn't stand the quiet, he said, "So what are your plans tonight?"

"Nothing much. I think I'll just go back home—"

"You could stay here. We could move your things in and—"

"God, I wish I could take you up on that."

"You could."

She nodded to the bathroom. "You need to try that shower. The water pressure is insane."

"You didn't answer my question."

"Was there one?" She glanced over again and exhaled. "Sorry. I'm being evasive, aren't I. And you're very sweet. I'll come see you here, though."

He had a compulsion to take her hand. So he did. "Please. Move in here and I—"

When she squeezed his palm, he stopped talking.

"Do you remember what I—do you remember everything I told you last night?" she said.

"Every word. You want me to replay it?"

"No, but thank you for listening." She took a deep breath. "So here's the thing. Do you know what the second worst thing in my life was, after finding out that I'd been lied to? The second worst moment . . . was when I decided to leave them. It wasn't the missing them or the fracturing-of-the-family thing. It was the fact that I didn't know how to do it. I didn't know how to take care of myself. I had seven hundred dollars to my name, a phone my parents paid for, an apartment I shared with my brother—I didn't have my own car, my own space. Even my job? My father got it for me. I was doing IT stuff for his oldest friend. I had nothing that was mine and no skills to take care of myself because my family had done everything for me. Or rather . . . those people I grew up with had done it all for me. I've never been more scared in my life as

I filled a duffel with some clothes and walked out of my apartment. Nowhere to go. No idea what I was going to do with myself. I was empty. Empty-headed, empty-hearted . . . lost in the world." She squeezed his hand again. "And I am never, ever going through that again. *Ever.*"

As her eyes met his, she was dead fucking serious. "I love this house," she continued. "I'd love to visit you in it. But I am going to make sure I don't rely on anyone else because that is the only way I'm going to make sure I'm not in that position again. I will make it on my own—and listen, I don't know where this is going between us, but trust me. You don't want a deadweight around your neck. You want someone who's a partner, not a problem that needs solving."

"You are not a problem." At least . . . not in the sense she was talking about.

"And I'm going to keep it that way." Her eyes were dead serious as they met his. "I need to do this. I have to prove to myself I can be strong."

Reaching up to her face, he caressed her cheek with the back of his knuckles. "Okay. I respect that."

"Thank you."

Trez had an impulse to kiss her, but she got to him first. She leaned forward and pressed her lips to his.

They stayed close for a time. And then he felt

compelled by her honesty, her openness. Or maybe it was more like guilted by it.

"I'm sorry," he whispered.

"For what."

"Being such a head case."

"You're not a head case. It's clear you have . . . something in your past that goes deep and is very painful. And I hate that for you." She shrugged. "But you are under no obligation to share it or anything else with me or anybody else. I only want the parts of you that you willingly want to give me. Those are the gifts I want, and I can be very patient with you."

Trez was so struck by her calm surety, her gentle strength, that he leaned in and kissed her. "You are . . . amazing."

And he was so grateful for the space she was giving him. The only problem was . . . he didn't think that time was going to ease his reticence. It seemed weird to tell her a story in which she was the heroine, a story of love and loss that she herself had lived—even if, at present, she didn't seem to consciously recall any of it. Still, she had been there at her death, she had suffered and—

Oh, bullshit, he said to himself.

The real reason he didn't want to tell her everything was because he wanted what he believed to be true to be reality, and if he laid it all on the table, his female had the ability—as no one else did—to blow it all up. iAm could talk in theory. People around him could worry about him. Reason could play endless matches against hope in his head.

But Selena . . . this female next to him . . . held the true detonator.

As a sharp, shooting pain went through his head, sure as if an arrow had penetrated his frontal lobe, he thought about his resolve after Xhex had spoken to him. His defensiveness when he'd fought with iAm. His certainty when he and his female had been having sex last night that it was, in fact, Selena and he reunited, the break that had come with her death resoldered, life not so much renewed as resumed.

Yeah, and then he'd cracked in half. So exactly how well was this shit working for him.

He felt torn in two for reasons he couldn't bear to look at too closely.

What if iAm was right. And Xhex had been kind rather than accurate that night of the shooting.

◆ ◆ ◆

Therese traced her lover's face with her eyes, the features so perfect to her, so sensual, so masculine, so . . . compelling. Those black irises, the dark skin, the skull trim.

"Sometimes I feel . . ." she whispered.

"What." Trez stroked her hair back. "Tell me."

"Sometimes I feel like I've always known you."

"You have," he murmured.

Therese laughed in a rush. "Fate, huh."

"Yes." He was so dead serious that she was taken aback. "I believe in fate. Don't you?"

Fantasies about a future with him aside, that question made her flinch. She had been born to someone who'd given her up. Just set her on a doorstep, and left her there in the cold, to die. So even as she spooled out whole destinies for her and this male, when it came to discussions of fate, she was troubled. Was she supposed to have been killed by neglect as an infant? Or was the saving that had happened, but that now felt temporary, what she was supposed to have gotten? On that theory, what if people's fates were doled out like pieces of mail, some of which, by the law of averages, inevitably were mislaid. Destroyed. Delivered to the wrong address.

Did she get someone else's parents by mistake? Did someone get hers?

And what of coming here and meeting Trez—

Okay, she really did *not* want to think right now, she decided. And what do you know, Trez didn't seem to either—especially as he brushed his fingers through her hair again and his hand lingered on her shoulder.

Smiling, she eased down against the pillows and ran her fingertip over her own jugular vein. Then she arched, desire curling inside her core.

"I don't want to talk anymore," she said.

Instantly, his scent flared, dark spices filling her senses.

"Right now, I want something else from you," she said. "And I want to give you something."

Eyes heating, Trez moved his own body down so they were face-to-face on the pillows. "I'm hungry."

"Me, too."

"Take from me first," he said as he cupped the back of her neck and urged her to his own throat. "Take from me so I can give strength to you."

She had a moment of pause. But then her own instincts took over.

Nuzzling into the side of his throat, she ran her sharp fang over the vein he was offering to her. She had a thought that she wanted to go slowly, but hunger clawed into her gut, a reminder that it had been too long since she'd done this. Since she'd taken care of herself in this way.

And it had been even longer since there had been a sexual component to it for her.

Licking up his neck, she reached down his body and found that he was hard again for her. Ready for her. Hungry for her.

With a hiss, she reared back and then punched her fangs through his throat—while at the same time, she began stroking him between his legs.

"Oh, *fuck!*" he barked as he rolled over onto his back and pulled her on top.

Throwing a leg over his hips, Therese sat his erection up and impaled herself on it. As she did, she began to suck on his vein, drawing him into herself. She didn't dare start moving, however. She didn't want to hurt him, and as the dark wine she swallowed warmed her gut, she was struck by such a greed, she was worried she would ride him hard and rip his throat open.

But if the goal was to bring him a release, it didn't seem to matter that she wasn't moving.

Trez started coming without any friction at all, the draws on his jugular enough to send him over the edge. And she was glad. She was so glad.

He had known such pain.

When he was with her, she wanted him to give him the pleasure he deserved.

And maybe even . . . the love.

CHAPTER TWENTY-ONE

N o, I better go back. At least for a little bit."

As his female spoke up at the sink in the kitchen, Trez glanced at his phone. It was almost eight now. They had come down here about twenty minutes ago, reclothed in what they had been wearing the night before, whereupon she had had another bowl of carefully apportioned raisins with bran, and he had rocked another set of dueling slices of toast.

They'd both had milk. In glasses.

Real hard partiers, high rollers they were.

Although upstairs, in that big bed? They had

nothing to be ashamed about when it came to having a wild time.

"Did you happen to get another phone?" he asked. "I mean, in the five minutes you've had to yourself since you lost your other one, of course."

"No." She smiled as she put her bowl in the dishwasher. Then she pointed inside the machine. "So you've got two items in here. At this rate, you'll have to run it in February."

"Can I take you to get a phone?" He put his hands up. "You'd pay, I swear. It's just we could drive by the Verizon store on the way to your apartment."

"Oh, it was just a burner, and I can get myself home." She turned around and leaned back against the counter. "I can dematerialize directly into my apartment. I know the layout and I left the window cracked."

Trez tried to keep a grunt to himself. "I can still drive you back."

"I know you can."

"Look, I'm not being a pain in the ass on purpose." Nah, it was just a gift he had. "But you should have a phone, and not because you're a female or anything—hey, what if iAm needed to get a hold of you? Or Enzo. To change shifts."

When in doubt, play the job card, he thought.

"It's Monday, remember." Her eyes grew low-lidded. "Which was why we got to stay in bed for a little extra . . ."

"Yes, we did." Trez purred. He couldn't help it. "And you know, I didn't realize how much I liked the start of the workweek until now."

There was a long moment. During which he had a feeling she was considering the idea of a change of elevation—namely to the second floor, back to that bed. And he would be a "yes" on that, go figure.

Except then she looked away with a blush. "You are too hot for me."

"No, you are."

They both laughed. Then she shook her head. "You know, you're probably right."

Trez deliberately put his fingers to the bite mark that she'd licked closed. "About what? The fact that you can take my vein anytime you want?"

"I need to return the favor, by the way," she drawled. "You didn't feed from me. We got distracted."

"In the best sense of the word. And I'd still be going down on you right now if I could."

His female let out a bark and then a snort. After which she clamped both hands over her mouth.

"Now why you gotta do that?" he asked. "You don't need to be quiet in this house."

"I have the worst laugh in the world."

Trez thought back to the time they'd spent together up at Rehv's Great Camp, on the lake near Saddleback Mountain, the two of them huddled in an old Victorian four-poster bed, a homemade quilt pulled up to their chins, quiet conversation, whispers of love, and a glimpse of eternity uniting them whether they were joined sexually or not.

He had told silly jokes. And she had laughed.

Stolen moments . . . on a timeline that had been far too short.

"I love your laugh," he said.

"You don't have to be charming." She walked over to where he was sitting at the table and put her arms around his shoulders. "You've got me already."

Trez put his hands on her hips. "And I want to keep you."

Her lovely eyes blinked. "I believe you do."

"Why wouldn't I?" God, that was all he wanted to do. "Why wouldn't anyone."

His female stroked his face. Then in a hoarse voice, she whispered, "That's not a rhetorical question to someone who was abandoned by her birth *mahmen* and sire."

Trez hugged her close. He'd never thought of the

Chosen like that, but he supposed it was true. They had no true parents. They were bred to serve, given no choice in the matter—in spite of their name—and expected to suck it up if they didn't like their role in the species. There was no love. There was only duty.

"I am so sorry," he said with emotion.

They embraced and held each other for a long time. And he told her he loved her in his mind because he briefly lost his voice.

When she pulled back, she cleared her throat. "Where were we?"

"Just where I want to be," he murmured.

She smiled. "Oh, right. My phone. Enzo and iAm. You do have a point—and I don't know why I'm being so stubborn about getting a new burner. I didn't pay a lot for it, and yet I resent like hell that I have to spend even a dime to replace the thing. And that's just stupid."

"So we're going to Verizon." He clapped his hands together in triumph. "Hot damn—"

"I have another phone."

She walked over to her purse, the one she had lost hold of at the club. Opening the top, she glanced in and glanced up again. "You know, it's really empty in here without a wallet. Thank God I'm not a human with a driver's license to lose or an identity to steal, huh."

His female reached in. Unzipped a pocket. And withdrew a cell phone.

As she held it in her hand, she stared at the thing, seeming to reacquaint herself with her own possession. "I haven't fired this up since I left. It's out of juice, though, I'll bet—yeah, no juice."

"We have cords." He got up and started looking in drawers. "Fritz always has something of everything in the houses he kits out—found 'em. What kind is it?"

"A Samsung." She came over and looked down at the various rolled black cords, all ready to use, the packaging removed. "Galaxy. But not the super-new one."

"Thank God it isn't an iAnything."

"Why?"

"Vishous doesn't like them. And given that he did the security system in this house, he would never have left anything like that behind in any drawer. He would have checked to make sure."

"Is that a Brother?" she asked. "Vishous, I mean?"

"You remember him," he said with distraction as he

started to try various options in the butt of her phone.

"Oh, was he at the club the night before last?"

"I got it. This fits." Stretching the AC/DC plug to the wall, he went to—

"Wait," she said as she stopped him.

◆ ◆ ◆

As Therese put her hand on Trez's arm, her heart was pounding. But come on, she told herself. It was crazy not to use her old phone. If she was trying to save money to move out of that rooming house, then getting another one was a waste if this was perfectly usable.

"Sorry," she said. "I'm just being weird."

"Are you afraid they've called?" His voice was low. "Your parents, I mean."

"No." *Yes.* "I mean, if they did, it's fine."

The initial charging took quickly, and as she waited, she found herself wishing she weren't so cheap. She also tried to decide what would be harder. If they had phoned . . . or if they hadn't.

"Turn-on time," she muttered.

Initialing the unit, she waited for it to fire up, and then—

There was no reason to enter her password. Her notifications flashed on the screen immediately.

And all she could do was stare at them.

"My brother," she heard herself say. "He's, ah, he's called."

"Recently?"

"Seven times. And yes . . . three nights ago was the last one."

"Are you going to call him back?"

Therese shook her head, but not in response to the question. She was trying to focus through her emotions to remember what the hell her password was. Her birth date—yes, she'd used that as her password because she got so sick and tired of remembering word-and-number combinations. Entering it, she got into the phone proper.

Her eyes watered as she looked through everything. There were texts, missed phone calls, other voice mail messages—not just from her brother.

It was all tangible evidence that her old life had continued without her. And the fact that none of the communications except for Gareth's calls were recent made her feel like she'd died and was witnessing people move on. Cousins, friends, professional contacts. Those had all stopped reaching out after a short while. Her brother had persisted, however.

Not texts, either. Calls.

He was a texter. Or had been. The only time he

ever called her was for emergencies: Accidents, car or person. Sicknesses, although with vampires that was rare. House problems that were messy, like burst pipes or blown electrical fuses that were smoking.

Or deaths.

Funny, Therese had heard people talk about seminal moments before, and she had always pictured them in the context of history. History was important, and involved many people—and sometimes the entire race: Like the raids of a couple of summers ago. The democratic election of Wrath, son of Wrath. The birth of Wrath's son, Wrath. All of those events were seminal in that they were origins of great change and the kinds of things that defined a given generation.

The lives of most individuals, on the other hand, were anecdotal rather than historic. The ins and outs of a person's life mattered solely to them, with minor extensions into families and friends. Rarely was there a span or sprawl that enveloped huge numbers. Rarely did things go so deep that breath was taken from you and you remembered exactly where you were standing when something happened or was told to you.

Rarely did you remember the shift, and not in terms of a left or a right.

Rather, like a glacier.

As Therese held her old phone in her hand and stared at the number of voice mails her brother had left her, she felt her heart move. Or maybe it was more . . . reopen.

Until she played the messages, she wouldn't even know if there was a problem. But the fact that there could be? Or might have been? And she didn't know? And she wasn't . . . there?

It was just wrong. And the whole who-birthed-who issue didn't matter in the slightest.

The next thing Therese knew, she was walking over to the table because sitting down suddenly seemed like a good idea. Except she didn't make it. The phone cord didn't reach that far from the wall.

"Here, I'll follow you," Trez said as he unplugged the charger.

There was little reserve battery, so she wondered, as she went and sat down, if the cell wasn't going to crash. But it didn't. Trez was quick to get another socket.

Holding the unit in her hands, she stared at the screen some more. "I hope they're okay."

Of course, she could find out if they were or weren't by playing the frickin' message(s). Hello. Except she was still grappling with the shift in the center of her chest. She was supposed to feel anger and resentment, hurt and betrayal—as she had since the moment she had left them all. She had had her reasons for all those negative emotions, and she had a right to be in that space. She had been lied to, the three of them conspiring to a fraud that they apparently had taken for granted would never be exposed.

Being mad was okay.

Now, though, instead of dwelling on the righteous indignation that had sustained her, all she could think of was that female's eyes, that female who had called herself *mahmen*: They had been as heartbroken as Therese had been feeling underneath her fury.

"Okay, enough of neutral," she muttered.

She called up the most recent message and prayed—*prayed*—that it was her brother chewing her out again for leaving.

His voice, coming out of her phone, was a shock, by turns foreign and familiar:

Well, it looks like you're not going to do the common courtesy of returning any of my phone calls. That's your decision. I hope you can live with it. We're taking her to Caldwell to be treated at the clinic. They say she has some time left, but it's limited, so if we're going to move her, it has to be now while she has the strength for the drive. Hope you're proud of this bullshit you're pulling. It's the only thing of your family you have left.

As the voice mail ran out, Therese's heart pounded so hard she couldn't hear anything and panic flooded her veins with the sting and the combustion of gasoline.

"I have to go," she said. "I have to go . . . see my *mahmen.*"

Leaping to her feet, she—

She immediately realized she didn't know where the Caldwell clinic was. And given how dizzy she was, dematerializing wasn't going to happen even if she had an address.

"Sit down." Trez urged her back into the seat. "You're very pale."

Therese's breath pumped in and out of her, fast but not far enough into her lungs. "This is my fault. This is all my fault—"

"Hold on. He doesn't say why she—"

She looked Trez square in the face. "She's always had a heart problem. That was why they were moving. The cold of the winters was getting too much for her. But what has always been even more dangerous? Stress." She grabbed onto his forearm. "Dearest Virgin Scribe, I've killed her."

CHAPTER TWENTY-TWO

Trez drove his female across the Hudson River, to the other side of Caldwell. Havers, the race's physician, had relocated his treatment facility to a forest over there after the raids, and although Trez hadn't been to the clinic since it had opened, he did know where it was. And he was able to make good time. The night was clear and very cold, so there was no falling snow to worry about, and the streets and highways had been plowed and salted well.

One good thing about having to deal with a hard winter every twelve months was that the city was very efficient about storm cleanup and road maintenance. They had to be. Businesses had to run. Schools had to teach their students. Hospitals needed to treat their patients.

If everything ground to a halt and stayed that way each time there was some serious accumulation? People in these parts would be indoors from mid-December to March.

He glanced across the BMW's cockpit. His female was staring out the window, but he doubted she was seeing anything. She was also unable to sit still, twitching in the seat, tapping her foot, moving around the safety belt that crossed her chest.

Refocusing on the road, he wanted to go back to having a conversation about the weather with himself. But maybe he could mix it up and think about sports. The club.

Particle-fucking-physics.

What he absolutely did not want to think about was the fact that his female was going to Havers's to deal with a family emergency.

A *family* emergency. As in . . . a group of people who, although she evidently was not related to them by blood, nonetheless counted as such as the result of her having been raised by and with them.

There was no reconciling this with her being

Selena. Nope. And the fact that he couldn't shoe-horn this fact pattern into the construct of her rein-carnation was shining a really fucking bright light on the number of things he had wedged and bent and twisted into vacancies in the puzzle.

And what do you know. There were more forced pieces than ones that fit—and he found himself des-perately grasping at the story he had constructed for himself. For them. It was impossible to ignore the sense that it was all about to be blown to shit, and the only thing he could think of was how much he wished she hadn't lost her purse in the chaos the night before last. If she'd just kept it with her, she would have had Rhage's tip money. And that burner phone.

So they wouldn't be doing this right now.

Instead, they would be driving to get her stuff at the rooming house, and then, while she got settled at the nice little Cape Cod, he would go to the club and shuffle some papers. In a couple of hours, he would come home to her and they would cook those steaks and watch a movie. And do other stuff in the dark.

He wanted *that* to be the plan.

Not this.

And goddamn, how selfish was all of that? Like he wanted her to not know this older female she cared for so deeply was sick?

Another thing for him to be proud of himself for. He had quite a fucking list.

"How much farther?" she asked tightly.

"Not far."

The subterranean clinic was hidden under acres of pine trees, and accessed through four kiosks, one of which was in a barn out behind the old farmhouse that served as a shell to the human world. The other three entries and their associated elevators were scattered through the forest, and convenient for those who could dematerialize. Needless to say, for them, it was going to have to be a park-and-ride situation, so he was going to bring them in the main road to the main driveway.

About ten minutes later, he wedged the BMW in between a minivan and a pickup truck. "You ready?"

"Yes," she said as she opened her door the six inches she could.

The fact that he didn't care about whether his side panels were dinged was something he tried to find virtue in. But the truth was, he didn't care about the car all that much, in spite of how beautiful it was.

He met her in front of the BMW and escorted her into that barn. Got them cleared by the security camera and into the hidden elevator. Hit the button for lower level. During the descent, they both stared at the little numbers above the doors, even though they did not light up because things had been retro-fitted to the purpose they served. L to 10, all dark. He found himself wondering what this Otis had been originally designed for. An office building, he decided. Or maybe a midsize hotel.

When the doors opened, he took her over to the registration desk and stood right behind her, in case she got dizzy.

The receptionist, who was wearing a white uni-form and one of those old-fashioned nurse's hats, looked up. "How may we help you?

He waited for his female to speak. And so did the receptionist, although on her side, she didn't seem surprised that it was taking a while. No doubt she was used to people in shock.

His female cleared her throat. "I'm looking for Larisse, blooded daughter of Salaman? I believe she came in here a couple of nights ago. For her heart?"

The receptionist's smile was kind as she typed on a keyboard. "All right. Yes, I have her. What is your relationship to her?" When there was a hesitation, the receptionist said softly, "I'm afraid she's in ICU and only family can be back there."

"I, ah . . ." His female cleared her throat. "I'm her daughter, Therese."

As the name was spoken, Trez's hearing checked out while directions were given to the room—or at least he assumed that was what was happening as the female behind the desk pointed in various directions.

Therese.

Not Selena.

Therese . . . a name that had been given to a female who had been born on earth, and then adopted into what clearly had been a loving home. The name that had been answered to during childhood, and written in a young's wobbly handwriting, and then, later, spoken as phones were answered. The name that had been lived with after the transition.

And was lived with now.

Not Selena.

As the walk to wherever the hospital room was commenced, Trez fell in step beside the female with the long, dark, curly hair. The female who was still wearing the server uniform from Sal's. The female who had called herself the daughter of a mortal *mahmen*.

Not the Scribe Virgin.

Passing through various double doors, proceeding down various corridors, following signage with various arrows, he put his hands in the pockets of his slacks and marveled at the brain's ability to construct reality.

With concrete and beams, Sheetrock and studs, he had built a belief that, if he were honest, had never really stood on its own. Even though the renderings had been stellar and promised a beautiful home to live in, from the beginning, there had been fault lines in the foundation, and cheap materials used, and shoddy workmanship all around.

Ultimately, that which could not hold itself up, did not.

But come on, as if this collapse was a surprise? He had vacillated the entire time, only his desperate need to believe shoring up the unsteady walls and loose, unreliable ceilings of the project he had thrown himself into.

The failure made him incredibly sad.

And he thought of something else, too.

So quick. This . . . hallucination of his . . . had come and gone so quickly. Hell, if you dismissed the prodromals, the actual tailspin had only been a matter of nights.

Abruptly, his female—

No, he stopped himself. *Therese. This was not his Selena. Never had been.*

Abruptly, *Therese* turned and looked over her shoulder. As her mouth moved, he realized she was talking to him.

"I'm sorry?" he said.

"I'm glad you're here." She reached out and took his hand. "Thank you."

* * *

The intensive care unit of the very extensive facilities was located behind a set of double doors that had to be open internally from a nursing station. Fortunately, there were glass panes you could lean into, and the instant Therese put her face in one of them, a female in a uniform looked up from a computer behind a counter.

There was a buzz, and some kind of lock was released.

Therese gave Trez's hand a squeeze, and then she released him pushed her way in. The instant she took a breath, she hated the antiseptic smell. And then her hearing checked in, and she was unnerved by the hush. Finally, as her eyes traveled around, she was disconcerted by the total lack of decoration.

This was the all-business part of the healthcare operation, and you were only here because you were either a seriously ill patient or a seriously trained professional.

Or a seriously worried family member.

She went up to the nurse at the counter. "I'm Therese. I'm here—"

"You're Larisse's daughter." The female in the uniform smiled. "The front desk called. She's in room thirteen thirteen. You and your mate are more than welcome to go down there."

Oh, God. Bad-luck number. Very bad luck.

And . . . um, Trez wasn't her mate. But like she was going to correct that if it allowed him to be in the unit?

"Thank you."

As she went to walk in the direction the nurse pointed her in, she glanced back at Trez. When he didn't seem to want to follow, she looked at the nurse, who nodded in support of his presence.

But he still stayed where he was, and in the awkward silence, Therese fiddled with the hem of her parka nervously. "You don't have to wait out here."

He looked over at a little arrangement of chairs and side tables just inside the ICU. Obviously, they had been provided as a break area of sorts for family members, the TV showing sports scores, a couple of half-finished coffees in Styrofoam cups left behind.

"Unless you'd rather?" she said.

"I think I better give you a chance to reconnect first."

As she considered the particulars, she saw the

logic to that. Her showing up here with a "mate"?
Yeah, that was one more layer of complication this
"reunion" didn't need.

"I'll come back and get you."

"Perfect." There was a pause. Then he came in for
a quick hug. "You've got this. You can do this."

Holding on to his strong body, she was struck
by how important it was for her to have him with
her. Trez was like a bridge between what had gone
before and where she was now. So even though she
hadn't known him for long, he seemed more permanent than a friend, more intimate than a lover.

Family, in a way.

"Thank you for being here." She'd told him that before. But she needed to say it again. "I won't be long."

Probably because her brother was going to toss
her out on her ass.

Breaking off from him, she walked down the hall
and refused to allow herself to look back. She was liable to lose her nerve.

The corridor was wide enough for two emergency
gurneys with associated medical staff and monitoring equipment to race into surgery side by side. Or
something like that. As she went along, it was impossible for her to think in any other terms than *Marcus
Welby, M.D.* scenarios involving life-or-death rushes.

Or maybe she needed to be more current. *ER.* Wait, that was like a decade ago.

Fine, *Grey's Anatomy.*

The *TV Guide* debate was what was on her mind as she walked by so many rooms, all of which had glass doors that were shut, most of which had drapes pulled closed for privacy. From time to time, however, she was able to see inside to family members at a bedside, cloistered around a very sick patient, holding hands. Holding each other.

Inevitably, the ill or dying were hooked up to a lot of machines.

What did she expect, though. This wasn't even a general floor. You were not here unless you were really, really sick.

Room 1313 was down at the end, on the left.

And she had to stop at 1311 for a minute and catch her breath.

Thank God she had taken Trez's vein. She wouldn't have had the strength for this otherwise.

Clearing her throat in anticipation of saying something coherent, she walked forward . . . and looked in through parted drapes.

Therese covered her mouth with her hand as her eyes filled with tears.

Her *mahmen* was lying so small and pale in a bed

that was surrounded by equipment. The males of the family, son and *hellren*, were sitting on either side of her, each cradling one of her hands in their palm. The arrangement of them all, the pervasive sadness, the obvious sickness . . . they formed a tableau of grief and suffering, the emotions and dying process eternal even in the face of so much technology and medical advancement.

Standing on the outside looking in, Therese greeted the three people she knew best in the world by reacquainting herself with their appearances, overlaying the present sight of them across the composite memory of the decades she'd known them. Her father looked older, much older. His hair, once salt-and-pepper gray, was now fully white, and his face was lined deeply, not wrinkles any longer but gouges around his mouth and at the corners of both his eyes. He had lost a great deal of weight, his plaid shirt hanging off his shoulders, his khaki pants pooling at his feet, and maybe that was part of the aging thing. But he was also exhausted, great bags under his eyes, his skin sallow and pasty.

Her brother, on the other hand, looked bigger and more vital. Gareth had nearly shaved off his hair, and his throat, shoulders, and chest had swollen up, the breadth of him not only so much greater than she recalled, but so much greater than his clothes could handle. His Michigan sweatshirt was stretching at the seams, and his jeans, though loose at his waist, seemed to be having trouble with the girth of his thighs and then his calves.

He had obviously been angry and had taken his emotions out in the gym. And he was obviously still angry. As he stared down at the female in the bed, his eyes were narrowed, his brows tight. The expression seemed like a permanent part of him, something he had been born with—except she knew that not to be true. He had been happy when she had known him. The life of the party. An older brother who had acted like a younger one.

Now . . . he was fully adult. There was no sign of the bluster and the fun to him, and as she replayed that voice mail he'd left for her in her head, she had a feeling this was not just because of the dire situation with their *mahmen* here in this hospital.

She had done this to him. She had done this . . . to all of them.

Staring through the glass, she felt a sinking feeling in her gut. The true depths of one's selfishness could not be assessed properly in the heat of the moment. Lost to emotion, to anger and retribution, you could be blinded to the effect you were having on those around you.

It was only from a distance, after a separation and recalibration, that you could see what you had done—and she knew that her absence had changed them, perhaps irrevocably.

And in the saddest of ways, it was proof of the very thing she had questioned, the very thing she had rejected so harshly.

They loved her. And they had mourned their loss.

As the conviction struck Therese, both father and son jerked to attention . . . and looked over at her.

CHAPTER TWENTY-THREE

Therese couldn't breathe as she put her hand on the lever to open the glass door to the room. She hesitated because she wasn't sure whether she would be told to go. Whether her brother would throw her out of the ICU as a whole. Whether her father would shun her.

But when neither of them moved, as if her presence was the last thing they had expected, she pushed her way into the—

The scents were the same. Dearest Virgin Scribe . . . their scents were the same. Beneath the acrid sting of bleach and antiseptic wash, she scented them all, even her *mahmen*.

As she entered, her father shot to his feet, his chair squeaking on the floor. "Therese . . . ?"

"Dad," she whispered as her eyes filled with fresh tears.

She didn't know who moved first. She just knew that between one heartbeat and the next, she was hugging her father and shaking and crying.

"Oh, you came," he said roughly. "Thank God, you're here. I think she's been waiting for you before she . . ."

Therese pulled back. "What happened? What's going on with her?"

In the corner of her eye, she noted that her brother had stayed seated—and obviously had no intention of going vertical anytime soon. He was leaning back in the hard chair, his arms crossed over his chest and his jaw rigid, like he was gritting his molars.

"It's the myopathy," her father said. "Her heart muscle is just not strong—"

Gareth cut in without looking over. "And stress is *so* great for her condition—"

"Gareth," her father interrupted. "Now is not the time."

"You got that right. She's too fucking late."

Gareth got up and strode out before anyone could say anything else. And as the door eased shut behind him, her father closed his eyes.

"Let's just focus on your being here, yes?" he said in his Old Country accent.

"Yes," Therese agreed. "There's time to talk . . . later."

Approaching the bed, she had to cover her mouth again to keep her emotions in check. Guilt sickened her stomach, freezing that Raisin Bran she'd eaten in its tracks, and before her legs gave up on their job, she sat down in the plastic chair her brother had been warming. Reaching out, she took her *mahmen*'s hand, and she was horrified at the bones: Beneath the paper-thin skin, there was no cushion in the anatomy at all. It was as if she were holding on to a skeleton.

"Mah-mah," she whispered. "I'm here. I'm so sorry . . . I should have . . ."

There was no response, of course. Then again, the female was intubated, a machine breathing for her.

"When did this all happen?" Therese asked. Even though she could guess.

Probably right around the first time her brother had left her a message. So about a week after she had left.

Her father sat back down. "Her condition has been a challenge for . . . a little while."

"After I left, right." She glanced up at her father. "You can say it. You can be honest."

"She was upset. It's true."

"I am so sorry."

"You're here now. That's what I really care about."

"I put her here—"

As Therese started to get emotional again, her father shook his head. "No, you did *not*. We've known all along that at some point she would transition into an acute period. It's the way her kind of heart disease works. This has been inevitable since she contracted that virus back in the seventies."

"I didn't help. I should have handled . . . everything . . . better."

"Well, none of us helped, either." He rubbed his face. "I don't want to go into it now, but . . . we all should have handled everything differently. Starting a long time ago."

While her father fell silent, Therese refocused on her *mahmen*'s frail face, the closed eyes, the veins that were showing under the skin. As she considered her righteous anger, she saw a truth that, like her selfishness, she had been blinded to.

She'd thought she had endless time with them. In

spite of the fact that she had known about her *mahmen*'s heart condition and the reason why her parents were moving somewhere warmer, she had never considered the possibility that she wouldn't be able to talk to her *mahmen* again. Never, not once. And as a result of there being an infinite opportunity to fix things, she had been totally inclined to let the situation fester.

Which was ridiculous.

Yet there had been no pressure to fix the rift. No super ordinal to wipe away the hurt and betrayal to reveal the love underneath. She had assumed she could dwell forever in the state of separation that she had created, justified in her hurt and anger— and in doing so, she had squandered a gift she hadn't realized she'd been given.

And now, as she sat at the bedside of her dying *mahmen*, the anger she had felt toward her parents and her brother was transmuted . . . and placed upon herself.

"I am so sorry," she said as she looked at her *mahmen*'s hollow face.

"You're here now," her father repeated for the third time. "That is all that matters."

Okay, that was so untrue.

She had learned her lesson, however. There was still time to make amends.

It would be an imperfect attempt, however, as who knew whether her *mahmen* could hear.

Oh, and then there was Gareth. She wasn't sure how much she had to work with when it came to him.

No, that was a lie.

Given where he was at, she had less than nothing to go on with her brother.

◆ ◆ ◆

Sitting in the waiting room, Trez hit up Xhex's cell and put his phone to his ear. *One ringy-dingy. Two ringy-dingies. Three—*

Down at the far end of the hall, a big male walked out of one of the patient rooms with an expression on his face like someone had just taken a hammer to the hood of his car. He was a sweatshirt-and-jeans kind of guy, and when he took a pack of Marlboros out of the back pocket of said Levi's, somehow it wasn't a surprise.

He looked like he could use a cigarette.

Or several hundred.

—four ringy-dingies. Five—

The male stopped in front of the nurse. "I need to have a smoke. There has to be somewhere in here that I can light up."

The female behind the counter opened her mouth

like she was going to out-of-the-question, against-regulations the guy. Except then she seemed to take pity on him.

"Just go out in the hall and down to the right," she said. "No one should bother you. But take this."

She handed him over a soda bottle with a screw top. "Do not ash on the linoleum. And if anyone asks you, do not tell them I said you could."

"Thank God," the male said with relief. Then he leaned in. "How long have you been trying to quit?"

"Three years, seven months, four nights . . ." She checked her watch and tacked on dryly, "and twenty-three minutes. And yes, I've done the patches and the gum, and nothing beats the real thing."

"Bless you."

As the male left, Xhex's voice mail kicked in. Which was to say an automated voice announced her number and instructed any callers to leave a message.

Trez killed the connection and stared at his phone. For no good reason, he thought about how much he hated people who didn't personalize their answering message. It made him feel like he was tossing whatever he wanted to leave on there into a trash can, never to be retrieved or replied to. At least his head of security had a reason to keep her ID on lockdown. But still.

Although even if she had recorded some kind of *Hey, this is Xhex, leave a message,* he didn't know what he would have said.

And actually, Xhex would be more likely to put out something like, "This is Xhex, I'm not going to tell you to leave a goddamn message. What the hell do you think this is for, asshat. Christ on a crutch, if I have to tell you what to do here you got more problems than me not answering your stupid call."

Beeeeeeeeeeeeeeeeeeeeep.

As he debated whether to try again—and found progress in the fact that at least he was not trying to phone his *symphath* friend just to be reassured about a fallacy he had created—he was also tempted to call iAm. Even though, as with whatever he was going to say to Xhex, he didn't have anything worked out in his head. The urge to hit them up was more a reflex born out of him feeling so adrift. But this was what people did, right? When things got off track, they called their nearest and dearest.

Maybe Rehv was right. Maybe he needed to get on meds and go for a little vacation—and not in a hang-himself-in-the-closet sense.

Or in a drown-in-the-Hudson kind of fashion.

As he shifted to the side and put his phone away, he looked down at his silk shirt and remembered his female—that female . . . *Therese*, he made himself say in his head . . . pointing out that he wasn't wearing a jacket. It made him realize that he had a matching double-breasted masterpiece to go with these slacks. He'd been in such a rush to get out of the house, to see that female, that he hadn't bothered to grab it and pull it on.

Which was kind of his theme song of late, was it not.

Moving so fast, he missed necessary pieces.

Glancing at the double doors of the unit, he told himself to stay put. For one, the female would be coming back out at some point, and she would want to know where he was. For another . . .

Oh, what did it matter. What did any of this matter?

"Therese," he said softly, trying out the syllables.

The sound of the name in his ears carried along with it a raftload of anxiety, and with a curse, he got to his feet and walked out of the unit, unable to stand still. In the corridor beyond, he put his hands on his hips and took some deep breaths—

"You got someone in there, too?"

As a male voice spoke up, he looked over to the right. It was the guy who had walked by the nursing station, the one who had been given permission to smoke on the DL. The one who had the same coloring as Therese. Who seemed to have come out of the same patient room she had gone into.

Trez nodded. "In a way, yes."

"You want one?" the male asked as he held out a packet of Marlboros.

"I don't smoke." He went over. "But sure."

"You don't smoke, or you don't want to smoke."

Trez accepted the soft pack and drew one of what was left out. "Does it matter."

"Nope, not in the slightest."

Catching the red Bic lighter that was tossed at him, Trez lit the tip of the cigarette and exhaled while he returned the flame-delivery device to its owner.

"I'm trying to quit," the male said.

"Not going well, huh?" Trez turned the cigarette around and stared at the glow. "I work in a club, so I'm used to smoke."

"I thought Caldwell has an ordinance against smoking indoors at public places. Doesn't everything over here?"

"Smoke machine. But it doesn't matter. My lungs are used to all kinds of secondhand shit." He pegged the guy right in the eye. "Gareth, right?"

The male frowned. "Do I know you?"

"I'm here with your . . . ah . . ."

"Sister?" The male straightened from his lean on the wall. "Therese?"

Trez nodded and held out the Marlboro. "You want this back now?"

There was a moment of tension as those yellow eyes went up and down his body. And before things could get aggressive, Trez shook his head. "I don't have a dog in this fight, okay? I drove her here so she was safe. She was so upset. She couldn't dematerialize. I didn't want her Ubering anywhere by herself, and there are no public transportation options on this side of the river."

Gareth took a hard inhale, like he was trying to suck part of the world through a straw. Except then he eased back against the wall. Bringing up the Coke bottle the nurse had given him, he unscrewed the top, ashed into the inch of flat soda in the bottle—and then offered the "ashtray" forth.

Trez tapped his own cigarette into the mouth of the bottle. "She just got the messages tonight. She came as soon as she heard them."

"I left them weeks ago."

"She had her phone stolen."

"Oh."

As her brother lost some of his bluster, Trez figured the lie about the phone felony was on the "little white" side of things. And worth it.

"Therese leaving broke our *mahmen*'s heart," the male said. "Just so you know."

"I think she is aware of that."

"And she still stayed away? Classy move."

Trez frowned. "I think you better talk to her about this."

"I intend to—"

The growl that came up and out of Trez's throat was a surprise—to both of them. As Gareth recoiled with shock, Trez got back to smoking what he'd been given. Shit. He did not need to get all protective here. That was not going to help.

There was no denying the impulse, however. And he was surprised to find . . . that it didn't have anything to do with Selena, either.

"You're more than a friend of hers," Gareth said.

After a moment, Trez shrugged. "It's complicated."

Motherfucker, he thought. His life was a goddamn Facebook status.

CHAPTER TWENTY-FOUR

An hour later, or maybe it was longer, Therese looked again at the bank of monitors around the head of the hospital bed. She had no idea what any of the numbers or the beeping meant. She supposed that the lack of alarms was a good sign—surely if things were taking a sudden turn for the worse, there would be a cacophony of sorts. Right?

That's how she would have designed them to work.

"When does the doctor come in?" she asked.

Her father sat up straighter in his uncomfortable chair. "Every noontime. His name is Havers."

Therese indicated around the high-tech room they were in. "Big change from back home."

"Sure is. She couldn't be in better hands."

Where they had lived, the only healer in a fifty-mile radius was a local vampire who came when it was necessary and did what he could with over-the-counter remedies and things that were traditional in the Old Country. Bricholt, was his name. Son of Bricholt the elder.

"How did you know to bring her here?" she asked.

"Your brother did research online."

"In the vampire groups?"

"Yes."

I could have done that, she thought to herself. *I should have done that.*

Looking at her *mahmen*, she exhaled. "You said she's waiting for something."

"Yes."

"I think I know what it is."

Turning to the closed glass doors, she wasn't sure she wanted to go find her brother and make up. If the discord was keeping their *mahmen* on the planet, maybe she could have some more time with the female.

But that was hardly fair.

"Will you excuse me?" she said. "I have to go make some arrangements with work."

"Oh, you have a job?"

"It's just a waitress thing. It's not a big deal."

"Work is work." Her father smiled hollowly. "Purpose is . . . well. I'm still proud of you. I've always been proud of you."

"Why?" she breathed. "All I've ever done is—"

"Be my daughter. And you have done that perfectly."

"No," she choked out. "Look at what I've—"

"Stop it." As the young in her instantly closed her mouth, her sire looked at the bed. "All we have ever wanted was for you to be happy. That's it. That's all you or your brother have to do for her and me."

"There's so much more, Dad. Especially as you two get older."

"We can take care of ourselves."

The fact that he didn't acknowledge that one half of that "we" was not going to be around for much longer broke her heart.

Therese got up. Leaning to her *mahmen*'s ear, she said, "I'm going to go talk to Gareth. I'm going to make things right with him. You don't have to worry, okay? I'm going to fix this."

On her way to the door, she went around and squeezed her father's shoulder. He patted her hand in response.

Stepping out of the room, she walked down the corridor. That Trez wasn't in the waiting area wasn't a worry. With his blood in her, she could sense him right out in the hall. And given the very distant scent of smoke, she knew who he was with.

The fact that she wasn't nervous at all at the idea of the two males talking was a good indicator of how much she trusted Trez.

But she already knew that.

Nodding to the nurse at the station, Therese opened one side of the doors and looked to the right. Her brother and her lover were sitting on the floor next to each other, smoking and talking in low voices.

As soon as she stepped out, they both looked over.

"Hi," she said.

Gareth looked away quick. But at least he didn't up and leave again. Or start yelling.

Trez's dark eyes were grave. "How are things in there."

"I guess the same as they've been, right, Gareth?" She took the grunt as a good sign. Okay . . . maybe it was more of a not-so-bad sign. Not-as-bad-as-it-could-be sign. "Mind if I join you two?"

Trez took out his phone and checked the time. "Listen, I was going to quickly go and check in with things at work—"

"Oh, of course." She lowered herself down next to him. "I don't mean to trap you here. But if you talk to iAm, can you please tell him I won't be in for a couple of nights? I'm not leaving until . . ."

As she let the sentence drift, her brother looked over at her. And kept looking.

"Absolutely." Trez took her hand. "What can I bring you?"

"Food, maybe?"

"Sure. What kind?"

"Gareth?" She glanced across. "Anything in particular?"

Her brother took a drag off his cigarette and then exhaled while shaking his head. "I'll eat anything. Dad's the same."

"Roger that."

When Trez hesitated, she answered the is-it-appropriate by making the move to kiss him.

"See you in a little bit," she said as their lips met briefly.

"Yup, you will." He ditched his cigarette butt in a soda bottle, then got to his feet. "Later, Gareth."

"Later."

Therese watched her male go—and was aware that the vibe changed immediately. But at least her brother didn't seem overtly hostile.

"How long you been seeing him?" Gareth asked as he dropped his own butt into that bottle. Before the hissing had even faded, he was lighting another.

"They let you smoke out here?"

"Don't start."

"I'm not. Honest." She sighed. "So how you been? And not long. To answer your question about the dating thing."

"So he's not why you picked Caldwell."

"No, I met him here. His brother is the chef at the restaurant where I work."

"Seems like a nice guy."

"He is."

Before the pause became a silence that grew long and awkward, she took a deep breath and jumped into it all.

"I'm sorry. I'm really sorry."

Her brother's yellow eyes twitched, and she braced herself for an argument. Instead, he just shook his head. For a while.

Sitting beside him, she gave him the space and time he needed to sort his emotions out. And she appreciated that he didn't do a rant-and-rave that would accomplish nothing and exhaust them both.

"I just really . . ." He started and didn't finish. Started again. "I just couldn't believe you would abandon us. You didn't just leave them . . . you left me, and whatever, I know you're my sister, but you're a friend, too. My roommate. You know. Whatever. It doesn't matter."

"You're only saying that because it does."

"Yeah. Maybe." He took another drag. "I need to stop smoking. Thank God vampires don't get cancer—and no, I absolutely do not do it anywhere around Mom."

"I never even considered for a moment that you would."

"I'm glad you came now, even though I wanted to scream at you when you walked in."

"I got that impression."

"That's why I left the room back there. I didn't want to make things worse. It's been so damned hard."

"Thank you for calling. I honestly didn't get the messages."

"I know. He said so."

As tears came to Therese's eyes, she glanced left and right, up and down—like she was giving herself an eye exam—so that none fell. "I've missed you. I've missed them."

"We've been empty since you left, too." He tapped the tip of his cigarette on the bottle's open neck. "Some people are the heart of a family."

"That's Mom."

"No." Gareth looked over at her. "That's you. That's always been you. You keep us going, keep us organized. You're . . ."

Clearing his throat sharply, he shifted his eyes down and then rubbed them hard, one by one, with the knuckles of his free hand. "Look, I can't talk about this. It's killing me, and I gotta pull it together for them—"

"Oh, Gareth," she whispered as she reached for him.

Except as she went to give him a hug, he put a hand up and leaned out of range. "Nope. None of that. I've got to get a hold of myself."

"I'm going to hug you later."

"Fine. Just not now."

Therese took her first full breath since the moment she'd marched out of her parents' house. Gareth, on the other hand, seemed to still be struggling with his emotions.

Trying to change the subject, she murmured, "So you've been lifting a lot, huh."

"I have."

"How's that female you were dating?"

He shook his head and kept his eyes on his cigarette. "She moved in right after you left, all ready to get mated. Like, are you kidding me? My family is imploding and you want to talk about the color theme of some reception out of the human tradition? It was a disaster."

"I'm sorry to hear that—"

"Here's what really bothered me," he said, looking up and staring directly into her eyes. "This is what got me about Mom." He pointed his rabbit-eared hold on the Marlboro at her. "You never gave her a chance to explain. You never got the story from her. You were so busy yelling and being all angry that she didn't have the opportunity to tell her side of the story. What's more, you acted like she owed you an apology for taking you in and giving you a home and caring for you all these years. That was what bothered me."

"I was blindsided. I didn't ever expect it. I thought . . . they were my parents, Gareth. You never tried to understand where I was coming from."

"You didn't know they weren't your parents because they *were*."

Therese put a hand on his now-thick forearm. "As you aren't in my position, you need to trust me about how it made me feel. I'm not saying I handled things well, but I know what it felt like, okay."

He cursed. Went quiet for a bit. "You're right. I apologize. And I didn't behave any better. I just was worried about *Mahmen* and worried about you as well. I'm your big brother. I'm supposed to take care of you."

"I need to take care of myself."

"No one can go it alone in this world, Milk Dud."

Therese started to smile, remembering how they had always given each other random nicknames. "Does this mean I can call you Ricola again?"

"I got an even better one for you." He pointed to his foot. "I dropped a weight on this thing a week ago. Right before we left to come here. Healed badly so now I'm wearing an orthotic."

"Oh, my God. I'm calling you Dr. Scholl's from now on."

The slow smile on her brother's face was so nice to see. "Good deal. Good deal."

Therese tilted forward and looked at the double doors of the ICU. "So Dad says she's been intubated for the last two nights."

"Pretty much right after we arrived here. We got her admitted in a nick of time."

"Do you think she'd want to talk to me?" Therese wondered out loud. "Maybe it would give her a reason to come back."

Gareth shrugged. "Anything. At this point, I'll take anything I can get. The idea of death separating those two? It doesn't bear thinking about. If she dies, we're going to lose Dad, too."

CHAPTER TWENTY-FIVE

The good thing about it being a Monday night, iAm thought, was that his fucked-up head didn't have to function: It wasn't required to coordinate his hands and arms, his memory or his reading skills, so he could cook food over a hot stove. He could just sit here in his office and stare at the paperwork.

Of course the bad thing was . . . all he was doing was just sitting here and staring at the paperwork.

"Fuck . . ." he said as he sat forward and put his head in his palms.

When there was a subtle beep from the security

system, he looked up. The rear staff door was opening, and he reached under the lip of his desk and put his palm on the nine that was mounted out of sight—

He knew immediately who it was.

Then again, he would recognize the scent of his blooded brother anywhere. Trez's outline, too.

iAm retracted his hand from his gun and straightened in the chair. "Trez?"

Stupid. To say the name. But he was relieved. Anytime he saw the male, it was a relief, one more night lived through. One more day, survived.

"Mind if I come in?" the guy said as the door closed behind him with a clap.

"You are always welcome anywhere I am."

"You sure about that?"

"Down to my marrow, brother mine."

Trez walked forward, and there was no anger in his face, but no expression to those familiar features, either. There was also a stillness to him that was eerie.

"What's happened?" iAm asked.

The other male paused in the doorway for a moment. Then he came in and sat down in the chair across the desk, curling up and balancing his chin on his knuckles. iAm recognized the pose. So he, himself, sat back.

"Tell me when you're ready," iAm said quietly.

It was a long time before his brother spoke, and when the words finally did come, Trez ran his fingertips up and back on the edge of the desk like he was anxious.

"That which cannot go on will not." As iAm's gut clenched, Trez shrugged. "It's a theory of economics that translates to so many other things—"

"I know what it is. How are you applying the theory is what I care about."

"Not to me." Those black eyes flipped up for a moment. "I'm okay."

iAm didn't want to argue. Shit knew they'd had plenty of that lately. But he wasn't sure if such an assessment was true—or if the male was even capable of making that call.

It was better than a lot of other options, however.

"Do you want to talk to Mary?" iAm blurted.

Trez smiled a little. "So many people asking me that lately. Rehv, you."

"It's because we're worried about you."

"I'm honestly not suicidal." Just as iAm was trying to hide his surprise, Trez looked up and shrugged. "I'm just not. I'm not saying I wasn't or that I won't be again. I'm just not right now. And after the shit I've been through, that's the only kind of reassurance I can give you—or myself, for that matter."

"I can't bear to lose you." iAm had to clear his throat. "Not now. Not ever."

Trez rubbed his face like his eyes were bothering him. "I'm sorry about all the shit that went down over Therese. You know, last night. And before."

"Me, too. And I should have—"

"You were right. I was wrong."

iAm shook his head. Fiddled with the paperwork in front of him. Regretted every bit of the argument—but not as much as he mourned the truth. "I don't want to be right. Not about any of it."

"It was just because I wanted to believe. You know, that she's back." Trez pointed to the center of his chest. "The pain here—I mean, it's not as bad as it was at first. But the problem is that I don't get any relief at all from this toxic pressure. It's always there. Always with me. As the love for her was, so is the grief over her death. Right here. Every second of the night and through each hour of my piss-poor sleep during the day. And I think . . . it kind of makes a male crazy, you know?" Touching his head, he continued, "Up here . . . it isn't working so well and I didn't appreciate exactly how badly until now. But

I think I'd guessed, though, which was why I lost it when you called me on my delusions."

iAm found himself, for the millionth time, measuring the extent of his brother's suffering. It had always seemed unsurmountable. Unsupportable. And now that iAm had *maichen*? It was incalculable. He couldn't imagine losing his mate.

"I think I was just desperate," Trez said. "I desperately don't want to feel like this anymore and the only way that happens is if Selena is back. And so I convinced myself . . . well, we've been through it."

"I hate this for you." iAm rubbed his stinging eyes. "I really do. I always have."

"Yeah, well. It is what it is."

"What can I do to help?"

Trez was silent for a while. And then he shook his head. "The only one who can walk over this bed of nails is me. But your just being here? It does help. And it really matters."

Before iAm could respond, Trez clapped his hands on his thighs, a clear sign that the conversation was over. And that did make sense, iAm supposed. Words only ever went so far. The rest of the distance had to be carried by the relationship that had always been between them. And always would be.

"So," Trez said brusquely, "what's new with you? It's dawning on me that I haven't asked that in a long while."

iAm blinked a couple of times. Then he ducked his eyes. "Oh, you know. Same ol'."

"How's *maichen*?"

Pregnant. Which is fucking wonderful and fucking terrifying. "She's, ah, she's good."

"Really?"

"Oh, yeah." *At least the priests said so. Although what the hell do they know?* "Just fine."

There was another pause. "Then why are you drawing blood right now?"

iAm frowned and looked down at his hand. Sure enough, he had gripped a pencil in his fist so hard that he'd broken it in half and the ragged parts were digging into his palm. Red drops were falling onto the paperwork, staining the bills. The payments. The schedules.

"Tell me what's going on," his brother said grimly.

◆ ◆ ◆

As Trez watched his next of kin bleed onto the desk, he had the first sense of what he had cost the male since Selena's death. And close on the heels of that revelation, he had a further one about how he had always taken, taken, taken—and though the narcissism had always been a product of circumstance, a door prize for the shit luck he'd always had, like that mattered when iAm needed something?

Just because the imbalance was understandable, and arguably forgivable, didn't mean it was a fucking party.

And now, on the far side of the cluttered desk, the other male was looking caught, an invisible cage locking down on him, his eyes lowering and likely to stay that way. Oh, and P.S., he was still bleeding at the palm, and doing nothing about it.

"She's pregnant," Trez said. "Isn't she."

iAm's eyes shot up. And the silence was the answer.

"Oh, my God," Trez said with a growing smile. "Really? You're going to have a young? That's incredible."

iAm's shock at the congratulations was apparent. And something Trez added to his list of regrets.

"Hey, I'm honestly happy for you." He leaned across the desk and took the broken pencil out of his brother's hand. "I'm so happy for you both."

"I didn't want to tell you."

Trez opened his mouth to ask why, but that would be two rhetoricals in as many minutes, wouldn't it.

"Well, I'm glad you did." Trez reached into his back pocket and took out his silk handkerchief. Pressing it to the wound, he found himself choking up. "It gives me something to live for."

iAm took a deep breath. "I want you to be the blessing one for her."

"It's a daughter?" Trez blinked. And then found himself smiling again. "A daughter . . . and yes, I would be her blessing one. I am honored."

"I would have no one else but you do it."

They sat there for a while, as the wound sealed up, and Trez was amazed. For the moments as he held his brother's hand in his own, and tended to the injury, and smiled at the good fortune that had befallen *maichen* and iAm, he felt something in the center of his chest that relieved the pain.

This is real, he thought to himself. And this moment . . . this present . . . was the first piece of his life since his *shellan*'s death that didn't hurt.

A next generation, born out of love, born into love.

"I can't wait to meet my niece," he said roughly.

iAm's smile was short and hidden, as was his way. He had always been the quiet one, the self-effacing, take-a-back-seat one. But like he'd had a choice? Trez had always been the marching band headed for a cliff.

Too much noise for anyone else to take up space.

"And she's going to love her uncle," iAm said in a hoarse voice.

"I'm going to make sure of it."

"You won't have to work too hard at that."

Trez peeked under the handkerchief. "Just a little longer, so it can take some wear and tear on the healed part."

"I didn't even know I'd broken the pencil." Then, as if iAm wanted to avoid any more emotional anything, he asked, "So . . . what brought you this way? Just a chat?"

"Well, that and I need some food. For, ah, Therese. And her father and brother. Her *mahmen's* at Havers's in the ICU. They need sustenance."

As iAm looked up sharply, Trez shook his head and peeked under the handkerchief. "And before you ask," he said, "yes, I am going to talk to her. I'm going to explain . . . everything."

"You could fall in love again, you know."

"I thought you didn't want me to be with her."

iAm put up his forefinger. "I don't want you to be with her if you think she's someone else."

"She is, though. Someone else, that is."

"Well, when you're ready, if you ever are, maybe you can give it a shot. If not with her, then with someone else."

"I can't think like that right now."

"I know and I don't blame you." iAm got to his feet and flexed his hand. "In the meantime, I will cook for her and her family. And I will make her the very best meal she has ever had."

Less than ten minutes later, iAm was at the stove, his injured hand gloved up, the spices flowing, the sauces simmering. He was cooking like the expert he was, nothing sloppy or distracted now, and the smells were heaven. What was even better? As Trez sat on a stool and watched, some of the tension left him.

Although he knew it would return as soon as it was time to go back to the hospital and see Therese again—

Hey, check it. He could think her name without hesitating now.

Great. Good job, sport.

Shit, he really needed to talk to her. But like it was appropriate with her *mahmen*'s condition?

"Oh, listen," he said, "Therese's going to stay with her *mahmen*. At Havers's, that is. Until the situation . . . resolves."

iAm started chopping a bundle of fresh basil leaves. "Tell her to take as long as she needs for that sad business."

"I will. Just keep the position open for her if you can. She needs this job."

"She has it. For as long as she wants it."

Trez thought of all the things he would change if he could. There were so many . . . but none of them involved that female morphing into his Selena. He'd lived that fantasy for ten minutes, and all he'd done was prove his brother's predication true.

Someone who deserved better was going to get hurt. And it was all Trez's fault.

"She's saving up to move out of the rooming house she's staying in," he heard himself say. "She wants to do things on her own."

Maybe that would be different now, though. With her reconciling with her family, maybe she would go back to Michigan with them. Surely they would return to her hometown there—no, wait. She'd said her parents were moving for her *mahmen's* health. Down south somewhere? North Carolina? South Carolina?

As he pictured her leaving Caldwell, and him never seeing her again, his heart ached, but he didn't trust the emotion.

He didn't trust his read on anything anymore.

CHAPTER TWENTY-SIX

Mahmen," Therese said. "We're right here. We're all right here."

There were now three chairs around the bedside. The staff had been so kind, so easy to deal with, so accommodating where and when they could be given the dire nature of that which they were treating. Then again, they didn't go into this particular division of medicine unless they were a special breed. Here, in the ICU, there was more death than life, the battle against the Grim Reaper lost more times than won.

So you had to be tough without losing your compassion.

Therese gently stroked her *mahmen*'s cool, dry hand and tried not to choke up. "I am so sorry I left like that." She glanced across at her father. Looked to the right at her brother. "I'm so sorry, but I'm here with you now, and Gareth and I have made up, and Dad is here . . . our family is back together, *Mahmen*."

"That's right, *nalla*," her father said.

"I want to understand, *Mahmen*," she continued. "You have a story to tell, I know this. And I want to know what it is, from you, and I want you to know that whatever it is, I accept it. You had your reasons for doing what you did, but you have to come back to us so I can know them from you. You have to . . . come back to us so you and I can be as we were."

Focusing on the closed eyes, she had no idea what to expect as she fell silent.

No, that was not exactly true. She knew what she wanted. She wanted the female to wake up, start breathing on her own, and resume life. Resume all their lives. Continue into the future that Therese had once taken for granted, but would no longer.

When nothing happened, when there was no response at all nor any recognition, Therese took a deep breath. "I'm so sorry, *Mahmen*."

And . . . that was how it went. They sat like that, on their vigil, with the machines beeping and staff coming and going silently, for God only knew how long. Every once in a while, Therese would repeat what she'd said in some form or another, or her father would tell an anecdote—like about the time Gareth had tried to paint the outside of the house as a Mother's Day present—or Gareth would stand up and pace in front of the glass wall that faced the rest of the ICU.

As there continued to be no change, time took on a surreal, elastic quality. Therese couldn't decide whether it was crawling . . . or flying . . . and that was because it was seeming to do both at once—

Except then, without warning, the scent of something absolutely not antiseptic in the slightest drifted into the room. And a second later, Trez appeared on the far side of the glass, a bunch of paper bags in his arms.

Therese smiled, her heart lifting in her chest. And as her father and her brother looked up, both males rose to their feet and Trez bowed out of respect.

"Is that . . ." her father started.

"Yup," Therese said as she patted the hand she had been holding. "Dinner has arrived, *Mahmen*. I wish you would join us. It's very good Italian, your favorite."

"They won't let us eat in here," Gareth said. "But just outside there's another sitting area. Right next door."

"The family waiting room," her father murmured as he sized up Trez.

"Come join us, *Mahmen*." Therese got up out of her chair and leaned forward, smoothing back the graying hair from the pale, drawn face that was breaking everyone's heart. "We'll be just in the next room if you need us, and we'll return very soon."

The three of them walked out, and Therese stood up on her tiptoes to kiss Trez. As she put her lips to his, he seemed to stiffen, but then again, he hadn't been properly introduced.

"This is my father, Rosengareth the elder," she announced, stepping back. "Dad, this is Trez."

"Quite a feast you have there," her father said as he nodded at the bags.

"My brother made it especially for your family." Trez transferred the bundles to one hand and put out his dagger palm. Switching to the Old Language, he said, "*Sire, it is a pleasure to make your acquaintance.*"

Her father seemed dumbfounded by the manners. But then he snapped to it and shook what was offered. "*And I, yours.*"

"I told them all about you," Therese said. "*Mahmen* as well."

Trez cleared his throat and looked like he wanted

to loosen the already unbuttoned collar of his silk shirt. Yeeeeaaaah, nothing like meeting the family under these circumstances.

"To the waiting room?" he said, indicating an open doorway.

"Right this way." Therese took a bag from him. "Let's try and eat before this gets cold. And then I'll take you in to meet *Mahmen*."

The family waiting room had no door, but plenty of space and lots of chairs to pull around a desk-like table in the corner. As Therese dove into the paper bags, she recognized the dishes that iAm served his best customers—and she thought about him turning on his stove just for them.

"Will you please thank Chef for us?" she said as she passed around the paper plates.

"I will," Trez murmured.

There were a variety of containers with foil tops, and they ate family-style, sharing the servings of pasta with different sauces and meats, as well as a great selection of desserts.

"So, Trez," her father asked between mouthfuls. "What do you do for a living?"

◆ ◆ ◆

Across the makeshift dining table, Trez nearly choked on his chicken parm. God . . . how to answer that to anyone's father? Probably best not to lead with pimp. Drug facilitator. Former skull cracker.

"I'm in . . . entertainment."

"He has a club," Therese said as she wiped her mouth with a paper napkin. "But it's totally legitimate."

Mostly legitimate, he tacked on to himself.

Okay, fine. Mostly illegitimate. But in a decent way. It wasn't like he got aggressive as long as everyone followed the rules. And hey, there had only been one shooting there. Well, this calendar year, at least—twelve whole months!

"I'm thinking about getting out of the business," he blurted

As he heard the words come out of his mouth, he surprised himself. Because it was true. But what the hell was his B plan? And weren't fresh widowers discouraged from making big relocations and decisions during the first twelve months after the death?

Whatever, he thought.

Sitting back, he found himself starting to talk. "I want to do something different. I've been in the same . . ." *Rut.* ". . . business, you know, for a while. And I think it's time for a change."

Rosen, as Therese's father went by, leaned in. "What are you thinking about?"

The older male was hard to look at, and not because he was ugly. Or mean. Or in any way unworthy. Instead, Therese's father was the kind of steady, strong, humble person that you instinctively knew you could trust with your taxes. Your house. Your kids and your dog.

"I want to go back to school."

"Education is very important. I've told my kids that all along." As both Therese and her brother nodded, the male smiled. "I never had much, but I've lived an honest life and gotten both of these two through college without leaving them with any debt. Larisse and I put our money into them, and it's the best investment we could ever have made."

See, Trez thought. His instincts about the guy were right.

Gareth spoke up. "I'm going back to school, too."

"You are?" Therese asked.

"I'm going to learn human law. There's an executive program at the University of Chicago. I figure the race needs people who understand how that side of things work."

Trez spoke up. "I think that's a great idea. I've had to use some non-species attorneys for real estate purchases, and it's a pain. I would have felt much better with one of us. Hey, you know, you should talk to Saxton, the King's solicitor. He could really help you—and maybe get you an internship at the Audience . . . um, House?"

He stopped talking. The three of them were looking at him with wide eyes.

"You've been to the Audience House?" Gareth asked. "Holy shit."

"Watch your language, son," Rosen mumbled. "Ah . . . have you met the King?"

"I live with him—"

As all three started coughing into napkins, Trez thought, *Well, crap.*

Therese's shock might have been comical. Except it was not. It was yet another reminder of how little they knew about each other.

"I guess I didn't mention that, huh," he said to her. "It's not a big deal, though."

"It's not a big deal?" she said. "That you live with—with the First Family?"

"I'm moving out, though. Into that house I rented."

Again, this was news to him. But hey, this was a surprise party for everyone, so to speak. So he might as well get in on the fun.

But yes, he thought. He was going to move out, and he was going to give the club over to Xhex. And then he had no idea what he was going to do with himself, other than the fact that he wanted to learn things. He wanted . . . textbooks to study, and tests to take, and things he had to focus on instead of what he had lost.

Surely school was like that? He'd never been to a formal one before. And he was smart. Anything he read he retained, and he liked words on paper. Hell, maybe he could take a page out of Gareth's proverbial book.

Whatever he decided to do, however, he knew it had to be a fresh start. A new life. A new . . . way of operating.

And hey, at least he wasn't suicidal. And with a niece on the way, a nice little house, and an open horizon? Things could be so much worse—

A nurse appeared in between the jambs. "Family, you're going to want to come into Larisse's room. Right now."

As the four of them jumped up, Trez took Therese's hand without thinking about it. But she was not going in there without him, that was for sure.

He was going to be by her side for what came next. God knew, he had plenty of experience with death.

CHAPTER TWENTY-SEVEN

Therese didn't remember much about the race to her *mahmen*'s patient room. But she knew she had Trez's hand, and was so grateful he was with her. Even though he was a new addition to her life, she needed his support. And he was there for her, their eyes meeting just as they ripped open the glass door and—

"Larisse?" her father cried.

Oh, God, she was—

Therese stopped dead such that her brother slammed into the back of her and nearly knocked her over. Except . . . wait, was she seeing this right? Were her *mahmen*'s eyes open?

"Larisse!" her father said as he threw himself down on the bedside. "My love!"

The nurse smiled. "Her vitals are stronger than they've been since she's come to us. She's back. And we're going to give her a little time, but if things stay like this, we'll try her breathing on her own."

Her father was whispering, and her *mahmen* was looking into the eyes of her *hellren*, the connection, the love between them, so tangible, it was as if there were another person in the room with everybody.

And then her *mahmen* searched out Therese.

Tears formed and rolled out onto the pillow, the frail hand lifting its fingertips from the white bed-sheet.

Therese surged forward, mirroring her father's sprawl. "I'm right here."

Those pale lips moved, but Therese sniffled and shook her head. "Don't try to speak. Not yet. Just know that we're all here, and we're not going any-where." She turned and motioned to her brother. As he came over, she smiled at her *mahmen*. "See? Everyone's here."

"*Mahmen*," Gareth said in a choked voice. "You're back."

"Wait, and there's one more." Therese reached out her hand. "Meet my . . . friend . . . Trez."

There was a pause, as Trez stared at them all from just inside the room. His face was remote, his eyes opaque, his body super still. For a split second, Therese had the sense he was going to leave. But then he pinned a smile to his face and stepped forward.

"Madam," he said, "it's my pleasure to meet you."

As he stood at the foot of the bed, his towering height and incredible strength seemed to dwarf the room.

Larisse lifted her hand again. And waved ever so slightly.

Therese wanted to hug Trez with all her might. Yes, this was a totally awkward situation—but he had more than risen to the occasion. As was his way, she was learning.

This is all going to be okay, she thought. *Absolutely okay.*

Strange . . . she didn't feel like she was reassuring herself just about her *mahmen* in that statement.

"Okay, folks," the nurse said. "We're going to do an examination on her, and I think some privacy is warranted."

Trez raised his hand. "I'll step out."

"I'll stay," Rosen said.

Gareth glanced around. "Would anyone be offended if I go back and eat? I'm starved."

Therese smiled, but felt like she had to force it as Trez stepped back. Even though he was still with them, she had the feeling he'd left.

"You can have my portion," she said to her brother. "I'm full."

"Good deal." Gareth patted their *mahmen*'s knee through the sheets. "I'll just be next door, *Mahmen*. And then I'll be back."

Larisse nodded ever so slightly.

"Me, too, *Mahmen*." Therese smiled and stroked Larisse's thin arm. "I'll be right back, too."

There was a quick discussion about the breathing tube—in which no promises were made, considering the workup hadn't been done yet—and then Therese walked out with Trez. There was a pause when he and Gareth said something back and forth, and that was when she learned Trez was leaving. Going back to town. But would be available by phone if anyone needed him. Numbers were exchanged between the males—at which point she made a joke about her being bad about answering messages about family crises.

"Too soon?" she said as her brother gave her a dry look.

Finally, she and Trez were alone.

"I'll walk you out?" she said.

"Just to the elevator. You're needed here."

When he offered her his arm, she took it with some relief, but she was pretty sure it was a reflexive gesture on his part. As they passed by the glass doors of the patient rooms, she did not look into any of them. She didn't want to be reminded of how easy it would be to lose the ground they'd so unexpectedly gained with her *mahmen*. And there were other things she didn't want to think about.

How ironic to get back her family and lose him in the same night.

"Trez?" she said as they passed by the nursing station and left the unit.

"Yes?"

They stopped and turned to each other at the same time. Abruptly, her heart skipped a couple of beats and her palms got sweaty.

"I know this is weird." She brushed her hair back and figured it was a mess. Or maybe it wasn't her hair that was tangled up and knotted. Maybe it was her brain. "I mean, this has gotten really intense, hasn't it. So it's got to be weird."

Please let it just be the drama-weird that's going on here, she thought.

"No, it's fine. I mean—" He shook his head. "It's great that your *mahmen* came back—"

"Where are you. And be honest. I'm too wrung out to sift through lies, even if they come from kindness."

Trez opened his mouth, like he was ready to go straight up platitude on her. But then he broke off and paced around. When the double doors of the unit broke open, she braced herself for the nurse coming back to get her with a report that things had been misinterpreted. Or that a crash cart was needed. But no. It was an orderly with a load of bed linens.

When he was out of range, Therese couldn't stand the waiting any longer. Her nerves were shot, she was exhausted, and all of iAm's amazing Italian food had formed a cement block spiced with oregano and basil in the pit of her stomach.

"I know I told you I was willing to be patient," she said. "But I think I may have overstated that virtue—"

Trez stopped abruptly and looked her right in the eye. "My *shellan* died. Badly. And like, recently. Very recently."

Therese exhaled the breath she had been holding. She didn't like the sad news, but she wasn't surprised, and at least this was nothing she needed to take personally.

"I'm so sorry." She nodded back at the doors. "So it must be really hard to see all that. Be around it—"

"Watching your father reunited with his beloved?" He held up a hand. "Not that I begrudge him her return. I hope your *mahmen* makes a full recovery. I really do. I totally do. But I didn't get that—and, listen, I didn't mean to lead you on. I really didn't."

Annnnnnnnd cue her not being able to breathe again. Which was what happened when you swerved off course into a tree. Him missing his *shellan* and being triggered by her *mahmen* and her father's tearful reunion at the bedside? That was tragic, but she could work with it. Talk to him. Help him in some way. "I didn't mean to lead you on," though? That was an exit sign over a doorway she was not going to be allowed to go through.

Trez shook his head slowly, regret tightening his features. But before he could go any further, she cut him off.

"It's okay. I know it's got to be . . . too soon," she heard herself say. "I understand."

Even though she didn't. Well, she did in the sense that a loss like that would make it impossible to fall in love with someone else for a while. A very long while. And who was she kidding? Love was what she wanted from him. Because it was what she had . . . for him.

Shit, she thought. She was in so much deeper than she'd been aware of.

How had she fallen in love with him over such a short time?

Trez came across and put his hands on her shoulders. His voice was low and intense, his black eyes grave, his muscular body still. "I don't want to hurt you. You have to know that. You have to believe it. I never meant . . . I don't want to hurt you."

So this is really happening, she thought. They were breaking up. Even though she wasn't sure exactly what they had to break up.

"I know you didn't do this on purpose, Trez." *You wanted to be independent, right?* she said to herself. "And . . . I'll be fine." She forced herself to smile tightly at him. "I'm totally going to be fine. I mean, I'll make sure of it. I have my family and—"

"I'm so sorry," he said as he brushed her face with his fingertip. "And I didn't want to do this here or now. I didn't."

She thought back to him weeping the night before and knew this made so much sense. All of that pain was still inside of him—locked down at the moment, but never far below the surface. It was going to be a long, long while before he was in any condition to love anybody, and she didn't question that he cared for her. He'd taken her hand as they'd rushed in to see her *mahmen*. And he had only ever tried to take care of her, with the house rental, with the financial arrangements, with . . . well, sexually, of course.

"I know you must still be in love with her," Therese whispered. "And I know she must have taken part of you with her unto the Fade. So this isn't . . . it's not about me. I mean . . ."

"No," he said. "It's not you. I swear to it."

＋ ＋ ＋

This is the right thing to do, Trez told himself.

In spite of the pain in Therese's eyes, the tension in her body, and the determined way she was keeping herself together . . . it was the right thing to do.

This was what iAm had warned him about. Therese was bearing the pain of something that should never have been started.

"You deserve," Trez said roughly, "to be loved for you, and you alone. Not because you're taking the place of someone else. Not because you're a tool for someone to try to save themselves with. This is all on me. Just because you looked like her, I should never—"

Therese frowned. "What?"

He tried to replay what had been coming out of his mouth, but he was caught up in his own emotions, so it was hard to recall. Instead, he just wanted to repair some of the damage he'd done—even though that was like trying to put a burned room back together with duct tape and twist ties.

"You're amazing," he said. "You're an incredible female who's beautiful and smart and funny—"

She stepped back. "No. About what I look like. What did you say?"

As he traced her face, her hair, her body, with his eyes, all he saw was Selena, and he allowed himself to linger on the comparison one last time. After this, it was unlikely he and Therese were going to see each other again because he knew, without asking, that she was going to go back with her family.

"You said I look like her," Therese repeated slowly. "But I don't just resemble her, do I."

When he didn't immediately answer, she crossed her arms over her chest. "I look exactly like her, don't I."

Taking a deep breath, he nodded once.

There was a long pause. And then she walked

off some distance down the corridor. As she strode away, he wondered if he shouldn't have lied about the appearance part. But that was a pussy move. She deserved the truth, and he deserved her anger.

Abruptly, she halted. Pivoted around to him. Came back.

"You said you lived with the King, right?" When he nodded again, she looked away. Looked back. "So the Black Dagger Brotherhood is his personal guard, correct. So that male I waited on—Rhage—with his *shellan*, they know you, right? Because they live there, too." He nodded again, aware of exactly where this was going. "So they knew her. Didn't they."

When he nodded once more, she started pacing again. "And that's why they did the double take when I went to wait on their table. And that's why your brother has always been weird around me. It's why the two of you fought last night—and it's why Xhex, your head of security at the club, also stared at me like that. They all saw it. They all saw what you did in me. Which was someone else."

"Yes," he said. "And I'm so sorry—"

She put her hand up. "Stop. Just . . . stop with that right now."

"I didn't mean—"

Jacking forward on her hips, she narrowed her eyes

on him. "You didn't *mean* to use me? Explain to me exactly how that argument works. How you somehow didn't intend to substitute me for your dead mate when I apparently look like the female. Explain to me how, when you were fucking me, you didn't think of her the whole time." When he went to say something, she talked right over him. "What you really need to tell me is how the hell you didn't call me by her—"

Therese stopped. Then massaged her temples like she had a headache. "You never used my name, actually. Did you. You never said my name when we were intimate. God, I didn't even see it. I didn't even—the feeding." As the color ran out of her face and she covered her mouth like she was sick to her stomach, he felt like he'd been kneed in the balls. "You didn't take my vein, even though you were starved, because you didn't want to know my blood tasted different. You didn't want anything to break the fantasy, to remind you I wasn't her."

As Trez watched the depth of his betrayal sink in for her, he wanted to take it all back. The whole thing, from that first night when he had tried to get her to take him to Havers to what they had done in the passageway at the club to everything that had happened at the little house. He wanted to spare her everything she was feeling now.

But to do that, he would have had to have listened to his brother's advice.

The reality of how wrong Trez had been, for some very right reasons, was a new low for him. And considering where he had started out from? That was saying something.

Therese took a deep breath. "I need to go now. And I need you to never seek me out again. Tell your brother I'm quitting without notice—something tells me he's going to understand exactly why—"

"Therese—"

"No!" she barked as she stamped her foot.

Then she clapped her hand over her mouth again as if she were stopping herself from either a rant or a crying jag. Or maybe both.

"Just go," she choked out. "I've fallen down a deep hole and I've got to start getting out of it right now—"

"I wish I—"

"No," she countered, "you don't get to wish anything. You knew what you were doing. You knew *exactly* what you were doing to me. I don't give a shit whether you're grieving or not. It was wrong. This whole . . . thing was wrong." Except then she laughed harshly. "But hey, it's also on me. I didn't question anything. I didn't ask why you were pursuing me. I didn't protect myself. And we never talked about ground rules, or whether we were in a relationship or—for fuck's sake, we had sex a couple of times. That was it. So I need to grow the hell up."

She said all that like she was trying to remind herself of the facts. Like she was reframing things—or trying to.

"I'm so sorry," he whispered.

"Okay, you can go screw yourself with that," she snapped at him. "It's way too late for apologies. And will you please leave? For crissakes, the only reason why you're standing here is because you don't want to say goodbye to someone who isn't me anyway. You've done enough damage. At least have the decency to let the cleanup begin. Don't ever contact me again."

Trez nodded, turned away, and walked down the corridor. He had no idea where he was going. But that had been true for quite a while now.

The only thing he was certain of was that he had hurt someone he honestly did care about, and the pain he was leaving behind was all his fault. As she had said, no matter what his intentions had been, or what state he'd been in, it had been wrong.

This was an all-new low. And the only good piece to it all? At least he wasn't suicidal.

Nope. He was not going to let himself get off easy. Selena's death and the grief that came along with it was nothing he had created by his own actions. But his regret over what he'd done to Therese? That was completely on him, and he was going to have to live with it for the rest of his nights.

However many there were. This was his punishment.

A life sentence he was not going to easy-way-out with a dirt nap. Or a watery grave—

As his phone rang, he grabbed for the cell, some stupid idea that it could be Therese calling making him desperate. But she didn't have his number in her old phone.

And she was not going to call him. Ever again.

It was Xhex. No doubt she had seen that he'd phoned and was hitting him back.

He didn't answer. He had nothing to say to anybody at the moment.

God . . . this was just as bad as when Selena had died, he thought.

Maybe even worse.

CHAPTER TWENTY-EIGHT

The next twenty-four hours in the ICU were a blessing. And a curse.

The following evening, as Therese walked into her *mahmen*'s patient room with a Styrofoam mug of surprisingly good coffee, she held on to the former and tried to let go of the latter. And wasn't sure how well she did with either of those goals.

Ever since Trez had walked away when she'd told him to, she'd been in a cold meat locker, numb and removed from everyone. Because, hey, it wasn't like she wanted to be the dimmer switch on everyone's tentative relief at Larisse's recovery—and for another, the relationship blowing up was nothing she had any interest in explaining.

She felt so stupid for rushing blindly into something like that. It had all felt so good, though. And he had been so—

Stop it, she told herself.

Focusing on the hospital bed, she pinned on a smile. "Good evening, *Mahmen*—"

"Good. Evening."

Therese stopped right where she was. Blinked a number of times. Tried to process what she was looking at. But sometimes, in the four hours since she, Gareth, and their father had left to catch some sleep in one of the facility's family apartments, a big change had come about.

"*Mahmen? Mahmen!*"

Therese rushed forward, spilling the coffee on the back of her hand and not caring. Larisse was sitting up, fully conscious . . . and breathing on her own.

"*Mahmen!*" Therese ditched the flimsy container on a rolling table, clasped the hand she had been holding for so many hours—and was surprised to feel it clasp back. "I knew they were going to take the tube out—but they did it early?"

"Yes." That voice was raspy, but it was wonderfully familiar. "Early."

"How are you feeling? Are you okay?" As soon as she asked the questions, she shook her head. Her *mahmen* was still so weak, she could barely lift her head off the pillow. "Wait, don't strain yourself answering—"

"Good. Good. Hi . . . hello. I love you. Back. Glad." Larisse was talking fast, as if she felt the need to get it all out fast. Just in case. "And I'm so sorry. I'm so very, very sorry—"

"Shhh. It's okay." Brushing her *mahmen*'s hair back, Therese lowered herself into the chair that had become her second home. "Let's just sit together."

"Dad . . . vein."

"You took his vein? When?"

"Nurse went to get him after tube out. Stronger now."

Therese smiled slowly. Her father must have left and then come back in while she and her brother were sleeping. "Good."

They fell silent for a while. And then her *mahmen* seemed to push herself up higher on the pillows—or tried to.

"Here, let me help," Therese said as she carefully rearranged her *mahmen*'s torso. "Better—"

Her *mahmen*'s hand squeezed hard. "Listen. Now. In case . . ."

"Don't say it. You're going to be fine. You're going to come out of this—"

"Always felt . . . you were mine. Always felt . . ." Her *mahmen* touched the center of her thin chest over the hospital gown. "In my heart, mine. That's why . . . never told you . . . never thought you hadn't been destined to be . . . mine."

Therese blinked. And swallowed hard. "Oh . . . *Mahmen*."

"You were left . . . doorstep. Delivered . . . no idea . . . who? How?" Her *mahmen* pointed to herself. "Wanted daughter. Prayed . . . prayed . . . prayed . . . then? Answered."

"*Mahmen*, don't use all your strength—"

"Paperwork to protect. You. Me. Your father and brother. Make sure no one could take . . . my young away."

As tears came to her eyes, Therese made soothing noises and stroked the hand that was gripping her own with such urgency. "It's okay, *Mahmen*. Take a deep breath."

She glanced up at the monitors. Things were changing on the screens. Heart rate up. Blood pressure up. She had no idea whether that was bad or good. At least there were no alarms?

"I'm right here," Therese said. "And I'm going nowhere. No one is going to separate us."

Even herself, she tacked on in her mind.

"Yes?" her *mahmen* said.

"Yes. I promise. I love you, and I wish . . . well, I wish a lot of things. But we're back together now. All four of us."

The idea that there wasn't a fifth made her sad—even though Trez hadn't been a member of the family, hadn't been around for long, had played her. And the mourning of him was frustrating as hell. But emotions weren't reasonable and couldn't be reasoned with.

"Come home?" her *mahmen* asked.

"Yes, I will. Absolutely." At this point, she was dying to get out of Caldwell. "But Dad said you didn't go down south. Maybe that's where we should head? Gareth can do his schooling from anywhere, he was saying."

"Good."

The tension eased out of her *mahmen*, and for a moment, Therese panicked that it was death that was making her go lax. But then no. It was peace.

"Sleep, *Mahmen*. You just rest. We're all here."

Sitting back, Therese watched over her *mah-*

men, another monitor working in concert with, but without the specificity of, the other machines in the room.

A young left on a doorstep? Really? At a regular family's home? She believed her *mahmen*, and Larisse certainly seemed clear on how it had all gone down. But jeez, it was like the storyline from a bad after-school special. How did something like that happen?

Time passed, again in that weird way it seemed to down here in the ICU. But maybe it was true all over the hospital. And her brother and father returned. And hugs were shared before Larisse took a nap. As she slept, everyone talked quietly, and Therese wanted to double-check the story, but not in front of her *mahmen*. That seemed disrespectful. Doubtful.

And the truth was, the details didn't matter. Just like shared blood didn't matter.

Family was so much more than DNA.

Eventually, Therese's strength lagged and she realized it had been a while since she had had anything more than fitful rest. With her lids drifting down, and her body jerking itself back awake, she was on the verge of—

"Honey?" her father said.

Therese shot up right. "*Mahmen*! Is she—"

"She's just fine." Rosen smiled down at her and put his hand on her shoulder. "You, however, need some real sleep. Why don't you go home for some rest and come back before dawn? Or you can stay in the apartment they gave us here?"

She hadn't yet told them about the rooming house, and now that she was leaving with them, she didn't feel the need to go into the details about that dump. And the idea that she could go there, grab some clothes, and then crash back here really appealed.

"You could ask Trez to give you a ride if—"

"No, Dad," she rushed in. "I don't want to bother him. I'll just get fresh clothes at my apartment and come back fast."

"There's no hurry. You have your phone. If something happens, we'll call—but things are really looking up."

Gareth nodded from his chair. "Yeah, you need some shut-eye."

"I'll snag my toothbrush and return right away."

Her father patted her shoulder. "Don't hurry. I think we've got a lot of time ahead of us now."

"Me, too."

Therese got to her feet. Hugged everyone goodbye and pulled on her coat, which she'd left on the floor in the corner. In a daze, she walked out of the patient room, and the unit . . . and then, after a brief elevator ride, out of a kiosk into the forest. It was bitterly cold, and she huddled into her parka. Before she dematerialized out, however, and in spite of the shock of the winter air on her warm cheeks, she paused and stared up at the sky.

The forest was sleeping around her. The world seemed in repose as well. No sounds of deer mincing over snow-sprinkled brush. No squirrels scrambling up trunks. No birds in flight, seeking far-between and forgotten nuts. Not even a breeze, as if the wind, too, were exhausted from previous efforts.

Silence. Stillness.

Like space.

Standing by herself, she felt alone, and not in the sense that she could not find a crowd of people in which to lose herself. And this specific sort of isolation made her reflect on how, no matter how many hearts had been broken in the great passage of time, when it was your own, it was the first time it had ever happened.

Why, she thought at the heavens.

Except as she asked the question without speaking a word, she wasn't sure exactly what "why" she was after. Why she had met Trez? Why she had happened to look like his mate? Why he had fallen into a whirlwind romance with her?

Well, she knew the answer to that last one. That, at least, was no mystery.

And as she considered the ins and outs of it all, as she replayed his kisses, his touches . . . the sex they had had . . . she came to understand the true nature of her pain. It wasn't that Trez had fucked her over on purpose. He wasn't some bastard like that. She had seen the regret on his face when everything had come out, and it had been an honest emotion—not that it had done anything to make her feel better in the moment.

It did keep her from hating him now, however.

No, it was more that she hadn't been the one to be loved like that. She hadn't been chosen by him. She had just been a vessel, nothing but a shell. A replacement vase swapped for the one that had been broken.

The sad truth was that she'd been bypassed even as they had been together, face-to-face, skin-to-skin. Invisible, though he saw her. Ether, even as he touched her body.

The pain was because she had felt found, when in actuality she had been nullified.

This was going to hurt for a while. It was also going to color how she saw males. How she interacted with them. How she did—or, more likely, did not—trust them.

It seemed the height of irony to be devastated

by the death of someone she did not know and had never met. Yet the loss of Trez's *shellan* had impacted her. Permanently.

Closing her eyes, Therese breathed the cold night air and calmed herself. She wasn't sure it was going to work, and she decided if she couldn't concentrate properly, she would just go back to the clinic and hang out there.

The next time she looked around, she was standing in the middle of her apartment.

Staring at the crappy furniture, she took another deep breath, and instead of clear Canadian air that was blowing in from the north . . . she smelled the complex bouquet of nose-death that seemed to emanate from the walls and floors of the flat.

Like everything had been sprayed down with Eau de Crime Scene.

Fates, she just wanted to go back to the ICU. And who'd have thought that would ever be a thing?

Still, instead of quickly gathering what she needed and getting the hell out of there, she walked around the empty space, her mind going places she'd rather it wouldn't while her body went in circles in a place she didn't want to be. But see, this was the problem with alone time—and the other reason that made her want to get back to her family.

Okay, she needed to get moving. Grab her toothbrush and an over-day bag. Return to where people she could trust were waiting for her.

Heading into the bathroom, she—

Stopped in front of the mirror over the sink.

Leaning into the glass, she stared at her reflection, and not because she had forgotten what she looked like. Instead, she was mining what was staring back at her for information about Trez's mate . . . as if the composite of her own eyes and nose, mouth and chin would tell her anything at all about what he had shared with his *shellan*, how much they had loved, how hard it had been for them to be parted by destiny.

But of course, there was nothing to be gleaned. And that was the point, wasn't it.

She had not been who he had thought she was, and that truth had come out as soon as he had met her parents and her brother. After that, there was no more pretending, no way of making the disjointed reality fit with his grief-relief fantasy.

And speaking of fantasies? She had no idea why she had convinced herself he was her shadow lover. In that regard, she supposed she had done a bit of the same to him. Not that the implications were in any way comparable. Besides, she had probably made all that up. Seduced by the sex, her brain had created a connection between him and her dreams.

After all, she'd had the best sex of her life with him—so she'd put it in the only context that had fit. Her shadow mate.

Man, it would be so much easier if she could just hate him, she thought as she looked away from herself.

As she reemerged with her toothbrush and her toothpaste—because she didn't want to linger in front of the mirror even long enough to use them—her keen vampire ears picked up on an argument across the hall. And then there were the two TVs on either side of her with their sound turned up high.

So it was business as usual in the rooming house.

Taking out her old phone, she triggered the screen and stared at the notifications. There was one from her brother. A random meme. It was funny. Another from her dad, reminding her to take it slow. Two from cousins who had heard about what was going on and had ascribed Therese's radio silence to worry over her parents. Which had been partially true—

The argument across the hall transitioned up a level, the voices, a man's and a woman's, increasing in volume, rising to the level of yelling. As Therese went over and grabbed a change of clothes from the duffel bag that served as her bureau, she knew that the banging and the crashing were going to start next. That was the way things seemed to go, no matter whether it was a couple, a set of roommates, or an entire floor. A lot of it was the drinking and the drugs, the desperation of so many shattered lives being burned off in any direction that was presented.

In that regard, she was no different from the others. In spite of everything, she was utterly depressed at the idea of never seeing Trez again—

As the smell of burning food reached her nose, she told herself to get with the program. She didn't belong here—and she didn't belong in Caldwell, either.

So screw just packing up for an over-day. She needed to get all her stuff and move the hell out. Right now.

◆ ◆ ◆

Trez's head blew up about two hours before shAdoWs's closing.

Which, considering the stress he was under and his history of migraines, was pretty much inevitable.

Unable to stay up in his office alone, because all he'd done was mentally beat the crap out of himself, he'd gone down to the dance floor and stuck to the periphery, watching the humans grind on each other, and wishing . . . well, wishing all kinds of shit that wasn't going to happen. He'd also been thinking about Therese. He couldn't get her out of his mind, it seemed, although he was going to have to get over that. She didn't want to ever see him again, and he did not blame her.

Standing in the lasers, squinting in the darkness, he hadn't envied the lost souls before him. So many of the men and women were regulars who routinely got drunk and drugged up and made bad choices, and you didn't do that if you had your shit together. You did that because you were running from something even as you stayed in one place, the toxic swill trapped inside your skin too much for you to handle, the outlet and distraction of the clubbing a Band-Aid made out of arsenic.

But at least they were getting a break from their problems, he supposed.

It was just as this thought was occurring to him that he abruptly noticed that the lasers had changed from piercing purple beams to multicolored sparkles. As he wondered who had ordered the new light show, and what kind of equipment must have been brought in without his approval, he realized that he was only seeing the fireworks in his right eye.

An aura. He was having an aura.

"Mother*fucker*."

Glancing around, he motioned to one of the security staff. As the guy came over, Trez said, "I've gotta go crash upstairs. Tell Alex to close up tonight."

"You okay, Mr. Latimer?" the human asked. "You don't look so good."

"Migraine. It happens."

"My sister gets 'em. I'll tell the boss. You need anything?"

Trez shook his head. "Thanks, man. Just gonna go lie down."

"Okay, Mr. Latimer."

As Trez walked over to the stairs to the second floor, he was grateful for the twenty-minute, quiet-before-the-storm part of the headaches. After the light show started, he had just enough time to get himself situated somewhere dark and quiet before the pain came. Of course, since he knew what was coming, his heart always pounded with adrenaline overload, his body's flight-or-fight response having no real options for expression.

There was nothing to fight, and as for the run-away side of things? Since everywhere you went, there you were, it wasn't like that was going to help.

Plus, hello, he was going to be throwing up soon, and a brisk jog was not going to be fun with that symptom.

Back up in his office, it was a relief to get out of the

paths of all those lasers and away from the pounding music. He didn't waste time as he shut himself in. Kicking his shoes off, he shucked out of his slacks, and got the little trash can from the bathroom. Stretching out on his leather sofa, he propped his head up with a throw pillow, crossed his ankles, and put his hands over his chest like he was a corpse. He could still see the aura even after he closed his eyes, and he watched it transition from a spot to a less-than sign . . . after which the bifurcated, sparkling angles flattened out and moved off to the side before disappearing.

Maybe this time the headache wouldn't hit. The nausea wouldn't cripple him. The floaty disassociation wouldn't pull him away.

In the eerie no-man's-land between the prodromal and the party time, an image came to him. It was of Therese looking up at him in the hospital corridor, anger and hurt darkening her pale eyes.

He had a feeling that memory of her was going to haunt him like a ghost. But before he could dwell on that, a thunderclap of pain lit off in one half of his skull, and—

As he wrenched to the side, and started to throw up that snack he'd had an hour ago, he decided he deserved this.

On so many levels.

CHAPTER TWENTY-NINE

It was hard to know exactly how long it took Therese to realize something was wrong in her apartment building—and not just minorly wrong. Eventually, though, she stopped shoving things in her duffel bag and frowned. Sniffed the air. Looked to the door to the outside hall.

For a moment, she wondered if she hadn't lost her mind . . . if maybe her lack of sleep wasn't causing olfactory hallucinations. But after having been at the rooming house for so long, she was well familiar with all kinds of food smells, whether they be rot or a case of over-roasting. And this was different. This was . . . not food.

Going over to her door, she put her hand on the panels, even as she felt like a paranoid fool. Just because part of her life was melting down, and she was taking her doomed romance far too seriously, did not meant her building was doing the same—and what do you know, the flimsy wood was room temperature under her palm. It was fine.

"Come on, now," she muttered to herself. "You're losing it."

A fresh round of shouting across the hall made her refocus and breathe in through her nose again. The strange odor was stronger, and there was a sweet undertone to it, something—

Alarms began to go off, the shrill sounds firing from both ends of the outer corridor. Alarmed—natch—Therese opened things and leaned out. Across the way, black smoke was seeping from the gaps around a closed door.

"What's going on?" someone said.

Therese looked to the right. A woman with a lit cigarette and sleep in her eyes had come out of the apartment next to the smoke.

"I don't know," Therese answered.

All around, other tenants emerged from their units, many of them similarly confused, although whether that was from a disturbance in sleep or an inconclusive assessment as to whether this was real or a drug-induced hallucination, Therese did not know.

"Has someone called nine-one-one?" she asked.

Without warning, an explosion blew open the door across the hall, the impact of the shock waves pitching Therese off her feet and throwing her back into her flat. As she landed, her breath was knocked out of her lungs, but she stayed conscious.

So she saw the fireball that expanded like a great beast, its breadth extending down the corridor in both directions.

And bursting into her apartment.

◆ ◆ ◆

From the depths of Trez's painful delirium, his brain coughed up a memory that made the agony of the migraine seem like a paper cut. He was back to the night he had sent Selena's remains unto the sky, her physical body set ablaze on the funeral pyre that had been built by his community of friends. He was standing as close as he could get to the flames, the heat so great that the skin on his face tightened and the front of his body roasted to the point of cracking. The blaze, which had caught quickly, burned brightly in the dense darkness of the night, the white smoke curling into the heavens—

It was as he brushed at his eyes to clear the tears of his soul that he realized . . . this wasn't a memory.

He was present at the actual scene, returned to the past through some kind of alchemy—no, not magic. This was a dream. This was one of those dreams when you found consciousness within your mind's subconscious, freedom of choice seeming to present itself in a reality that wasn't real except for the way it felt.

Why couldn't he have gone back to a happy time? To when he had rented out Storytown just for him and his queen, when they had danced between the headlights of his car, when he had been able to hold her against him once more?

If he could pretend to be in any scene from their relationship, pretend to feel anything, see anything, be anything, why was it the heat of Selena's funeral pyre upon his aching body, the sight of her remains being consumed, the mourning cranked up to an acute suffering that took his breath away?

Was this never going to end, this cycle of sadness, loss and pain.

Trez stared at the curling orange and yellow fire, the pyrotechnic monster devouring the food it was provided, the wood, the body, breaking down, becom-

ing the smoke that rose and the ashes that fell. And as the consumption continued, rage and anger became a blaze within his own body, burning him, destroying him, as his beloved was likewise alit, the two of them united for this one last time, both of them in flames.

Unable to hold the emotion in, he started to scream, an explosion of sound propelled out of his lungs by the constriction of his rib cage, the force so great he felt the veins in his neck and his forehead bulge, his arms and his shoulders turn into cords of twisted steel, his legs threaten to propel him into the pyre. He screamed until he was out of oxygen, and then he dragged in the night air. As soon as he had breath in his lungs, he screamed again. And again. And again—

It was during an inhale that he sensed a figure standing off to the side, and he wheeled around, panting. When he recognized who it was, he was confused.

"Lassiter?" he said hoarsely.

The angel's body was nothing but an outline, only the glimmering wings that rose over his torso seeming to have weight and substance. As wind came up from all four directions, ghostly tendrils of the male's blond and black hair swirled around.

Catching his breath, Trez wiped his mouth. "What do you want? Why are you here?"

The angel didn't answer. Didn't seem to hear him. Lassiter was focused on the pyre, a holy silver light radiating out of his eye sockets.

A feeling of disassociation compelled Trez's own stare back to the roiling flames and his heart began to pound. The strange wind that swirled around the blaze changed the pattern of the fire, the flashes of yellow and orange coalescing—

From out of the pyre's pulsing heat and flaring light, Selena's white-wrapped body rose, the resurrection happening with an inexorable elevation that had Trez trembling from fear and love combined. This wasn't right. This dream . . .

It wasn't a dream, either.

He didn't know what this was—but he didn't care.

Selena was risen from both the cold embrace of death and the inferno of the funeral pyre, her arms lifting from out of the wraps he himself had wound round her lifeless body, her torso straightening, her legs standing strong. And now came her hair, the long, dark locks spooling free of the confines that abruptly loosened and fell away into the inferno beneath her feet, revealing her face and her shoulders.

She was of flesh and flame combined, an apparition that called to him without saying his name, that captured him without chains or bars, that held him without laying a hand upon him.

"Selena?" he said desperately. "Selena . . ."

In the midst of the violent glow, he could see that her mouth was moving. She was speaking to him.

"I can't hear you," he called out. "What are you saying?"

In a panic, he tried to close the distance, but the heat was too great, a barrier even his love and need for her could not help him cross.

"What are you saying?" he yelled again.

When he couldn't hear her, he turned to Lassiter, but the angel was gone. Maybe he'd never been?

Wheeling back toward the blaze, Trez was terrified Selena, too, might have disappeared. But no, she was there, still yelling for him, still trying to get her message across the pyre and through the strange wind, her growing frustration and fear killing him.

Just as he had the thought that he would jump in there with her and join her in the flames, even if he was destroyed, she stopped, crouched, and held her arms up as if to protect herself from something that was falling on her. Then the funeral pyre seemed to explode, sparks and heat pushing out at him so that he had to cover his head and bow away also, even with his desire to get in there with her—

Trez jerked upright with a strangled cry, sure as if

his physical form had to be ripped free of whatever thrall had captured him.

Covered with sweat, panting like he'd run for his life, lost in the dreamscape he'd been in, he looked around and tried to ground himself.

His office. At the club. Except there was no noise down below, no thumping of music that would indicate things were still open, no smattering of talk that would tell him it was just after closing and the staff were—

His keen hearing, made even more sensitive because of the headache, picked up the howl of sirens outside of the club, and it was the distant, quiet persistence of them that made him realize that everything at shAdoWs had been wrapped up for the evening and the staff had gone home.

What the hell time was it, anyway?

Getting to his feet made him aware that he still had the headache, but considering the sharpshooter behind his sternum, that ouch in his gray matter was a drop in the fucking bucket. His phone was facedown on his desk, and he picked it up, hoping for . . .

But of course Therese hadn't called.

Why would she?

As more sirens sounded out, from a different quadrant of the city than the first set, he entered his password and went into the call section. You know, just in case—

All at once, the image of Selena yelling out for him from the pyre, and then crouching down to protect herself, took over everything.

Like a movie inserted into his conscious mind, it was all he could see, and all he could smell, too, the stench of burning wood flooding into his nasal passages until he sneezed as if it were real.

"Fucking migraines."

The headaches had made him go weird places in his mind on occasion, and olfactory hallucinations were not uncommon, although, from what Doc Jane had told him, they were usually prodromals rather than active symptoms of the neurological event. She'd even said that some people smelled bananas or citrus instead of experiencing an aura.

Who fucking cared.

As still another round of sirens lit off and streaked right by the front of the club, he put his phone down and went back to the couch.

Must be some fucking fire somewhere in the city tonight, he thought as he lay back down and closed his aching eyes.

All those fire trucks, from different districts.

It sounded like a whole city block was on fire.

CHAPTER THIRTY

As Therese lifted her head, flames were everywhere around her, the explosion's incandescent core having retreated from its advance, leaving greedy subsidiaries in its wake. Part of her wall was fire. The rug was smoking. Molding at the ceiling was curling with flames. But none of that compared to the origin of the blast.

That apartment across the hall was engulfed with deadly fire.

Dizzy and disoriented, she sat up and was aware of a ringing in her ears—unless it was the fire alarms? What had happened? What had exploded?

Who cared, she had to get out—

Across the corridor, something emerged from the source of the blaze. It was on fire. It walked and swung its arms, but it was made of fire. And it was screaming as it fell to its knees and landed facedown on the worn carpet.

"No!" Therese yelled as she jumped to her feet.

Her first thought was to help whoever it was, but then the heat registered properly, her higher verticality bringing her into a force field of intense hot air that was thickening with toxic smoke. Coughing and covering her mouth, she couldn't imagine how that person was suffering and she had to do something. Bending down and looking around, she knew the slipcover on her sofa was her best bet, and ill-fitting as it was, the heavy fabric came off the ratty superstructure underneath without much effort. Dragging it out into the hall, Therese covered what turned out to be a writhing woman—and desperately tried to ignore the smell of cooking meat as she stayed in a crouch and attempted to get the flames to die.

"Help!" Therese yelled out through the heat and the smoke. "I need help!"

No one was paying any attention to her. Like rats escaping floodwaters, humans were pouring out of their apartments, all but trampling the burning woman in their rush to get to the stairwells.

Except there was no chance to save the woman, anyway. Death claimed her, the body beneath the slipcover falling still—

A creak directly overhead made Therese look up. Flames were licking out of the doorway in front of her and clawing at the corridor's ceiling, eating away at the plaster and the studs beneath, the heat doubling and tripling; the more the fire consumed, the more powerful it became.

Just as she started to back away, something let loose and swung free, coming at her. Raising her arm to protect her head, she reared back from the origin of the blast, but she didn't get far with that. She bumped into something, someone, and couldn't get out of range. The flaming weight hit her hard, crushing her to the floor by the body that was under the slipcover, still alit, still smoking.

Dazed, Therese's sense of survival took over as her brain faltered, her arms shoving her out from under, fast as a blink. Damage had been done, however. Her back was stinging, and one shoulder refused to move. Frightened, she half-dragged, half-crawled back toward her apartment door. Phone.

She needed to get to her phone. She had to call her brother. He would help her—

A second explosion came from somewhere else. Maybe it was the original apartment, maybe it was another one—but it was definitely behind her instead of ahead of her.

No time for phone. No time for purse.

She had to get out of here if she was going to live. The pain in her back and the panic of the situation meant dematerializing was out of the question, but she could damn well use her legs. Planting her hand on the wall, she hauled herself to her feet and started to run—but she didn't make much progress at all. She stumbled, landing badly on her knee. When she tried to get up again, she couldn't understand why her balance was off—

It wasn't her balance. Her ankle on the left side was unable to bear her weight.

She was going to have to use the wall to steady herself.

As she pulled herself back up, she took a hit from behind, somebody banging into her and sending her to the rug again, before another fleeing human stepped on her bad arm. Yelling out in pain, she curled in a ball, protecting her head and her torso, bracing herself for more impacts from some kind of stampede. When none came, she risked a glance around.

Smoke had filled the hallway and was crowding out the usable oxygen, the deadly level descending fast, leaving only a couple of feet of visibility.

Yanking up the front of her shirt, Therese covered her nose and mouth and started to crawl, but that proved to be inefficient. She needed both hands, and that shoulder was a problem. Dropping the hem, she moved as fast as she could, keeping her head down and trying to control her breathing. The noxious chemical swirl above her made her cough and her eyes watered so badly it was as if she were crying, but she wasn't.

Shock. She was in shock.

Totally disorientated, she was grateful for the worn pattern of the runner. She knew if she followed it, she would get to the staircase eventually—

She came up to the first body some thirty feet later. It was that of a man, and his clothes had been burned off his back and legs, his skin charred, the smell the kind of thing that made her want to vomit. He was facedown and not moving, and as she came up to his head, she looked into his wide-open eyes. They were fixed and dilated, unblinking because they were lidless, and his mouth was open, the lips peeled off yellowed teeth from the pain.

With a strangled sound, Therese kept going, especially as a fresh rumble vibrated up through the floor and made her terrified the whole building was collapsing. Faster, she tried to go faster. But it was not fast enough. As the smoke continued to get lower and lower, she lost visibility, only her elbow on the wall leading her at all, and soon her lungs started to burn so badly, she was coughing more than she was inhaling.

More rumbling. Someone screaming. Another body she had to crawl over.

All she knew was that she had to keep going or she was going to die.

◆ ◆ ◆

Back at shAdoWs, Trez sat up on his sofa and looked to the observation wall behind his desk with a frown. Something was tapping on the glass, the knocking sound repetitive, insistent. Annoying as fuck in the quiet.

Getting up, he walked over and turned on the lights down below from the control panel by his office phone. One by one, the banks of fluorescent lights made noontime out of the club's darkness, the black dance floor with all its scuffs and stains illuminated with the kind of clarity that did its wear and tear no good whatsoever.

No one was down below. Nobody hovering in front of the glass.

And it was too soon for the housekeeping staff to come in. Besides, humans couldn't levitate without wires.

What the hell had he been hearing?

Under his skin, something was itching at him, and he ran his blunt nails up and down the backs of his arms. An unbearable sense of restless adrenaline flooded his veins, and without a lot of options, he walked back over to his bathroom. Inside the black marble jewel box of a loo, he ran the water and kept it cold, splashing his face. As he straightened and turned to the black hand towel, he looked through the water dripping into his eyes at the blinds that covered the tall, narrow window. Wiping his face with one hand, he used the other to twist the rod.

The view that was exposed between the tilting slats was of the long-and-low rooftops of the buildings between him and the river. Beyond them was that water. That icy, sluggish water that had previously called his name, but which was now silent—

Trez frowned.

The amount of smoke drifting across the Hudson and tangling in one of the span bridges' arches was enough to obscure the far side.

Huge amount of smoke. Billows of it.

Trez's brain was not working very well, the migraine dulling him up, that horrible disturbing dream making things even slower. And that was what made the lickety-split conclusion he came to as to the source both impossible and arguably irrational.

But it was just . . . if he triangulated the direction from which the wind was taking all that smoke, and the sound of the sirens that were still calling out into the night, and the glow off in the distance . . . there was only one place the fire could be.

No, that can't be right, he told himself. *It can't be Therese's rooming house.*

Okay, it could be, but there were dozens of buildings, large and small, between him and her. It could be any one of them—

She was there. He could sense her.

Because she had taken his vein, he knew exactly where she was . . . and she was in that building.

But was she in a fire?

Trez's heart rate tripled, another conclusion reached with the kind of certainty that facts did not support and his instincts could not deny. Closing his eyes, he dematerialized through a seam in the panes of glass, traveling through the cold night air across many, many roofs, passing by many, many buildings, flying over many, many streets.

He re-formed in the freezing wind on the roof of an apartment building directly in front of the blaze, and what his eyes focused on took his breath away. It was her rooming house. It was the three floors in the middle. It was on the side that Therese's flat was located on.

And she was in there. Goddamn it . . . he could sense her.

For a split second, his mind spun out of control, his senses over-heightened by urgency and panic, his body braced to pounce, his blood racing. There was just too much to assess: the ten fire trucks that were parked around the inferno, the arcs of water being trained by human firemen onto the blaze, the ambulances arriving, the crowd gathering in the cold and husbanded by cops.

But he couldn't afford to be scattered.

Scanning the front of the rooming house, he saw people streaming out of an exit at street level on the far side of the building. She was not among them, and he knew this without being able to see faces or bodies clearly.

No, he knew where she was. And her location terrified him.

Closing his eyes, he forced himself to calm down and then ghosted forward, entering the building through the last set of blown-out windows on the left-hand corner on the third floor. It was an incredibly stupid and dangerous thing to do, given that he could have killed himself if he'd re-formed in the middle of a bed or a sofa. But he lucked out. He was dead center in a shallow living room with an open door, the tenant having clearly escaped the apartment.

Not that he could see much of anything.

The smoke was so thick he had to bend down, and as he headed for the open doorway, he grabbed what turned out to be a baseball shirt to cover his nose and mouth. Its smell of marijuana, embedded in the synthetic fibers, was quickly eclipsed by the stench of melted plastic and steaming metal, and goddamn it was hot. He was sweating already, and all he had on was his silk shirt.

Out in the hall, he looked both ways and saw fuck all. The smoke was down to the floor and coming in waves, the heat wafting it to and fro.

She was close by. He could sense her. But he couldn't see a fucking thing.

"Therese," he called out.

If he could sense her, she had to be alive. She just . . . had to be.

The water from the hoses of the firemen was pounding on the outsides of the building, creating a din that was impossible to hear through, and that was before you added in the alarms that were going off throughout this floor as well as the ones above and below. And the fire itself was loud, the crackling and hissing, the hot breath of the flames forming a background noise level that was going to drown out his voice.

"Therese!" he yelled anyway. "Therese!"

In the back of his mind, he knew no one could survive in this hallway, not without protective gear and a breathing apparatus—and even with that kind of equipment, it was going to be dangerous.

"Therese!"

The heat was all around, even though the fire was still ahead of him, his body flushing, sweat breaking out across his chest, under his arms, down his back. As the skin on his face tightened, he thought of the funeral pyre. Of the dream that had woken him up.

This was the sensation he had. Exactly the sensation he'd had.

As he forced his way forward, his mind played tricks on him. Sometimes what was ahead was the fire in the rooming house. Sometimes it was the fire Selena was calling him from.

Either way, he had the bizarre sense that he was trying to save both of his females.

CHAPTER THIRTY-ONE

Therese had known heat before: Steamy August nights when there hadn't been any air-conditioning or breeze in her parents' house. Fevers from the occasional virus to which vampires were susceptible. Hearths that were over-enthusiastic, and also the hot flashes associated with her needing.

Nothing came close to this.

As she lay facedown on the hallway's worn runner, her hands cupped around her mouth and nose, her head tucked in against her collarbones, her breathing labored and wheezy in between coughing spells, she felt like she was in an oven. There was no sweating, even. That had stopped a while ago. She was crisping on the outside, her skin crackling up . . . her muscles cooking on the inside.

This is how I die? she kept thinking. *This is it?*

In Caldwell, in a shitty rooming house, on a cold night in December, in a fire?

Determined not to have that fate be what separated her from her family, from her life, from the future years that she felt like she deserved, Therese got herself moving again. But the momentum didn't last long, and she didn't make it far. She was running out of strength, and her thinking was getting muddled—

-ese! Therese!

The sound of her name, repeated over and over above the fire's beastly temper, had her lifting her head. Except how could she be hearing this? Who would be here for her? It must be a hallucination, a last-ditch effort in her mind to—

A ghostly apparition appeared before her, coalescing from the smoke. It was a female, with dark hair, just like her own, a face . . . just like her own . . . and a body . . . just like her own.

This is me, Therese thought. *This is what I was.*

The conviction made absolutely no sense, so she focused on the strange white robe, and the fact that whoever it was was utterly unaffected by the flames and the lack of oxygen. And she was impossibly ethereal. The female was positively glowing in the midst of the horrible, billowing smoke, an angel straight from the Fade.

No . . . not an angel, Therese thought. *She is* me.

So great was both her confusion and her certainty—the two poles of cognition existing in the same moment about the same thing—that for a split second, Therese forgot all about the fire's deadly heat.

Oh, wait, so she must have already died, she decided. That must be herself risen unto the Other Side, her soul looking down upon the broken body it had had to disinhabit.

Just as this thought occurred, a flood of memories deluged her mind, all the images and sounds making no sense, yet being totally familiar: She saw an all-white world that turned colorful, grass becoming green, tulips becoming pink and orange and yellow, a forested rim now verdant instead of dressed in shades of pearlescent cream. And there were people in the sanctuary, females in white robes, and males who were warriors. And there were temples and loggias made of white marble, and seeing bowls that showed the history down on the earth below, and quill pens that recorded the events on parchment, and a library of leather-bound volumes detailing narratives collected and cherished as the history of the race.

And there was something else.

Someone else.

There was *Trez*.

All at once, the vision of the female in front of her, the one of herself in a white robe from that other place, was broken through, a huge figure scattering the apparition with his own, solid, very real body.

Except it couldn't be. Why would he know she was trapped in here?

"Therese!" he yelled as he saw her sprawled on the hallway floor.

As the tremendous male before her crouched down, she decided that this was her last thought, the final cognitive spasm of her consciousness: On the edge of her death, she had conjured not her *mahmen* or her father, not her brother or any of her cousins or her friends, but . . . him.

Somehow, she was not surprised.

"Oh, God, Therese!"

Except then things got weird. Well, okay, weirder. The hands that reached out to touch her did not seem like something she was imagining. They seemed very real, and she screamed at the contact with her burned skin.

"I know this hurts," he said roughly, "but I've got to get you out."

As the Trez vision spoke over the din of the fire, she was very impressed by the hallucination. It was so accurate, the way his voice cracked, the coughing, the fact that her body's nerves went haywire with pain as he dragged her up off the carpet and held her against his chest and turned away from the center of the inferno.

Running now. He was running, and it was terrible, the jangling of her limp arms and legs causing her to retch from the agony as her raw skin rubbed against his shirt, his muscles, his bones. And there was even less oxygen to be had up off the floor. As she gasped and gagged, she had no idea how he was breathing through the exertion. Or how he knew where he was going. The smoke was blinding, not that she could have tracked anything, because pain was making her go in and out of consciousness, her eyes checker-boarding and then clearing . . . only to phase out again.

And then there was pause. And an explosion.

No, wait, he was kicking down a door.

But it wasn't to the stairwell. It was to an apartment, and she was rushed into the space.

Trez—or what seemed to be him—slammed the

door shut behind them and went farther into the apartment, all the way to the back, to a bathroom. The air was clearer now, and he yanked down the shower curtain with one hand, and laid it out on the tile.

"I'm going to put you down now," he said.

He was careful as he did so, but she moaned in pain as her body was shifted, and as soon as she was on the hard flooring, a coughing fit curling her onto her side—and she was pretty sure she vomited. She didn't know. She was just trying to breathe, but all she could seem to draw in was smoke, even though her eyes, unreliable as they were, were telling her that there was none in the cramped room.

Trez turned away. Opened the window. Got out a phone.

Then he was back down beside her, leaning over her as he spoke to someone.

All she could do was study his face.

He was totally familiar to her, she realized in her delirium. But not just because she had met him at the restaurant. Or because she had had sex with him. Or because she had been thinking of him all day and night since their breakup.

It was because she knew him . . . from before.

And this conviction made her study him all the

more closely—although what she saw terrified her. Soot streaked the dark skin of his beautiful face, and part of his short hair was gone, singed off from the heat. The collar of his thin silk shirt was black, but not because the fabric had come in that color. The smoke had seeped into the fibers that had been white, and she had a thought that their lungs were the same, now clogged with particles.

What if he died here, too—

He was talking to her. Urgently.

When he took her hand, she moaned in pain, and he immediately stopped. In the strange, surreal silence between them, he looked as terrified as she felt, and she knew he feared he was too late when it came to having saved her. Just as she was scared she had endangered his life.

She wanted to tell him she loved him. Because she did. In a way she could not understand, the clogging, blinding smoke had brought in its thick, impenetrable folds a clarity that revealed everything: She had been his at an earlier time, and he had been hers, and they had been separated by death. After which she had been placed on the doorstep of her parents' house and destined to find him here, in Caldwell, some decades down the line, in this specific moment right here.

This was the reunion that he had recognized first and then doubted.

And that she now saw for what it was.

A Christmas miracle.

Desperately, she wanted to tell him all this, but her strength was draining fast, as if, now that they were in relative safety, the adrenaline load that had kept her barely alive was leaving and taking the functioning of her vital organs with it. She was out of time.

Therese thought of her *mahmen*. Her brother. Her father.

And then she focused on Trez's face.

With the last vestiges of her energy, she lifted her hand. As it entered her line of sight, she had a momentary horror at the bald anatomy that was showing. But then not even that mattered.

Touching Trez's cheek, she knew she had come home to him.

"My love . . ." she whispered roughly. "How I have missed you."

◆ ◆ ◆

Trez couldn't hear what Therese was saying as he leaned over her. But he wanted her to keep talking. Needed her to. She had been terribly injured, whole sheets of her skin . . . gone. Parts of her clothes melted onto her. Soot covering her to the point where the whites of her eyes glowed as if backlit in contrast to her smoke-stained skin. He had no idea how she had survived at all.

Reflexively, he went to take her hand again and had to stop himself. It had hurt her too much the first time.

"Stay with me," he begged. "Help is coming—"

Her eyes locked on his, and the light behind them made the back of his neck tingle. Then she smiled. Even through her pain, she smiled at him and was beautiful.

"My love . . . ," she whispered. "How I have missed you."

As she spoke the words, a cold shock went through him—and a vision of his *shellan's* face overlaid Therese's, or maybe it was more that his Chosen's was revealed through Therese's. Revealed to be . . . the same.

"Selena?" he choked out.

"Yes," she whispered. "I don't know how . . . but yes."

Without warning, her eyes fluttered closed and a sound that was more animal than anything remotely civilized ripped from his throat. He lunged forward, as if he could go into her failing body and drag her soul out of the burned shell.

"No!"

Planting his palms on either side of her, he was yelling, babbling, crying. He had done this once— he had already done this! He was not losing her again—

Someone touched his shoulder, and he bared his fangs and snapped at the hand, nearly biting it off at the wrist.

Doc Jane, instead of falling back, grabbed the front of his throat with a hard grip. "It's me! Trez! I'm here!"

He blinked, aggression and agony warring for control as his faulty brain tried to pull some kind of rational anything out of the no-sense-anywhere that just happened. That *was* happening.

Oh, God . . . was it possible they were the same people after all? But how?

Or was he just getting back on the train he'd gotten off of, the one that had hurt a female he . . . loved?

"Back off," Doc Jane commanded. "If you want her to have a shot at surviving, you need to back off right now."

When he didn't move—because he couldn't—the Brotherhood's physician put her hand out behind her, and snapped, "And you stay there. I do *not* need any help. I got this."

Trez shifted his eyes up and over. Vishous, Jane's mate, was standing off to the side, his diamond eyes flashing a bonded male's urge to kill, his enormous body poised to attack, his fangs likewise bared. Which was what you got when you tried to bite someone's *shellan*.

"I'll fucking kill you and not even care," the Brother ground out.

"Vishous! Lay off—"

Trez reared away from Therese, holding his palms up like someone was pointing a loaded gun at him. "I'm sorry—just help her! Please! I can't lose her again—"

His voice broke, and then he was collapsing, his body refusing to hold his weight, what was left of him pitching to the side and slamming into the hard floor. Even as he went down, his eyes did not leave his female and he had to swipe his face with his hand to try to clear his vision.

"Just save her," he kept saying, over and over again.

And he wasn't only talking about Selena. It was about who Therese was, as well. It was both of them, a single life that had been lived in two parts, in two different eras, but with one true love.

This was the solution to the equation. Provided she lived.

Thank fuck Doc Jane was on it. She had come with a backpack strapped to her shoulders and an oxygen tank mounted on her chest, and she moved fast, putting a mask on his *shellan* and checking for a pulse at the neck. Then she was injecting things into an arm—no, an IV. She was setting an IV and then injecting things.

"Come here," someone said to him. V. It was V.

Trez felt his position get moved, his torso lifted from the floor and laid in someone's lap. And then something was passed over his face. He tried to bat it away, but his hands were unceremoniously slapped aside.

"It's oxygen," V said in a dry voice. "You're wheezing."

Was he?

"I need you to breathe slow and steady for me."

Trez did what he was told because it was easier than arguing. All he really cared about was trying to keep track of what Doc Jane was doing—and the fact that she was still moving so fast was the good news and the bad news. It meant that his *shellan* was still alive, but it also meant that the injuries were serious. Like he didn't already know that, though? Dear God, his female's skin had been ravaged by the fire.

As he started coughing, he nearly vomited.

Doc Jane put a cell phone up to her ear. "Where are you. Right. ETA? Got it. Yeah, we're going to have to move her."

Trez's body inflated with strength. Shoving himself up off of V's lap, he pushed the oxygen mask onto his forehead. "I'm going to carry her. No one else."

Doc Jane ended her call and opened her mouth, no doubt to hell-no him.

"That's the way it's going to be," he said grimly.

"Not if you want her to live." Doc Jane rezipped her backpack and got to her feet, the thin, clear tubing running between the oxygen tank and Therese's mask terrifying because it seemed so fragile for its critical purpose. "You hold the oxygen mask in place and the IV bag. That's just as important as her body. V, you're going to have to pick her up. I haven't given her any morphine, but I can't run the risk of depressing her respiration any further."

When he opened his mouth to argue, Doc Jane shook her head sharply. "Let's make this fast, gentlemen, so I can stabilize her properly in the mobile unit."

Trez was of a mind to disregard it all, but something in those forest green eyes got through his possessiveness. Doc Jane wasn't giving him a choice, and not because she was playing games or didn't understand how bonded males were. It was because she understood everything that mattered medically.

V's face barged into Trez's line of sight again. "I'll get her down safe. You can trust me."

Trez nodded numbly. "Okay. Let's do this."

He was given her oxygen tank and a flappy plastic IV bag full of God only knew what.

"Put that mask back on yourself," V said. "The tank's in my pack, so we need to stay close."

"I love her," Trez explained. "Even though it doesn't make sense."

V was known for empathy to the same degree one would expect it from a loaded shotgun. Nonetheless, the sadness and regret that transformed his harsh face was not so much a testament to a character transformation, but the life-or-death situation they were all in.

"I gotchu, true?" Vishous said softly. "And you and I are going to get her out together."

Trez nodded and got to his feet. Or . . . tried to. The fact that he lurched and had to throw out a hand to the wall was a good indication Doc Jane had made the right role assignments. To help himself, he snapped his oxygen feed back into place, and took as much as he could of the plastic-scented, force-fed air.

As V bent down and gathered Therese's arms and legs, she stirred. But when he lifted her from the floor, she cried out in pain under the mask, her eyes flaring open, her hands clawing, her legs kicking.

"We gotta be quick," V said urgently. "*Fuck.*"

"I'm right here!" Trez repositioned the mask on her face, making sure the seal was tight around her lips and nose. "We're getting you to help!"

"Down the stairwell. It's to the left," Doc Jane ordered as they moved as a group out of the bathroom.

"Stay with us," Trez yelled through his own mask. "We're almost there!"

Bullshit, they were almost there. They had countless landings, dead humans in the way, and God, Manny's mobile surgery unit had better be where he said it'd be. Wherever the hell that was.

"Not long!" Trez said loudly.

As Doc Jane opened the outer door and they reentered the smoky, hot corridor, he stayed as close as he could to Therese and kept talking, for all the good it was doing. Her eyes had rolled back in her head, and he worried that the shock of the relocation was killing her.

"I'm behind you," he said as V rushed out with his precious cargo, turning sideways through the jambs to fit Therese's head and legs.

Left, Trez thought. They had to go left.

Faster, now, through the smoke, the level of which rose as they left the fire behind, now at their chests. Now above their shoulders. Better visibility and less heat—and then they were passing under the EXIT sign and entering the stairwell. Amid the screaming alarms and blinking lights, there were stragglers descending, some with bags in their arms, others with TVs they either had stolen or were protecting from theft or water damage. As Team Therese joined the rush, Trez struggled to keep his legs moving. He couldn't feel anything in his body, his head dizzy even with the supplemental oxygen.

He was going to pass out. He was going to fucking pass out.

"Stay with me," he repeated. "Stay with me . . ."

He didn't know whether he was talking to Therese.

Or himself.

CHAPTER THIRTY-TWO

Trez didn't make it.

As he stumbled on a landing, and his knees failed to catch him, he twisted around and held out the IV bag and oxygen to Doc Jane.

"Stop," she yelled to her *hellren*. V froze on the dime as she caught everything Trez threw at her.

Coughing, he tore off his oxygen mask and blinked in the flashing lights. "Go! Fuck me! Take her and go!"

"I'm sending help!" Doc Jane said as she turned her mate around and removed the tank that fed Trez's mask. "I'm sending help!"

As she dropped the thing by him, Trez pushed himself back out of the way. "Go!"

It was a relief to see them continue the descent, Therese's lax head bouncing off the crux of V's elbow as the Brother jogged down the stairs.

Putting his mask back in place, Trez could not seem to get any oxygen into his lungs. As his vision faltered, two other humans—both men—came down, their arms laden with electronics. They didn't spare him a glance, and he had a worry they would catch up to Therese. Although what they would do to her, he didn't know. Like they were going after oxygen tanks?

He wanted to move. He wished he could move. He tried to move.

But his body had given out, to the point where even his heart was slowing down. Was it shock? He didn't know—

Boom, boom, boom . . .

Thunderous footsteps. Ascending the stairwell. Coming at him.

And there he was.

Tohrment, son of Hharm. The sensible leader of the Brotherhood. The one who took care of all the others.

Who else could it have been? Trez wondered mutely.

The Brother was dressed for war, covered in leather with weapons hidden but never out of reach. And there were no wasted words, no salutations, as Tohr picked Trez up like he weighed nothing more than a toaster oven.

"Is she alive," Trez said. Or tried to. He didn't know what came out of his mouth.

"Hold on to that tank," the Brother told him.

Trez did the best he could with that, but he couldn't seem to make his arms work right. They mostly hung like ropes from his torso, useless, inanimate. And his breathing got worse as they hit the stairs. Like the words he had attempted to speak, nothing was working right in his throat, inflow and outflow jammed up.

On the bottom floor, Tohr kicked open a steel door, and the cold was a shock, not a relief, the icy air stinging Trez's face. As a serious fucking coughing jag stole his breath and his eyesight, at least Tohr's arms remained strong, and the Brother's boots made fast work over the dirty snow. The mobile surgical unit came to them—or at least it seemed that way. Trez couldn't tell. All he knew was that he was suddenly thrown into the back of the RV, and Manny Manello caught him. As he was stretched out flat on the metal floor, he had a brief impression of Therese on the treatment table, all blistered and burned skin with medical people around her, but then there were too many things on and in his face for him to see anything.

Down his throat.

Air. Being actively forced into his lungs.

There was a pinch on the back of his hand. An IV.

In confusion, he looked up and saw Ehlena. "Am I really that bad?" he asked.

Rehv's *shellan* didn't stop to answer him. Or maybe he'd done another one of his not-really-made-it's with the words. Either way, she was giving him a shot of something, and abruptly, his head cleared a little. It was a false reconnoitering, however, short-lived and insubstantial.

As he began to lose consciousness, he forced his eyes to focus on Therese.

When he had looked into her face back in that fire, he had known what he had seen: A soul crossing the divide of death, returning to him. And not just because she looked like the one he had lost.

Because she was Selena. And Therese. At the same time.

Somehow, Xhex had known this.

Somehow, he had sensed this all along.

And more than that, his love had called unto him

for help. From out of the depths of his migraine, and the strange, phased-out sleeping he often had with those headaches, she had come to him in that vision that was of another realm, pleading to him that she needed to be saved.

"She's coding!" Jane yelled. "V, get those paddles on her."

Oh, God, he had been too late, he thought with despair as he lost his hold on the present catastrophe and sank deep into an abyss that offered no respite from his fears or his sorrow.

♦ ♦ ♦

Bumpy.

Bumpy, bump, bump . . . bumpy. Then smooth. Perfectly smooth. And finally, there was a sudden decline, the mobile unit tilting forward onto its front wheels—

Trez gasped and jerked upright. Disoriented and in a panic, he flailed at the stuff on his face—

Tohr captured his hands, the Brother's deep blue eyes grave. "No, leave that on. You need it."

As Trez looked at the treatment table in a panic, Tohr put his face in the way. "She's still with us. They're just working on her."

Trez tried to stand up off the mobile surgical unit's floor, thinking he could help—in spite of the fact that he had no medical training and was totally compromised physically. Fortunately, Tohr gently yet firmly kept him where he was.

"You don't want to get in the way." The Brother shook his head. "You want to stay right here. And as soon as we come to a stop, I need to get you out fast. Okay? It's going to move really quick the second we pull up. Do we understand each other?"

Trez started to hyperventilate. But he nodded.

And it happened exactly as the Brother said. The descent ended, the mobile unit stopped, and the doors were opened. Eager to be more than an inanimate object, Trez tried to shuffle out the back, but Tohr was the one who actually moved him, the Brother scooping him up and rushing him forward as Zsadist and Qhuinn ran a gurney to the RV.

With Tohr gunning for the training center's entrance, Trez wanted to see whether Therese was okay—he knew the answer to that question, though, didn't he—whether they were getting her out of the—

His brain was making no sense, his thoughts like pennies spilled on a hardwood floor, spinning all willy-nilly before falling down in random disorder. And then the next thing he knew, he was in an exam room, on a table. Determined to get with the program, he lifted his hand up to reasonably remove the mask so he could communicate better.

He didn't recognize his forearm or what was attached to it. Everything was blackened with smoke, and he had some burns on him, although when that had happened, he had no clue. Looking up, as if Tohr, who had not been with him, could explain anything, he found the Brother taking off his leather jacket with hands that shook.

Tohr was normal. As in not sooted up the fuck, but he was pale and it wasn't just his extremities that were shaking. His whole body was on vibrate, a phone on silent waiting to be answered.

As Trez nixed his mask, he realized he was connected to the Brother by thin tubing, him with the breathing apparatus, Tohr with the tank.

"This should be with Therese," Trez said in a raspy voice.

"No, they have her on a big tank now."

"That's my *shellan*, and I need to get intohelpherfeedingfeedingneedstohappen—"

"Shh." Tohr put his palms out. "It's going to be all right. Put the mask back on until someone can check you out."

Even though Trez was like a soda bottle with the cap cracked, all kinds of words rushing to get out around the too-small seal of his mouth, he recognized that if he wanted to be taken seriously, he needed to pull it together.

"She needs to feed," he said in a more even tone. "And I don't want anyone else doing it."

"They're working on her."

"Then she's not dead yet and she needs me." Trez grabbed the Brother's arm. "If that was your *shellan*, who you could help with your vein, would you want to be stuck in here?"

The Brother blanched. "You're not well."

"Maybe. But can you argue for even a second that she's not so much worse off?"

There was some cursing on the Brother's side, low and nasty. "Stay here."

Tohr put the oxygen tank on the floor next to the exam table and Trez resumed breathing through the mask, not because he was worried about himself, but because he was anticipating the need to give Selena the very best blood he could.

When the Brother didn't immediately come back, Trez got anxious. And then terrified. He imagined the medical staff doing chest compressions and shouting demands for more meds across Therese's lifeless body—

Before he was aware of deciding to move, his

body slid off the table and stood on its own—and as something didn't feel right, he looked down. He'd lost one of his loafers. Who knew when or where.

Limping over to the door, he opened it and looked out.

Down on the left, Tohr was arguing with someone. Vishous. And their voices were low and intense.

"He's half dead," V hissed.

"What's it going to hurt? He probably thinks it's Selena. Everyone says they look alike—"

They both stopped talking and stared at Trez.

"Come on," Tohr said, "I'll take you in."

V threw up an f-bomb and went for his Turkish tobacco, the rest of his curses staying mostly under his breath.

But Tohr held out his hand, and Trez went to the Brother. Linking his palm with the other male's, as if he were a young, as if he needed guidance—because he did—Trez allowed himself to be drawn into the treatment room next door.

It was the same one.

The same one Selena had died in before.

On the table, under the medical chandelier, Therese was lying under a sheet. Tubes were going in and out of her, fluids pumped in, fluids pumped out, and there was a stand of monitoring machines by her head. Dr. Manello and Doc Jane were speaking softly and quickly by her feet. Ehlena was at the ready with a crash cart.

Doc Jane looked up. "What is he doing in here—"

Therese moaned on the table, and Dr. Manello said, "Heart rate is getting stronger. Blood pressure normalizing."

Doc Jane glanced at her patient. Looked back at Trez. "Come closer."

Trez limped over, and Therese turned her face to him, even though her eyes remained closed.

"I'm here," he said.

"Heart rate stabilizing. Blood pressure continuing to improve."

"Get him a chair," Doc Jane barked. "Before he falls over."

When something hit the back of his legs, Trez let himself go down. He wanted to take his female's hand, but he remembered when they had been in the corridor, in the fire. It had hurt her.

"Take from me," he said urgently. Bringing his wrist up, he struck his own vein with his fangs. "Take my strength."

As he held the puncture wounds over her mouth, Dr. Manello said something sharply, as if he did not approve. But then a drop of blood fell on Therese's mouth and she moaned. After which, her lips parted, and her head lifted ever so slightly.

Trez put his wrist right down. "Take from me, my queen. And come back."

He worried she wouldn't be able to do it, but then she latched on and took from him, even in her compromised state. And as he watched her neck work as she swallowed, his eyes watered. He had been here before with her. He had done this before, and he had lost her.

Not this time, though.

This time . . . he had won the fight.

Therese would survive, and they would be together, and he was going to accept the complex truth that all was as it should be, even though it defied logic and explanation.

But that was kind of what true love was, wasn't it. Against all odds and probability, two souls could indeed find each other in the soup of time and humanity, and forge a trail to walk along, hand in hand, forevermore.

It made him think of an old proverb:

Blessed are those who believe in all that two hearts aligned achieve. For once united, no matter where winter finds them, they will always be warm.

CHAPTER THIRTY-THREE

Female: *Her vitals are stable.*
Male: *What about the pain?*
Female: *I'm still worried about her breathing. She's too close to the edge.*

The back-and-forth voices were close by, but from behind Therese's closed lids, she couldn't exactly place them. Were they in front of her? To the side? Behind? And what was the beeping. There was incessant beeping.

Some kind of fear, transient yet persistent, dogged her, but as with the voices, she couldn't place its source. She knew only of its existence. And what were they saying about pain? She felt nothing. Were they talking about someone else?

No, wait. She did feel something. As she swallowed, her throat was sore.

And she could taste. Dear Lord, could she taste . . . there was the most incredible dark wine in her mouth, and down the back of her throat, and deep within her gut. It was a source of warmth, of strength, like a banked hearth—

Therese's eyes flipped open, and as she gasped, three heads leaned over her. A male and a female she did not recognize—the voices, probably? Because they were in doctor garb—and then—

"Trez," she croaked.

As she lifted her hand, the male she wanted to see above all else captured her palm in the gentlest of holds.

"I'm right here," he said roughly. "I'm right with you."

Yes, she thought. He always had been with her. Even though . . . well, he didn't look so hot. His face was an unnatural red, and he had one eyebrow singed, and a section of his hair was missing—

Something was on fire, she thought. She could smell the smoke.

Therese opened her mouth to say something, but abruptly she became distracted by the bandages that ran up her forearms. Lifting her head, she looked down at her body. She was wound up with white bands from collarbone to ankle.

That was when the pain registered. Except how was it possible that every square inch of her body hurt? And there was heat, too, not like the sustaining, sultry engine of life in her belly, but a burning—

Fire. She'd been in a fire. In her rooming house.

As with the sensation in her body, memory came back in a rush that nearly knocked her unconscious, so great was the barrage of images, sounds, smells. She remembered everything, from the scent of something burning right before the explosion, to the blasts, to the flames and the smoke along the corridor. She recalled trying to douse the fire out on that female with the slipcover and then something swinging down on her from the ceiling. Then the crawl on the filthy runner and her trying to get to safety. She remembered going as far as she could to get herself away from the heat, but it had not been fast enough. Far enough.

Her skin had burned. All over her body.

That was the reason she was bandaged.

And she was here in this hospital because Trez had gotten her out.

Therese sought his face, while, off in the distance, alarms sounded. Still, she met his gleaming black eyes.

"Thank you," she said. "For saving me."

The doctors were talking fast again, but she couldn't concentrate on what they were saying. It was all she could do to speak what she needed to to Trez. With her pain level shooting up as high as it was, the sensations ricocheting around her body, in her skull, were so dominant that she felt like she was shouting through a concrete wall.

But she had to let him know.

"My queen," he whispered, "I would never have left you there."

Strange, but it seemed completely normal for him to say such a thing. *My queen*—

That was when the other half of it all came to her. The female in the white robe emerging from the smoke, seeking her out . . . because that was her, in a different form, in a different life.

Abruptly, over the shoulder of the Shadow, Therese saw someone standing in the corner of the hospital room. At first, she wasn't sure what she was looking at, but then . . . it was herself. Again. Just as it had been in the burning hallway.

She was staring at herself staring at herself.

As Therese smiled, the female—the other version of her—smiled back.

All will be well, the vision mouthed. *All is as it should be.*

"This should help the pain," someone said.

Therese looked at the person who spoke. Just as she was going to ask what they had given her, a cooling entered her body, coursing through her veins, calming the raucous firing of so many nerves.

Shuddering in relief, she was able to focus better on Trez.

"How did you know I needed you?" she breathed.

"Because you told me."

Therese looked back at the ghost of herself, still hovering in the corner.

"Yes," she whispered, "I must have."

The ghost of her raised a hand and waved ... before slowly dissipating, as if her job was done. And then where she had been standing, someone else took her place, like an existential baton had been passed and only one could inhabit the space. It was an angel. An angel with gossamer wings, and blond and black hair, and gold rings around his throat and his wrists.

Part of her wanted to dismiss all of it as the product of some really good drugs. But she knew this was real. How else could a miracle like this be explained? Yes, it was all as it was supposed to be. She had been gone for a while, but now she was back where she needed to be, with Trez.

The angel smiled at her. She smiled back at him.

"Do you see him?" she whispered to Trez. "The angel . . . ?"

"Shh, don't talk. Save your strength."

Funny, that's what she'd said to her *mahmen*.

Refocusing on Trez, she studied his face. "I am the one you lost. I don't know how that is possible, but I lost you and now I'm back. And I love you."

Abruptly, there was total silence all around her—and not because she had died. All of the medical staff, and the other people in the room, froze where they stood and stared at her, at Trez.

"The fire," she said. "I saw myself in the fire in a white robe. And then there you were."

"I saw you in the fire, too," he explained. "You came to me out of the funeral pyre. You . . ."

With a jerk of his head, Trez looked to the angel. Then everyone looked at the angel.

As if he had been waiting for the group's attention, beneficent illumination emanated from the heavenly messenger's body, the great, warm, healing light, enveloping them all. Then the angel started to laugh.

"Hot damn, it worked!" he said, clapping his hands and then boom!'ing his hips. "This is my first frickin' miracle, and I rocked the shit out of it! High fives all around for me." He smacked the air with his palms over his head. "I mean, I wasn't sure whether it was going to work. After Selena died, I delivered her soul to those nice people's house in Michigan. I left her on the doorstep in a bassinet— I mean, come on, who doesn't love a young in a basket on the doorstep at Christmas!" He swooned as if he was admiring a piece of art. "And then, after some difficulty—because, come on, even in my world, there was to be a *little* balance—everything works out! It's perfect! I mean, seriously—I impressed even myself."

Walking over to Trez, he put his palm out, and Trez slowly raised his own. The angel made the clap happen, and then he very gingerly did the same with Therese.

"High fives," he whispered to her.

Then he stepped back. "Now. I gotta go 'cuz *Home Alone* is about to start. It's a marathon for eight hours, but if you miss the pizza scene in the beginning you really can't get Kevin's motivation right. Plus, hello, Fuller's a bed-wetter, so you get why Kevin has to go to the attic—"

The angel stopped and looked around at all the dumbfounded faces.

"Are you guys keeping up here?" When there was no collective response, he *pshaw'd* them all. "S'okay, I know you're in awe of my greatness. I get it. Happens all the time. Anyway, you guys talk amongst yourselves, but she's going to be fine and he's going to be fine, and Merry fucking Christmas. Just call me Lassi-claus!" Turning away, he made like he was going to walk through the wall to disappear, but then he turned back and lifted his forefinger. "Yeeeeeeah, so one thing. I'm afraid we're going to have to forget about this little behind-the-scenes revelation just now, m'kay? The rules say I have to tidy up after myself, so none of you can technically know about the particulars. I'll just stipulate that you're so grateful, you can't contain yourself, and listen—if you feel the need to buy me really expensive gifts for under the tree? Don't fight it. I like animal prints, the color pink—I'm a forty-four long in pants and you can forget shirts 'cuz I work out."

Abruptly, he grew serious as he looked at Trez and Therese. Then he smiled, wistfully. "I'm a sucker for true love, what can I say. I only wish I could fix everyone's problems like this."

With a fetching wink and sashay, he abruptly disapp—

EPILOGUE

New Year's Eve, Two Weeks Later

Upstairs, in the little Cape Cod house, Therese stepped out of the shower—and stopped. On the counter, by the toothpaste she shared with Trez, there was a small wrapped gift. It was nothing big in terms of size—which mean it had to be jewelry.

She immediately looked to the open doorway. "I thought we agreed," she called out. "No presents!"

When she didn't get an answer, she rolled her eyes and smiled. Wrapping a towel around herself, she picked up the little box with its bow. There was a tag on it that read, "Open Me Now."

Laughing, she held the present to her heart. Took a deep breath. And counted her blessings.

After the fire at the rooming house, thanks to Trez's blood and the Brotherhood's excellent medical care, she had bounced back to health within a week. Which, even being fully fed by her mate, and having a vampire's incredible healing capabilities, had been faster than anyone could have expected, given the seriousness of her injuries.

They'd been so extensive. And the recovery had been very painful.

Also, if it wasn't for the fact that vampires healed without scars as long as they weren't exposed to salt, she would have been permanently disfigured.

So, yes, it was the longest seven days of her life, and she was still going to physical therapy, but dear God, it could have been so much worse.

And Trez, along with her father and her brother—and her *mahmen* in spirit from her own hospital stay—had been there the whole time. Or rather Rosen and Gareth had gone back and forth between the two clinics, ferried by Fritz, the Perfect Butler, as she had taken to thinking of him as. And she and her *mahmen* had FaceTimed a lot.

After which, she had come home to this wonderful little house.

To her mate.

She looked down at the little box and marveled at Fate.

During the fire, something had happened, something that had shifted her internally—and her new perspective was not just the result of her appreciating life so much more after such a close brush with death. No, whatever it was went even deeper than that. She had an awareness of some other part of herself, something that had always been, she now recognized, just under her surface. Not a separate identity, no. It was more . . . like a prism of her identity, another facet that enhanced the colors she saw and the people she now knew—especially Trez.

She was just . . . utterly at peace with him. As if some kind of answer had been given to her. And Trez felt the same.

Somehow, the discord, the strife, the confusion about who she was to him and who he was to her had all washed away. And anytime her mind was tempted to return to the angst, the warmth in her soul, her happiness, shooed away any doubts. All she knew, all she needed to know, was that she was exactly where she needed to be.

With exactly who she needed to be with.

Trez was likewise. As her discharge from the

Brotherhood's clinic had approached, the two of them had talked things out and decided that they would take things slowly. And then they had promptly moved in here together as soon as she was released from that hospital.

They had never looked back.

It was as if they had always lived together. And always would.

"What did you do, Trez," she murmured as she took off the wrapping paper.

Yes, it was indeed a jewelry box. A little blue velvet jewelry box.

Opening the lid, she gasped. Inside, was a gold pendant ... of an angel with diamond wings.

"I figure since we're believers and all."

She looked up at Trez, who had settled in the doorway. "You shouldn't have."

"But I will, anytime I like." He smiled as he came forward and took the chain the charm was on out of the packing. Hanging the angel around her neck, he smiled at her reflection in the mirror. "Besides, it's not like a huge rock or anything."

"I do not want one of those. I told you."

"I'm getting you one anyway."

"But I'm going back for my PhD in another three weeks. That's expensive." When he just cocked an eyebrow at her, she laughed, held the pendant out, and looked at the angel. "Where did you get this?"

"Little shop downtown in the financial district. They have a lot of engagement rings there. Maybe we should go look—"

Therese turned away from the mirror and put her arms around his neck. "Kiss me?"

"Are you trying to distract me? Because it's working."

Even though they had guests coming in less than an hour, his talented hands found her skin under the towel, and she promptly forgot about all the reasons she needed to rush to get ready.

Besides, this could be the last time they were alone-alone in the house.

She eased back. "Are you sure you want my whole family to move in with us?"

"We have two bedrooms downstairs. And besides, your *mahmen* needs to be close to Havers's."

"You're wonderful, you know that?"

"Yes, I do, but tell me again."

Therese opened her mouth to say so, but he put her up on the counter and found his way in between her thighs. There was the sound of a zipper being lowered, and then she gasped.

Every time they made love, it was a revelation. New and fresh.

"I'm so happy," she said as she arched into her male.

"Me, too," he moaned as he began to thrust inside of her.

Moving together, her breasts against one of his perennial silk shirts, her thighs split wide around his hips, his bonding scent in her nose, she revisited the sense that a circle had been completed, and they were safe.

Together.

♦ ♦ ♦

Everyone came to the NYE party in the house Trez was busy buying for Therese behind the scenes. All the Brothers. All the *shellans*. The fighters. Only the King and the Band of Bastards stayed back at the mansion for security purposes. But there was all kinds of FaceTiming going on, so no one felt left out.

Although thank God for the finished basement and the wide-screen TV, Trez thought as he got out the first of the champagne bottles from the fridge. Lassiter had insisted that the Times Square special be put on, and at least half of the people ended up down there.

The other half was avoiding *New Year's Rockin' Eve* like the plague.

*cough*V*cough*

The food had been a great hit all around, however. Trez had ordered the event catered from the very best Italian restaurant in town, and iAm had more than delivered on the eats. Everybody had tucked into the food, and with the clock closing in on twelve midnight, it was Korbel time.

"You need someone to ride herd on the flutes?" Xhex asked from over at the kitchen table.

The two of them had been catching up on all things shAdoWs, and he was almost ready to sign the club over to her. Saxton was drawing up the paperwork, and Trez was looking forward to surprising her with the gift. And after that?

Well, he was thinking about joining Gareth on the human-law train. And getting into real estate.

"Sure do," Trez said as he popped the first cork.

There was a cheer from the living room, and he leaned around the archway and waved as Butch and Marissa came in the front door.

Then, he shifted his eyes over to the love seat. Therese's parents were sitting together, holding hands and smiling like newlymateds. Then again, they were newly back together, in a way. Larisse had rebounded beautifully, and there was hope, with more aggressive management, that she had plenty of good, healthy years ahead of her. And hey, she was making it to midnight, which was awesome considering she had only been released the night before.

Under doctor's orders, though, Trez was closing the party down at 12:45 on her behalf. And also because he and his Therese had some more private celebrating to do. That quickie on the counter in the bathroom had only whetted his appetite.

As Xhex brought the tray of flutes over, Trez started pouring—

"Uncle Trez, that's my card!"

He glanced behind himself. Bitty was standing in front of the refrigerator and pointing at the Christmas card she had made for him.

"Yes," he said. "I told you I love it."

"Right on your door!" She skipped over and tugged him down to give him a kiss on the cheek. "I need to go find Auntie Therese."

"She's playing *Mario* in her brother's room downstairs."

"Thank you," the little female said as she skipped off through the crowd.

For a split second, Trez stared at the drawn image of him next to his female, her with her silver skin and her smile, him holding her hand, a big gold star over them both.

It was the most perfect depiction he could imagine of his life, of the union between him and his mate. Somehow, he knew the truth behind the impossibility. He knew that his female was back with him, had never really left him. He couldn't describe the particulars—somehow, they were out of reach, but he was at peace with the blind spot.

As was everyone else.

It all just made . . . sense, somehow.

A puzzle completed, with no missing pieces.

And yup, today, when he'd been downtown, heading for the club in his car, he'd passed by a jewelry store with this display of engagement rings and glittering things in the window. Not really understanding why, he'd felt compelled to park in a surface lot and walk three blocks in the cold to stand in front of the store. There had been a lot of those rings, but Therese wasn't flashy like that. As she'd said, she'd much rather have the money go to her PhD in civil engineering.

Which was going to help when she worked with Wrath on some building projects. She just didn't know that was going to happen yet.

Trez had looked at all the jewelry store's wares, all the crosses, too, but nothing had really felt right. Except then he'd seen the angel.

Perfect, he'd thought. Even though he'd never really had an affinity for them before.

"Trez?" Xhex said softly. "You okay?"

He shook himself back to the present and smiled at his old friend. "I think you know the answer to that."

Those gunmetal grays were warm as she smiled back. "I do. I really do."

"This is going to be a great year coming up, I can just feel it."

"You know, I have to agree with you."

As the minutes got tighter before midnight, somehow they all squeezed into the basement, with Therese's parents being given the best seats in the house, right in front of the TV. With champagne at the ready, and the ball in Times Square beginning to drop, Trez put his arm around Therese, drawing her in tight against him.

The crowd started to chant. "Ten, nine, eight . . ."

He leaned to her ear. "I love you."

She smiled up at him. "I love you, too."

". . . seven, six, five . . ."

Glancing to his left, he smiled at iAm and *maichen*, who was just starting to show. They smiled back at him.

". . . four, three, two . . ."

With one, unified voice, everybody in the house yelled, "Happy New Year!"

As "Auld Lang Syne" started up, and couples kissed, Trez stared into the eyes of his one true love.

"Forever," he said.

Therese nodded. "Forever."

They kissed, and as he straightened, he caught sight of Lassiter, the Fallen Angel. The male raised his champagne glass in their direction with a self-satisfied expression. Then he pointed to his throat and gave the thumbs-up, like he approved of Trez's gift.

"A job well done indeed," Trez murmured as he hugged his female and thanked every blessing he had ever been given.

Turned out that star he'd been born under? It had been a pretty damn good one, after all.

ACKNOWLEDGMENTS

With so many thanks to the readers of the Black Dagger Brotherhood books! This has been a long, marvelous, exciting journey, and I can't wait to see what happens next in this world we all love. I'd also like to thank Meg Ruley, Rebecca Scherer and everyone at JRA, and Lauren McKenna, Jennifer Bergstrom, and the entire family at Gallery Books and Simon & Schuster.

To Team Waud, I love you all. Truly. And as always, everything I do is with love to and adoration for both my family of origin and of adoption.

Oh, and thank you to Naamah, my WriterDog II, who works as hard as I do on my books!

Keep reading for an exclusive excerpt of J. R. Ward's

THE SINNER

The eighteenth Black Dagger Brotherhood novel!

Coming March 2020 from Gallery Books

CHAPTER ONE

Behind the wheel of her ten-year-old car, Jo Early bit into the Slim Jim and chewed like it was her last meal. She hated the fake-smoke taste and the boat-rope texture, and when she swallowed the last piece, she got another one out of her bag. Ripping the wrapper with her teeth, she peeled the taxidermied beef free and littered into the wheel well of the passenger side. There were so many others like it down there, you couldn't see the floor mat.

Up ahead, her anemic headlights swung around a curve, illuminating pine trees that had been limbed up three-quarters of the way, the puffy tops making toothpicks out of the trunks. She hit a pothole and bad-swallowed, and she was coughing as she reached her destination.

The abandoned Adirondack Outlets was yet another

commentary on the pervasiveness of Amazon Prime. The one-story strip mall was a horseshoe without a hoof, the storefronts along the two long sides bearing the remnants of their brands, ghostly laminations and off-kilter signs with faded names like Van Heusen/Izod, and Nike, and Dansk. Behind the dusted glass, there was no merchandise available for purchase anymore, and no one had been on the property with a charge card for at least a year, only hardscrabble weeds in the cracks of the promenade and barn swallows in the eaves inhabiting the site. Likewise, the food court that united the eastern and western arms was no longer offering soft serve, Starbucks, or lunch.

As a hot flash cranked her internal temperature up, she cracked the window. And then put it all the way down. March in Caldwell, New York, was like winter in a lot of places still considered northerly in latitude, and thank God for it. Breathing in the cold, damp air, she told herself this was not a bad idea.

Nah, not at all. Here she was, alone at midnight, chasing down the lead on a story she wasn't writing for her employer, the *Caldwell Courier Journal*. Without anyone at her new apartment waiting up for her. Without anyone on the planet who would claim her mangled corpse when it was found from the smell in a ditch a week from now.

Letting the car roll to a stop, she killed the lights and stayed where she was. No moon out tonight, so she'd dressed right. All black. But without any illumination from the heavens, her eyes strained at the darkness, and not because she was greedy to see the details on the decaying structure.

Unease tickled her nape, like someone was trying to get

her attention by running the point of a carving knife over her skin—

As her stomach let out a howl, she jumped. And went diving into her purse again. Passing by the three Slim Jims she had left, she went straight-up Hershey this time, and the efficiency with which she stripped that mass-produced chocolate of its clothing was a sad commentary on her diet. When she was finished, she was still hungry, and not because there wasn't food in her belly. As always, the only two things she could eat failed to satisfy her gnawing craving, to say nothing of her nutritional needs.

Putting up her window, she took her backpack and got out. The crackling sound of the treads of her running shoes on the shoulder of the road seemed loud as a concert, and she wished she wasn't getting over a cold. Like her sense of smell could be helpful, though? And when was the last time she'd considered that possibility outside of a milk-carton check.

She really needed to give these wild-goose chases up.

Two-strapping her backpack, she locked the car and pulled the hood of her windbreaker up over her red hair. No heel-toeing. She left-right-left'd with the soles of her Brooks flat to quiet her footfalls. As her eyes adjusted, all she saw were the shadows around her, the hidey-holes in corners and nooks formed by the doorways and the benches, pockets of gotcha with which mashers could play a child's game of keep-away until they were ready to attack.

When she got to a heavy chain that was strung across her path, she looked around. There was nobody in the parking lots that ran down the outside of the flanks. No one in the promenade formed by the open-ended rectangle. Not a soul on the road that she had taken up to this rise above Route 149.

Jo told herself that this was good. It meant no one was going to jump her.

Her adrenal gland, on the other hand, informed her that this actually meant no one was around to hear her scream for help.

Refocusing on the chain, she had some thought that if she swung her leg over it and proceeded on the other side, she would not come back the same.

"Stop it," she said, kicking her foot up.

She chose the right side of the stores, and as rain started to fall, she was glad the architect had thought to cover the walkways overhead. What had not been so smart was anyone thinking a shopping center with no interior corridors could survive in a place this close to Canada. Saving ten bucks on a pair of candlesticks or a bathing suit was not going to keep anybody warm October to April, and that was true even before you factored in the current environment of free next-day shipping.

Down at the far end, she stopped at what had to have been the ice cream place because there was a faded stencil of a cow holding a triple-decker cone by its hoof on the window. She got out her phone.

Her call was answered on the first ring. "Are you okay?" Bill said.

"Where am I going?" she whispered. "I don't see anything."

"It's in the back. I told you that you have to go around back, remember."

"Damn it." Maybe the nitrates had fried her brain. "Hold on, I think there's a staircase over here."

"I think I should come out."

Jo started walking again and shook her head even though he couldn't see her. "I'm fine—yup, I've got the cut-through to the rear. I'll call you if I need you—"

"You shouldn't be doing this alone!"

Ending the connection, she jogged down the concrete steps, her pack bouncing like it was doing pushups on her shoulders. As she bottomed out on the lower level, she scanned the empty parking lot—

The stench that speared into her nose was the kind of thing that triggered her gag reflex. Roadkill . . . and baby powder?

She looked to the source. The maintenance shed by the tree line had a corrugated-metal roof and metal walls that would not survive long in tornado alley. Half the size of a football field, with garage doors locked to the ground, she imagined back in its heyday that it housed paving equipment as well as things like snowplows, blowers, and mowers.

The sole person-sized door was loose, and as a stiff gust from the rainstorm caught it, the creak was straight out of a George Romero movie. And then the panel immediately slammed shut with a clap, as if Mother Nature didn't like the stink any more than Jo did.

Taking out her phone, she texted Bill: *This smell is nasty.*

Aware that her heart rate just tripled, she walked across the asphalt, the rain hitting the hood of her windbreaker in a disorganized staccato. Ducking her hand under the loose nylon of the jacket, she felt for her holstered gun and kept her palm on the butt.

The door creaked open and slammed shut again, another puff of that stink releasing out of the interior. Swallowing through throat spasms, she had to fight to keep going and not because there was wind in her face.

When she stopped in front of the door, the opening and closing ceased, as if now that she was on the verge of entering, it didn't need to catch her attention and draw her in anymore.

So help her God, if Pennywise was on the other side . . .

Glancing around to check there were no red balloons lolling in the area, she reached out for the door.

I just have to know, she thought as she opened the way in. *I need to . . . know.*

Peering around the door, she saw absolutely nothing, and yet was frozen by all that she confronted. Pure evil, the kind of thing that abducted and murdered children, that slaughtered the innocent, that enjoyed the suffering of the just and merciful, pushed at her body and then penetrated it, radiation that was toxic passing through to her bones.

Coughing, she stepped back and covered her mouth and nose with her elbow. After a couple of deep breaths into her sleeve, she fumbled with her phone to call Bill again.

Before he could say anything over the whirring in the background, she bit out, "You need to come—"

"I'm already halfway there."

"Good."

"What's going on—"

Jo ended the call and got out her flashlight, triggering the beam. Stepping forward again, she shouldered the door open and trained the spear of illumination into the space.

The light was consumed.

Sure as if she were shining it into a bolt of thick fabric, the fragile illumination was no match for what was before it.

The threshold she stepped over was nothing more than weather stripping, but the inch-high lip was a barrier that felt like an obstacle course she could barely surmount—and then there was the stickiness on the floor. Pointing the flashlight to the ground, she picked up one of her feet. Something like old motor oil dripped off her running shoe, the sound of it finding home echoing in the empty space.

She found the first of the buckets on the left. Home Depot, orange and white—and the logo was smudged with a rusty, translucent substance that turned her stomach.

The beam wobbled as she went over and looked into the cylinder, her hand shaking. Inside, there was a gallon of glossy, gleaming . . . red . . . liquid. And in the back of her throat, she tasted copper—

Jo wheeled around with the flashlight.

The two men who had entered the facility and come up behind her without a sound loomed as if they had been born of the darkness itself, wraiths conjured from her nightmares, fed by the cold spring rain, clothed in the night. One of them had a goatee and tattoos at one of his temples, a cigarette between his lips, a downright nasty expression on his hard face. The other wore a Boston Red Sox hat and a long coat, the tails of which blew in slow motion even though the wind coming in from the open door was choppy. Both had long black blades holstered handles down on their chest, and she knew there were more weapons where she couldn't see them.

They had come to kill her. Tracked her as she'd moved away from her car. Seen her as she had not seen them.

Jo stumbled back and tried to get out her gun, but her sweaty palms had her dropping her phone and struggling to keep the flashlight—

And then she couldn't move.

Even as her brain ordered her feet to run, her legs to run, her body to run, nothing obeyed the panic commands, her muscles twitching under the lockdown of some invisible, external force of will, her bones aching, her breath turning into a pant. Pain firework'd her brain, a headache sizzling through her skull.

Opening her mouth, she tried to scream—

As Butch O'Neal stared at the woman's vacant, frozen fear, he had a wicked-odd thought. For some reason, he recalled that his given name was Brian. Why this was relevant in any way was unclear, and he chalked up the cognitive drive-by to the fact that she kind of reminded him of his first cousin on his mother's side. That connection wasn't particularly relevant, either, however, because in Southie, where he had been born and raised, there were only about a thousand red-haired women.

Well, and there was also the fact that he hadn't seen any member of his family, extended or otherwise, for what, two years now? Three? He'd lost count, although not because he didn't care.

Actually, that was a lie. He did not care.

And besides, the reality that this woman was a half-breed on the verge of going through the change was probably more to the point of the connection thing. Not exactly his own experience coming into the species, but close enough.

"Am I scenting this right?" He looked over at his roommate. His best friend. His true brother, in comparison to the biological ones he'd left in the human world. "Or am I nuts."

"Nah." Vishous, son of the Bloodletter, exhaled a cloud of Turkish smoke, his hard features and goatee briefly obscured by the haze. "You ain't nuts, cop. And I am getting really sick and tired of scrubbing this woman, true?"

"To be fair, you get sick and tired if you have to do anything more than once."

"Feeling a little judgey tonight, are we." V waved at the woman to send her off. "Buh-bye—"

"Hold on, she dropped her phone."

Butch went further into the induction zone and gagged as he shined his light around. Fucking *lessers*. He'd rather have sweat socks shoved up his nose. But at least he didn't have to wade around long to find her cell. The thing had landed face-up in the oily mess, and he took a handkerchief out and wiped it off as best he could.

Going over to the woman, he put the thing in the pocket of her windbreaker and stepped back. "Okay, she's good to go."

Are you certain about that, some quiet part of him wondered.

"Whatever, I'm sure I'll see her again," V said dryly. "Bad penny this human is."

As she exited and walked off, Butch watched her cross the asphalt and disappear up the concrete stairs. "Is she the one you've been monitoring?"

"She just won't leave it the fuck alone."

"The one with the website about vampires."

"Damn Stoker. Real original. Remind me to ask her when I need help with puns."

Butch looked back at his roommate. "She's searching for herself. You can't turn that kind of thing off."

"Well, her change needs to shit or get off the pot. I got better things to do than check on her hormones like I'm waiting for a goddamn egg to hard-boil."

"You have such a way with languages."

"Seventeen, now that I've added 'vampire conspiracist.'" V dropped his butt and crushed it with his shitkicker. "You should read some of the shit they post. There's a whole community of the crackpots out there."

Butch held up his forefinger. " 'Scuse me, Professor Xavier, given that we do actually exist, how can you call them crazy?"

"You ready to do this, or do you just want to stand there in that wet cashmere coat of yours."

Butch brushed at the shoulders of his Tom Ford. "It is so unfair that you know my triggers."

"You could have just put on leathers. Or stayed home."

"Style is important. And I didn't want you to come alone. That's what she said."

"Nice joke, Lassiter. Besides, I can handle this by my little lonesome. You know I come with my own special kind of backup."

V lifted his lead-lined glove to his mouth and took the tip of the middle finger between his sharp, white teeth. Tugging the protective shield off what was underneath, he revealed a glowing hand that was marked on both sides with tattooed warnings in the Old Language.

Holding his curse out, the interior of the storage building lit up bright as noontime, the blood on the floor black, the blood in the six buckets red. As Butch walked around, his footsteps left patterns that were eaten up quick, that which covered the concrete consuming the prints, reclaiming dominance.

Lowering down onto his haunches, Butch dragged his fingers through the shit and rubbed the black stink, testing for viscosity. "Nope."

V's icy eyes shifted over. "What?"

"This is wrong." Butch hit his handkerchief again for cleanup. "It's too thin. It's not like it was."

"Do you think . . ." V, who never lost track of a thought, lost track of his thought. "Is it happening? Do you think?"

Butch straightened and walked over to one of the buckets. It was a bog-standard drywall container that still had the brand name on it. Inside, the blood that had been drained from the veins of what had been a human was congealing from the cold. And there was something else in there.

Huh. The inductees took their hearts home in a jar. Or used to.

Clearly the Omega wasn't doing that anymore to his boys. Then again, none of the new slayers lasted long enough to establish a residence to keep their jar safe. And back in the good old days, if they lost their heart, they got into trouble—which was why the Brotherhood had a tradition of taking those containers whenever they could. Plus, hello, trophy.

It was so weird. The slayers could lose their humanity. Their souls. Their free-agency. Just not that cardiac muscle they didn't need anymore to exist.

Although the rules had changed, apparently.

"Cop?"

Butch pivoted back around to his roommate and did not like the expression on the brother's face. "Don't look at me like that."

"Like what."

"Like I got answers. Like I'm the solution to it all."

There was a long moment of silence between them, nothing but the pitter-pat of rain on the metal roof marking the stillness, the quiet.

"But you are, Butch. And you know it."

Butch walked over and stood chest-to-chest with the male. "What if we're wrong?"

In the Old Language, V said, "*The Prophecy is not ours to claim. It is the property of history. As it was foretold, so it shall be. First as the future, then as the present when the time is nigh. After which, with recording, it shall be the sacred past, the saving of the species, the end of the war with the Lessening Society.*"

Butch thought of his dreams, the ones that had been waking him up during the day. The ones that he refused to speak to his Marissa about. "What if I don't believe any of that."

What if I can't believe it, he amended.

"You assume destiny requires your belief."

Unease scurried through his veins like rats in a sewer, finding all kinds of familiar paths. And meanwhile, as freely as it roamed, he became trapped. "What if I'm not enough?"

"You are. You have to be."

"I can't do any of it without you."

V's familiar eyes, diamond with navy-blue rims, softened, proving that even the hardest substance on earth could yield if it chose to. "You have me, forever. And if you need it, you can take my faith in you for as long as you need it."

"I didn't ask for this."

"We never do," V said roughly. "And it doesn't matter even if we did."

Vishous shook his head sadly, as if he were remembering parts of his own life, routes taken by force or coercion, dubious gifts pressed into his unwilling hands, mantles tossed over his shoulders, heavy with the manipulations and desires of others. Given that Butch knew his roommate's past as well as he knew his own, he wondered about the nature of the so-called destiny theory V spoke of.

Maybe the intellectual construct of fate, of destiny, was just a way to distance a person from all the shitty fucking things other people did to them, all the proverbial bad luck that rained down on the head of an essentially good guy, all that Murphy's Law, which was actually not luck at all, just the impersonal nature of chaos at work. And then there was the disappointment and injury, the loss and alienation, the chips off the soul and the heart that were inevitable during any mortal's tenure upon the ashes and the dust to which they were doomed to return.

Butch pushed damp cashmere aside to grip his heavy gold cross through the thin silk of his shirt. There was a balance, though, he reminded himself. Love, in all its forms, was the balance.

Putting his hand on V's shoulder, he moved down that heavily muscled arm until he clasped the thick wrist above the curse. Then he stepped in beside his brother and lifted the glowing, deadly palm, the leather of V's jacket sleeve creaking at the repositioning.

"Time for cleanup," Butch said hoarsely.

"Yes," V agreed. "It is."

As Butch held up the arm, energy unleashed from that deadly palm in a great burst of light, the illumination blinding Butch, his eyes stinging, though he refused to look away from the power, the terrible grace, the universe's mystery of origin that was housed within the otherwise unremarkable flesh of his best friend.

Under the onslaught, all traces of the Omega's evil work disappeared, the structure of the shed, those comparably fragile walls and rafters of the roof, remaining untouched by the fearsome glory that reclaimed the humble space that had been horribly used for as evil a purpose as ever there was.

What if the prophecy itself is not enough, he thought to himself.

After all, mortals weren't the only things that had a shelf life. History likewise decayed and was lost, over time. Lessons forgotten . . . rules mislaid . . . heroes dead and gone . . .

Prophecies dismissed when another future came along to claim the present as its victim, proving that that which had been taken as an absolute was in fact only partially true.

Everyone is talking about the end of the war, but is there ever really an end to evil? Butch wondered. Even if he succeeded, even if he was, in fact, the *Dhestroyer*, what then. Sweetness and light forever?

No, he thought with a conviction that made his spine tingle with warning. There would be another.

And it would be the same as what had been defeated.

Only worse.